Australian author **Ally Blake** loves reading and strong coffee, porch swings and dappled sunshine, beautiful notebooks and soft, dark pencils. Her inquisitive, rambunctious, spectacular children are her exquisite delight. And she adores writing love stories so much she'd write them even if nobody else read them. No wonder, then, having sold over four million copies of her romance novels worldwide, Ally is living her bliss. Find out more about Ally's books at www.allyblake.com.

National bestselling author **Nancy Robards Thompson** holds a degree in journalism. She worked as a newspaper reporter until she realized reporting "just the facts" bored her silly. Now that she has much more content to report to her muse, Nancy loves writing women's fiction and romance full-time. Critics have deemed her work "funny, smart and observant." She resides in Florida with her husband and daughter. You can reach her at www.nancyrobardsthompson.com and Facebook.com/nancyrobardsthompsonbooks.

Also by Ally Blake

Falling for the Rebel Heir
Hired: The Boss's Bride
Dating the Rebel Tycoon
Millionaire Dad's SOS

The Royals of Vallemont miniseries
Rescuing the Royal Runaway Bride

And look out for the next book
Amber and the Rogue Prince
Coming June 2018

Also by Nancy Robards Thompson

The Cowboy Who Got Away
A Bride, a Barn, and a Baby
The Cowboy's Runaway Bride
His Texas Christmas Bride
How to Marry a Doctor
A Celebration Christmas
Celebration's Baby
Celebration's Family
Celebration's Bride
Texas Christmas

Discover more at millsandboon.co.uk

RESCUING THE ROYAL RUNAWAY BRIDE

ALLY BLAKE

MADDIE FORTUNE'S PERFECT MAN

NANCY ROBARDS THOMPSON

MILLS & BOON

First Published in Great Britain 2018
by Mills & Boon, an imprint of HarperCollinsPublishers,
1 London Bridge Street, London, SE1 9GF

Rescuing the Royal Runaway Bride © 2018 Ally Blake
Maddie Fortune's Perfect Man © 2018 Harlequin Books S.A.

Special thanks and acknowledgement to Nancy Robards Thompson for her contribution to the Fortunes of Texas: The Rulebreakers continuity.

ISBN: 978-0-263-26492-0

38-0518

MIX
Paper from
responsible sources
FSC® C007454

This book is produced from independently certified FSC™ paper to ensure responsible forest management.

For more information visit: www.harpercollins.co.uk/green

Printed and bound in Spain
by CPI, Barcelona

RESCUING THE ROYAL RUNAWAY BRIDE

ALLY BLAKE

For my husband, Mark,
who loves nothing more than looking to the stars.

CHAPTER ONE

THE DAY COULD not be more perfect for a royal wedding, thought Will as his open-topped hire car chewed up miles of undulating Vallemontian roads.

The sky was a cerulean-blue dome. Clusters of puffy white cumuli hovered over snow-dusted mountains and dotted shadows over rolling green hills filling the valley that gave the small European principality its name.

By Will's calculations, snow should fall on the valley any day. Instead, the delicate bite of a warm sun cut through the washed-clean feeling that came after lashings of rain. It was as if the influential Vallemontian royal family had wished for it to be so, and so it was.

But Will Darcy did not believe in wishes. He believed in the human eye's ability to find millions of colours in a drop of light; the resultant heat of distantly burning stars; that weather forecasting was an inexact science.

This coming from an astronomer; his field truly a game of extrapolation, using ancient evidence to build current theory, relying on calculations that pushed against the edges of the range of known values. One had to be part cowboy, part explorer, part decoder, idealist and seer to do well in the field—something he'd addressed as the keynote speaker at the Space and Time Forum in London the night before.

It had been a late night too. Hence the fact he'd flown

into Vallemont only that morning, and would arrive at the palace just as the ceremony was about to start.

The delayed flight had also given him plenty of opportunity to back out if need be. There was the lecture on worm holes he was due to give at the University of Amsterdam a few days from now, after all. The podcast with newyorker.com. The notes from his editor on the second edition of his graduate-level astronomy textbook due any day. And then there was the virtual-reality game set in the Orion Nebula for which he was both investor and technical advisor.

Reasons enough to forgo the trip.

But only one reason to get on that plane.

To see his old friend tie the knot.

A day for knots, Will thought, choosing to ignore the one that had formed overnight in his belly at the thought of what this day might bring.

He pressed down on the accelerator on the neat little convertible his assistant had hired for him in the hope he might "realise how damn lucky he was and take a moment to enjoy himself". The chill wind ruffled his hair as he zoomed through the bucolic countryside until the road narrowed, heralding yet another idyllic Arcadian village.

Around a tight bend and he was in the thick of it—tightly winding cobblestone streets dotted with gaslight-style street lamps, stone houses with thatched roofs tucked tightly together and wedged into the side of a steep hill, their windowsills abundant with brightly coloured flowers; history in crumbling stone walls, mossy pavements and the occasional brass sign telling of times past.

The engine on the low-slung sports model growled as Will changed down a gear. The suspension knocked his teeth together as it struggled against the ancient stone beneath, but it was all he could do to avoid the crowd spilling from the thin footpaths onto the road.

Festive they were. All smiles as they headed to pubs and parks and lounge rooms all over the country to watch the wedding on television. Pink and gold ribbons had been strung across the road. Handmade banners flapped from weathervanes. Pink flower petals covered the footpaths and floated in tiny puddles.

All because Will's oldest friend, Hugo, was getting married to some woman named Mercedes Gray Leonine, no less. Though those who had strung the ribbons and scattered the petals knew the guy as Prince Alessandro Hugo Giordano.

Then the roadway cleared and Will aimed for a stone bridge crossing the rocky river that trapped the village against the hillside and hit open space again.

It was all so very green, rain having brought a lush overabundance, shine and glisten as far as the eye could see.

And on he drove. Until he reached a tunnel of trees running parallel to the river.

Glimpses of fields pushing into the distance sneaked through the dark foliage. The ever-present mountains cast cool shadows through the sunshine. And, if his GPS wasn't glitching, any moment to the east...

There. Sunlight bounced off arched windows and turned pale sandstone turrets into rose-gold. Pink and gold banners flapped high in the breeze while the Palace of Vallemont sat high and grand on its pretty bluff, like something out of a fairy tale.

And the knot in Will's stomach grew so that it pressed hard against his lungs.

The first time he'd been invited to the palace had been well over a decade before. Circumstances—by way of a skiing accident—had seen to it that he'd been forced to stay at his grandparents' mausoleum of a townhouse in London that summer, leaving his sister, Clair, to visit the royal family as Hugo's special guest on her own.

Only a few weeks later, Will's life had been irrevocably, tragically altered. The boy who'd already lost so much became a young man who'd lost everything. And Vallemont, this postcard-pretty part of the world, had been a throbbing bruise on his subconscious ever since.

Memories lifted and flurried. He'd handled things less than admirably at the time. This was his chance to put things right. He held the steering wheel tighter and kept moving forward.

The thicket filled out, the view narrowing to the curving tunnel of green and rutting muddy road that hadn't had the benefit of recent sunshine. A herd of sheep suddenly tripped and tumbled their way across the road.

Will slowed again, this time to a stop. He rested his elbow on the windowsill, his chin in his hand, his finger tapping against his bottom lip. If life wasn't so cruel, random and insensate, he might one day have attended a very different wedding in this storybook place. Not as a ghost from the groom's past, but as best man and brother, all in one.

He shook his head.

What ifs were not relevant. The world simply kept on turning. Day would dissolve into night. And tomorrow it would start all over again.

The last of the sheep skittered past, followed by a wizened old man in overalls holding a crook. He tipped his hat. Will returned with a salute. And then he and the knot in his belly were off again.

He kept his speed down as rain had dug deep grooves into the ancient mud and stone. The trees hung dangerously low over the road, dappling sunlight over the windscreen, shadow and light dancing across his hands, hindering his vision for a second, then—

Will slammed on the brakes. He gripped the wheel as

the car fishtailed, mud spattering every which way, the engine squalling, the small tyres struggling to find purchase.

Then the car skidded to a jarring halt, momentum throwing him forward hard against the seatbelt, knocking his breath from his lungs. At which point the engine sputtered and died.

His chest burned from the impact of the belt. His fingers stung on the wheel. Blood rushed like an ocean behind his ears. Adrenaline poured hotly through his veins. And beneath it all his heart clanged in terror.

He'd heard a noise. He was sure of it. The growl and splutter had been punctuated with a thud.

Expecting carnage, axle damage from a fallen log, or, worse, a lone sheep thrown clear by the impact, Will opened his eyes.

Sunlight streaked through the thicket. Steam rose from the road. Wet leaves fell like confetti from a tree above. But there was no sheep in sight.

Instead, dead centre of his windscreen, stood a woman.

He blinked to make sure he wasn't imagining her. So pale, sylph-like in the shadows of the dark, dank vegetation, she practically glowed.

As if in slow motion, a leaf fluttered from above to snag in a dark auburn curl dangling over her face. Another landed on a fair bare shoulder. Yet another snagged on the wide skirt of a voluminous pink dress three times bigger than she was.

Those were details that stampeded through Will's mind during the half-second it took him to leap from the car. The mud sluicing over the tops of his dress shoes and seeping into his socks mattered only so far as the fact it slowed him down.

"Where are you hurt?" he barked, running his hands through his hair to dampen the urge to run them over her.

Not that she seemed to notice. Her eyes remained

closed, mouth downturned, black-streaked tears ran unstopped down her cheeks. And she trembled as if a strong gust of wind might whip her away.

Best case scenario was shock. Worst case... The thud still echoed against the back of his skull.

"Ma'am, I need you to look at me," he said, his voice louder now. It was the kind of voice that could silence a room full of jaded policy-makers. "Right now."

The woman flinched, her throat working. And then she opened her eyes.

They were enormous. Far too big for her face. Blue. Maybe green. Not easy to tell considering they were rimmed red and swollen with dark tears.

And every part of her vibrated a little more, from her clumpy eyelashes to the skirt of her elaborate dress. Standing there in the loaded silence, the hiss and tic of his cooling engine the only sound, he knew he'd never felt such energy pouring off a single person before. Like the sun's corona, it extended well beyond her physical body, impinging on anyone in its path.

He took what felt like a necessary step back as he said, "I cannot help you until you tell me whether you are hurt."

She let out one last head-to-toe quiver, then dragged in a breath. It seemed to do the trick as she blinked. Looked at his car. Lifted her hands into the air as if to balance. Pink diamonds dangling from her ears glinted softly as she shook her head. *No.*

Will breathed out, the sound not altogether together. Then, as relief broke the tension, anger tumbled through the rare breach in his faculties.

"Then what the holy hell were you doing jumping out in front of my car?"

The woman blinked at his outburst, her eyes becoming bigger still. Then her chin lifted, she seemed to grow an inch in height, and finally she found her voice. "I beg your pardon, but I did *not* jump out in front of your car."

Will baulked. The lilting, sing-song quality of the Vallemontian accent that he had not heard in person in years was resonant in every syllable. It took him back in time, making the ground beneath his feet unsteady.

He refocused. "Jump. Leap. Swan dive. It's all the same. You had to have heard me coming. My car engine isn't exactly subtle."

That earned him a surprisingly unladylike snort. "Subtle? It's a mid-life crisis incarnate. *You* should have been driving your overcompensation more slowly! Especially with the roads being as they are after the rain we've had."

"It's a rental," he shot back, then gave himself a swift mental kick for having risen to the bait. "Speed was not the issue here. The pertinent fact is that you chose to cross at a bend in the road shaded by thick foliage. You could have been killed. Or was that your intention? If so it was an obtuse plan. Nearly every person in the country is already at the palace or sitting by a TV to watch the royal wedding."

At that she winced, her pale face turning so much paler he could practically see the veins working beneath her skin. Then she broke eye contact, her chin dipping as she muttered, "My being right here, right now, was never part of any plan, I can assure you of that."

Okay. All right. Things had gone astray. Time to bring everything back to fundamentals. "So, just to be clear, I did not hit you."

She shook her head, dark red curls wobbling. "No, you did not."

"I could have sworn I heard a thud."

Her mouth twisted. Then she looked up at him from beneath long, clumping eyelashes. "When I saw you coming I did the only thing I could think to do. I threw a shoe at you."

"A shoe?"

"I'd have thrown both if I'd thought it would help. But alas, the other one is stuck."

"Stuck?" Will was aware he was beginning to sound like a parrot, but the late night, early morning, the knotty reality of being in Vallemont after all these years were beginning to take their toll.

He watched in mute interest as the woman gathered her dress and lifted it to show off skinny legs covered in pale pink stockings. One foot was bare. The other foot was nowhere to be seen—or, more precisely, was ankle-deep in mud.

Will glanced back at his car. Then up along the road ahead.

Time was ticking. Hugo's wedding was looming. Will wasn't sure of the protocol but he doubted a soon-to-be princess bride would be fashionably late.

The woman in pink was calmer now, the static having dulled to a mild buzz. Best of all she was unhurt, meaning she was not his problem.

Will did not do "people problems". His assistant, Natalie—a jolly, hardworking woman who performed miracles from a desk at home somewhere in the Midwest of the United States—was the only person in the world to whom he felt beholden and only because she told him every time they spoke that he should. Even then her efforts on his behalf were well-compensated.

He preferred maths problems, fact problems, evidentiary problems. His manager would attest that time management was Will's biggest problem as he never said no to work if he could find a way to fit it all in.

And yet... He found that he could not seem to roust himself to wish the woman well and get back on his way.

There was nothing to be done except to help.

Decision made, he held out both hands as if dealing

with a wounded animal. "Any way you can jiggle your foot free?"

"Wow. That's a thought." It seemed she'd hit the next stage of shock—sarcasm.

"Says the woman who threw a shoe at an oncoming car in the hope of saving herself from getting squished."

Her eyes narrowed. Her fists curled tighter around her skirt. Beneath the head-to-toe finery she was pure street urchin itching for a fight.

Shock, he reminded himself. *Stuck*. And she must have been cold. There wasn't much to the top part of her dress but a few layers of lace draped over her shoulders, leaving her arms bare. The way the skirt moved as it fell to her feet made it look like layers of woven air.

Air he'd have to get a grip on if he had any hope of pulling her free.

Will slid the jacket of his morning suit from his shoulders and tossed it over the windscreen into the car. Rolling his sleeves to his elbows, he took a turn about her, eyeing the angles, finding comfort in the application of basic geometry and calculus.

She looked about five-feet-eight, give or take the foot stuck in the mud.

"What do you weigh?"

"Excuse me?"

"Never mind." It would come down to the force of the suction of the mud anyway. "If you don't mind, I'm going to take you from behind."

A slim auburn eyebrow rose dramatically. "I thank you for asking first, but I do mind."

Will's gaze lifted from the behind in question to find the woman looking over her shoulder at him. Those big eyes were unblinking, a glint of warmth, laughter even, flickering in the blue. Or was it green?

Right. He'd heard it too. He felt his own cheek curving

into an unexpected smile. "My intentions are pure. I only wish to get you out of your...sticky situation."

Her right fist unclenched from her skirt, her fingers sliding past one another. Then her eyes dipped as she gave *him* a thorough once-over to match the one he'd given her.

Will crossed his arms and waited. He was the pre-eminent living name in modern astronomy. Eyes Only at NASA. An open invitation to the UN. On first-name terms with presidents and prime ministers alike.

Yet none of that mattered on this muddy country road as, with a deep sigh of unwitting capitulation, the woman waved an idle hand his way and said, "Fine. Let's get this over and done with."

First time for everything, Will thought as he moved into position. Adrenaline having been sapped away, he was now very much aware of the damage incurred by his footwear. He attempted to find purchase on the boggy ground. "Ready?"

She muttered something that sounded like, "Not even close." But then she lifted her arms.

Will wrapped his arms around her waist. There really was nothing of her. More dress than woman. He grounded his feet, and heaved.

Nothing happened. She was well-bogged.

"Grip my arms," he said. "Lean back a little. Into me."

In for a penny, she wrapped her arms over his, her fingers shockingly cold as they curved over his wrists. But right behind the chill came that energy, like electricity humming just beneath her skin.

Will said, "On three I need you to press down strongly with your free foot, then jump. Okay?"

She nodded and another curl fell down, tumbling into his face. He blinked to dislodge a strand from his eyelashes. And a sweet, familiar scent tickled his nose till he could taste it on the back of his tongue. *Honeysuckle.*

"Here we go," he grumbled. "One. Two. And…three!"

He felt her sink into the ground and as she pushed he pulled. With a thick, wet *schlock* her foot popped free.

She spun, tottered, her feet near slipping out from under her. And finally came to a halt with her face lodged into his neck.

There she breathed. Warm bursts of air wafted over his skin and turned his hair follicles into goose flesh.

Then he felt the moment she realised she had one hand gripping his sleeve, the other clamped to his backside for all she was worth.

The breathing stopped. A heartbeat slunk by. Two. Then she slowly released her hold.

Only, the second she let go, she slipped again.

With a whoop she grabbed him—the sound shaking a pair of bluebirds loose. They swooped and twittered before chasing one another down the tunnel and away.

And suddenly she was trembling in earnest. Violent shakes racked her body, as if she were about to self-destruct.

Dammit. Computing how best to separate her from her trap was one thing, but this was beyond his pay grade.

She made a noise then. Something between a squeak and a whimper. The next time she shook she broke free with a cracking laugh. Then more laughter tumbled on top of the first. Braying, cackling, riotous laughter—the kind that took hold of a person until they could barely breathe.

Will looked to the sky. He wasn't built for this kind of roller coaster of emotion. It was so taxing and there was no logical pathway out.

Ready to take his leave before things turned again, Will took her firmly by the arms.

Another curl fell to dangle in front of her face. She crossed her eyes and blew it away with a quick stream of air shot from the side of her mouth. When she uncrossed her eyes she looked directly into his.

Spots of pretty pink sat high on her pale cheeks, clear even beneath the tracks of old tears. As her laughter faded, her wide mouth still smiled softly. Light sparked in the bluish green of her huge eyes, glints of folly and fun. And she sank into his grip as if she could stay there all day.

Instead of the words that had been balanced on the tip of his tongue, Will found himself saying, "If you're laughing because your other foot is now stuck I will leave you here."

A grin flashed across her face, fast and furious, resonant of a pulse fusion blast. "Not stuck," she said. "Muddy, mortified, falling apart at the seams, but the last thing I am any more is stuck."

Will nodded. Even though he was the one who suddenly felt stuck. For words. For a decision on what to do next. For a reason to let her go.

Which was *why* he let her go. He unclamped his fingers one at a time, giving her no reason to fall into his arms again.

The woman reminded him of a newly collapsed star, unaware as yet that her unstable gravitational field syphoned energy from everything she touched.

But Will wasn't about to give any away. He gave every bit of energy to his work. It was important, it was groundbreaking, it was necessary. He had none to spare.

"Look," he said, stopping to clear his throat. "I'm heading towards court so I can give you a lift if you're heading in that direction. Or drop you…wherever it is you are going." On foot. Through muddy countryside. In what had probably been some pretty fancy shoes, considering the party dress that went with them. From what Will had seen there was nothing for miles bar the village behind him, and the palace some distance ahead. "Were you heading to the wedding, then?"

It was a simple enough question, but the girl looked as if she'd been slapped. Laughter gone, colour gone, dark tears suddenly wobbled precariously in the corners of her eyes.

She recovered quickly, dashing a finger under each eye, sniffing and taking a careful step back. "No. No, thanks. I'm... I'll be fine. You go ahead. Thank you, though."

With that she lifted her dress, turned her back on him and picked her way across the road, slipping a little, tripping on her skirt more.

If the woman wanted to make her own way, dressed and shod as she was, then who was he to argue? He almost convinced himself too. Then he caught the moment she glanced towards the palace, hidden somewhere on the other side of the trees, and decidedly changed tack so that she was heading in the absolute opposite direction.

And, like the snick of a well-oiled combination lock, everything suddenly clicked into place.

The dress with its layers of pink lace, voluminous skirt and hints of rose-gold thread throughout.

The pink train—was that what they called it?—trailing in the mud behind her.

Will's gaze dropped to her left hand clenched around a handful of skirt. A humungous pink rock the size of a thumbnail in a thin rose-gold band glinted thereupon.

He'd ribbed Hugo enough through school when the guy had been forced to wear the sash of his country at formal events: pink and rose-gold—the colours of the Vallemontian banner.

Only one woman in the country would be wearing a gown in those colours today.

If Will wasn't mistaken, he'd nearly run down one Mercedes Gray Leonine.

Who—instead of spending her last moments as a single woman laughing with her bridesmaids and hugging her family before heading off to marry the estimable Prince Alessandro Hugo Giordano and become a princess of Vallemont—was making a desperate, muddy, shoeless run for the hills.

Perfect.

CHAPTER TWO

"YOU CAN'T BE SERIOUS."

Sadie swallowed as the man's voice echoed through the thicket. Or she tried at the very least. After crying non-stop for the last hour, her throat felt like sandpaper.

In fact, her entire body felt raw. Sensitive. Prickly. As if her senses were turned up to eleven.

Adding a near-death experience hadn't helped a jot.

Well, pure and utter panic had got her this far and she planned to ride it out until she reached the border. Or a cave. Or a sinkhole that could swallow her up. Where was a batch of quicksand when you needed it?

She gathered as much of her dress as she was able and kept on walking, hoping her sardonic liberator would simply give up and drive away.

Unfortunately, his deep voice cut through the clearing like a foghorn. "You've made your point. You can stop walking now."

Sadie's bare foot squelched into a slippery patch of mud. She closed her eyes. Took a breath. Turned. And faced down the stranger in her midst.

When she'd heard the car coming around the corner her life had flashed before her eyes. Literally. Moments, big and small, fluttering through her mind like pages in a picture book.

Not yet school age, screaming, pigtails flying behind

her as she was being chased through the palace halls by a grinning Hugo. Her mother waggling a finger at her and telling her to act like a lady.

At five, maybe six, Princess Marguerite gently reminding her not to hold her hand up to block the bright lights from the TV crew. Hugo standing behind a camera making faces as she sat on a couch in the palace library, answering questions about growing up as a "regular girl" in the palace.

The blur of high school without Hugo at her side—the first sense of feeling adrift without her safety net.

Her attempt to overcome that feeling—wide-eyed and terrified, landing in New York when she was twenty. Then grabbing that safety net with both hands as, teary and weary, she fled New York and moved back into the palace at twenty-five.

Her memory had not yet hit the anxious, fractured, out-of-control mess of the past few weeks when she'd spied the driver on the muddy road.

For time had slowed—imprinting on her mind wind-ruffled dark hair, a square jaw, a face as handsome as sin. A surge of drama at the end. *At least the last thing I'll ever see is a thing of beauty*, she'd thought.

Of course, that was before he'd proceeded to storm at her for a good five minutes straight.

Quite the voice he had. Good projection. With those darkly scowling eyes and that muscle ticking in his impossibly firm jaw she'd first thought him a Hamlet shoo-in. From a distance, though, with those serious curls and proud square shoulders he'd make a fine Laertes. Then again, she'd had a good grip on that which was hidden beneath the suit. A dashing Mercutio, perhaps?

Though not in one of her high-school productions, alas. One look at him and her twelfth-grade drama students would be too busy swooning to get anything done.

That, and she'd been "encouraged" to take a sabbatical from her job the moment she'd become engaged. The palace had suggested six months for her to settle into her new role before "deciding" if she wished to return.

"Ms," he said again, and she landed back in the moment with a thud.

Focus, her subconscious demanded, lucidity fluctuating like a flickering oil lamp during a storm. Her brain seemed to have kicked into self-protect mode, preferring distraction over reality. But, as much as she might wish she was living a high-school play, this was as real as it got.

"Ms—"

"Miss," she shot back, levelling the stranger with a *leave me be* glance. Oh, yes, she was very much a "miss". Her recent actions made sure of that. She remembered the rock weighing down her left hand and carefully tucked it into a swathe of pink tulle.

"As I said I'll be fine from here. I promise. You can go." She took a decided step back, landing right on the cusp of a jagged rock. She winced. Cried out. Hopped around. Swore just a bit. Then pinched the bridge of her nose when tears threatened to spill again.

"Miss," said the stranger, his rumbling voice quieter now, yet somehow carrying all the more. "You have lost both your shoes. You're covered in mud. You're clearly not…well. It's a mile or more to the nearest village. And the afternoon is settling in. Unless you have another mode of transport under that skirt, you're either coming with me or you're sleeping under the stars. Trust me."

Trust him? Did he think she was born under a mushroom? *Quite possibly*, she thought, considering the amount of mud covering the bottom half of her dress.

Not witness to the conversations going on inside Sadie's head, the stranger went on, "How could I look myself in the mirror if I heard on the news tomorrow that a woman was eaten by a bear, the only evidence the remains of a pink dress?"

Sadie coughed. Not a laugh. Not a whimper. More like the verbal rendering of her crumbling resolve. "Bears are rare in Vallemont. And they have plenty of fish."

"Mmm. The headline was always more likely to be *Death by Tulle*." He swished a headline across the sky. "'*Woman trips over log hidden entirely from view by copious skirts, lands face-first in puddle. Drowns.*'"

Sadie's eye twitched. She wasn't going to smile. Not again. That earlier burst of laughter was merely the most recent mental snap on a day punctuated with mental snaps.

She breathed out hard. She'd walked miles through rain-drenched countryside in high heels and a dress that weighed as much as she did. She hadn't eaten since... when? Last night? There was a good chance she was on the verge of dehydration considering the amount of water she'd lost through her tear ducts alone. She was physically and emotionally spent.

And she needed whatever reserve of energy, chutzpah and pure guts she had left, considering what she'd be facing over the next few days, weeks, decades, when she was finally forced to face the mess she had left behind.

She gave the stranger a proper once-over. Bespoke suit. Clean fingernails. Posh accent. That certain *je ne sais quoi* that came of being born into a life of relative ease.

The fact that he had clearly not taken to her was a concern. She was likable. Extremely likable. Well known, in fact, for being universally liked. True, he'd not caught her in a banner moment, but still. Worth noting.

"You could be an axe murderer for all I know," she said. "Heck, *I* could be an axe murderer. Maybe this is my *modus operandi*."

He must have seen something in her face. Heard the subtle hitch in her voice. Either way, his head tipped sideways. Just a fraction. Enough to say, *Come on, honey. Who are you trying to kid?*

The frustrating thing was, he was right.

It was pure dumb luck that he had happened upon her right in the moment she'd become stuck. And it was dumber luck that he was a stranger who clearly had no clue who she was. For her face had been everywhere the last few weeks. Well, not *her* face. The plucked, besmeared, stylised face of a future princess. For what she had imagined would be a quiet, intimate ceremony, the legal joining of two friends in a mutually beneficial arrangement, had somehow spiralled way out of control.

She'd had more dumb luck that not a single soul had seen her climb out the window of the small antechamber at the base of the six-hundred-year-old palace chapel and run, the church bells chiming loud enough to be heard for twenty miles in every direction.

Meaning karma would be lying in wait to even out the balance.

She looked up the road. That way led to the palace. To people who'd no doubt discovered she was missing by now and would search to the ends of the earth to find her. A scattered pulse leapt in her throat.

Then she looked at the stranger's car, all rolling fenders and mag wheels, speed drawn in its every line. Honestly, if he drove a jalopy it would still get her further from trouble faster than her own feet.

Decision made, she held out a hand. "Give me your phone."

"Not an axe murderer, then, but a thief?"

"I'm going to let my mother know who to send the police after if I go missing."

"Where's your phone?"

"In my other dress."

A glint sparked deep in her accomplice's shadowed

eyes. It was quite the sight, triggering a matching spark in her belly. She cleared her throat as the man bent over the car and pulled a slick black phone from a space between the bucket seats.

He waved his thumb over the screen, and when it flashed on he handed it to her.

The wallpaper on his phone was something from outer space. A shot from *Star Wars*? Maybe underneath the suave, urban hunk mystique he was a Trekkie.

The wallpaper on the phone she'd unfortunately left at the palace in her rush to get the heck out of there was a unicorn sitting at a bar drinking a "human milkshake". Best not to judge.

She found the text app, typed in her mother's number.

But what to say? *I'm sorry? I'm safe? I screwed up? I would give my right leg to make sure they do not take this out on you?*

Her mother had been a maid at the palace since before Sadie was born. It had been her home too for nearly thirty years. If they fired her mother because of what Sadie had done…

Lava-hot fear swarmed through Sadie's insides until she imagined Hugo's response to such a suggestion. No. No matter how hard he might find it to forgive her for what she'd done to him today, he'd never take it out on her mother. He was that good a man. The best man she'd ever known.

Maman

Good start.

By now you know that I'm not at the chapel.

Another deep breath.

I couldn't go through with it. It wasn't right. Not for me and certainly not for Hugo. If you see Hugo...

She paused, deleted the last line. Whatever needed to be said to Hugo, she would say herself.

I'm so terribly, desperately sorry for all the confusion and complications that will come of this and I promise I will make everything right. But today, right now, I have to lick my wounds, clear my head and prepare. Know that until then that I'm whole and I'm safe. xXx

Before she could change her mind, she pressed "send". Only remembering belatedly that her mother wouldn't recognise the strange phone number.

In fact...

She found the camera app, held up the phone and said, "Smile!" Her benefactor turned and she took a photo.

She quickly started a new message. Added the picture.

I've borrowed this phone from the gentleman in this picture, so do not message back. I'll call when I can. Love you.

The picture slid up the screen as the message was sent. The top of his head was missing, and an ear, but it was still him in all his grumpy glory. His hand was at his tie, giving it a tormented tug. His dark eyes bored into the lens. He wasn't smiling but there was something about the shape of his mouth, a curving at the corners, the barest hint of what might—under just the right circumstances—become a dimple.

Her thumb hovered over the screen as she thought about sending a text to Hugo too. What if the poor lady-in-waiting she'd sent off into the palace with the note to Hugo clutched in her white-knuckled grip hadn't managed to get through to him? Even if she had, Sadie still needed to tell him…to explain…

What? That she was nothing but a scaredy-cat?

She slid her thumbs away from the screen.

"Done?" the phone owner asked.

Sadie deleted the conversation. She hoped her mother would heed her warning or her cover as a possible axe murderess would be blown.

She solemnly gave him back his phone. "And now I'll go in your car with you."

"You're a brave woman."

"You have no idea."

His mouthed twitched and…there. Dimple. Heaven help the women of the world who got to see that thing in full flight.

Not *her* though.

If her mother had taught her anything it was to beware instant appeal; it had everything to do with genetic luck and nothing to do with character. A handsome smile could be fleeting, and could be used to hide all manner of sins.

With that in mind, it had taken her twenty-nine years to agree to marry Hugo and he'd been her best friend since birth. And still, when it had come to the crunch, she'd run. Something she'd learned from her father.

Sadie felt the backs of her eyes begin to burn as the home truths settled in. But she was done crying. She mentally forced the tears away.

She'd made a choice today. One that had sent her down this road alone. And alone she had to remain if she was to get her head on straight and figure out what the heck she was going to do with the rest of her life. But Grouchy Dimples wasn't going to leave her alone unless she let him do his knight-in-shining-armour bit and get her safely out of sight.

So Sadie picked her way back through the rivulets of rock and dirt and mud.

The stranger moved around to the passenger side of the car, opened the door, bowed slightly and said, "My lady."

Sadie's entire body froze. Only her eyes moved to collide with his.

She looked for a gleam of knowledge, a sign that he knew exactly who she was. But the only sign she got was the return of the tic in his jaw. He couldn't wait to get rid of her either.

"Sadie," she said before she even felt the word forming. "My name, it's…just Sadie."

"Pleasure to meet you, Just Sadie. I'm Will."

He held out a hand. She took it. He felt warm where she was cool. Strong where she was soft. His big hand enveloped hers completely, and for the first time in as long as she could remember she found herself hit with the profound sense that everything was going to be okay.

The sensation was so strong, so unexpected, so unsought, she whipped her hand away.

Will held the door for her once more. "Let's get this show on the road."

Taking a deep breath, Sadie gathered up as much of her skirt as she could, tucking and folding and looping the fabric under her arms. Then she squeezed backside-first into the bucket seat.

After Will closed the door with a soft snick, Sadie let the fabric go. It sprung away, filling the space right up to her chin. Relief at not being on her feet, on the run, in the open, rolling over her like a wave of bliss.

Will slid into the driver's seat and curled long fingers over the leather steering wheel. He surreptitiously checked his watch again. He still thought he had a wedding to attend, Sadie realised, and for a fraught second she thought he might simply drive that way.

"You mentioned a village," Sadie said, pointing over her shoulder in the opposite direction to the palace.

"The village it is." Will gunned the engine, carefully backed out of the muddy trench, executed a neat three-point turn and drove back the way he had come.

A minute later, Sadie glimpsed the palace through the trees. The afternoon sunlight had begun to cast the famous pink and gold highlights across the sandstone walls which had lent the small principality the beautiful, romantic, quixotic colours of its banners.

Home.

But after what she had done, could she ever go back there? Would they even let her through the door? And what would happen to her mother, a maid who had lived and worked under the palace roof for the last twenty-nine years?

Sadie put the flurry of unpleasant questions to one side and closed her eyes, letting the dappled sunlight wash across the backs of her eyelids. There was nothing she could do about all that right now.

Later. She'd figure it all out later.

Will leant his elbow against the window of the car, feigning a relaxedness he did not feel as he drove over the bridge he'd navigated not long before. Back in the village, banners still flew. Music poured out into the streets. The roads were now bare, since everyone had moved inside to be in front of their TVs in order to see the bride make her first appearance. Little did they know they were looking the wrong way.

If Hugo hadn't yet discovered his bride was missing, he soon would. Search plans would be afoot. Containment plans.

Will was forced to admit that his immediate plans would need to become fluid for the moment as well. But first...

As the engine's throaty growl gave him away, Sadie sat upright. "What are you doing? Why are you slowing?"

"We need petrol," he said as he pulled off the road and up to a tank wrapped in rose-gold tinsel that flapped in the light breeze.

He used the collective noun very much on purpose. He'd read enough books to know that, in hostage negotiations, making the hostage-taker feel they were on the same side was paramount. Though which one of them was the hostage here was debatable.

He pulled over and jumped from the car. But not before surreptitiously sliding his phone into his pocket.

Meanwhile, Sadie had slunk down so far in the seat she was practically in the footwell. All he could see was acres of crinkled pink and a few auburn curls.

"Can you breathe down there?"

A muffled voice professed, "Most of the dress is organically grown Australian cotton. Very breathable."

"And yet I'm not sure it was intended to be worn over the face."

Two hands curled around the fabric and a small face poked out. "Point made."

She blinked at him through huge red-rimmed eyes above a pink-tipped nose. Her full lower lip was shiny from nibbling. When she wasn't acting so bolshie and stubborn she was rather pretty.

Will pushed the thought away. He turned his back and splashed a nominal amount of petrol into the tank before heading for the shop. Inside, he gave the guy behind the counter a wave. Then, finding a private corner, he made the call, using a phone number he could only hope still worked.

It answered on the second ring.

"Yes?" came the voice from Will's past. The voice of the Prince.

Will leaned against a shelf. "Hey, mate, how's things?"

A beat. "Darcy? Look, I can't—"

"You can't talk because you're meant to be getting married but your bride seems to have gone missing."

The silence was deafening. Then footsteps echoed through the phone as Hugo obviously set to finding himself a private corner of his own.

"How the hell can you possibly—?"

"She's with me."

Will gave a very quick rundown of the events. Leading to his decision to keep her close.

Hugo's voice was uncommonly hoarse, even a little cracked, as he said, "I was given a note just before you rang by a maid refusing to leave my doorway. Written in lipstick, on the torn-out page of a hymnal no less, telling me she couldn't go through with it. I didn't believe it until just now. Yet at the same time it felt like I'd been waiting for that note all my life. I— *Dammit*. Excuse me a moment."

Hugo's voice was muffled. Will imagined him covering the mouthpiece of the phone. His tension was palpable in his short, sharp responses to whomever had disrupted their conversation.

It had been years since he'd seen Hugo in person. Even as a teenager there'd been gravitas about the Prince, the weight of the world sitting easily on his shoulders. Until his own father had died in a car crash and that world had collapsed.

Will had born Hugo through that horrendous time. Hugo had tried to return the favour after Clair's death only a few months later, putting aside his own grief, but Will had rejected Hugo's counsel out of hand.

Will had been mistaken then. He would not turn his back on the Prince now.

Will waited, glancing around the petrol station. Pink and gold streamers hung limply from the ceiling to the cash register. The guy behind the counter hunched over a small TV while sipping pink milk through a straw. The vision showed a variety of invited guests smiling and waving as they walked up the gravel path to the palace gates.

A frisson of tension pulled tight across Will's shoulders. Everything had happened so fast—the near crash, the rescue, the discovery, the uncommon decision to get involved—the repercussions that went far beyond his inconvenience didn't hit him until that moment.

An entire country held its breath in anticipation, clueless as to the axe that had already begun to swing, while Hugo sat somewhere in the palace, looking into the face of an emotional ruination that he did not deserve. Again.

"Apologies," said Hugo as he came back on the line.

"Mate," said Will, his own voice a little rough. "What the hell happened?"

The silence was thick. Distant. Elongating the miles and years between them.

Hugo's voice was cool as he asked, "Is she injured? Is she distressed?"

"She's shaky but unhurt."

"I'd very much like to talk to her."

Will thought *he'd* very much like to kick her out of his rental car, and dump her on the side of the road; force her to face the bedlam she had unleashed. But it was clear Hugo was not of the same mind.

If Will's intention in coming to Vallemont had truly been to put things to rights with his oldest friend, then it seemed he'd been gifted the opportunity to do just that. The fact it would not be easy was ironically just.

"In full disclosure, she doesn't know I'm talking to you. In fact, she doesn't know that I'm aware of who she is at all. I believe that's the only reason she agreed to let me give her a lift."

He let that sit. When Hugo made no demur, Will went on.

"I can give her the phone or I can keep her with me until you send someone to collect her. Unless, of course, you want me to bring her back right now so you can work your magic and marry the girl."

He half hoped Hugo would say *Bring back my girl*— then Will could deliver her and tell himself he'd achieved what he'd come to Vallemont to do.

"If you could stay with her I would very much appreciate it," was Hugo's eventual response. "I'll send for her when I can. Till then, keep her safe."

Will nodded before saying, "Of course. And you? Where do you go from here?"

"That, my friend, would be the question of the hour."

"As opposed to, *Do you take this woman?*" Will imagined a wry smile filling the silence. And suddenly the miles and years contracted to nothing.

"Yes," was Hugo's dry response. "As opposed to that."

The Prince rang off first. No doubt plenty on his to-do list.

It left Will to stare at the picture he'd linked to Hugo's private line; the two of them at seventeen in climbing gear, grins wide, arms slung around one another's shoulders, mountains at their backs. Clair had taken that picture the day before Will had broken his leg.

By the end of that summer Clair had been taken ill. A week later she'd been diagnosed with an incurable brain disease. Mere months after she'd taken that photo she'd left them for ever.

Will slid his phone into his pocket. He tucked the memories away too before they started to feed on him rather than the other way around.

Hugo wasn't the only one with things to do.

Only, while Hugo would no doubt be fending off a buffet of advisors as he determined the best way forward, Will had to go it alone.

It was a concept that didn't come easily to a twin, a concept that had haunted him for a long time after his sister was gone. Until one day, while hiding from his economics professor at Cambridge, he'd slipped into a random lecture hall. Taken a seat at the back. Discovered it was *Stars and the Cosmic Cycle*. And found himself skewered to the seat.

For Clair's last gift to him, one she'd planned to give to him on what would have been their eighteenth birthday, one he'd only found in her bedroom after she'd died, was a telescope.

As a man who'd never believed in signs, he'd gone with it. As the lecturer had talked of the universe as unmapped, unchartered and mostly incalculable, many in the lecture hall had twittered and shifted on their seats, finding the concept overwhelming.

For Will it had changed the concept of being "alone" for him completely. And it was that ability to dissociate from the everyday, to enjoy a high level of dedicated solitude, that had paved the way for his being the pre-eminent voice in modern astronomy.

Will paid for the petrol, steadfastly refusing to look at the pre-wedding coverage on the monitor. He was halfway to the car when he remembered.

He wasn't alone.

He had Sadie.

She peered up at him from the mound of wriggling pink as he slid back into the car, her curls flopping onto her pale shoulders, her big eyes filled with pandemonium. This woman was chaos incarnate, and she was leaving a widening swathe of trouble in her wake.

"Everything okay?" she asked. "You were gone for a while."

"Was I?" Will started the car with more gusto than required.

He'd come to this country, pained at the thought of having to watch Hugo marry someone who wasn't Clair, quietly wondering if the invitation was his penance for having laid the blame for what had happened at Hugo's guiltless feet for all these years.

Now he realised he'd miscalculated. *She* was his penance. Mercedes "Sadie" Gray Leonine. Looking after her on Hugo's behalf, keeping her out of sight until he could send word to Hugo where he could find her would go some way to ameliorating past wrongs.

And when it was done, he might even be able to get an earlier flight out. It was meant to be an unusually clear night, a rare opportunity to spend some time with London's night sky.

Feeling better about the world, Will shot Sadie a smile, which faded a tad at the way her eyes widened as he did so.

"The tank is full, the sky is blue." Will tapped the car's GPS. "North? South? East? West? Coast? Mountains? Moon? Where are we going?"

CHAPTER THREE

SADIE NIBBLED SO hard on the tip of a pale pink acrylic nail, the thing snapped right off, so she carefully hid it in the door pocket and racked her brain for an answer.

Where are we going? Will had asked. As if she were following some kind of plan.

Her only goal had been to get as far from the palace as possible without being seen. Her luck would not hold out for much longer. Her best bet now was to hole up, get in touch with Hugo somehow. Apologise, grovel, make him see that while her timing had been terrible it had been the right decision, for both of them.

"A room," she said. "To stay for a night. That's what I'd like."

"Excellent. Do you have a place in mind?"

"Not exactly. Some place…quiet would be fine." Discreet. Not one of Hugo's palatial resorts, for example. "Where are those dodgy motels you see in American cop shows when you need them?"

"I'm sorry?"

Sadie glanced at her companion, thankful to find he was back to looking at her as if he was barely containing his impatience. That momentary flash of perfect white teeth as he'd smiled had been disconcerting to say the least.

She usually went out of her way to make people feel comfortable. Hugo joked that her need to be liked by everyone was pathological. Sadie simply wanted to make sure everyone around her was happy. But in these circumstances a little distance felt safer. It was easier to think of the man as a means to an end rather than a collection of dimples, warm hands and crinkles at the edges of his eyes as he smiled. Especially now, when she was feeling so untethered. In the past her decision-making skills had not been at their peak at such times.

She turned on the seat; her skirt bunching under her hip. "You know, the kind where the anti-hero in the vintage brown Cadillac hooks around the back of some dreary, anonymous, flat-roofed roadside joint where the ancient woman with a cigarette dangling from her cracked lips doesn't even bother to look up from her crossword as she signs the guy in?"

He glanced at her and said, "Flat-roofed?"

How odd that he focused on that. It was the kind of detail that usually tickled only her. When she found herself looking into those dark eyes of his a beat too long, she glanced at her fake fingernails instead. One down, nine to go. "You know—squat. Like it's been flattened by the weight of the world. Why doesn't Vallemont have places like that?"

"Because it's Vallemont," he said, and he was right.

The sentiment wouldn't have made as much sense to her as a kid.

Watching Hugo go away to school had made Sadie itch to see the world, to see life outside the borders of the peaceable country in which she'd been born. And eventually she'd managed to talk her way into a four-year acting course in New York.

At first it had been a dream. Auditioning, waitressing, living in near-squalor with three strangers in a studio in Brooklyn. Walking streets where nobody knew her story, with its urban canyons, subway smells, its cracked sidewalks and manic energy, as different a place from Valle-mont as it was possible to find.

Halfway through she'd begun to feel lonely, the brilliant, fraught, nerve-racking, ugly, beautiful and eye-opening experience taking its toll.

By the end of that year she'd realised that it wasn't the noise and hustle and energy of a big city she had craved, but control over her life. Taking control over her narrative. That's what she loved about theatre. Not acting, but the chance to shape a play from beginning to end.

She'd lasted another year before she'd come home. Giving up a dream many would kill for.

And oh, that land of rolling hills and green pastures. Of crystalline streams fed by snow-capped mountains. And towns of cobbled streets and dappled sunshine and quiet, happy lives. The relief had been immeasurable.

And here she was again—gifted a rare opportunity and she'd thrown it all away.

Sadie groaned and let her head drop back against the seat.

"If it's accommodation you're after, what about this place?" said Will, the car engine growling as he slowed.

Sadie cracked open an eye to find herself looking at a place as far from a dreary, anonymous, flat-roofed roadside joint as possible.

A sign reading "La Tulipe" swung from the eaves of a ramshackle dwelling, three storeys high, with a pitched roof and balconies all round. Bright purple bougainvillaea was starkly stunning as it crept over the muddy brick. Oddly shaped, it dissected two roads, one heading up the hill to the left, the other dipping down the hill sharply to the right, creating an optical illusion that made it look as if it had a slight lean down the hill. Or maybe it *was* falling down the hill. It had an ancient, ramshackle appeal either way.

A skinny black cat skittered across the way as Will pulled into a spot on the low side of the building. He turned off the engine, got out of the car and reached into the back seat for a soft black leather bag.

Sadie sat up straight. "Ah, what are you doing with those?"

"I plan on seeing you inside. And I'm not leaving my bags in the car while I do so."

Sadie peeked over her shoulder. A gentle breeze skipped autumn leaves over the cobbled road. A small brown bird danced from one semi-bare tree to another. Other than that, there was no one as far as the eye could see. "We're not exactly a crime capital here."

Will followed her gaze, paused a moment, then, ignoring her, heaved his other bag—a big square silver case—out of the car and set it on the footpath. "Coming?"

Sadie heard voices—a couple laughing as they crossed the street at the bottom of the hill. Time to get inside. Except...

"I can't go in there dressed like this. I look—" Like the girl who'd left the country's most eligible bachelor standing at the altar. She'd be less likely to be recognised naked than in that dress. She'd heard knock-offs were already available. "A total mess. What do you have in your bag? Or your case?"

Will's hand went to the battered silver case. It was big enough that she might even fit inside. For a brief moment she considered asking.

"Anything I might be able to borrow? I'll take it off the minute I get inside a room."

That muscle ticked in his jaw. Another flickered below his right eye. He appeared to be making a great effort at keeping eye contact. And Sadie realised what she'd said.

Feeling a wave of pink heat rising up her neck, she backtracked. "I mean I'll find something else to wear, even if it's a bed sheet, then you can be on your way."

Her reluctant knight breathed for a beat or two, his dark eyes pinning her to her seat. Then, muttering under his breath, he lifted the leather bag and plonked it onto the driver's seat.

Then he moved down the footpath and away from the car, his back to her, giving her some privacy. Not ideal, but needs must.

Inside his bag she found an expensive-looking knit sweater. Black. Soft as a baby's bottom. It smelled delicious too. Like sandalwood, and fresh air and man. Like the scent she'd caught in that strangely intimate half a second where Will had put his arms around her, pulling her back into the nook of his strong, warm body, before yanking her out of the mud.

She cleared her throat and shoved the sweater aside, rifling until she found a utilitarian tracksuit top. Black again. And some black tracksuit pants. The guy sure liked black. Maybe he was a spy. Or a magician. Or clinically depressed.

She glanced over her shoulder to find he still had his back to her as he stood on the footpath, hands in pockets, face tilted to the sun.

Even in a suit it was clear he was built like a champion diver—all broad shoulders and thick, roping muscle. His profile as he squinted down the street was strong, sure, forbearing. He might not be the most easy-going man she'd ever met, but there was no doubting he was very comfortable in his own skin.

Not depressed, then. Perhaps he simply liked black.

She pulled out the tracksuit pants, shuffled up onto her knees, twisted her hands over her shoulder to attempt to rid herself of layers of lace embedded with tiny pink crystals...no luck. She twisted around the back of her waist. Still no luck. As panic tickled up her spine she thought about ripping the thing over her head, but it was so dense she'd probably find herself caught in a straight-jacket of her own making.

Sadie bit her lip and looked up at the sky. Cloudless. The brightest blue. Such a happy sight. She muttered a few choice words under her breath.

Then, "Ah, excuse me. Will? I need some help here."

He spun on his heel so the sun was behind him, his face in shadow. Resistance was evident in the hard lines of his body as he said, "Help?"

She flapped her hand towards the trillion pearl buttons strapping her in.

It was his turn to mutter a flurry of choice words before he took a few slow steps her way. "What do you need me to do?"

"Start at the top? Truth be told, I wasn't paying much attention as I was strapped in." Trying not to panic had been higher on her list of priorities.

Will took in a long, deep breath before his hands moved to her neck, surprisingly gentle as they pushed her hair aside. So many curls had dropped during her run from the palace. She helped, taking them in hand as she tipped her head forward.

A beat later, Will's fingers worked the top button, which was positioned right against a vertebra. That was what it felt like anyway, as if he'd hit a nerve cluster. Goosebumps sprung up all over her body.

With a sweet glide, it unhooked, Will's warm thumb sliding against her skin as he pressed the fabric aside.

"Sadie?" he asked, his voice deep and low and close enough to cause a rumble.

"Yes, Will?"

"There are about a hundred-odd buttons on this thing."

"One hundred and eight." One for every year the Giordanos had been the governing family of Vallemont. Seriously. When the small wedding she and Hugo had planned had twisted into the kind of circus where the number of pearl buttons on her dress had a backstory, that was when she ought to have put her foot down and called the whole thing off.

Will said, "Take this as a serious question, but are there…layers underneath the dress?"

"Layers?"

"Ah, under…garments?"

She'd not been able to pin down his accent until that moment. It was crisp and clear, but worldly. As if he'd travelled a great deal. In that moment it was pure, upper-crust, Queen's English.

He sounded so adorably repressed, she was unable to stop herself from saying, "Are you asking if I've gone commando?"

A beat, a breath. Then, "Sure. Why not?"

"No, Will. I am not naked beneath my dress. There are undergarments to spare."

"Glad to hear it. And are you planning on wearing your dress again?"

"Once this thing is off I never want to see it again, much less wear it!" A tad effusive perhaps?

"Excellent. Here goes." Solid nails scraped lightly against her shoulder muscles as his fingers dived beneath the fabric. Then with a rip that split the silence he tore the dress apart. Buttons scattered with a pop-pop-pop as they hit the dashboard, the steering wheel, the metal skin of the car.

As the fabric loosened and fell forward across her chest, Sadie heaved in a big, gasping breath. The first proper lungful of air she'd managed in hours. Days even. Weeks maybe. It might well have been the first true breath she'd taken since she and Hugo had shaken hands on an agreement to wed.

She felt the moment Will let the fabric go, the weight of his warm hands lifting away. More goosebumps popped up to fill the gaps between the others.

"Thank you," she said, her voice a little rough, as she wriggled free of the thing until she was in her bra, chemise and stockings.

Out of the corner of her eye she saw Will turn away again, this time to lean his back against the car.

As the chill autumn air nipped at her skin she hastened Will's clothes over the top. There was that scent again. This time she also caught layers of leather and skin and cologne. Subtle, expensive and drinkable. The sooner she was out of his clothes the better.

Kicking her dress into the footwell with more force than was probably necessary, Sadie got out of the car.

The stony ground was freezing against her bare toes. Bracing.

When Will's tracksuit pants—which were far too big for her—began to fall, she twisted the waistband and shoved it into the top of her knickers. The jacket falling halfway down her thighs covered the lump.

At last, she bent to check herself in the side mirror. And literally reared back in shock at the sight. Her hair was an absolute disaster. Her cheeks were blotchy and wind-chafed. She could barely recognise herself beneath the rivers of dried mascara bleeding down her cheeks.

Licking her thumbs, she wiped her face clean as best she could. Then she set to pulling out the thousand pins from her hair. Dislodging the hairpiece was a blessed relief.

Once her hair was all her own again she tipped over her head, ran fingers through the knots, and massaged life back into her skull. With practised fingers, she tied the lot into a basic ponytail. No longer a clown bride. Now she was rocking more of an athletic goth look.

An athletic Goth with a mighty big engagement ring on her finger.

She glanced Will's way. He was checking something on his silver case.

She looked back to the ring. It was insanely ostentatious, with its gleaming pink diamond baguette in the rose-gold band. But was it her? Not even close.

Hugo's face slid into her mind then, with his oh-so-familiar laugh.

"My grandmother left it to me, which was a matter of contention in the family, as you can imagine. Her intention was that I give it to my bride. I'm sorry."

"Sorry for what?"

"It looks ridiculous on you."

"Thanks a lot!"

"Seriously. Your fingers are so scrawny, it looks like you're trying to balance a brick on the back of your hand. Take it off."

"No. Never. Do you remember the first time you said you'd marry me? I do. I was four and you were seven. Kind woman that I am, I never planned to hold you to it back then. But I'm not letting you off the hook now. This ring is what it is: a symbol. If a brick is what will help keep roofs over both of our families' heads, then it seems like a pretty fine symbol to me."

Another promise broken, Sadie slid the brick from her finger. The fact that it came right off, without even the slightest pressure, seemed like a pretty big sign in and of itself.

She quickly tugged down the track pants, found a ribbon hanging from her garter and tied the ring to it with a nice tight knot. Then she gave the jacket one last tug. "Okay, I'm ready."

Will pressed away from the car and turned. His dark gaze danced over her clothes—*his* clothes—her bare feet, then up to her hair. It paused there a moment before dropping to the hand clutching the bouffant of fake curls. At which point his mouth kicked into a smile. Dimple and all.

As it had been the first time, it was as unexpected and magnificent as a ray of sun slicing through a rain cloud and Sadie's heart thumped against her chest.

"What?" she shot back.

Will held a hand towards the doorway of La Tulipe. "I didn't say a thing."

Sadie grabbed the hood of his jacket and pulled it over her head. Then, scooting past him, her chin imperiously high, she said, "You didn't have to."

As soon as they entered the lobby of the old hotel, Sadie's adrenaline kicked up a notch. For all her efforts to escape, everything could fall apart right here, right now.

She tucked herself in behind Will, breathing through her mouth so as not to drink too deeply of the deliciousness of his cologne. Skin. Washing detergent. Whatever.

"Sadie," he said, turning so she was face to face with his strong profile. The heavy brow, nose so perfect it could have been carved from marble, the hint of that dimple.

"Mmm?"

"Have you heard of a little something called personal space?"

"Sorry," she said, searching desperately for a sane reason why she might be snuggled into him as she was. "I'm… cold."

If Will didn't believe her, he didn't say so. No doubt he already thought her a lunatic, considering her behaviour thus far.

As they approached the desk, over Will's shoulder Sadie

saw a girl in her late teens wearing jeans and a plain pink T-shirt, her long brown hair in a side ponytail.

Will came to a stop, tipping his big silver case back onto its wheels and readjusting his leather bag on his shoulder.

The girl smiled as they approached. "Hello!" she sing-songed. Then she seemed to notice Will anew, as along with a little sigh came a breathy, "Oh, my. Oh… Ah. Didn't think we'd see a soul today. The entire country has its nose up against its collective TVs. Waiting for the wedding to begin!"

She motioned to her computer monitor and Sadie was bombarded with a montage of images—crowds lining the path leading to the palace waving Vallemontian flags and throwing pink peony petals into the street. The front doors of the St Barnabas Chapel were open, inviting, a mouth waiting to swallow a bride whole.

"Prince Alessandro is so dreamy," said the girl, "don't you think? Those eyes. That voice. He's like the hero from some novel. To think, there is a woman out there who gets to be his heroine."

Sadie let her head fall, gently landing on one of Will's shoulder blades. "A room," she stage-whispered. "Ask about a room."

Will cleared his throat. "We were hoping for a room."

The girl blinked, seemed to suddenly notice Sadie hiding behind Will's shoulder.

Having been seen, Sadie fixed the hood tighter over her head, then gave the girl a little wave. She held her breath, waiting for the moment of recognition. But the girl merely gave her a nod before her gaze slid right back to Will.

"Right. Well, lucky for you the Tower Room has just come free. The couple using it had a wicked fight. She stormed out. He followed, looking most chagrined. It was all very exciting. Like Beatrice and Benedick in person."

Sadie perked up. The girl was into *Much Ado About*

Nothing? It was Sadie's absolute favourite play. She taught it to her senior students every year. Perhaps this place was a good choice after all.

"Anyway," said the girl, "it's our finest room. Canopy bed. Kitchenette. Balcony with views that extend all the way to the palace."

Sadie's perk was short-lived. Views of the palace? No! *No, no, no...*

She must have said it out loud, as Will leaned back an inch. "No?"

Sadie bit her lip.

"Oh. Well, I'm afraid that's the only room we have. And you're not likely to find another this close to the palace. We've been booked out for weeks. Ever since the date of the royal wedding was announced. Prince Alessandro is a favourite. Many a heart broke the moment the news came through that he was to settle down for good."

"Did they, now?" Will asked, with something akin to humour edging his voice. A catch. An aside. Like an inside joke. Or was she imagining it? "The Tower Room sounds just perfect? Thank you."

A beat slunk by, followed by another, after which Sadie realised Will was waiting for her. As this was the point at which she was meant to give her details. And her money.

She lifted herself a little higher, high enough she could mutter near Will's ear, "I don't exactly have my wallet on me right now."

"In your other dress?" he muttered back.

"Uh-huh."

His hand slid between them, grazing her belly through his tracksuit top. She gasped, her breath shooting past his ear.

He turned to stone. "Sadie," he said, his voice seeming even lower than normal.

"Mmm-hmm?"

"Wallet's in my back pocket," he said.

"Right. Sorry."

Sadie rocked back onto her heels, giving Will room. When he slid a shiny black card from inside, Sadie wasn't exactly trying to catch his name...not really. But catch it she did.

Dr William Darcy.

Dr Darcy, eh? Doctor of what? William suited him more than Will. Will was a friendly name. Will Darcy—

It was Sadie's turn to turn to stone.

Surely Mr Tall Dark and Grouchy wasn't *the* Will Darcy—schoolfriend of Hugo's from his murky boarding-school days and the only person Hugo had insisted they invite to their wedding back when the plan had been to keep it small?

Her gaze danced over the back of the man's head and neck, as if hoping for clues. But alas his collar gave nothing away.

All the while, Will's finger pressed down hard on the card and stopped its counter-slide. "Dare I ask what might the room rate be at this late date?"

The girl looked at Will, looked at his shiny card, then with a bright smile quoted an exorbitant nightly price more suited to a famous Fifth Avenue penthouse than a crumbling old village building. "Blame the wedding."

"Oh, I do," Will grumbled as he slowly lifted his finger from the card.

And Sadie felt the ground tip out from under her.

It *was* him. It had to be.

It was him and he knew. He knew who she was, he knew what she'd done. It all made sense! His coolness towards her, his insistence she go with him, the fact he was being so obliging, despite the fact he ought to have been fretting about getting to the wedding late.

The cad had been lying to her about who he was the entire time!

Okay, fine. She was lying too. But her reasons were *life and death*. Or near enough. In the olden days she would have been stoned for the move she'd pulled.

His motivation could not possibly be so clean.

"Lovely," said the girl after swiping and checking Will's card. "All set. Here are your keys."

What was that? Keys? Plural? Hang on a second. Sadie opened her mouth to let the girl know she only needed one, but Will had already picked them up.

"I'm Janine," said the girl as she came around the desk. "If you need anything, anything at all, I'm your girl. Until then, head up both sets of stairs; your door is the last on the right. I trust you'll find it wonderfully comfortable. The Tower Room also has its own fireplace. Fur rugs throughout. Super-comfortable sofas. And the most gorgeous bed you will ever see. There's no TV, of course, because it's our honeymoon suite."

Of course it is, thought Sadie, right at the moment Will said the exact same words.

A bubble of crazed laughter escaped her throat, though it sounded more like a whimper.

"Have a lovely stay, Dr Darcy and…friend."

"Thank you, Janine," he said, tapping his forehead in a two-finger salute and earning himself another sigh.

Then he turned to face Sadie. "Ready?"

Sadie gave him the same salute.

When his mouth twitched, that dimple showed for one brief second. Sadie ducked her chin and took off for the stairs.

The Tower Room was as advertised.

Exposed brick walls covered in romantic prints by Waterhouse and Rossetti. Polished wood floors gleamed in the fading light of day. Soft couches looked as if you'd fall in and never want to get out. A fireplace big enough to sleep in.

It was charming, inviting and terribly romantic.

Only then did she see the bed.

For there it was, perched on a slightly raised platform at the end of the room. Soft, cream-coloured blankets covered the mattress. Pretty gold gauze trailed from a canopy, falling into pools on the floor at each corner while fake ivy twisted around its beams and posts.

It looked like something a fairy-tale princess would sleep in.

Panic welling within her once more, Sadie looked for an out. Stumbling to one side of the room, which from the outside mirrored a classic castle keep, she pushed open the French windows and stepped onto the tiny, round balcony.

Gripping the cold metal, she gulped in great lungs full of crisp, late autumn air, hoping not to be sick all over Will's clothes.

When she finally got her stomach under control she opened her eyes.

Janine was right. The view was breathtaking.

The village lay before her, all warm, tumbling brick and thatched roofs. Early lamplight laced together rambling cobbled paths. Flower pots, green corners and naked-branched trees were scattered prettily about.

And then she looked up.

The glorious jagged mountains that surrounded their landlocked little corner of the world thrust up into the sky. And right smack dab in the middle of the view, like a gem in the centre of a ring, sat the Palace of Vallemont.

Pink ceremonial flags flapped in the breeze, all across the rooftops, heralding the big occasion. And then, as if someone had simply been waiting for her to watch, the flag atop the highest tower slid slowly down the flagpole.

If the raising of the flag signified glory, honour, rejoicing, the lowering was a sign of a death in the family, a tragedy in the country, a moment of great national sorrow.

The news was out.

Soon everybody would know she had run.

Talk about breathtaking.

CHAPTER FOUR

SADIE BACKED SLOWLY into the room, feeling as if her insides had been scooped out.

When she'd come home from New York she'd felt like such a disappointment. She'd let down everyone who'd rooted for her. Having to tell the story of her withered dream over and over again had been an out-of-body experience.

This was way worse. Millions of people she'd never met would be reeling with dismay.

Sadie was not used to being disliked. In fact, her likeability was the cornerstone of her identity.

Her story was well-known all across Vallemont, she having been born literally on the road to the palace.

Her father—a less than exemplary model of manhood who had been dragging his pregnant girlfriend across the country to avoid debt collectors—had taken one look at newborn Sadie and fled. Luckily, the wife of the reigning Sovereign Prince—Hugo's Aunt Marguerite—had been driving past when she found them, huddled on a patch of grass. The Princess had famously taken them in and given Sadie's mother a job as a palace maid, allowing Sadie to grow up as a palace child. Sadie had been a firm favourite ever since.

The very thought of all that hatred coming her way

drained the blood from her extremities until she could no longer feel her toes.

Someone cleared their throat.

Sadie's focus shifted until she saw her reluctant rescuer, the living embodiment of unfavourable judgment, standing in the centre of the room holding his bags.

The only person she could possibly turn to, the only person she could lean on, ask for advice, was looking at her with all the warmth of a shadow. His dark energy added layers to her discomfort, making her feel edgy. Awkward. Hyper-aware.

Okay, she thought. This situation seems overwhelming, impossible even. But all you can expect yourself to do is handle one thing at a time. Starting with the thing right in front of you.

Dr Will Darcy.

He was the right age to have gone to school with Hugo. That elevated level of self-confidence was certainly comparable. Though where Hugo oozed sophistication and class as if he'd been dipped in them at birth, Will had the personality of a wounded bear: gruff, unpredictable. Dangerous.

She nibbled on one of her remaining fake nails.

In the end it didn't matter. What mattered was thanking him and sending him on his way.

She moved to the small table behind the couch and grabbed some La Tulipe stationery and a pen. "Will. Thank you. So much. Truly. You've gone above and beyond. If you leave your contact details I'll know where to send the money to pay you back. Petrol, car cleaning, laundry, the hotel bill. Whatever expenses you've incurred."

He slowly shook his head. "Not necessary."

Sadie flapped the stationery his way. "But it is. Necessary. I don't like being beholden to anybody."

"Really."

Wow. Passive-aggressive, much? Sadie's shoulders snapped together, annoyance rising in her belly. He *really* didn't like her and wasn't even trying to hide it. Well, he was no prince either. Sadie held back the desire to tell him so. Barely. Years of practice at being nice coming to the fore.

"Okay, then. I officially relieve you of your knight-in-shining-armour duties." Sadie waved her fingers as if she were sprinkling fairy dust in his general direction.

Will's expression changed. It was a miniscule shift. Barely akin to an intake of breath. But she felt it. Like a ripple of energy beneath the gruff exterior. *Game on.*

He hefted the smaller bag onto the couch. Then he nudged his muddy shoes off his feet in the way men did— using the toes to shove them past the heels. He picked them up, dropped them at the door, then padded into the small kitchenette.

"I'm thirsty. You?" he asked.

With an exaggerated yawn, she said, "I am exhausted though. I think the first thing I'll do after you have your drink and go is take a nice long nap."

Will took his time filling a glass with water from the tap. Then he turned, leaning against the bench. His voice a rumble across the room. "I'm not going anywhere just yet."

A strange little flicker of heat leapt in her belly before she smacked it down. *That* wasn't what he meant. Even if it was, now was not the time, or place…

The corner of his mouth lifted, as if he knew exactly what she was thinking. It was unnerving. *He* was unnerving. She'd been so sure he didn't like her. But maybe she had it all backwards and—

Then he said, "My tracksuit. I'd like it back."

Right. Of course! He was waiting to get his clothes back. What was wrong with her?

She was a mess, that was what was wrong. Scared,

disoriented and emotionally wrecked. Not at all herself. She felt a small amount of relief at the realisation that that was why every little thing Will did—his every look, every word, every dig—was getting under her skin.

She managed a laugh. "Right. Sorry! What a goof. I'll just…find an alternative. Get you your clothes and then you can be on your way."

He took another sip of water and gave her nothing in response.

She spun around. Near the bed was a pair of doors. Behind one was a bathroom. Ooh, how lovely! A bath the size of a small car. That would go a long way to getting her back on track. But first… *Voilà!* A closet! With a pair of fluffy pink robes with rose-gold stitching and matching slippers, no less. *Viva Vallemont!*

She turned around. Will had moved to the lounge room and was sitting on the couch, looking right at home.

Sadie thought of the bath. Her head felt like mush. Her muscles ached. Even her bones were tired. Happy-go-lucky reserves fading like an empty battery, she said, "Give me ten minutes."

With that she headed into the bathroom.

There she stripped off Will's clothes and took off her chemise.

Something rubbed against her thigh. The garter. Thankfully the ring was still attached. Hugo's grandmother's ring. Not only was it part of the royal collection, and worth more than the building she was standing in, but also it didn't belong to her any more.

Not that it ever really had.

She carefully slid the garter down her leg and over her foot, placing it on the bathroom sink.

Last came her stockings, mud-covered and torn. Without a shred of remorse she threw them in the bin.

Then she turned the taps on the gorgeous big bath to as

hot as was manageable. She found complimentary bubbles and squeezed until the bottle was empty and watched as the room became misty with steam and the bubbles threatened to topple over the sides.

And, as water tended to do, it began to unlock and unwind the knotty thoughts, opening the way to the simplest plan for dealing with the problem in front of her—moving Dr Will Darcy on.

Will leant back into the big, soft couch, checked his watch and adjusted the map of his day yet again.

He hadn't given up on making the late flight home, even as the afternoon faded, but then evening began to creep in, painting golden tracts of sunlight across the wooden floor.

It flipped a memory to the front of the pack. A crumbling cottage made of stone; cosy and warm, with a fireplace and rugs on the wooden floor. His parents' house—his and Clair's—before his mother and father had died.

His grandmother had insisted he'd dreamt it. No Darcy would dare live in such a place.

But something about this place made the memory feel solid. Perhaps it was the surrealism of events. Or the fact he was thinking so much about Clair.

He rubbed his hands over his face, then reached for his phone, dashing off a quick message to Hugo giving him their location.

Within seconds a message came back:

Well done.

As if he'd known Sadie-wrangling wouldn't be easy. Needing a distraction, Hugo made another call. The phone was answered. "Boss man!"
"Natalie. How are you?"

"Frantic. Busy. Overworked."

"Happy to hear it."

Will's assistant laughed, the jolly sound coming to him from somewhere in the Midwest of the United States.

Natalie had worked for him going on seven years now, after having been attached to his case by a publicity firm the week his textbook was first published. Finding her tough, keen and pedantic, he'd offered her a permanent position as his assistant and she'd snapped it up. They'd never actually met, working purely online and over the phone which suited him. Less time wasted on personal chit chat that way. She ran his bookings, planned his travel and was the gatekeeper between him and his business manager, clients, institutions, conglomerates and governments the world over.

"Now," said Natalie, "Garry is breathing down my neck like a dragon with a blocked nose, wanting to set up a meeting."

Will's business manager. Probably wanting to talk career strategy, aka Slow Down Before You Break Down. He'd heard it before, mostly from whoever he was dating at the time. Perhaps it was time for a new business manager too.

"When are you coming home?"

Will knew that by "home" Natalie didn't mean London. He had an apartment there, as he did in New Mexico, Sweden, Chile and many of the best star-gazing spots in the world, but he was rarely in one place longer than any other. By "When are you coming home?" Natalie meant, when was he getting back to work?

"What's coming up?"

Natalie listed a string of upcoming engagements. Full to bursting. Just as he liked it.

Without the onus of family, his work was the sun around which his life revolved. Whether he was looking through a telescope, hooking a crowd of eager-faced college students, putting the hard word on funding to a room filled with industry leaders, chipping away at the whys and wherefores of the universe, he was as engrossed now as he ever had been.

The rare times he loosened his grip, took a short break, said no to opportunity, he felt his life touching on the ordinary—and with it a creeping sense of futility. Of being indolent and inadequate. Just as his grandmother assured him his parents had been.

"You've also had meeting and speaking requests from a talk show in LA, a finishing school in the south of France, and…this is my favourite." She rattled off the name of a big-time rapper, who was keen on investing in new digital mirroring technology that Will had funded from day dot. NASA were liking the looks of it and the musician wanted in.

"Fit them in."

Not surprised with his answer, Natalie barrelled on. "And the prime minister would like five minutes next week."

Will perked up. "The agenda?"

He could all but see Natalie's grin as she said, "The Templeton Grant."

Will smacked his hand on his thigh. "Finally! Make the time. Day or night. I'm there."

Professor Templeton was the man who had conducted the first lecture Will had ever attended. He had become a mentor over the years until he had passed away a few months before. The long-running grant the professor had directed for the university was in danger of being phased out. Will was determined not to let that happen. He'd petitioned parliament to ask they continue in perpetuity, and to rename it in Templeton's honour. So far unsuccessfully.

The prime minister—a smart man, a good man, a man of science—was his last hope.

"You bet," said Natalie. And Will was certain she'd make it work.

Until then, so long as he was on the first plane out in the morning, he could roll from one commitment to the next like the human tumbleweed that he was.

"Anything else I can do for you, Boss Man?" Natalie asked.

"Tell Garry we'll make time soon. And send through the changes to the calendar when you have them."

"Shall do." A beat then. "So is it true?"

"What's that?"

"That the royal wedding didn't go off as planned?" Her sing-song voice dropped, as if they were sitting across from one another at a café. "It's all over the news. Apparently, the bride-to-be had a change of heart."

"You don't say."

Will glanced towards the wooden door when the sound of running water stopped. He listened a moment before he heard a splash. He imagined Sadie stepping a muddy foot into the bath. Then a long, pale calf, then...

Natalie sighed, bringing his vision to a halt. "She looked so nice too. Fun. Smiley. Someone you could be friends with. What did you think? I mean, before she did a runner? Did she seem as lovely as she looked in the magazines?"

Will knew better than to engage. He rubbed his temple instead.

"Aw, come on, Boss Man! My cousin Brianna works for a reality TV producer. I don't get many chances to one-up her in ways she understands."

"Alas."

"Fine. I'm guessing by the stoic silence she's not all she's cracked up to be. I mean, did you get a load of the

Prince? Oh, me…oh, my. I guess a real-life, normal girl marrying a prince is simply too much to hope for."

"Hang in there, Natalie."

"I'm all right. You're the only man I need."

"Lucky me."

And then she was gone.

It seemed word was out. If Natalie was busy making negative assumptions, tucked away in her cottage in Wisconsin, it wasn't looking good. Things had gone up a notch. This was no longer simply a case of keeping Sadie in sight until Hugo came to get her, but actually keeping her safe.

Something he'd not been able to do for Clair.

Throat feeling unnaturally tight, Will lifted a hand to his neck, tugged his tie loose, then pulled it free and tossed it on top of his bag.

He wasn't built for this. All this…emotional disarray. It wore down a man's sharp edges. He liked his edges. On a day like today—with the whole world looking to others with a need to "share"—those edges were a requirement.

Ironic that he'd thought Clair's memory would be the biggest battle he'd fight today, instead it was the reality of Sadie. Yet somehow it was all intertwined. Choices, decisions, reactions, repercussions.

The door to the bathroom opened. He pulled himself to standing. Turned. And whatever ethical dilemma he'd been mulling over disintegrated into so many dust motes as his eyes found Sadie.

Gone was his oversized tracksuit, the piles of messy curls, the tear-soaked make-up.

Her hair was wet, and long, and straight. Her cheeks were pink from the heat of the bathroom. Freckles stood out on the bridge of her straight nose. Without the black make-up her eyes were even bigger. *Blue*, he thought, catching glints of sky. Wrapped in a big, fluffy, shapeless robe, she seemed taller. Upright. More graceful somehow. Long, lean and empirically lovely.

Something tightened in his gut at the sight of her. Something raw and unsettling and new. Like the deep ache of a fresh bruise.

Her brow knotted and she ran a self-conscious hand over her hair.

Will came to; realised he'd been staring.

"Better?" he asked.

"Much. I did wonder if you'd still be here when I got out."

Will held out his hands. "Not going anywhere without my favourite running gear."

Sadie seemed to remember she was holding his clothes. She padded over towards him and handed them over. She was careful not to touch him.

He threw them atop his bag and her eyes followed, glaring at the clothes as if by sheer force of will alone she could unzip his bag, pack the clothes away and make him leave.

"Now that you have them..."

Will put his hands into his pockets. Right. How to convince her to let him stay without coming across as a Neanderthal. Or a Lothario. Without giving her actual cause to run.

"Will," she said.

"Yes, Sadie."

She lifted her gaze, bright eyes snagging on his. Then she laughed, a sound both sweet and husky. But there was no humour in it. "I was going to eke it out. To keep you hanging. Make you suffer. But you look like you're about to pull a muscle with the effort at keeping this up. I saw your credit card downstairs. You're Will Darcy. You were heading to the wedding at the palace today because you were invited by Prince Alessandro himself."

Will should have been prepared for this eventuality.

He was a man of angles after all. And control was an illusion. The universe chaotic. Any number of factors altered the possible futures of any given body, making accurate projections near impossible. Still, he found himself unprepared.

"Are you going to deny it?" she asked; gaze steady, that humming energy of hers now turned up to eleven.

He shook his head, *No*.

As if she'd been hoping for a different answer, Sadie deflated, crumpling to sit on the arm of the couch. "Okay. Next question. I know the answer but I want to hear it from you. Do you know who I am?"

Will crossed his arms over his chest as he decided how to play this; fast and loose as he had so far, or absolute truth. As a man of science, the decision was elementary, and a relief.

"You were Hugo's intended. Now you are his runaway bride."

Her eyes were wide, luminous in the fading light. "How?"

"The dress. The tears. The determination to be as far from the palace as you could be. But it was the ring that clinched it. I'd seen it before. We were at school when his grandmother sent it to him. After…"

"After Prince Karl—Hugo's father—died in a crash," she finished, her gaze not shifting a jot. She was far tougher than she looked.

Then she shifted, her robe falling open. The slit separated at her ankles, then her knees, revealing one long, creamy pale leg. She had freckles on her knees. A small bruise just below. Her hands delved up inside the robe and, before Will could even look away, with a wriggle she pulled a frilly pink garter down her leg.

The fact that this rather intimate move had been meant

for Hugo later that evening was not lost on him. Neither was the heat that travelled through him like a rogue wave.

Will pressed his feet harder into the floor and thought of England.

Holding the garter scrunched in her hand, she took a deep breath and opened her palm. And there, tied to the thing with a length of pink ribbon, was the Ring of Vallemont.

Then, tucking the ring back into her palm, she held out her other hand. "Mercedes Gray Leonine. Pleased to meet you."

He took it. Her hand wrapped around his—soft and cool and impossibly fine. He could all but feel the blood pulsing beneath her skin, the steady vibration of the perpetual electric impulses that made her tick.

His voice was a little rough as he said, "Will Darcy. Pleasure's all mine."

She let go and used both hands to slide the garter back into place. "But it's not your pleasure, not really, is it?"

Will said nothing, holding his breath so long it grew stale in his lungs.

"I'm a drama teacher, you know. Or I was...before. Body language—understanding it and duplicating it—is my job. You've hardly hidden the fact that you would rather be anywhere but here." She blinked at him. "If it helps any, I'd rather be pretty much anywhere but here too."

It didn't. It only made his task more complicated than it already was. He didn't want to see her side of things. He certainly didn't want to empathise. He wanted to keep her from running away again and gift her back to Hugo in one piece. Then leave.

He saw the moment she realised it too. She sat taller, and narrowed her eyes his way. Something hardened in her gaze, like steel tempered by fire. And Will couldn't press his feet into the floor hard enough.

Her eyes drilled into his as she said, "He'd never mentioned you before, you know."

A deliberate barb, it scored a direct hit. Will crossed his arms tighter.

She noticed. A small smile tugged at one corner of her mouth. "And suddenly, with the wedding, you loomed large. This friend from school he hadn't seen in years. A falling-out he never explained, no matter how maddeningly I prodded. With all that, I imagined you hunched and brooding. More Holden Caulfield, less…"

"Less?"

"Mr Rochester." She waved a hand his way as if it was obvious, her eyes dashing from his chest to his hair and back to his face. Her cheeks came over such a sudden pink he knew he'd have to track down this Rochester fellow the moment he had the chance.

She looked down at her toes, where he could see the nails painted in some kind of animal print, making him wonder if this palace rebellion of hers had been coming on for some time. Then she asked, "How did you imagine me?"

"I didn't." It was true. He'd done everything in his power not to know anything about her. He was no masochist. Though the longer he chose to stick around this woman, the more he'd question that fact.

Sadie crossed her arms, mirroring his defensive position. "Seriously? Then you have a better hold over your curiosity than I do. Well, how about now? Am I the kind of girl you imagined Hugo would one day marry?"

Will ran a hand through his hair. Hell. This was worse than masochism. He'd found himself on the pathway to hell.

"Forget it. It doesn't matter," she said, shaking her head. "Okay. So, cards-on-the-table time. What are we doing here, Will? What's your end game? I know something happened between you and Hugo, something regrettable. If your intentions aren't above reproach, if you're out to humiliate him in any way…I'll…I'll cut off your whatsit."

Even though he knew she was all bluff, Will's whatsit twitched in response. "I think he's had quite enough humiliating for one day, don't you?"

Her gaze dropped to his…whatsit.

Will's voice was dry as he said, "I was talking about Hugo."

Another hit. This one flashed in her eyes like a bonfire. "Leave him out of this."

He shook his head.

"Why? Wait. Have you spoken to him? Is he okay? Does he know we're here?"

Will pulled the phone from his pocket. "Call him. Ask him yourself."

Sadie's arms loosened, her hands dropping to grip the arms of the couch on which she sat. She pulled herself to standing. Then reached out and took Will's phone.

Their fingers brushed, static electricity crackling through his hand.

Her eyes shot to his. She'd felt it too. Breathing out hard, she asked, "Are you sure? I mean, will he even take my call?"

"Call him."

She nodded and took a few steps away, before turning back.

"Today—not going through with the wedding… It wasn't a decision I made lightly. I usually make a much better first impression. I'm very likeable, you know."

"I'm sure."

She looked at him then, all ocean-blue eyes and electric energy. With her brow twitching a moment, she said, "No, you're not."

And then she stepped out onto the balcony and was once more gone from his sight.

With leaden feet, Will sat back on the couch. Feeling like he'd gone ten rounds.

She was right. After what she'd done today, to his oldest friend, he wasn't convinced that he would ever come to like her. But there was no denying she'd made an impression he'd not soon forget.

CHAPTER FIVE

SADIE'S HEART STAMMERED against her ribs.

In front of her, the palace was glowing gold in the final throes of the dying light.

Through the gauzy curtains behind her, a man was all but keeping her hostage. A man who'd made no bones about the fact he wasn't a fan. A man who made her feel unsettled and antsy and contrite.

And in her hands was a link to her Prince. Her friend. The man she'd wronged.

With the fall of night came a brisk wintry breeze cascading off the snow-topped mountains in the distance, skipping and swirling through the narrow valley and tossing Sadie's damp hair about her shoulders.

She pulled her gown tighter, sat on a small wrought-iron chair and tucked her feet up beneath her. And typed in Hugo's private number.

As unexpected as it was sudden, Hugo's picture flashed onto Will's screen as the phone rang. Will was in it too. They had their arms around one another as they stood atop a mountain somewhere. Young men. Grinning. Happier times.

The phone stopped ringing.

"Darcy?" said Hugo, in his deep bass voice. "What's happened?"

Sadie pictured him sitting behind the grand old desk

in his study, foot hooked up on the other knee, hand gripping his chin.

Sadie closed her eyes and swallowed. "Hugo—" Her voice cracked. She cleared her throat. "Hugo, it's me."

Sadie couldn't remember a time when she'd been so scared of a response. Not since calling her mother to let her know New York hadn't worked out as hoped and that she was coming home.

She'd felt like a failure then. As though she'd let everyone down. Right now, she *knew* she was a failure. She *knew* she'd let everyone down.

Finally he spoke. "Leo."

Sadie nearly sobbed with relief. Hugo was the only person in the entire world who called her that and the fact he used her nickname now meant so much. It meant everything.

"Hey, big guy. How's it hanging?"

"Tight and away."

Her laughter was croaky. "Yeah. Figured as much. I'm assuming you got my note?"

"The one about deciding not to marry me after all?"

"That's the one."

The moment she'd realised there was no way she could go through with the wedding, she'd also known she couldn't go without letting him know.

Finding him would have been impossible without making a huge scene. At the time not embarrassing Hugo in public had seemed the most important thing. Now she realised she'd simply postponed the inevitable.

So she'd torn a page from a hymnal, grabbed a stick of lipstick left behind by the make-up artist and scribbled down the best short explanation she could. She'd given it to the sweet maid who'd been left to "keep her company" and, using every ounce of charisma she had in her arsenal, had convinced the young girl to deliver it to the Prince.

Then she'd climbed out of the old stone window and run.

"The poor girl who gave it to me was so terrified she left fingerprints in the thing."

Sadie laughed, even as a rogue tear slithered down her cheek. She dashed it away with the sleeve of her gown. "She needs a raise. A big one." Then, "Is it crazy over there?"

"That's one way of putting it. It was agreed that Aunt Marguerite would make the announcement to the guests. One line—the wedding would not go ahead but the after-party would. Then everyone was promptly herded into the ballroom. The champagne is flowing. The music is loud. The doors are bolted shut."

"She's hoping they'll not remember any of it in the morning?"

"Very much."

Sadie heard a squeak. He was definitely in the leather chair behind his desk. She wished she was in there now, lying on the big, soft rug, using a throw cushion as a headrest, annoying him as he tried to work; chatting about her latest class play or Netflix addiction; niggling him about some movie star who'd claimed to have a crush on him; listening as he took calls from foreign leaders, or those interested in his divine resorts.

"So," he said, his voice nothing but a rumble. "You've met Darcy."

"Mmm-hmm." Suddenly uncomfortable, Sadie adjusted her gown. Then her sitting posture. Then the garter which had begun to feel scratchy now her tights were gone.

"What do you think?"

"About?"

Hugo waited. No surprise that he saw right through her. Born two years apart to the day, they'd grown up in one another's pockets. The Prince and the daughter of a palace maid. As the story went, she'd told anyone who would listen that she'd one day marry Hugo before she could even pronounce his real name properly.

"Oh," said Sadie, "you mean Will? He's..." *dogged, grouchy, brooding, infuriating, enigmatic* "...a very good driver."

Hugo's chuckle was pained. "You playing nice?"

"Of course I am! I'm the epitome of nice. Ask anyone." A beat. "Well, maybe give it a few days." *Weeks. Months. Millennia.* "I'm not sure there's a person in the world who'd have a good thing to say about me right now. Hugo—"

"Leo. It's okay."

"But—"

"Truly."

"No. I need to say it. I wronged you. Terribly. I screwed up more than even I ever imagined I could and that's saying something. And I plan to do everything in my power to fix it. I'll write an official apology to the palace. I'll take out a full-page ad in the *Vallemont Chronicle*. I'll go door to door telling every man, woman and child that my running away had nothing to do with you. That you are the Prince they know you to be, while I am a complete flake. Anything."

"Anything except marry me."

She opened her mouth to...what? Tell him to give her another chance? That this time she could go through with it, if it was what he really wanted. What he needed. But for some reason Will's face popped into her head right at that moment. Those intensely dark eyes of his boring into her as if he'd accept nothing but the truth. Her truth. However unpopular it might be.

The tears flowed fast and furious now. "God, no. Anything except that."

Hugo laughed, as she'd known he would. Never in the

history of history had there been a better man, meaning that he deserved a better woman.

Sadie shifted on the seat. "He doesn't like me, you know."

"Who?"

Right. They hadn't been talking about him, she'd just been thinking about him. "Your old friend, Will Darcy."

"Not possible."

"Something to do with my actions today, perhaps?" But even as she said it, Sadie knew it wasn't that. Not entirely. It was something deeper. Something about her made him uneasy. Not what she'd done but who she was. And to think she'd thought she couldn't feel worse!

"I know you. Making people feel comfortable is your special skill. You'll work him until he adores you. You always do."

"Alas, once I give him his phone back he's outta here." No response from Hugo. Which gave her pause. "Unless I'm missing something."

"I'd like him to stay."

Sadie sat up so fast she nearly fell off the chair. The thought of being *stuck* in the hotel room with Will— "working him until he adored her", no less—made her feel itchy all over.

"Hugo—"

"I'd feel better knowing that you had company. At least until I can send for you."

"A babysitter, you mean. So that I don't get up to more mischief than I already have."

"If you like."

The ease of his about-turn gave him away. "You don't think I need a babysitter. You think I need a bodyguard."

How bad was it out there? For the first time since she'd run she wanted access to a TV. She remembered Janine from downstairs saying "the honeymoon suite" didn't have one. Maybe she could ask Will if she could check out the news pages on his phone.

"Send Prospero," she tried, imagining Hugo's big, neckless, mountain-sized, actual bodyguard.

"Prospero wouldn't leave me if ordered him to by royal decree. It has to be Will."

She dropped her forehead into her hand.

"Humour me," Hugo said.

He didn't say, *You owe me this much at least*, but Sadie read between the lines. He'd been born into a royal bloodline, a flourishing principality run by very smart, savvy, forward-thinking people. Hugo could be a master manipulator when he wanted to.

If making things right meant having to put up with Will Darcy's disquieting presence, then Sadie would just have to handle it.

"And what would you like me to tell your friend about this arrangement? Not my biggest fan, remember."

"Just tell him I asked."

"Really? He doesn't come across as the kind of man who blindly follows."

"Just tell him."

"Fine. And when things die down? What then?"

"Then I'll send someone to bring you home."

Home.

Sadie stifled a whimper.

That Hugo could sit there, in the middle of the scandal of his life, and truly believe she could ever move back into his venerable ancestral home after what she'd done… He was the best man she'd ever known times ten.

"Anything you need until then?" he asked.

Clothes. A phone. Money. Her mum. A hug. A new place to live. For her students not to be out there thinking badly of her. For the people who knew her best to believe she'd had no choice. For the world to forget her name.

"I'm fine."

"As for Will?"

"Mmm?"

"Take it easy on the guy. If he's the same man I knew back then, he comes across as a big, gruff loner, but deep down he's a good guy."

"It'd have to be *waaaay* deep down."

"Leo."

"Fine! I'll be sweetness and light."

"I know you will. Now… Sorry. Hang on a moment." Hugo put her on hold.

The village below was quiet in the looming gloom of late autumnal dusk. Through the curled iron of the balcony she watched a small, battered Fiat bump slowly along the street below. When a group of revellers pushed their way out the front door of a pub down the road, she ducked down so they wouldn't see her.

And she suddenly felt terribly alone.

But while he had people clamouring to do his bidding, Hugo was far more alone than she was. He always had been. It came with the position, with the expectations thrust upon him from birth, with not knowing if people liked you for who you were or what you had to offer. And now, without her at his side, she feared he always would be.

Was that why she'd planned to marry him? Maybe. Partly. If so, at one time it had seemed like reason enough.

After a most inauspicious entry into the world, Sadie's life had been blessed.

Educated by royal tutors. Given music lessons, dance lessons, drama lessons. During the latter, she'd discovered the direct link between putting on a show and having people look to her with smiles on their faces. Thus her love of theatre had been born.

But who deserved that kind of luck? Truly? People who earned it, who were grateful for every ounce; who were nice and kind and likeable; who made sure not to let down all those who'd been instrumental in giving her the chances she'd had.

The Muzak stopped as Hugo came back on the line. "Apologies. It was Aunt Marguerite."

"Ruing the day she rescued my mother and me?"

"Asking if you are all right."

Of course. "What did you tell her?"

"That if you're not yet, you soon will be."

Sadie let her feet drop to the ground, the freezing cold tiles keeping her in the here and now.

"I should go," Hugo said.

"Me too. Busy, busy! You don't have to send someone for me, you know. I'm a big girl."

"I don't have to, but I want to."

Her eyes fell closed. Giving him that was the least she could do. "Do it soon."

"As soon as I'm able. Stay safe."

With that, Hugo rang off.

Sadie uncurled herself from the chair, shivering as she stood. The temperature had dropped fast as night closed in quickly. The sky was now a soft dusty blue, the mountains guarding the borders of her tiny country glowing white.

Just before she turned to head back inside, the first star popped into sight. She thought about making a wish, but had no idea what to wish for.

Will was on the couch, one foot hooked over the other knee, fingers running back and forth over his chin.

He looked up at the sound of the French door sliding closed, a slice of moonlight cutting his strong face in half. "All's well in the state of Denmark?"

Sadie's mouth twitched. She could count on one finger the number of men who'd quoted Shakespeare at her without knowing what a geek-fan she was.

She walked over to Will and gave him back his phone,

then took a seat on the other couch. "Princess Marguerite is hosting the party to end all parties in the hope of either giving everyone the night of their lives so they leave with only good to say, or they are too hungover to speak of it."

"Seems a pity to be missing it."

Sadie coughed out a bitter laugh. "For some strange reason, I'm struggling to imagine you partying. You seem a little straight for all that. More of a cognac and non-fiction tome kind of guy."

Will breathed out hard, his hands coming together, fingers running over fingers in a hypnotic pattern. "Is that what you came in here to say?"

Well, no. But it had felt good to have a dig at the guy anyway. Hugo clearly thought more highly of her "working it" skills than she did.

Enough dilly-dallying. Time to get this over with. Hugo seemed to think Will would stay simply because he'd asked him to. Hugo believed Will was a good guy. And that had to count for something.

So, while the words felt like stones in her mouth, she managed to say, "While I feel like I'm taking the feminist movement back decades by asking this, is there any chance you could stick around until Hugo sends someone to whisk me out of here?"

Will sat forward. His hand went to his watch—big, fancy, classy—twisting it about his wrist as he made his decision.

It hadn't occurred to her until that moment that he might say no—claim work, or play; claim a jealous wife or a sick child or a job that needed him more. That he might leave her here, in this honeymoon suite with its princess bed and its view of the palace.

"And how long might that be?"

"I...don't know. As soon as humanly possible."

"Is this a request from you, or Hugo?"

"Does it matter?"

The slight tilt of his head told her it did.

Well, buddy, you rub me up the wrong way too. The funny thing was, though, sitting there beside him, her hairs standing on end, a tornado in her tummy, prickling under the burn of his hot, hard gaze, being on his bad side felt like the safer option.

Sadie shuffled forward on the chair, held her hands out in supplication and said, "Look, I get that I'm not your favourite person."

There, now it was out there. Maybe that would alleviate the tension sapping the air from the room.

"But neither am I some damsel in distress, if that's what you think."

To that he said nothing.

"The truth is, you don't know me. You just happened upon me at just about the crappiest moment of my entire life. And now I'm exhausted. And hungry. And stuck in a hotel room with a stranger. Which isn't going to bring out my best. I promised Hugo I'd be sweetness and light, but I'm not sure how long I can keep that up. So, stay, don't stay; right now I'm done caring."

Will looked cool as a cucumber as he said, "Is self-sabotage a habit of yours?"

"*Excuse* me?"

"I'm simply going by the evidence. I've known you a couple of hours and in that time you've rejected a prince and done your all to convince me to throw my hands in the air and give up on you."

"I'm not! I—"

"Then my staying won't bother you."

Oh.

"Not a jot," she said.

She lied. *He* bothered her. But that was just the price she had to pay.

"Then that's that," said Will.

Sadie breathed out hard and flopped back into the couch, feeling better about having a plan, even if it wasn't hers.

Will opened up his battered silver bag to pull out a laptop. He flipped it open, long fingers tapping in a password. "Now, if you don't mind, I'm going to get some work done."

Sadie flapped a hand his way, barely wasting a thought wondering what that work might be. He was a doctor of some sort. Did they give doctorates in such pedantic things as forensic accounting, or comment moderating?

She closed her eyes for a second. When she peeled her eyes open—five seconds later, or five minutes, she couldn't be sure—it was to find Will looking at her strangely.

Sadie followed the path of his gaze to find her gown had fallen open. Not much—enough to show her collarbone and a little shoulder. Maybe a swell of something more, but nothing to get excited about.

When she found his eyes again his jaw clenched, as hard as stone. His nostrils flared with the fervour of a racehorse, then with patent effort tore his gaze away.

Sadie was surprised to find her hands shaking as she surreptitiously tugged her dressing gown back together. And her heart beat like gangbusters.

He didn't like her. But it turned out he was very much aware of her.

The horrible truth was that she was aware of him too. The sure strength of his arms, the scent of his neck, the intensity of his gaze had been playing like a brutal loop in the back of her mind whenever she felt herself begin to relax.

And now they were stuck here, in this romantic hotel room.

It was going to be a long night.

* * *

Sadie had fallen asleep on the couch almost instantly.

A few hours later she lay there still, breathing softly through open lips, her lashes creating dark smudges beneath her eyes. Her gown...

Will looked away from her dressing gown and ran a hand over his face. A move he'd made so much in the past day he was in danger of rearranging his features permanently.

Will refocused on his laptop—not that it looked any different from the way it had ten minutes before. The internet was prohibitively slow, meaning he couldn't check Natalie's updates to his calendar. Or access Hubble's latest infrared take on Orion that was due to land, eyes only, that morning. Or open the latest incarnation of the Orion's Sword game sitting temptingly in his inbox.

And he'd had no word from Hugo.

Edgy and frustrated, Will rolled his shoulders, got up, started a fire and checked out the kitchen, to find only a few mini-bar items. He could have done with some real food, but, since he wasn't lucky enough to be at the non-wedding reception—aka the party to end all parties—he had to make do with instant coffee and a bar of chocolate-covered ginger.

The fire made short work of the cold room, so, needing some fresh air, Will headed to the balcony. The village was spread beneath him like something on the front of a Marks and Spencer biscuit tin.

Sipping on the bitter brew, he looked up. And promptly forgot to swallow.

For the perfect day had given way to an even more perfect night.

The combination of minimal light pollution from the old-fashioned gas lamps below, the elevated position of the hillside hotel and a first-quarter moon had made the galaxy come out to play.

* * *

From his cramped position tucked into the corner of the small balcony, Will found a nice angle on his target and racked up the focus.

His serious telescope—with long exposure CCD camera attachment—which lived in the permanent glass box atop his London town house, had collected more detailed images of the nebula's famous irregular, translucent fan-shaped cloud, and ultraviolet glow. But this telescope—smaller, older, less sophisticated—was the one he took with him all over the world.

It was the last gift he'd received from Clair.

He'd added to it over the years. Modified it to keep it relevant. And right now, as always, it did right by him, giving him a really nice shot of vivid grey-green mist enshrouding a distant star.

But what he was really hoping for was—any moment now— *There!* A shooting star. And another. The annual Orionid Meteor Shower in all its glory.

Will sat back in the freezing wrought-iron chair and did something he rarely took the time to do nowadays: he watched the sky with his own two eyes. The moment seemed to require it.

It was late. A ways after midnight. And the entire world felt quiet. Still. Slumberous and safe within the cradle of jagged mountains all around. It was as though this spot had a direct link to the heavens.

"Will?" Sadie's voice cut through his thoughts.

His chair scraped sharply against the tiled floor of the small balcony as Will arose.

Sadie stood in the French windows, nibbling on a bag of peanuts. "What are you doing out here? It's freezing. You should… Oh." Her eyes widened comically as she spotted the apparatus taking up most of the balcony. She stepped out onto the tiles, wincing at the cold beneath her bare feet. "Was this here the whole time?"

Will laughed, the rough sound drifting away into the darkness. "I brought her with me."

"Her?"

Will put a hand on the body of the telescope. "Sadie, this is Maia. Maia—Sadie."

"Pretty name. An old flame?"

"A young star. Found on the shoulder of Taurus." Will pointed unerringly towards the bull constellation without even having to look.

"So *that's* what you had hiding in your silver case! By the measly contents of your other bag I'd have bet you were planning on skedaddling tomorrow at the very latest. And yet you lugged this thing all the way here? Why?"

"Did Hugo not mention what I do for a living?"

She grimaced. "No. Maybe. He mostly told stories about your time at school. How you led him to the dark side, teaching him how best to ditch class. Or the time he dared you to petition the school to reinstate Domestic Science and you won. So many *Boys' Own* adventure stories I may have drifted off now and then." Her eyes darted to the telescope and back again. "So…this. This is what you do? What are you? Some kind of…*astronomer*?"

Will nodded.

And Sadie's eyes near bugged out of her head. "Really? But that's so cool! I imagined you in a career that was more…phlegmatic. No offence."

None taken. In fact, he took it as a compliment. A high level of impassivity was necessary to doing his best work. Besides, Will was too busy noticing she seemed to imagine him a fair bit. But he kept that noticing to himself.

"Hugo's friends are all in their family business—money, politics, ruling." She scrunched up her nose. "But not you. Unless astronomy *is* your family business…?"

"My family business was holding on tight to old money. And my grandmother's version of ruling was browbeating the butlers until they quit. This seemed a better choice."

Her hair rippled in the light breeze. "I would have thought that kind of thing was done by computers nowadays. Super-robots."

"Computers can certainly extrapolate data, make comparisons, find patterns in big, random, violent actualities that rise and fall over billions of years before we've even seen their first spark of light in our sky. But—as my old university mentor, Professor Templeton, used to remind us—the first step, the human element in all that, is to wonder."

"I like the sound of your professor."

"He was one of the good ones."

"You've surprised me just now, Will Darcy. Quite a bit. So what are you looking for?"

"That's a big question."

Sadie laughed. And waggled her fingers at the telescope.

"Ah," said Will. "You mean in there."

She laughed again, her eyes gleaming. The quiet, the dark, the late hour...they all promoted a sense of playfulness. Or maybe that was simply her: mischievous, bright, irreverent, with an agile open mind.

Will rubbed a hand over his chin to find it rough. Somehow he'd forgotten his nightly shave. Reminding himself to fix that tomorrow, he said, "This telescope isn't big enough for any serious research. I bring it with me more out of sentimentality than anything else."

"You? Sentimental?"

"Apparently so. It was a gift." *Swallow.* "From my sister." He braced himself against the jagged knot tightening in his belly. Then he moved on. "What would you like to see?"

"Me? Wow. I suddenly feel really ignorant. I don't know all that much about what's out there apart from, you know, moon, stars. The earth is the centre of the universe."

Will's mouth twitched. Then he leaned down, adjusted direction and focus and found the general direction of his telescope's namesake. Then he pushed back the chair, and motioned for Sadie to have a look.

Adjusting her robe, Sadie shuffled in closer to the telescope. Will had to press himself hard against the railing so as not to be right behind her as, fingers lightly gripping the eyepiece, she bent to have a look.

Sadie's mouth stretched into a slow smile. "Oh. Oh, Will. That is...spectacular."

"Pleiades," he said. "Otherwise known as the Seven Sisters. Maia is the fourth brightest."

She stood and blinked up into the cosmos. "Show me more. Show me your very favourite thing out there. Show me something that makes a man like you gasp with delight."

Will cocked an eyebrow. "I'm not sure I've ever gasped, in delight or otherwise."

Her grin was bright, even in the low moonlight. "Maybe you're just not doing it right." She flicked a glance to the sky. "Maybe you could lighten up a little. Put that frown of yours away for a bit and find the delight. Maybe you just have to look harder."

He looked, but not at the sky. At her profile, open and bright. At the dishevelled way she'd tied her gown. At her leopard-print toenails as her toes curled into the cold floor.

For the first time since Natalie had rung him about the invitation, Will purposely wondered about the girl Hugo had planned to marry, opening the part of himself he preferred to keep under lock and key—that place that bred *what ifs* and *if onlys*.

It was his turn to imagine as he attempted to picture the

Hugo he knew with this restive, indefatigable, unkempt creature.

And couldn't.

Deep down in a place both unfamiliar and disquieting, Will wondered how Hugo could have chosen a woman who was so clearly not meant for him.

Will cleared his throat and did a mental about-turn.

Nothing was *meant* in this world. Nothing was for ever. Planets collided, suns faded, worlds were destroyed by their own cores, imploding in on themselves in utter self-destruction. The universe was random and chaotic and it was foolish to think otherwise.

"Move aside." He gave her a nudge with his hip so that he might shift the telescope a smidgeon.

"Should I prepare myself to be amazed?" she asked as they swapped places again, this time the front of her dressing gown brushing against his arm. His hairs stood on end, chasing the sensation.

His voice was gruff as he said, "I would think the purpose of preparation was to avoid surprise."

"We shall see," she said. This time Sadie held her breath. Her voice revenant, she whispered, "What am I looking at now?"

"That would be Orion. A diffuse nebula in the Milky Way. Around one thousand five hundred light-years from here and containing thousands of stars, it is the nearest star-forming region to Earth."

Will had heard Orion, so optically beautiful, described as "angel's breath against a frosted sky". He believed its true beauty was that it was their best glimpse into how the universe had begun.

Sadie pulled back. She looked up at the sky for a good while. Then, her voice rusty, she said, "I can't even find the words, Will. It's beautiful, to be sure. But also…somehow hollow. Like if you look at it too long, all that darkness would see your darkness until it becomes one. 'Stars, hide your fires; Let not light see my black and deep desires.'"

Her last words had been so soft he wasn't even sure she'd meant to say them out loud. The order tickled at the corner of Will's brain. He sorted through the databanks of information he'd stored over the years and found a match. *Macbeth*.

Catalogued under cosmic quotes he'd kept note of over the years, he found, "'When beggars die there are no comets seen; The heavens themselves blaze forth the death of princes.'"

She blinked as if coming out of a trance, then turned to him, incredulous. "Seriously?"

"Seriously what?"

"You're quoting Shakespeare. Again."

"I'm very well-read."

"I'm beginning to see that." She shook her head. "Because that's my thing, you know. My mission in life is to show attention-deficient young adults how to concentrate long enough to get through an entire Shakespearean play. Huh. I just realised. Will. Will Shakespeare. You have the same name."

As her gaze held his and didn't let go, Will felt the air shift between them. A wind of change. A disturbance in the force. Electric currents zapped and collided until he was all but sure he'd see sparks.

But deeper, beneath it all, a sense of recognition; of shared experience; of lives lived parallel; of truth. Will felt its pull like a physical thing.

People spoke of chemistry being the reason people were drawn to one another. But it was gravity that caused one body to revolve around another. That said the denser gravity of a planet could draw on the lesser gravity of a meteor, leading to destruction, sometimes on a grand scale.

Sadie's gaze snapped to something over his shoulder.

"Did you see that?" Sadie gasped. "Keep watching. Keep watching... There!"

Will looked up. He watched as another shooting star flashed, flew and disappeared, disintegrating into a mass of scattered space dust.

If he'd believed in such things he might have taken it as a sign.

CHAPTER SIX

SADIE WOKE UP with a start.

It was deep in the heart of the witching hour; that time of night when every sound, every thought felt heightened. Her skin prickled with sweat. Unfamiliar sheets twisted around her legs. Her chemise had ridden high enough to nearly strangle her.

She wriggled and rolled, kicking off blankets, and scrambled up towards a mound of pillows. Holding her legs to her chest, she stared into the semi-darkness. Embers crackled in the fireplace below, the eerie golden glow casting light and shadow over the room. And over the man sleeping on the couch.

She couldn't make out much detail bar one bare arm dangling off the edge, fingertips nearly grazing the floor. A large naked foot hooked over the arm rest.

It was more than enough.

She looked away, towards the French door, towards the palace; towards her bed, her pillow, her home. She wondered if Hugo had managed to fall asleep or if he was still awake, lamenting what might have been, or relieved she'd let him off the hook.

She slid back down into the big, soft bed, pulling her sheets up to her neck and trying to recapture her dream. But all she remembered were insubstantial threads, like ribbons in a storm.

A few moments later she lifted her head, checking to make sure Will was actually asleep. His arm lifted and fell, as if in time with long, slow breaths.

Whatever. Sleep or no sleep, as soon as Hugo sent someone to get her, chances were she'd never see Will again.

There hadn't exactly been time or opportunity to uncover why Will and Hugo had been estranged since school, despite the fact there was clearly great mutual respect. But it must have been significant. A great fight? A deep betrayal? Or had she simply read *Macbeth* so many times she saw potential drama everywhere she looked?

No. Something must have happened. In her experience, men didn't lash out like wounded animals unless they felt cornered.

Her father had been the first. Taking umbrage to the fact Sadie's mother had dared love his child as much as she loved him. For that he had left and not looked back.

Then there had been her acting coach in New York. An older man, a faded Paul Newman wannabe, he'd been her teacher, then her mentor, dangling the string of success for a couple of years. Once she'd bitten he'd become her agent. Not a good one, but the fact he'd seen something in her had felt like enough. Until the day he offered her a part—not the lead—in the "adult" film he was producing. When she'd refused, point blank, he'd kicked her to the kerb, leaving her homeless, the entire experience telling her it was time to head home.

She'd even seen how implacable Hugo could be, if those in his care were under attack. It was the very reason he'd wanted to marry her, after all.

Will's "self-sabotage" accusation hovered on the edge of her subconscious, but she brushed it away.

She'd heard them called "the rational sex", but in her experience men made decisions based on emotion over common sense far more than women.

From what she'd seen of Will Darcy so far, he'd not proven to be any different.

More awake than asleep now, Sadie laid herself out as flat as she could, becoming one with the mattress, and closed her eyes. She breathed slowly through her nose and wondered... Did Will dream? If so, of what? Supernovas and little green men? Or was he a classicist—dreaming of memory, hope, wishes, flying, falling, desire...

Just like that, her own dream came back to her in a rush. Hurtling through a sky filled with planets, a great, hot sun and bright, thrusting comets. Only she wasn't falling, she was being held. Protected. By a pair of strong, warm arms. While also being shown the moon and stars.

She grabbed a spare pillow and shoved it over her head.

Will woke feeling as if he'd been hit by a truck.

Every muscle, joint and bone ached from trying to curl six feet two inches onto an over-soft two-seater.

He pressed himself to sitting, then rubbed both hands hard over his face in an effort to put all the bits back into the right place.

Will checked his phone. It was a little after seven. He had had eleven missed messages overnight. Not unusual. The stars were always out somewhere in the world. He listened to them all, took mental notes and sent word to Natalie how to deal with each.

She hadn't yet sent word about a meeting time with the prime minister regarding the Templeton Grant. He nudged her to make it the number-one priority.

The moment he'd heard the grant was in jeopardy he'd felt a strange compulsion, a knowledge deep in his bones, that he had to use the power of his reputation for more than simply work.

For Professor Templeton's gentle patience had been Will's deliverance at a time when things had gone either way, and it seemed only right that he make sure the next generation of students would have the chance to find their path as he did that long-ago day.

Following that one random astronomy class, Will had doubled up on his degree, joined as many research projects as would have him. He'd worked nights, checking the university's telescope minute by minute for whichever project needed data at the time. And eventually he'd earned the Templeton Grant himself for his independent study on the Orion Nebula. It had paid his way through university, in one fell swoop giving him complete independence from his grandparents and showing them he was neither indolent nor inadequate. He was bloody hardworking and exceedingly bright. Despite them.

Clair would have been the same, if she'd been given the chance. So what choice did Will have but to take every opportunity she'd never had?

Keeping watch over Sadie had nudged him off course, which was not a comfortable place for him to be. Nevertheless, after a prolonged beat, he sent another message to Natalie asking her to cancel or postpone—with apologies—everything he had on for the next twenty-four hours. To keep the day after that on standby. And please not to injure herself when she fell over in shock.

Then he threw his phone into his leather bag and stood.

He rolled his shoulders. Cricked his neck.

Glancing towards the raised platform, he could make out the lump of Sadie's form. Fast sleep.

Weak, dreary sunlight attempted to breach the curtains before seeming to give up.

Hunger gnawed at his belly. If Hugo wasn't here soon he'd have to head out and source some real food.

But first…needs must.

He grabbed his leather bag and headed to the bathroom. Since he couldn't get there without passing Sadie's bed, he found her splayed on her stomach like a human starfish, one hand hanging off one side, a toe hanging off the other. The sheets were twisted around her and tugged from their moorings. Her hair was splayed out across the white sheets like a red wine spill.

An empty chocolate packet lay open on the bedside table. And below it, in a pile on the floor, was her dressing gown. Meaning beneath the twisted sheets she wore…

Will kept his eyes straight ahead as he moved into the bathroom and shut the door. Two minutes later he was stripped and standing beneath a hot shower. And he did what he always did near water: he closed his eyes and let his mind go.

It wasn't an unusual phenomenon that his most complete theories had come to him while in the shower. Having nothing else to worry about, the mind travelled in disparate directions and made random connections it would otherwise miss.

He waited for his mind to mull over tricky calculations he'd been asked to weigh in on. Or the three-dimensional graphics of the Orion Nebula the gaming team in Oxford were working on.

But instead his head filled with silken, wine-red hair, soft, cool skin, eyes so deep they seemed to go on for ever.

Jaw clenching, he dragged his tired eyes open.

So, no stream of consciousness, then. Purposeful analysis was the order of the day. He began, as he always did, with known data.

Fact: he'd been on edge for days. Weeks even. Knowing he was set to face Hugo, to face his part in the derailment of their friendship, knowing that watching someone else take his sister's place at Hugo's side would be…difficult. No, it would be insufferable.

Fact: stress led to surges of adrenaline, a natural human response to an extraordinary amount of stimuli. Biological readiness for a fight or flight led to heightened senses. Which then led to a natural physical response to the attractive woman he was sharing a hotel room with.

Fact: he clearly wasn't the only one suffering this... natural human response.

He was suddenly back on the balcony the night before, Sadie's energy tangling with his, the stars shining in her eyes. Gravity, attraction, the heady pull of mutual intrigue, of the thrill of discovery drawing them together.

He was not unduly attracted to his old friend's runaway bride. It was simple science.

And yet he turned off the hot water and stuck his head under the cold until it began to burn.

When he'd punished himself enough, Will turned off the water, shaking off the chilly droplets. And stilled. Listening.

He'd heard something. A knock at the front door?

Hugo.

He reached for a towel to find the nearest towel rail empty. A quick glance found Sadie's towel flopped over the side of the bath.

Upon a thorough search he couldn't find another. So, grabbing her towel, he rubbed himself down, straining to hear voices. But the room seemed quiet.

"Sadie?" he called, his voice echoing in the small, steamy room. No response.

There. The front door opening. And closing.

"Dammit. Sadie!"

He couldn't seem to get himself dry. Because the towel was damp. Redolent with the scent of honeysuckle.

"Saaadiiie!"

The bathroom door swung open and with the rush of clear air came Sadie. "What's wrong? Are you okay?"

Will swept the towel around his waist, clamping it together with one fierce hand at his hip. "Hell, Sadie!"

"What?" she said, swallowing a yawn. "You were the one bellowing my name."

Her hair was crushed against one side of her head where it had dried while she was sleeping. A crease from her pillow lined her cheek. Thankfully she was now wearing her dressing gown, though it sat twisted, half falling off one shoulder. When she absently tugged the sash tight it made no difference.

"I thought maybe you'd slipped, or…something." Her words faded as she seemed to realise his state of undress.

Under her unchecked gaze, Will felt the water dripping off his hair and rolling over his shoulders. His skin felt tight, and sensitive. Even with the heat of the shower still filling the room, goosebumps sprang up over his arms. When he felt other parts of himself beginning to stir he gathered the towel more tightly and growled, "Sadie."

She blinked. Slowly. Then she swallowed. Her next breath in was long and slow. Then her eyes rose to his. "Hmm? What? No? Wait… What on earth…?"

She took a full step towards him. Close enough that he saw the genuine worry in her eyes, the constellation of slightly darker freckles on her left cheek. Close enough that her hand hovered an inch from his chest.

She reached a hand towards his chest. Will clenched all over. Now what was she playing at?

Then she asked, "Is that a bruise?"

Will looked down to find a dark variegated stripe angling across his chest. He lifted a hand and ran it over the contusion. Thinking back, he came to a likely conclusion.

"I slammed on my brakes," he said, his voice rusty. "My seatbelt did its job."

Her eyes whipped to his. Energy crackled through the fog, the level fit to reach the back of a large theatre. "That's happened when you stopped for *me*? Does it hurt?"

She lifted her hand again, and this time he knew she was set to touch him.

Will caught her an inch from ground zero, holding her hand at bay. Her skin was cool against his. His thumb rested on her wrist, picking up the scattered throb of her pulse. Or perhaps it was his own.

Her pupils were huge and dark. Her cheeks high with colour and her breath no longer at ease.

Gravity. Attraction. Intrigue. Discovery.

"I'm fine." Will pressed his hand towards her before letting go. Then he turned and dug about inside his bag. Needing a break from those eyes. "Who was at the door?"

"The door?"

"The reason I called your name. I heard a knock."

"Right. Yes. I thought it might be Hugo… Alas. When I checked no one was there. But there was a gift basket left outside. Decorated in little love hearts for the honeymoon suite, no less."

Will gripped the edges of his bag. He was not a praying man, but in that moment he understood the impulse.

"Thank goodness, right? Because I'm starving."

Starving. Will's belly felt empty and his head a little light. A man his size couldn't live on adrenaline and chocolate-covered ginger alone. Food would help. It would alleviate the pangs. And he could recalibrate from there.

Oblivious to his internal bargaining, Sadie went on, "There's champagne, strawberries, chocolate, almonds, Vallemontian ginger. Some crackers and crisps. Even a tub of honey. I call the ginger."

"All yours," he managed, contemplating the veritable cornucopia of aphrodisiacs. "I don't have much of a sweet tooth."

"What a shock."

He looked up then. To find her gaze was on his chest once more. Not the scar—the rest. He could have told himself the aspiration in her gaze was all due to the food talk, but what would be the point?

Clearly a cold shower and rationalisation weren't going to do the trick.

He'd been on the back foot since this entire escapade began—a feeling he was neither used to nor welcomed.

Enough was enough. It was time to take charge.

He turned, reached into his bag, grabbed the tracksuit she'd worn the day before and threw it at her.

She caught it. "What's this for?"

"Put it on. It'll be warmer than what you're wearing. And it's a grey old day out there."

"Thanks. That's really nice of you."

It was completely self-serving. "Was there something else?"

"No, but...I was just thinking about what the gift basket fairies might leave next? A collection of sonnets? Some massage oils? There's no TV so I guess that rules out—"

"Sadie."

"Yes, Will?"

"Get out."

"Yes, Will." She spun on her heel, all but scurrying from the room, closing the door with a loud snick.

That left Will to dress in the only clean clothes he had remaining—jeans and a black cashmere sweater.

He wiped his face, hung up his towel and tidied away his toiletries. He left no trace of himself behind.

And prayed when he checked his phone again Hugo would have sent word.

Will was back at the couch, repacking his bag for the tenth time that day, clearly wanting to be ready to go the moment she was off his hands. While Sadie—after living off strawberries, chocolate and champagne all day—felt super-twitchy and a little claustrophobic.

"Bored, bored, *bored*," she chanted under her breath.

Will turned, jaw tight, brow furrowed as if she'd interrupted him doing something terribly important. "Did you say something?"

"Nope. Maybe. I'm bored."

Will gave her a look. "Why don't you tidy up a little?"

"Nah."

"You are clearly used to having a maid."

"Are you kidding? My mother *is* the maid. At the palace. So was I, at times." She shuddered. "When Hugo was away ditching school with you, I begged Marguerite to put me to work. I helped look after the smaller royals—teaching them to clean up after themselves, to make their beds, to cook easy meals. Have you ever had to clean up the same Lego day after day after day?"

His blank look gave him away.

"That's right, you had a butler. Well, if you spend enough time cleaning up that stuff, one day you wake up and think, what's the point?"

"I never cleaned up my own Lego, Ms Gray, because my grandmother was rather old-fashioned when it came to the raising of children and did not believe in frivolous toys. That said, if the zombie apocalypse ever comes I'll be able to fence myself to freedom."

He went back to packing and she poked her tongue out at his back. Then she spun, held out fake pistols and muttered, "This room ain't big enough for the both of us."

"You definitely said something that time."

She blew invisible smoke from the top of a finger before sticking it back in her imaginary holster.

Things couldn't go on like this. This constant tension was messing with her equilibrium.

Like out on the balcony the night before—there'd been a moment when the wintry air had turned thick and steamy, when she'd looked into Will's dark eyes and seen something. Seen *him*. It had felt intimate, and thrilling, and terrifying. It was the kind of moment where something might have happened. The kind of something you couldn't take back.

And then in the bathroom this morning…she'd woken with a fright to the sound of his voice, the grit as he'd called her name. It hadn't occurred to her she might walk in on him half-dressed. Make that quarter-dressed. It had been too early in the morning to react sensibly to so much man. And how close had she come to feeling the guy up? He'd had to physically stop her from running her hand down his hard, muscular, naked—

Sadie sucked in a breath and shook her head.

Hugo had been right. Making friends with Will had to be better than…whatever was going on between them now.

She lifted her chin, manufactured a blinding smile and said, "So, Will, do you have a girlfriend waiting for you back in…wherever it is you're from?"

Wow. Excellent sentence-making skills, Sadie. Had she left her renowned charm in her "other" dress too? Apparently so, because Will wasn't charmed.

He kept on folding, waiting until everything was precise and in its place before deigning to reply. "No," he said. "And I was born in London."

No surprise. Grey, damp, so much snarling traffic they all but outlawed it, London was the polar opposite to the wide open, verdant green that was Vallemont. Though Hugo had taken her there for her eighteenth birthday, to see *The Tempest* in the West End, and that had been phenomenal.

Huh. Funny that Hugo hadn't made the effort to get in touch with Will, then, either. So whatever had happened between them was already in play. She'd get to that. But first:

"Really? No saucy smart girl with a lab coat, glasses and big brain to go home to?"

He gave her a sideways glance, still not giving an inch. And she knew there was no point even trying. He was just too…Will. He seemed to respond best to cool, clinical honesty.

Oh, well, here goes. "Come on, Will. Give me something. I'm drowning here."

"And what exactly do you mean by *something*?"

His deep, gravelly voice did things to her spine. Zappy, tingly things. She decided that was a little too much honesty and kept it to herself. "A little light small talk to while away the hours might be nice."

"Small talk?"

"Sure, why not?"

"Because it's asinine."

"Asinine? There you go. Something juicy for me to chew on." She took a deep breath and once again put on her best cowboy voice. *"Now, who do you think you are, calling me asinine?"*

He blinked. "I didn't. I said *small talk* was—"

She flapped a hand at him before plopping down on his couch, one foot under her backside, the other knee hooked up on the seat. Then she smacked the cushion, requesting he join her. "Sit. Let's get to know one another better. We might be here for days, after all. We might be here for ever."

Will lost a little colour at that last prediction.

"Sit. I dare you."

The colour returned.

He sat. The couch seemed to shrink, leaving her bent knee mere inches from his. But she held her ground. *All good here! My physical nearness to you is not a problem at my end!*

"So, where were we? No girlfriend. Great. I mean… fine. Okay. Glad we have that sorted." Then, because champagne and chocolate and boredom and…some new level of sadomasochism seemed to have taken her over, "But you do like girls, right?"

A slightly raised eyebrow and a flicker of his dimple was his only response.

"So, you *like* girls but you don't *have* a girl. Got it. I'm assuming it's that you're simply between girls and not because you're as much of a relationship screw-upper as I am."

His only response to her eventual silence was a look; dark and broody and gorgeous. Did she just say gorgeous? Only inside her head this time, which was okay. Except it wasn't even slightly okay!

Maybe it was some kind of Stockholm Syndrome. He'd practically kidnapped her, after all, and dragged her off to an actual tower, where he was keeping her hostage... Who knew what he had in mind for her?

Sadie wriggled on the seat, trying to shake off the tingle in her spine that didn't seem to want to go away. While also trying desperately not to let her knee touch his, because every time they touched, every time she bumped into him in the kitchen, or shuffled past him on the balcony, or passed him a cup of tea there was this spark, and warmth, and fast-spreading heat, and...

Will was still looking at her. His gaze locked on to her, not letting go. She could feel her heart rate speeding up and was getting that fuzzy feeling at the back of her skull. Like when a man was about to...

"My work is very important to me," said Will, thankfully cutting off her train of thought before it got away from her completely. "More than important. It's critical. It's also not conducive to long-term relationships."

She swallowed, hard, before managing, "How's that?"

"I work a great deal. I travel often. My plans change daily. I have a place in the Americas and Scandinavia as well as London, but my mail forwards to my assistant in

Wisconsin. My publisher is in New York. The stars are always out somewhere in the world and so can I be too."

"Doctors work a lot. Firefighters too. Soccer players travel constantly. Many manage to settle down, have families." She could have just said, *That's nice*. Why was she pushing this?

"Ask those families if they'd prefer to have their partners and parents home more. I believe you'll get an unequivocal yes."

"So your singlehood is benevolent."

"Entirely." The way he said it, with a hint of humour in that whisky-rough voice of his, hit a spot deep down inside. Echoing. Reverberating. Before making itself at home.

"Well, good for you."

He nodded. The best she could manage was a toothless smile. Then, before she even felt the words coming, she said, "You must have questions."

Will's eyebrow twitched. "Many. Though they usually bend towards the esoteric—why are we here, how did we get here, what might happen next?"

"I meant about me...and Hugo."

Will went straight into his statue impersonation. Not moving, not breathing, not giving anything away. He was very good at it.

"No? Then let's start smaller. How about what's my favourite colour? Do I prefer ice cream or sorbet? What did I want to be when I—?"

"How long were you together?"

"Together? You mean Hugo and me? Hugo and I were never *together*."

The guy could win a statue competition, hands down.

"We were the closest of friends since we were tiny tots. He'd pull me around in his little red wagon when he was three and drive me around in his big red Maserati when he was eighteen. And, because it never failed to bring a smile to someone's face, I'd declare to anyone who would listen that one day I was going to marry him."

"But you didn't mean it."

Sadie's breath caught. He'd known her a day and he got her. Those who'd known her a lifetime didn't have a clue.

She dragged her gaze away, the break of eye-contact a blessed relief. "Sure, we kissed a couple of times over the years—spin the bottle, three minutes in heaven, that kind of thing—in case it actually worked. But it never did. Not the way it should. It was to be a marriage of convenience. Separate quarters. Separate beds—"

Now Will moved, holding up a hand. "I know what a marriage of convenience means."

"Okay."

"But what I don't understand is why. Why get married at all?"

It was entirely her fault, but now they were moving into territories she wasn't comfortable talking about. It wasn't just her story to tell after all.

With a smile she said, "You've met the guy, right?"

"Several times. Wouldn't marry him, though."

"If you remember, neither would I."

Will shot her a look. Intense, intrigued. A life lived in the public eye, and she'd never felt quite so much as if she was under a microscope as she did now. Then, "Wait. Are you in some kind of trouble? Is that why he agreed to marry you?"

"Wow. You make him sound so gallant, deigning to stoop to—"

"Sadie."

"No," she allowed. "Not in the way you mean."

"Then in what way?"

She wondered if Will had a clue that he'd suddenly sat up taller—shoulders back, fists braced on his thighs as if preparing to take on the as yet unknown trouble that had her in its thrall.

While she was trying so hard to appear cool and unaffected, it unglued her. He unglued her. Every time he went all gruff and protective on her behalf.

In the short time they'd been thrown together, he'd managed to see through her plucky façade to the truth. Her truth. In a way no one else had ever managed. She wondered now if anyone else had even bothered to try.

"Stop it," she said, her voice raspy. Her hands gripping one another in her lap, hanging on for dear life.

"Stop what? I didn't say a word."

She licked her lips. "But you were thinking it. I can see it. All those big, heroic, take-over thoughts whipping around inside that ginormous brain of yours. Synapses firing at supersonic speed, sparking lights in your baby blues."

"Baby *what*?"

She waggled a hand towards his face. "Your eyes. Why, do you have something else blue on your person that I don't know about? Inner nostrils? Belly-button lint? No, I would have seen it when you called me into the bathroom this morning. And what was that really all about? You couldn't have pulled on some clothes beforehand?"

Sadie's gaze dropped to Will's chest, saliva actually pooling in her mouth as she remembered.

"Wasn't it Shakespeare who had something to say about a lady protesting too much?"

She coughed out a laugh as her eyes swung back to his. So intense, so clever, so unrelenting. "Seriously? This is the conversation you want to be having?"

When he didn't demur, she knew she had to get out of there. But where? The steamy bathroom and her memories of Will half-naked? The balcony, where anyone could see her? With its palace view and memories of looking at the stars with Will? Maybe it was time to run again. At least she was wearing a tracksuit this time…

She made to stand, but as soon as her foot hit the floor she realised it had gone numb. Unable to take her weight, it collapsed and with a *whoop* she toppled.

Will reached out and caught her with all her gangly limbs and flailing panic. He braced, taking the worst of the impact as they landed in a heap on the couch. A telling *oomph* shot from his lungs as her knee jabbed him in the thigh, her elbow slamming him right in the solar plexus.

As she waited for her own aches and pains to show themselves, she couldn't feel anything bar the fact her body was all up against Will's. She felt as if she had a hundred senses, not the normal five. Each one focused on hard muscle, strong arms, warm, masculine scent.

"Sadie," he said. "Sadie, are you hurt?"

She squeezed her eyes shut and shook her head.

"Are you sure? Because you're shaking."

Trembling. She was trembling. Emotion, adrenaline, lust, fear, exhaustion, confusion—all were rolling through her in satiny, liquid waves.

Will reached up to brush her hair from her face, tucking it behind her ear.

Her eyes flickered open in surprise and landed on his.

He should have let his hand drop then. They both knew it. Instead his thumb lingered, just a moment, brushing over the high sweep of her cheek. Following the sweet, warm rush of heat rising in her face.

The move was so unexpected, so gentle, so *tender*, she couldn't handle it.

She shifted, and he grimaced. Not with agony. She knew the way a woman knew. He was bracing himself against the slide of her body against his.

Even before Will's hand moved around her back, sliding up her ribs, into her hair, he said, "Stop. Moving."

"Okay." She licked her lips. "But I have to move eventually."

"Just not yet."

When he breathed she felt it against her mouth, her neck, everywhere. It was a rush. A terrible, wonderful, overwhelming rush, asking too much, not asking for enough.

She could not want this man. Not the way her body was trying to tell her she did. He was Hugo's friend. A man Hugo had trusted to be on her side, meaning that Hugo thought Will was on his side.

If this whole debacle had taught her anything, surely it was to stop thinking she could make it work with men she couldn't have.

Her acting coach in New York had adored the way she had looked up to him. The estimable Prince of Vallemont adored her as a friend. And insular, unreachable, closed-off Dr Will Darcy...

There was no adoration here. Only attraction. Compulsion. And a sweet, raw, formidable urge to pack away her need to be liked and simply get real.

"Will," she said, her voice soft, her heart aching with regret.

"Mmm?"

"I'm sorry you got caught up in all this. But I'm also not sorry at all."

The look in his eyes was tragic. Tortured.

Then he opened his mouth to speak—

But Sadie never got to find out what he'd been about to say next because just then someone knocked on the door.

CHAPTER SEVEN

FEELING AS IF he'd swallowed a lead balloon, Will said, "Expecting anyone?"

Sadie shook her head, her hair sliding over his collarbone like silk. Her next breath in she was shifting her body over his, her next breath out she seemed to melt over him like chocolate on a summer's day.

Then she blinked, her oceanic eyes widening. "Well, apart from whoever Hugo plans on sending in to whisk me away." She swallowed. "Has he sent word?"

"Nothing since yesterday."

The knock came again. Not the dainty taps that had heralded the gift basket but harder, more insistent, like a secret code.

Then, even though he was not in the right frame of mind, or body for that matter, to talk to anyone, Will found some reserve of inner strength in order to lift her bodily away, place her back in the chair and heave himself to standing.

He took a few moments to bring himself back under some semblance of control before he moved to the door and looked through the peephole.

What he saw made him take a literal step back. As time contracted, and his gut squeezed tight, he considered ignoring the knock. The moment passed, as moments tended to do. And good sense returned. *This* was what he wanted. This was what he'd been waiting for.

"This'll be cosy," he muttered, widening the door.

And there stood Hugo.

Taller than Will, just. Lines fanning out from the edges of his eyes where there'd been none before. A short dark beard now covered his jaw, but the chronic wealth and the resplendent royal Vallemontian bloodline was evident in every cell. With the antiquated newspaper rolled up under one arm, the way the collar of his button-down shirt was turned up at the neck it was simply so particularly Hugo, Will burst into laughter.

And reached out a hand.

Hugo's face split into a matching grin as he shook it. "Good to see you too, my friend."

Hugo glanced back towards the neckless, black-clad man-mountain with the bald head and the frown standing guard at the end of the hall. "I'll message when we're done."

The man-mountain nodded and hulked down the hall.

Only then did Hugo step into the breach to wrap Will in a manly hug. Double back-slap and all. And just like that the years between them faded to nothing.

"Hugo?"

Sadie's voice cut through and both men turned to face the room.

"Oh, my God! Oh, my God!" Like the Doppler effect, Sadie's voice lifted and grew as she vaulted over the back of the couch and ran towards them, her hair flying behind her.

Hugo had about half a second to drop his newspaper and the overnight bag he'd had slung over his shoulder before she leapt into his arms. Like a teddy bear with Velcro hands, she buried her face in his neck. Hugo's eyes squeezed closed, his voice rough even though muffled by her hair.

"Leo."

"What the heck are you doing here, you great fool? I assumed you'd send a lackey. Or maybe just a car. You didn't have to come."

"Of course I did."

Imagining them together was one thing. Theorising why it made little sense was another. Watching them, like this, their affection a real, live, pulsing thing, Will gripped the door handle so hard the thing creaked in protest. "Perhaps we ought to move this reunion inside."

Hugo's eyes found Will; filled with a level of understanding Will knew the man couldn't possibly have. Then he nodded his agreement and walked inside with Sadie still attached like a limpet.

Will shut the door, perhaps a tad harder than necessary.

At the sound, Sadie lifted her head. She tapped Hugo on the back and when he placed her on the ground she peeled herself away. "I can't believe you're actually here."

"Yet here I am."

"Excellent. This is just excellent." She glanced at Will, her cheeks now pinking like crazy.

And what Will thought was, *She's about to give us away entirely.* Except there was nothing tangible to give away. Only a little gravitational theory. And a whole lot of misplaced heat energy.

It didn't matter now. Hugo was here. Will's job was done. It was time for him to bow out. To get on a plane. To get back to work.

"Come in!" said Sadie. "Tell me everything. No, not everything. I might need a little Dutch courage before we get to that."

Hugo smiled as Sadie took him by the arm, but the look in his eyes showed he was pensive.

And from one breath to the next Will knew he wasn't going anywhere. Not just yet.

Not that he didn't trust Hugo, but the Prince's interests were divided. Naturally so. He had his own legacy, his own future to consider. He also had an entire royal house breathing down his neck. Will had been charged with keeping Sadie safe, so he'd stick around a little longer and finish the job properly.

He moved the overnight bag—Sadie's by the looks of it—to the door and picked up the newspaper Hugo had dropped, giving the front page a quick glance. The non-wedding was the headliner. No surprise there.

When he looked up, Will noticed Sadie had bypassed the nearest couch to sit Hugo on the other. The one Will *hadn't* slept on. The one on which they had not just been wrapped up in one another...

Will cleared his throat. When Hugo looked over he pointed to the newspaper, asking, "Any concern with this lot on your way here?"

"We were careful."

"Be grateful you're not British," said Will. "Or they'd be camped out on the roof, climbing the trellis, crawling out of the toilet bowl by now."

"I'm grateful of that each and every day."

Old jokes. Old friendship. All new tension in the air as Sadie sat on the edge of the couch, leg jiggling, nibbling at her bottom lip, energy levels spiking.

"How long have you and the man in black been special friends?" Will asked.

Hugo's cheek twitched. "Since an attempt was made on my uncle's life a year ago. While he was picnicking with Princess Marguerite and the twins."

That was half the Vallemontian succession plan right there. Another tragic event would have brought Hugo within sight of the throne. "I hadn't heard."

"It was kept quiet."

"Were they all right?"

"Shaken up. But unharmed." Hugo sent Sadie a comforting wink. "Against my express wishes, Prospero turned up the next day. I have offered him gainful employment in any number of positions since, and yet I can't shake the guy."

"It must be a constant struggle, being so beloved."

"And yet I never let the hardship get to me."

Sadie laughed. Quieted. Laughed again. "Who the hell are you two and what have you done with Hugo and Will?"

Hugo gave her a pat on the knee. Chummy. Friendly. "Don't tell anyone but all men are teenaged boys in the bodies of grown-ups. Now, I'd kill for a glass of water."

Sadie sprang out of the seat. "I can do better than that. Will, you start the fire. Hugo, you tidy the coffee table. I'm sure I saw designer beers in the bottom of the fridge."

Will watched her bounce into the kitchen. "Where's the, *Please, Your Majesty*?"

"Ask her," said Hugo. "I dare you."

"Hey, Sadie?" Will called.

Sadie pulled her head out of the fridge. "Mmm?"

"I hid some cheese and crackers in the pantry so we wouldn't starve."

"Perfect!"

Hugo laughed under his breath. "Coward."

Will crouched to pick out kindling and a good-sized log. "At least she gave me the manly job. She has you on tidying duty."

"Fair point. Leo?" Hugo called.

"Mm hmm."

"Do I have to tidy?"

"It builds character."

"Fine," Hugo mumbled, before making space on the coffee table.

Leo? Will thought. Oh my god. *Leo.*

Will had quietly wondered why he couldn't remember Hugo mentioning Sadie while at school, if they'd known one another as long as she'd intimated. But flashes came back to him now. Hugo talking about *Leo's* terrible taste in music. Rock climbing with *Leo.* Plans to hit Oktoberfest with *Leo.*

Hugo had spoken as if talking about a great mate. Not even the slightest hint of romance. While the stories had been about Mercedes Gray *Leo*nine, naturally Will had thought "Leo" was a boy.

Giving in to a sudden urge to whistle a happy tune, Will set to starting a fire. Out of the corner of his eye he saw Sadie with a packet of crackers hanging from her teeth, cheese hooked into her elbow and a knife between two knuckles, three beers in one hand. Barefoot, hair cascading over her shoulder, her small frame swamped by his tracksuit.

Either Hugo had become less observant over the years or he was holding off from passing comment on the story behind the outfit. Odds were the latter; the question was *why.*

When Will stood it was to find Hugo leaning back in the chair, hands behind his head, looking content.

"Here you go, big guy," said Sadie.

Hugo held out a hand and Sadie dutifully handed him a beer. "Much appreciated."

Then Sadie placed a hand on Hugo's knee as she leant over his legs to hand a beer to Will. "And one for you."

He took it with a nod.

She smiled quickly and pink heat flushed her cheeks again. He felt it too. The echo of a pulsing red haze that had come over him on the couch; her soft body flush against his, her hair sweeping against his neck.

Will tipped his drink towards her. She took a big swig of hers, then dumped the rest of the picnic on the coffee table.

"S'cuse," she said, nudging her way past Hugo's legs, taking a quick survey of the space and choosing a piece of floor in between them. "Tell me, in gory detail, how is it out there?"

"I'd say it's pretty mild for this late in the year."

"Jeans and jumper weather?" Will asked.

Hugo nodded. "I'd take a coat, just in case."

"Boys," Sadie chastised, shooting each of them a glare. "This is a war meeting. Not a party. Now, what do I need to do from here? How can I help mitigate the damage? For you. Your family. My mother—"

"Your mother is fine," said Hugo. "In fact…"

"In fact what?"

"She handed in her resignation."

"She *what*?"

"Apparently she told Marguerite she has been wanting to retire for years. She has quite the nest egg, an eye on a small cottage in the village near your school and a penchant to travel."

"Why didn't she say anything to me?"

"She didn't want to disappoint you."

"Disappoint *me*? But the entire reason I agreed to marry you was so that she could stay on after she stops working. I mean, *part* of the reason, because, well, I'd been told there'd be a tiara in it for me. A really big one. And you are, of course, you."

Hugo waved an understanding hand her way.

But Will realised he'd stopped with his beer halfway to his mouth. "Can we rewind just a second?"

Hugo and Sadie glanced his way—expressions of barely restrained patience exactly the same.

"Did I just hear that you were marrying this lug so your mother could live in the palace after she retires?"

Sadie answered, "That was a deciding factor. Yes."

Will sat forward, and turned on Hugo. "And why the hell were you marrying her?"

"Whoa," said Sadie. "A tad too effusive in your level of disbelief there, cowboy."

Hugo laughed. "He makes a fair point. I am ridiculously eligible."

Sadie batted her lashes at Hugo. "And rich."

"And devilishly handsome."

Sadie ran a hand through her hair; most of it settled back into place but some hooked on the hood of Will's track top. Light from the fire inside sparked off the russet tones like flares from the sun. It would take nothing to unhook it for her, to let it run through his fingers.

Nothing but his dignity.

Will's voice was a growl. "Get a room already."

Hugo looked around. "I could say we already have one, but this has a little too much chintz for my taste."

Will let his half-drunk beer drop to the coffee table and rubbed a hand over his chin as he attempted to sort the actual evidence from the white noise, only to find he'd forgotten to shave yet again. Unlike him.

He ran his hands through his hair instead, as if that might massage his brain into gear, and said, "The attempt on Sovereign Prince Reynaldo and his family—it was more of a near thing than you made out. If it had been a success, you would have been damn near the front of the succession line. Reynaldo is a serious ruler. A serious man. That realisation had him rethink the leeway you've enjoyed since your father passed. He made you an offer. Or a threat."

"Wow," said Sadie. "You're good."

Hugo's smile was flat. "Since my mother is not of royal blood, and Australian-born, her position here is precarious. Especially now that she has remarried—a Frenchman, and a commoner no less. The law is clear: without my father she lives at the palace at the grace of the family until I come of age."

"At…?"

"Three and thirty."

"Next year. And then?"

"If I marry she may stay. If not…"

"I see."

"Do you?"

"She must leave the palace."

"Without citizenship, without naturalisation, without a partner from Vallemont to sponsor her, my mother would be forced to leave the country."

Will coughed out a laugh. It was laughable. Archaic. Nonsensical. And by the twin expressions looking back at him, true. And then he was laughing no more. "So he was marrying you for real estate and you were marrying for the sake of…" He looked to Sadie. "What? Security?"

"Don't knock it. Security is pretty sought after. Especially for those who don't have it."

Hugo offered up a hand for a high five.

"So you were both being altruistic to the point of sadomasochism?" Will was right to stay a little longer. He ran a hand through his hair, tugging at the ends. "You're cracked. The both of you."

"And you're so very British," said Hugo.

"Isn't he?" Sadie agreed. Then, to Will, "Our sensibilities are not as draconian as yours. It is normal for Vallemontians to openly marry for any number of reasons: business, property, partnership, companionship. Even— shock, horror—for true love."

Hugo stopped her there. "Don't bother, Leo. They say no man is an island, but even before he discovered the stars Will was always a planet."

"Hugo," Sadie chastised.

But Will stayed her with a smile. "I was trying to remember why we hadn't seen one another in an age, but now it's all come back to me."

Only it hadn't. Not until that moment. Somehow he'd been so caught up in protecting Sadie—from herself, it turned out—he'd not seen Hugo and thought *Clair*.

From the flash of pain in the Prince's eyes Clair's ghost was now on his mind as well.

"What?" said Sadie. "What just happened there? What am I missing?"

But words were not possible. Will's throat had closed up. The edges of his vision blurring. Clair was not something he spoke of. In fact, he hadn't spoken to anyone who'd actually known her in years. It was too brittle. Too terrible. The loss of her was as much a part of him as his ribs.

But Hugo, it turned out, was not so bound. "Do you remember my friend Clair?"

Sadie looked at Hugo and back to Will. "Clair. You mean from the high school near yours? Of course. She came to stay that summer."

"Clair was Will's twin sister."

Will had seen Sadie shaken, seen her scared and he'd seen her cry. He'd seen her eyes warm and melt. But he had not, until that moment, seen her focus, the cessation of energy coming from her position like a sudden black hole.

Then she said, "You're *Clair's* brother. The one who was meant to come to Vallemont that summer, but couldn't because you…"

"I broke my leg."

She clicked her fingers at him. "Yes! From what I remember Hugo had quite the crush on young Clair. Followed her around like a puppy. I might have even been a mite jealous—because I hadn't had him to myself for months—if not for the fact I had a bit of a girl crush on her too. She taught herself to play the guitar, remember, Hugo? From nothing. And she was obsessed with Marguerite's accent. She had the impression down pat. She was rather too taken with Ibsen to truly be trusted. But she was fun. And you say you're her twin? Will wonders never cease?"

On her saunter down memory lane Sadie was clearly missing the undercurrents. For Hugo had gone deadly quiet, while Will was eating up her every word. He was swimming in visions of Clair laughing, creating, keeping the palace in thrall. Filling in gaps of the time he'd missed. He'd spent so long blaming Hugo for stealing those last days, when the truth was Will's old friend had given her a wonderfully rich final summer.

It wasn't Clair's death that had ripped their friendship apart. It was Will's anger. His grief. The fact that he'd been eviscerated. The next couple of years were a wretched blur. Until he woke up again in that astronomy lecture, and never looked back.

Never truly faced his grief. Never truly let go.

"Whatever did happen to Clair?" Sadie asked. "Why isn't she here? Too heartbroken over the one that got away?"

Will's gaze shot to Hugo to find the Prince looking deep into his beer. *Come on, Hugo, give me a hand here.* Hugo took a long, slow swig, but refused to look Will's way.

It seemed Will would have to find the words after all. "She fell ill."

"Oh, poor thing."

"No... I mean, years ago. Clair died not long after that summer."

Sadie's hand went to her mouth as she rose to her knees, her gaze zapping between the men. "No. I can't believe it."

Will nodded.

"I'm so sorry, Will, I had no idea. And there I was, fluffing on about ridiculous impressions and how gaga we were over her."

"It's okay," Will said, surprised to find he meant it. "It

was actually good to hear. To think of her having a good time."

Sadie looked into his eyes, deep, searching, demanding honesty. "How did she die?"

"Sadie," said Hugo, speaking up for the first time.

"If Will doesn't want to talk about it he'll tell me. You on the other hand don't get to weigh in here because this is all news to me and that is your fault. What happened?"

Will twisted his knuckles, easing out the tension, and soon found himself saying, "It started with memory loss. Personality changes. Depression. You met her, she was… sunny. When we'd all gone back to school I started receiving letters in which she sounded anxious, aggrieved. I figured she must have fought with Hugo even though he denied it. I asked my school to allow me to check in. As a known truant they refused me, so I begged my grandmother to intervene. My grandmother was not moved. It wasn't until the first seizure that anyone else thought anything was wrong. By the time they had Clair in hospital her speech was impaired, her balance dysfunctional. Pneumonia hit three weeks later. And then she was gone." Will's voice didn't feel like his own. It felt a hundred years old. "I had not seen her in person since I broke my leg."

"Since Vallemont?"

"That's right." Out of the corner of his eye Will saw Hugo shift in his seat.

"Is it hereditary?" Sadie asked.

A note of concern in her voice had Will lifting his eyes. "No. It was the spontaneous misfolding of a protein. Nothing anyone could have done."

"So, you're okay?"

"I'm okay."

"Okay, then." Her eyes caught the reflection of the fire as she turned on Hugo. "Alessandro Hugo Giordano, what were you thinking in not telling me?"

Hugo refused to answer and Sadie rocked back onto her feet and stood. "I'm sorry to hear about your sister, Will. But I can't look at him right now. I need a moment."

And with a withering look sent Hugo's way, she went. The creak of the French windows opening was followed by a stream of chilly air.

"That went well," said the Prince.

"Oh, hello," said Will, grabbing his beer once more. "You've been so quiet I'd forgotten you were here."

"Nowhere else in the world I'd rather be."

"I vote for the Bahamas."

Hugo raised his beer. Will gave it a clink. And together they drank. Unlike the beers they'd secreted during not-so-secret parties their American dorm-mate used to host in his room after hours, this felt more like a wake. A toast. To Clair.

The girl they'd both loved. The girl they both missed. And just like that Will felt as if a weight that had rested on his shoulders for years lifted.

Hugo shifted. Cleared his throat. And changed the subject. "So, Will, how's life been treating you these last million years?"

"Can't complain."

"My mother showed me an article about you in a magazine a month or so back. Which one was it?"

"Time? New Yorker? American Scientist?" He could have named dozens.

Hugo clicked his fingers. *"Top Twenty: sexiest living scientists* issue. I particularly liked the 'living' addendum. Clearly if they'd opened up the field to intellectuals of eras past you wouldn't have stood a chance."

Will's laughter now came without restraint. No one in his life today had known him before he was someone. Before the university awards, the publishing deal, the infamy in his field. No one in his life had known him as a troubled kid with an incorrigible twin sister he'd loved more than anything.

But he was that kid. He'd had that sister. Pressing it deep down inside, never to be talked about, had not made it go away. Did not make it hurt any less. It only made it fester.

Time to let in a little sunshine. Time to heal.

"So how do you like my Leo?" Hugo asked.

And as if he couldn't stop himself now, Will laughed again. "I like her just fine."

"Really? Because every time you look at her you roll your shoulders as if trying to shake her off. She's under your skin, my friend."

Will's gaze slid to the open French window. Like a moth to the flame. "Stick anyone in a room with her for twenty-four hours and she'd get under their skin."

"And that's the truth. She had a hard beginning to things, you know. Father left her and her mother on the side of the road the day she was born."

Will ran a hand up the back of his neck. "Hell."

"Could have been. Marguerite found them and took them in. The entire country adopted her as their own. It would be difficult to find one's feet under so many watchful eyes. I've handled it by creating a life, a purpose, separate from the renown. She handled it by being the sweet, funny, happy, grateful kid she thought everyone expected her to be."

Hugo rested a finger over his mouth.

"She's the one person in my life I can trust to call me on my bullshit. And I care for her more than I care for anyone. But I also clearly misread her. What she must have suffered—to go through with my plan for this long and then run. I know she is determined to take the blame, but this is entirely my fault. She'll forgive me when she finally realises it—she's all heart. But I'm not sure I'll ever forgive myself."

Will knew Hugo wasn't looking for a response, merely a listening ear. So he listened. He heard. And he tried with all his might not to let it colour his feelings for Sadie. They were convoluted enough as it was without adding pathos to her tale. She had a sweet, determined kind of dauntlessness. But it was best to remember her as an unexpected variance in his life's path. And nothing more.

"Anyway." Hugo pulled himself to standing and Will did the same. "I'll just make a quick stop and then it's time for us to leave."

Hugo reached out a hand. Will took it.

The Prince tipped his head. "Thank you for stepping up in my stead, old friend. She couldn't have landed in better hands."

Will's gut clenched, looking for signs Hugo meant the words in a way other than how they appeared. But he seemed only grateful.

Will nodded. "I'm glad I could be of help."

Hugo let go, patted Will on the shoulder, then jogged towards the bathroom. The moment his friend was out of sight, Will turned his gaze east. Towards sunset. Towards night. Towards the stars.

Towards the open French window and goodbye.

Sadie looked up into the sky. The first stars had begun to twinkle high above her, the deep red sunset over the mountains masked the rest. The small village below was even quieter than the evening before. As if everyone had simply gone on with their lives.

She breathed in long and hard as her mind flipped through memories of Clair, her breath shaky as she let it go. It was silly really, feeling so bereft about a girl she'd known for a few weeks so long ago. She could barely even remember what she looked like apart from dark wavy hair. A quick smile. Bright, mischievous eyes.

When Hugo had come back from school at the end of that next year, and not mentioned her again, she'd assumed they had drifted apart. And, knowing Hugo as she did, she'd let it go. All the while he must have been in such pain.

And to think that warm, funny girl was cool, clever Will's sister. His twin sister, no less. How must losing her have affected him? He'd been, what? Sixteen? Seventeen?

Sadie felt swamped. Off kilter. As if everything she thought she knew about Will had shifted just a fraction to the right. Where there was a two-dimensional thorn in her side, now there was warmth, sorrow, angles, depth, adding rabid curiosity to what had been, up until that point, rabid physical attraction.

None of which mattered a jot.

Hugo was here.

She was leaving with him.

Will would...do whatever it was Will did with his time wherever in the world he did it. The fact that she couldn't quite imagine what that might look like made her feel even worse.

She gripped the railing hard. The air had turned so bitterly cold it felt as though it might even snow.

Her breath hitched before she even knew why. And she turned to find Will stepping over the threshold and onto the balcony.

She gave him a small smile. He gave her one back. Then he moved to stand beside her, his hands gripping the freezing cold railing mere inches from hers. But not touching. Things unsaid swirling about them like a storm.

"Time to go?" she asked.

Will nodded.

"But where?" she said. "That is the question."

"Home?"

"I'm not sure where that is any more."

"Not a bad thing in my experience. Where would you like to go now you have the chance?"

"I have no idea. I truly hadn't let myself think past yesterday. Not to the honeymoon, or to my new living quarters, or to how I was going to get my job back. I think, deep down, I was sure someone would call us out, that it would never actually happen." She shook her head. Old news. The future was now. "Anyway, I should... I was going to say pack, but I have nothing. No home, no prince, no job. Just me."

"Sounds like you have plenty."

At the note in Will's voice—husky and raw—Sadie's eyes swept to the man beside her. The dark curls, the strong face, those profoundly deep eyes—he looked like some Byronic hero. He looked...so beautifully tragic, her entire body began to unfurl. To reach for him. To ease his aches and pains. And, yes, her own.

How had she come to be so used to having him in her life? It had been a day and a half, for Pete's sake. How had she become so attuned to the subtlety of his movements, his expressions, his breaths? So responsive to the quiet questions in his eyes?

She closed herself back in, crossing both arms over her chest. "Thank you, Will. For the tracksuit, for the bed, for putting up with me."

"I won't say it's been my pleasure—"

She smiled, as she was meant to do.

"But it has been educational."

Sadie reached out, laid her hand on Will's arm. "From a smart guy like you I'll take that as a compliment."

"From a generous spirit like yours, I wouldn't expect anything different."

Sadie should have let go. Instead she stepped forward, tipped up onto her toes and pressed her lips to Will's cheek.

Even as it happened she knew she would never forget

the scent of him—soap and heat and man. Or the warmth of his body, enveloping hers. The scrape of his stubble against her lips. Or the telling shiver that rocketed down his arm and into her hand. Like a perfect circuit.

When she pulled away, her heart was clanging in her chest. Breaths were difficult to come by. The intensity in his eyes was nothing like she'd felt in her entire life.

And once again the spell was broken by a knock at the door.

Shaking her head, literally, she landed back on her heels. Then she took a step towards the room. "Did Hugo go out?"

But Will put a hand over the door, protecting her. "No. Wait here."

She didn't wait, she followed. He might harbour a protective streak a mile wide, but she could look after herself. To find Hugo was already at the door, eye at the peephole.

He opened the door with a flourish to reveal Prospero filling the doorway.

"Prospero," said Hugo. "Excellent timing. We're ready to—"

The big man held out his phone. "Your Highness."

Hugo winced. "For the hundredth time, it's Hugo, please."

The big man's expression didn't falter. "Your Highness, you need to see this."

"Fine." Hugo took the phone, his expression blank. Until it wasn't. His brow furrowed, his mouth thinned. He seemed to grow out of his shoes until he looked for all the world a king. His voice was sharp as he demanded, "Where did you find this?"

"Internet alerts," said Prospero. "Any hint of a news article about you comes into my phone. I need to be prepared." The big man's throat worked ever so slightly, the only sign he was in any way concerned. "I blame myself.

They must have followed us from the palace. I have failed you at the first sign of trouble. I will resign the moment I get you to safety."

Hugo gave him a look. "You're not quitting. I've only just got used to having you around. And it looks like I'm going to need you tonight."

When Will stepped forward, Sadie realised she'd been tucked in behind him, taking his protection for granted. She moved past him and tugged on Hugo's sleeve. "What is it? What's going on?"

Hugo glanced over her shoulder at Will.

Sadie took Hugo by his royal chin and forced him to look at her. Out of the corner of her eye she saw Prospero move in. To the big bald man she said, "Back away." To Hugo, "And you. Tell me what's going on. Right now."

Hugo gave over his phone.

Sadie recognised the website. It was the kind that traded in online gossip, most of it made up. All salacious. Whatever their opinion on the wedding upset, no one would take it seriously, surely.

And then she saw the art.

There was Hugo walking into a building. Crumbling brick. Bougainvillaea. A swing sign with a tulip carved into the wood.

She looked up at Hugo. "That's you. Walking in here. This afternoon."

"Keep going."

Finger shaking now, she scanned down. Her hand moved to cover her mouth as she saw the worst of it.

More pictures. This time it was later, darker. The shots angled up at the Tower Room balcony. Some images weren't even in focus but every one of them was all too clear.

Picture after picture of Sadie and Will. Hands an inch

apart as they held the railing. Looking into one another's eyes.

Sadie's throat tightened as she madly scanned through the lot. Thankfully the pictures stopped before she had taken Will by the arm. Leaned in. Kissed him.

Small mercy. For under each picture the banner read, "Prince Alessandro busts Lady Sadie with new lover in secret village pad."

She'd known the balcony wasn't secure. The entire village was spread out below with its houses and shops and bars. Will's self-sabotage theory grew roots and shoots and twisted around her like a creeping vine.

"Hugo, we were just talking." That was Will, looking over Sadie's shoulder as she slowly scrolled back.

"I know," said Hugo.

"I mean, it was right now. Just happened. Look at the clothes. The angle of the shadows—"

"Will, I know. I trust you weren't just romancing Leo on the balcony like something from one of her plays. It's okay."

Head swimming, tummy tumbling, Sadie shoved the phone at Hugo before it burned her hand, clueless as to whether to apologise or smack him.

She turned to Prospero, ready to flay him for bringing the press here, but the big guy looked so desperately disgraced that in another place, another era, he might have popped an arsenic tablet and been done with it.

She looked around the room for answers. It really was a sweet room. If one had to get stuck somewhere for any length of time it was a wonderful choice. She'd miss it. Or maybe it was the simplicity. The time to do nothing but reflect on the life choices she'd made. The company...

It didn't matter. For now it was time to go.

Hugo broke into her reverie. "Will, what's your plan?"

"London."

"Take her with you."

In the gap left by Will's revealing silence, Sadie said, "Am I the *her* in this situation?"

Her eyes flickered between theirs. Hugo had gone full prince—looking down his nose imperiously, as if he was about to bestow a knighthood. While Will was pulling his statue move. These men...

"Will can't just take me with him. He works. He has a life." Sadie realised she wasn't sure what that entailed. Despite the intensity of the past couple of days, she didn't really know the man at all. "Tell him, Will."

But Will was watching Hugo, the two men having some kind of psychic Man Conversation of which she was no part.

Sadie looked to Prospero for help. "Prospero, tell them they're overreacting."

Anguish passed over Prospero's face. "Sorry, m'lady. But His Highness is right. The sooner you are gone, the easier it is for me to protect the Prince. It's best."

Sadie threw her hands in the air. "'It's best'? *It's best* is how we got into this mess in the first place!"

Knowing the barb was meant for him, Hugo finally looked at her. She took her chance. "If Will and I are seen together, leaving the country no less, those pictures will take on loaded meaning where right now there is nothing but two separate, uninvolved people on a balcony. Chatting. About...stuff."

Only she couldn't stop the strangely guilty warmth rising in her cheeks, because for her it had meant more than simply chatting. If Hugo noticed he didn't say, but something passed over his face, nevertheless. Ruefulness? Or maybe it was release.

Sadie turned on Will, getting desperate now. "Will. You say the word and we can put an end to this idea."

Will's gaze turned to Sadie. All deep soulful eyes and tight, ticking jaw. And he said, "It's fine."

"Wow, how to make a girl feel wanted."

A flash of fire lit the depths of his eyes, of *want*. It lit a twin fire in her belly, lower. Higher. All over. This was going to be a disaster.

"Don't you see you're off the hook? You're not my baby-sitter any more. You're not my bodyguard."

"Then what is he?" Hugo asked.

"He's… He's…" So many conflicting answers rushed to the front of Sadie's mind, none of which she could say out loud.

Hugo took her silence for acquiescence. "Exactly. It's done. Prospero?"

"I'm on it." And then the big man was off, striding down the hall.

Hugo shoved an overnight bag at her. "I had your mother pack for you, just in case you decided against coming home right away. Clothing, toothbrush, et cetera. A book. Your phone. Charger. And your passport."

Passport? She'd run out of excuses. Unless she wanted to be hunted in her own backyard, she had to go. It was best.

Will gathered his leather overnight bag and his battered silver case. *He'd* been packed, ready to go, from the moment they'd arrived. "Let's do this."

And then they were off. Hugo at the head, Sadie in the middle, Will at the rear.

"Breathe," Will murmured.

"Don't want to."

Then his hand slipped under her elbow and he walked beside her. "Do it anyway."

"Story of my life."

His rough laughter made her feel as if she'd stepped

into a warm bath. The tingling in her toes diminished and her anxiety eased.

Striding down the hall, down the stairs and into Reception, they saw that Prospero had taken up residence with his back to the front door.

Janine of the ponytail was at the desk once more, watching Prospero like a hawk. When she looked up to see Will bearing down on her, her whole face brightened. "Why, hello! If it isn't the lovebirds from the honeymoon suite!"

Sadie blanched. Not that Janine would have noticed. Her eyes were now comically jumping from Will to Prospero to Hugo.

"Heading out?" Janine called. "It's cold out there—" Her voice came to a halt as her mouth dropped open into comical shock. "You're…him. You're the… Oh, my."

Hugo stepped up to the plate, blinding smile in place. "Prince Alessandro. Pleased to meet you. Is there, by any chance, a back entrance to this place? We seem to have collected some unsavoury hangers-on."

Janine, good girl that she was, did not need to be asked twice. She was out from behind the counter in a flash. "This way," she stage-whispered, tiptoeing dramatically.

Will, Hugo and Sadie followed, edging through the old kitchen, and out into an alleyway filled with limp bougainvillaea petals, bins and a half-dozen stray cats. As luck would have it they could see the bumper of Will's hire car out the other end.

To Will Hugo said, "Take care of her as if she is your most precious possession. Take care of her as if she is family."

Will's nod was solemn.

"Thanks again, Will," said Hugo, shaking the other man's hand. "I owe you."

"You owe me nothing."

"Can you let Maman know?" asked Sadie.

"Of course." Hugo gave Sadie a quick bear hug. "Try not to cause too much trouble."

She laughed. "Way too late for that."

"Go. Now."

Will grabbed Sadie's bag from her shoulder and strode towards the car. Sadie followed, noting it had started to snow. Big, soft, romantic flakes that dissolved the second they hit skin.

Her feet ground to a halt as she neared the end of the alley, and moonlit hit her toes. "Just a second."

She ran back to Hugo, who was waiting in the darkness, delved deep into the zip pocket in the side of her track top and found the ring which was still attached to the garter. She gave it to Hugo.

He winced. "Maybe I ought to gift this thing to the twins and be done with it."

"Don't say that. You'll find someone one day. Someone wonderful. Someone who adores you. Someone who doesn't cringe at the thought of kissing you. Someone who doesn't answer back all the time and isn't such a bad sport at board games as I am. Someone, maybe, a little like Clair."

A moment of torment crossed her old friend's face like a cloud passing the moon, and she wondered that she'd never noticed before.

Then he pulled himself free of it and gave her a smile. "Take care, Leo."

"You too, Hugo."

And with that, Sadie ran and hopped into the car. Or she tried, but her wedding dress was still smooshed into the footwell, her hairpiece sitting pathetically on top.

She hopped out of the car, dragged out the wedding stuff, went to the bin in the alleyway and threw it all away.

Back in the car she looked at Will, his face a familiar expression of barely reigned-in patience.

"Are you ready?" he asked.

Her heart clunked against her ribs just at the look of him. "Not even close."

But as the engine growled to life, Sadie felt lighter. Like an untethered helium balloon. Even though, as they took off into the night, leaving Vallemont behind, she knew not when, or if, she might ever return.

CHAPTER EIGHT

DARKNESS HAD LANDED by the time their private plane—
organised with stunning speed by Will's apparently un-
flappable assistant, Natalie—hit English soil. While the
snow falling through the crisp Vallemontian air had felt
dreamy and romantic, London's weather was damp and
grey.

A driver was waiting for them at a designated point.
"Where to, sir?"

Will gave an address in Borough Market and it wasn't
long before they were pulling down a dark concrete alley
to a warehouse conversion with rows of arched leadlight
windows and striped metal security bars.

Sadie walked hesitantly inside.

Will dragged his battered silver case with Maia the telescope inside to a spot beside a long, black leather couch,
then moved about, turning on lights, turning on the heat.

Industrial lamps splashed pools of cool light against
walls of rustic exposed brick. Insanely high ceilings criss-
crossed with massive steel and wooden beams. There was
a fantastical Art Deco staircase that went up, up, up. Huge,
gunmetal-grey barn doors shut off whatever rooms were
behind them. Everything was dark, seriously arty and
hyper-masculine. There was an old wooden plane propeller mounted to the wall above the TV, for Pete's sake!

It was an amazing place, to be sure. Only it didn't mesh

with what she thought she knew of Will. Not even close. She would have said Will's defining feature was how confident he was in his own skin—in his cleverness, his quirks, his self-containment. This place was pure mid-life crisis—all it was missing was wood chips on the floor, a Lamborghini in the lounge room and the scent of beer in the air.

Coming here had been a mistake. A huge, colossal mistake.

Will touched her on the shoulder and she near leapt out of her skin.

When she realised he was taking her overnight bag she let out a shaky laugh. "Sorry. I was half expecting the bogeyman to have followed us here."

"We weren't followed. I'm sure."

"Prospero was sure and he's a professional."

"Prospero's neck is so thick he can't turn his head to check his side mirrors."

Sadie laughed and a small measure of her nerves faded away.

Then she realised Will's fingers were still hooked into her bag, on her shoulder, the heat of them tingling through her arm. She let him slide the strap away.

Then she moved further into the space. So much space. "How long have you lived here?"

"I've owned it about eight years. Ten maybe. Quite a place, isn't it?"

"Quite."

"But?"

"Did you hear the but?"

"It's written all over your face."

His arms were crossed as he watched her move through his home, but his face was gentle. He didn't seem to mind her hesitance, he was more…curious than anything else. The Will she knew was curious. Painfully so. It made her nerves fade a little more.

"But…where's all your stuff?"

He looked around. "In its place."

What place? There was nothing there. No rugs to soften it, no cushions to add comfort. No bookshelves, even though Will was an educated man. No knick-knacks, no family photos. Not even a telescope pointing out the expanse of windows. No sense of Will at all.

"I wasn't expecting company."

She dragged her eyes away from the man cave to shoot Will a flat stare. "Big shock. But even if you were, all of this feels more like a concerted effort to scare people away."

He didn't react. Didn't even blink. But then a smile kicked at the corner of his mouth and his dimple came out to play. Sadie tried to settle the resultant shimmer in her belly, as she wondered if maybe she had him figured out after all.

The she turned on her toes and came to a halt, her mouth dropping open at the huge, twenty-foot-high wall covered in the most stunning wallpaper—a black background scattered with the names of constellations and such in chunky white font.

"That was the clincher," he said, his voice near as he moved in behind her. "My publisher had rented the place and a stylist had decked out that wall for a publicity shoot before my first book came out. I found I wasn't comfortable pretending the place was mine for the book jacket photographs, so I bought it. As is. *Stuff*—or lack thereof—and all."

Sadie wasn't au fait with London real estate but she knew enough. "Who knew gazing at the stars paid so well?"

"It's not all star-gazing, Sadie," he said, his voice going gruff in that way it did when she had him on the ropes. He was so easy that way.

"No?"

"Consultancy, publishing, speaking, teaching. I do okay. Not as well as a prince, mind you."

"Ha! Turns out, for me, that's not all that much of a selling point."

Will's brow clutched. And Sadie, belatedly, heard what she'd said.

"Not that you were *trying* to sell me anything, of course." *Stop. Stop talking right now. Nope, more words coming.* "But if you were… I'm out of a job, out of a home and on the shelf. You in the market for a wife?"

It had been a joke. *Absolutely.* She had meant to alleviate the tension that had been humming between them since they'd taken off in Will's car. Or maybe it had been since the first night on the balcony. Or the first time she'd seen Will's smile.

It didn't work. Tension rippled through the air like a living thing, smacking against the stark brick and overwhelming glass and rocketing back at them like flying knives.

Feeling the pink beginning to rise up her throat, Sadie flapped a lazy hand at Will. "I changed my mind. Now I've seen this place I realise the neat freak thing wasn't a one-off. And I'm a delightful slob. It would never work."

She feigned a nonchalant yawn which turned into the real thing.

"You look exhausted."

"Why, thank you," she said on yet another yawn.

"You hungry?"

"Not a bit," she lied. Knowing she had to head somewhere quiet, alone, to collect her thoughts before she said something even less appropriate than mock-proposing to the guy.

"Then I'll show you to your room."

Sliding the strap of her bag over his shoulder, Will headed for the stairs, leaving Sadie to follow. The heating system must have been state of the art as she was starting to feel all thawed and fuzzy already.

Up the big black stairs they went, past more barn doors—she spied a sliver of sterile-looking office behind one, fancy gym equipment behind another, which explained the man's physique—until Will stopped in front of a neat, light room with huge, curtainless windows and a view of a whole lot of rooftops of post-industrial London.

Will handed over her bag and waited on the threshold as she went inside. "There's a private bathroom through that door. The remote on the bedside table darkens the windows." A beat. Time enough for his cheeks to lift before he said, "Knowing how much you like borrowed clothes, there are spares in the cupboard."

She sat on the corner of the neat grey bed and patted her bag, holding it close to her chest to try to stop the *ba-da-boom* of her heart at the sight of that smile. "I'm all good."

"Excellent. If I'm not here in the morning there'll be food in the fridge. I'll leave my assistant's contact details on the kitchen bench. She knows where I am at all times."

"Okay."

"Okay. Goodnight, Sadie."

"Goodnight, Will."

Will went to slide the door closed, but Sadie stopped him with a breath. "They'll figure out who you are, you know."

"I know."

"They'll make assumptions without fact and write about it. They'll take those pictures and turn them into something ugly. Over and over again, the stories getting bigger, wilder, further and further from anything resembling truth." She knew. She'd seen it happen to other members of Hugo's family. Tall poppies ripe for cutting down.

"I'm aware."

"Are you? Because the thought of it impacting your career, of you having to explain me to your friends... I sense that, for all the speaking and publishing and teaching and consulting and international jet-setting, you're a private man, Will. Should you call your family?"

"No family to call."

"None?"

"Sadie, don't worry about it."

"But I will. I do. I worry all the time. The thought of someone out there not liking me, or being angry at me, or blaming me..." She ran a hand over her eyes. "You're right. I am exhausted."

Will's toe nudged over the line at her door before he stopped himself. "Whatever happens tomorrow, or next week, the sun will rise, the earth will turn, and it will be forgotten. We all will be forgotten. Nothing lasts for ever."

Sadie laughed. "Was that meant to make me feel better?"

"You're laughing."

"So I am."

"Sleep."

"Yes, sir."

With that Will slid the door closed, leaving Sadie in his big grey room, in the big, bold house, in a big, strange city, her thoughts a flurry, her heart confused, her oldest fears playing on the edges of her mind.

Alone.

"I'm back."

"The Boss Man's back!" Natalie paused as she mulled over Will's words. "Back to work or back in London? Or back in Vallemont? I've lost track."

Will lay back on his uncomfortable couch in the main room, staring up at the propeller jutting out from the floating wall, wondering if there might be a button somewhere to make it work, he'd simply never cared enough to find out. "London. Work."

"Fantastic! I'll set up newyorker.com for you for... tomorrow afternoon your time. No appointment set up with the prime minister as yet, but I've managed to become firm friends with his secretary, Jenny. She gave me an amazing recipe for mulberry jam. And I can let Garry know he no longer has to berate you for never taking a break, as you've just had two whole days in the gorgeous countryside of Vallemont! Was it amazing?"

"Amazing," Will said.

"You're not even listening."

Will sat up straight. Focused. He checked his watch to find it had been five minutes since the last time he'd looked. And twenty-five minutes since he'd left Sadie to sleep in his spare bedroom.

He rubbed a hand over his chin to find his beard now long enough to leave a rash, and said, "New Yorker. Jam. Sadie. I got it."

"Will."

"Yes, Natalie."

"Who's Sadie?"

Will held the phone away from his ear as if it had just grown legs. Dammit. How distracted was he.

"Will? Will!" Natalie's voice chirped through the phone.

Will slowly brought it back to his ear. In time to hear his assistant ask, "Is that what you were doing the past two days? A girl?"

Will pinched the bridge of his nose. For all her voracious work ethic and killer travel-arranging skills, Natalie was ridiculously focused on his private life. She had been since she saw a photo of him once in *GQ*, attending the Kennedy Centre honours for a previous president with a Victoria's Secret model on his arm.

The fact that his date was a space buff who'd been in

contact with Garry, his manager, asking for advice on which university was best for post-grad studies was beside the point as far as Natalie was concerned.

"Will," she shouted. "Don't you lie to me. It's the one non-negotiable of our contract together."

"No, it's not."

"Fine. But tell me anyway. I worry about you. From all the way over here. Garry does too. And Cynthia."

His publisher? Please don't say they'd all been talking about him.

"Knowing you had a nice girl in your life would go a long way to alleviating our concerns."

"Natalie, do I not pay you enough?"

"Oh, no, Boss Man. I cannot complain on that score. Not a single bit."

"Do I push my luck, ask too much of you, underappreciate you?"

"Often, sometimes and absolutely no."

Not the answer he'd expected. Into the moment's pause Natalie said, "Will, did you or did you not meet a girl in Vallemont?"

He stared up at the propeller once more and thought of the look of incredulity in Sadie's eyes as she'd spotted it. He'd had dates in his London pad before. They'd either not noticed the thing, or they'd thought it inspired. Sadie had known, in a second, that it wasn't something he'd ever have chosen.

"It's complicated."

Natalie whooped. And clapped. For so long he wondered if she was giving him a standing ovation.

"It's not what you think."

"You have no idea what I think."

"You think I'm skiving off work because I've found myself a woman who's made me realise human relationships are more important than work can ever be."

A long pause. "Well, have you?"

"No, Natalie. I have not. For which you ought to be thankful, as it is my work that keeps you in mulberry jam."

Natalie went quiet. Then, "Will Darcy, it is my skill that keeps me in mulberry jam. It's your work that keeps you from rocking in a corner. Check your calendar; it's updated. And packed to the rafters, just as you like it. Goodnight."

Will threw his phone to the end of the couch, where it bounced and settled. Knowing he ought to check his calendar in order to be prepared for the next day's work, he instead headed upstairs, ignoring the lift of his pulse as he passed Sadie's closed door, and headed into his room.

He showered—and shaved, *hallelujah*—put on fresh pyjamas, and hopped into his own bed.

Then stared at the ceiling knowing he'd never been further from sleep in his entire life.

Natalie's words floated around and around his mind like so much space junk.

He had relationships. They were simply shorter, more condensed or more peripheral than others might be used to.

And, while his work was at the centre of his life, it wasn't the thing that held him together. If he had to give it up one day, he could. Yup, even he heard it—he sounded like a junkie. *Who's Sadie?* Natalie had asked.

Sadie was the reason he felt a gnawing self-reproach at having missed work for two days apart from a little gazing at the Orionid Shower.

Sadie was the reason he was holed up in his London house, when he should be in the outback, a desert, anywhere but the high-density cityscape that was London, where it was so grey out he'd see nothing but soup.

Sadie was the reason he was wide awake.

He rolled over, and closed his eyes. Sleep would come. This restlessness wouldn't last.

Nothing ever did.

Sadie was used to things going bump in the night. She'd grown up in a several-hundred-year-old palace after all.

But it didn't make a lick of difference. As tired as she was, knowing Will was out there was making her restless.

Restless in a way she hadn't been before the kiss on the cheek.

Before the photos of them looking so...so...

Before he'd gone above and beyond, whisking her away to his private residence.

She rolled over, rifled through her overnight bag. Hello! Her phone.

It was only slightly charged. And she had so many messages her mailbox was full. She paused a half-second before deleting it all. And she made the only call she needed to make.

"This is Genevieve."

Sadie rolled her eyes. "It's *me*, Maman. And I know you know because my number comes up when I call."

A beat slid by in which Sadie imagined her mother's imperious stare. Only then did her mother launch into a series of very important questions.

"Mercedes Gray Leonine, did I not teach you anything about getting into cars with strange men?"

"No. You did not."

"Really?"

"It never came up."

A beat, then, "Are his eyes as blue as they look in the photo?"

"Oh, yeah."

"Some might call that extenuating circumstances."

Some, but not Genevieve. It had been her life's mission

to make sure her daughter thought once, twice, three times before taking anyone at face value. Men in particular. The better looking, the more charming, the more she was encouraged to stay away. It was as if she'd had to defy her mother by falling for her acting coach in New York—an older man, beautiful but fallible—to finally see she had a point.

Leading her to Hugo. The one man in her life, and her mother's life, who had always been the exception to the rule.

Still Sadie had run. And where had she learned that, again?

"Now Hugo tells me you are *living with* this man?"

"Not living. Staying. In his spare room. He is a dear old friend of Hugo's. He's been amazingly...unruffled by the situation. A self-contained sort of man." Yikes, she was making him sound like a doddering uncle. She heard Will's voice accusing her of *protesting too much* and eased back. "It's easier this way."

"Hmmm. And how good-looking is he?" her mother asked. "Because if that photograph was even close you need to beware—"

"Maman. Any chance we can talk about something other than Will?"

"But why?"

"Because I ran away from marrying a prince yesterday and I thought you might have an opinion on that. And I hear that you have retired and moved out of the palace and I wondered if you would like to hear my opinion on that?"

"Not so much."

Sadie rolled onto her back and stuck her legs in the air, the huge, lacy white nightie she had never seen before that her mother had so kindly packed for her falling to her hips as she twirled her ankles one way and then the other. "I've been thinking."

"Yes?"

"About my father."

Never a fun topic.

Sadie's toes clenched as she waited for her mother's, "I see."

"About the similarities between us."

"You do have his eyes." Genevieve sighed. The love of melodramatics also an inherited trait.

"I mean, that he was a runner. And so, it seems, am I."

"Oh, darling. My sweet girl. What you are is discriminating. You will not be shaken. You will not be swayed. You know kindness and you know how to put people at ease."

"I know when I'm being hustled."

"That's my girl. No point being sweet unless it's wrapped around a core of steel."

"That's right, Maman." Sadie let her feet drop. She rolled to her side, watched moonlight play over the painted wood floor. "Have you really moved out already?"

"I really have. To a lovely little cottage on the edge of the grounds. Marguerite has been saving it for me for years. You have a room here too, my darling. If you want it."

Sadie rolled onto her front, to the foggy grey view out the window, to the light from the converted homes nearby, the city beyond. Growing up in the country, she'd dreamed of living in a big city one day—close to the best theatres, surrounded by crowds and people who had no clue who she was. Who didn't watch her every move. Where she could be anonymous.

New York hadn't worked out. Maybe this was a second chance.

"Thanks, Maman. I'll let you know as soon as I know what I decide to do."

Her phone started to buzz. Low battery. She promised to call soon and hung up.

She rolled to sitting. Her toes reached to the floor before curling away from the cold grey. Only... Her toes tapped against the floor to find it warm. Toasty, in fact. Under-floor heating. Naturally.

She was thirsty. Or hungry. Or something.

Whatever she was she couldn't sit here pretending to sleep. It was early—maybe that was it. She needed to stretch her legs. Or watch a little TV. Hugo had mentioned a book in her bag... No. A book wouldn't do it. Surely this place had a TV somewhere.

Grabbing the heavy comforter off the end of the bed, she wrapped it around her shoulders and heaved open the door and—

The comforter slid off her shoulders and landed in a puddle on the floor as she came face to face with Will.

He'd stopped in the hallway, a cup of coffee in his hand. A pristine white T-shirt—creased from where it had just come out of its packet— did magical things to his chest. Or was that the other way around? Dark grey pyjama bottoms hung low on his hips. His feet were bare.

Moonlight sliced across his strong face. He'd shaved, making him look younger somehow. Clean-cut. All crisp edges, and smooth lines. Much like the statue he seemed too fond of incarnating. Except for the banked heat in his eyes.

"I don't remember that being in my spare-clothes drawer."

"Hmm?" Sadie followed his gaze, glancing down at her matronly nightgown with its neck-to-ankle pin-tucks. "My mother packed it for me."

"Is there a chance she wants you living at home with her for ever?"

Sadie laughed out loud, recalling the phone call she'd literally just had. "Could be."

For a man who came across as so dry, he had a way at cutting to the heart of things. The humanity. Like this strange house of his—cool and intimidating on the outside, but warm to the touch.

"Did you need something?" he asked. His deep voice rumbled over her skin like a blast of heat.

Did she? Did she need something? Maybe. Maybe what she needed was right here in front of her.

No. Don't be stupid. You don't need Will. You've just gotten used to having him near. You like having him near. You want to have him nearer still.

Boy, was that a bad idea. He was Hugo's friend, for one. He was a self-confessed workaholic, existing in the rarefied air of the intelligentsia, whereas everything she did was navigated by her heart. And security was crucial to her; knowing she had a safe place to go home to if everything else in her life fell apart. His home clearly meant nothing more to him than a place to occasionally sleep.

If she stood a chance of doing this right one day, she'd need a stayer. Someone solid and settled and present. Someone to pin her feet to the floor. Someone she could trust not to bolt. Someone not like her father. *Someone not like her.*

She needed someone else.

But she wanted him.

He took a step closer and she gripped the comforter for all she was worth.

"Are you hungry? We could go out— No. Bad idea."

Will smiled. It did things to his face, encouraging things, that had Sadie feeling warm all over. It had to be some kind of glitch in the space-time continuum to find the only astronomer in the universe who could do more for a white T-shirt than Marlon Brando.

"I could order food in. I think Natalie had my cleaning agency pin some takeaway menus to a door somewhere."

She shook her head no.

"How about a book? I know there are plays in my library. Funny, I hadn't remembered until that moment that Clair used to read herself to sleep when it wouldn't come on its own."

Funny; she wondered if he realised that here, alone with her, he was able to say Clair's name and not look as if he was being stabbed in the heart as he said it.

Funny how well he knew her that he understood she was a lover of words.

Not so funny that all of that burned him a little place marker onto her heart.

"The building came with a fully stocked library when I bought it. I'm sure even Shakespeare is in there somewhere."

Maybe it was the moonlight, maybe it was the man—heck, maybe it was the fact that he kept quoting Shakespeare—but Sadie dropped the comforter on the floor, stepped over it, took Will by the front of the T-shirt, pulled herself up onto her toes and kissed him.

Time seemed to stand still as her lips met his. Her fingers curled harder into the cotton as every nerve ending zinged as if all the energy in all the world had coalesced into her body in that moment.

Which was why it took a moment to realise he wasn't kissing her back.

Her eyes fluttered open to find his dark. Impenetrable.

She pulled back. A fraction. A mile. It didn't matter. So long as she had those eyes on hers. For she knew she hadn't misread the signs—the way he looked at her, how he found excuses to touch her—had she?

The urge to let go, to step back, to apologise, make a joke, make light, to *run* was near overwhelming.

But this time the want was stronger.

She squeezed the cotton tighter in her grip, holding on for dear life. And…there. The thump of his heart against her knuckles gave him away. It was galloping, out of control.

"Will?" she said, her voice barely a breath.

With a growl that seemed to come from some primal place inside of him, Will's arms were around her, holding her so close not a sliver of light could get through, then kissed her like there was no tomorrow.

Colour exploded behind her eyes as heat and want and desire and relief swirled together in a heady mix of intense sensation. His kisses were like a dream, pulling her under until her thoughts were no longer her own.

Her hands ran over his hard shoulders, diving into his curls. Her knees lost all feeling and she felt an almost insatiable need to cry.

Then, just when she thought she might dissolve into a puddle of trembling lust, his arm slid under her knees and she whooped as her feet left the ground.

Laughter spilled from her as Will stepped over the comforter and carried her to the bed. He dropped her so she bounced. Her laughter grew patchy, breathless, as he hovered at the end of her bed.

He stood perfectly still in a patch of moonlight, every inch of him illuminated in its silvery spotlight.

She felt as though she could see past the impermeable Will wall and into the heart of him for the very first time. Substantial, stoic, strong and sure. But above all solitary. A lone wolf.

Her belly fluttered in warning. *Be careful. Be sure.*

This had all the markers of self-sabotage he'd observed in her. Only it didn't feel the same. It didn't have the same breathless desperation with which she made so many big decisions. She felt…calm. Present. As if she'd been waiting for this moment her entire life.

"What are we doing, Will?"

"If you need me to tell you that—"

"You know what I mean. This, us, it's just a normal re-action to the stress of the past few days, right?"

He said nothing. But she'd been stuck in close quarters with him long enough now to read his supremely subtle body language. The heat was no longer banked, the spark of attraction was aflame. But he was as conflicted as she was.

But then his gaze travelled down her body, roaming over her hair, her shoulders, down her voluminous nightdress to her feet, leopard-print toenails curling and uncurling in the soft grey sheets. It left a trail of warmth, of anticipation, of promise in its wake.

And he said, "I've never been comforted by the idea of normal. Not when there's the option to reach for more."

"All the way to the stars?"

He smiled then, a deeply sexy smile in which his dimple came out to play. Then he climbed onto the bed and thought became something other people did.

His hand started at her ankle, then moved slowly up her calf. She jerked as it hit the back of her knee. Then it was gone, over the top of her nightgown now, sliding over her hip, slowly moving over her ribs. Her muscles melted one by one. All except her toes. They curled so far back on themselves they hurt.

She grabbed him by the T-shirt and dragged him towards her. He caught himself so he didn't hurt her, muscles in his arms straining as he pressed her back, even as she pulled him down.

Then his fingers were at her neck, tracing the edge of her nightgown. She realised he was looking for a button. A release.

She reached down to her knees to grab the hem, before wriggling the acres of fabric over her head. Dangling it daintily over the edge of the bed, she said, "Unless you'd prefer I fold it and place it neatly in my bag..."

Will shoved it to the floor, and hauled her into his arms. The heat of him burnt through his clothes, searing her bare skin. It was as if now he had her he couldn't stand to let her go.

Dangerous thought.

This was a man for whom sentimentality was a four-letter word. He *would* let her go. And that was okay.

Funny; the fact that he would never expect anything from her made him all the more of a prize.

As she hovered on the edge of no turning back, her eyes once more found his, moonlight no longer giving her insight, forcing her to respond to the truth of his touch, his pulse, his presence.

"Nothing's going to be the same, is it?"

He smoothed her hair off her face. Kissed her nose. Her forehead. Her chin. And found her eyes again. "Nothing ever is."

Then he lowered himself to drag his lips across hers, slow, gentle, before settling perfectly into place and stealing her breath away, taking her to some other place where thought was lost, memory became a dream and nothing mattered but the moment.

And neither of them said a thing for a good long while.

CHAPTER NINE

WILL WOKE LATE. Not that he could remember what he might be late for. Or what day it was. Or what country he was in.

Then he heard Sadie shift, muttering and murmuring as she rolled onto her belly, the sheets twisting with her, her hair cascading down her back, like liquid fire in the morning light.

The urge to join her again hit fast and furious. To sweep her hair away and run his hand down her back. To trace her spine with kisses. To see her smile.

To feel her open to him. To silence her moans with a kiss. To see that look in her eyes, the raw emotion, something beyond attraction, beyond a mere spark, as she tumbled over the edge.

But, while the night before had felt inevitable, the burning away of the tension that had simmered between them from the moment he nearly ran her down, waking her with a kiss would be a very different thing.

For he was in London, it was Monday and he had work to do.

Will slid out of Sadie's bed, picked her nightgown up off the floor and shook it out, preparing to fold it. He stopped himself, tossing it on the edge of the bed instead.

Stretching out his limbs, he turned at the door and looked back. Took stock.

He would give her sanctuary so long as she required it, and he could get back to real life, driven by a brutal calendar, living on the rush of his work, banking his meticulously architected reputation to make sure he was in the rooms of power.

But now he had finally slayed the sentimental obstructions that had been dogging him for years, he did not intend to replace one kind with another.

Stepping over the comforter in her doorway, Will went back to work.

Sadie felt like herself for the first time in days. Weeks even.

It could be the jeans.

While packing her a nightgown fit for Queen Victoria, Sadie's all too clever mother had also packed her favourite jeans. Soft from wear, skin-tight and worn away at the knees. Add a warm top, an oversized cream jumper and a leopard-print scarf and she was happy as a clam.

It could also have been the coffee.

She'd managed to find an espresso machine in Will's concrete kitchen and actual ground coffee. Not instant, or pods, but fresh ground: manna from heaven.

Of course, it might well have been Will.

Last night had been…unexpected. Not the fact that it had happened. Something had had to give, what with the tension that had been building between them in incremental steps for days. But the way of him—intense as he was in the everyday, all dark, brooding eyes and devastating detail. But also tender. Cherishing her. Making her ache so sweetly, all over, so deeply, she'd lost all sense of place and time. She didn't remember falling asleep so much as drifting away as if on a cloud.

Then, as though she'd closed her eyes and opened them again, it had been morning. And she'd been fully awake.

Every fibre, every cell, every hair follicle switched on. As though the night before had acted like some kind of psychic system reset. As if things would be different from hereon in, she just had to figure out how.

But first...coffee.

Sipping, she stared across the great expanse of Will's plane-hangar-sized abode. The weak morning sunlight did nothing to make the living space appear homelier. While stunning in its über-masculine detail, it was sterile. The perfect pad for the man who'd leapt from his car and accused her of being obtuse.

But what about the man who'd held her in his arms, caressing a length of her hair, breathing softly into her neck as they'd floated into slumber together? There had to be proof of him here somewhere.

She began a room-by-room reconnoitre.

The kitchen cupboards were mostly bare. His office had not a pencil out of place. It was as if he'd deliberately not left his mark on the place. As if being packed, ready to leave a place, wasn't the mark of a well-seasoned traveller but a way of life.

Despite the underfloor heating and the coffee in her system, Sadie suddenly felt the cold.

What brought a man to the point where being alone was the only choice?

The few times Sadie had managed to solicit her mother to talk about her father, Genevieve had admitted she'd been smitten. That his passion, his joie de vivre, his dashing good looks had been hard to resist. That she'd been so blinded by it she'd never for a moment imagined he'd desert her the way he had.

Cradling the cooling coffee, she wandered aimlessly about the upper level, bypassing small doors probably leading to storage areas and a ladder that went up to who knew where.

And then she found the library.

She stepped inside the cool, shadowy room. The heavy dark shelves were covered in books organised by colour and shape rather than author or title. Visually stunning, but futile.

Nevertheless, she searched. For something she couldn't be sure was there but was certain all the same. Going over each row, each column until... There.

She pulled down the textbook, its pages soft and heavy in her hands. Then she turned it over to see the cover, her heart lodging in her throat at the words on the cover— *Waiting to Be Known* by Dr Will Darcy.

Swallowing hard, she looked inside. The title, it explained, was taken from a quote by Carl Sagan. Reviews included praise by famous scientists. The dedication read simply, *"For Clair."*

She flicked through the rest to find that from there it went into full scientific-textbook mode. Words upon words, diagrams, maths and the occasional colour picture to break it up. Clever man, this friend of Hugo's. This friend of hers.

But waiting to be known? Could it be?

She put the book down and looked a little further until she found a large, softcover book amongst the hardbacks. Its spine was creased with use. A book someone had actually read.

She pulled *The Collected Works of William Shakespeare* from the shelf. Opened it to find dog-ears. A handful of notes in the margins. The sign she'd been looking for. The sign *someone* had lived here. Someone had left something of themselves behind.

A piece of paper fell out. A receipt that had been used as a bookmark. By the date, it had been bought after Will had moved in, meaning Will had bought the book himself. Read it. Made notes.

She brought the heavy tome to her chest, pressing it against her rocketing heart. The brand he'd burned there the night before pulsed like a fresh wound as the tendrils of his life twisted a little tighter around hers.

Why was she doing this to herself? Looking for connections? Just because she felt as if she'd glimpsed the core of the man, it didn't mean she ought to keep digging. It didn't mean that knowing him, understanding him, would get her what she wanted.

And she wanted... No.

Will had said it himself—she had a predilection for self-sabotage. Or maybe, she was beginning to wonder, was it more of a compulsion? Do unto herself before someone else did unto her.

If so, not any more.

She'd woken up that morning and she was never going to fall asleep to her life again.

It was long dark by the time Will returned.

And it had been a hell of a day. Determined to get back on track, he'd made a dozen phone calls, finished research papers and begun others, fitting a trip out to the Royal Observatory with a meeting with the gaming crew. He felt as if he could only remember half of it. Probably for the best, as the game had major holes—meaning he had to front up more money, and agree to replace one of the designers, in order to get it back on track. A paper was rejected, as the core theory had already been covered by a fellow scientist from Tulsa. And Natalie was still stubbornly unhappy with him for not being more "sharing".

Music was playing as he headed to the front door and for a second he found himself checking he was outside the right warehouse. When he opened the door he was overcome with the scent of home cooking.

It was so foreign, so specifically outside the basic absolutes of his life, and yet so sorely welcome after such a long, difficult day, he nearly shut the door.

But then he heard the clang of pots and pans. His natural curiosity had him edging inside to find Sadie behind the kitchen bench wearing an apron he didn't know he had, using pots he'd never seen, dancing along with Otis Redding coming from a record player somewhere, cooking up a storm.

She looked up, lips puckered around the end of a wooden spoon, then slid the spoon away before calling, "Honey, you're home!"

It was so sexy Will found himself in the middle of an out-of-body experience—pleasure warring with good judgment. He gripped his briefcase hard enough to break.

Then she burst into laughter. "I'm kidding! Oh, my God, you should see your face. Come in. Put down your stuff. Sit. And wipe that look of abject terror off your face. All this is me going a very small way to making it up to you for being my babysitter, and my bodyguard, my newfound friend."

Will found himself holding his breath as he waited for another title. When none came it felt insufficient.

He dropped his briefcase by the couch, then moved towards the kitchen. Antennae on the blitz, he wasn't sure whether to kiss her on the cheek and ask after her day, or keep the bench safely between them.

In the end, he moved around to the working side of the bench. Plates and cutlery, napkins and wine glasses were lined up ready to be filled. He looked in the pot. Some kind of soup was bubbling away. It smelled amazing. Rich, decadent and wholesome.

"Where did you find all this?"

"In the cupboards. And a local grocery store delivered the ingredients."

"You cooked this?"

"Of course I cooked this. I'm fixing things in reverse, you see. Stitching up the mess I've made, starting with thanking you."

He looked up to find her nudged in beside him. Not touching, but close enough to see the light dusting of flour on her cheek. The sparks of gold in the ends of her hair sticking out of the messy topknot on her head. Her jeans fitted like a second skin and on her feet she wore a pair of socks he would have sworn were his.

Tendrils of attraction curled around him like a fast-motion creeper, twisting and tugging, shooting off in random directions until he couldn't tell where it all began. "I assumed..."

"That I lorded it up in the palace? I *learnt* in the palace. Thank goodness too. When I lived in New York I shared a tiny studio apartment with three other starving actors who waited on tables on the side. I worked in hotels, so I didn't get any of the leftover food they did. For me it was cook or starve."

"You lived in New York."

Her gaze swept to his. Snagged. Whatever she saw in his gaze had her pupils growing dark. A pulse beat in her neck.

Brow furrowing, she moved away from him to clean a bench that already looked pretty clean. "For a few years, in fact. In order to...expand my dramatic education. Why? Do I seem that parochial?"

"Yes."

She laughed, the sound tinkling up into the rafters. And Will found himself imagining coming home to this every day. Not the food, though his taste buds were watering like crazy. The woman. Her smile, her impudence, her interminable optimism.

"I get that," she said. "But, as I keep telling you, you didn't meet me at my best. I can be quite erudite when the situation calls for it. Charming too. And I know some of the best dirty jokes you will hear in your life."

Will breathed out hard, trying to find some kind of equilibrium. He was so out of sync, he felt like coming through his own front door and trying again.

It was his fault. Work or no work, he shouldn't have left as he had, not without discussing what had happened. Without putting their night together into some kind of sensible model—with margins, and objectives, and a deadline.

He'd just have to do it now.

First, he turned to pour himself a large glass of water, but he stopped when he saw the open book on the bench next to the fridge. His textbook. Open to a page about a third of the way through. A couple of bookmarks fashioned out of kitchen towel poked out of the top. And she'd scrawled question marks in the margin.

"You read my book?"

"You read Shakespeare. Seemed a fair exchange. Hungry?" she asked.

"Famished," he said, his voice a growl.

She ladled a hefty amount of soup into each bowl, tore some bread apart and lathered it in butter, then finished the look with a small pinch of herbs. *"Voilà!"*

Will breathed it in. And rubbed a hand up the back of his neck.

"You okay? You look like no one ever cooked you soup before."

"The kitchen at my grandmother's place was three floors down and locked away in the servants' quarters. The house smelled like demoralisation and thousand-year-old paintings. It never smelt like this."

"Well, then, you're welcome." A second slunk by before she said, "You were raised by your grandmother, weren't you? Were your parents not around?"

"They died when we were five."

"That's rough. I can't imagine not having my own mother around, baffling woman that she is. Is that why you always call it your grandmother's place and not home?"

"As you call the place you grew up 'the palace'."

"Huh. Do I really?"

He looked to Sadie, hip nudged against the bench, holding a glass of wine in her hand, watching him. She was the very picture of friendly nonchalance.

Except he knew better. For all the happy chatter, she was on edge. Her energy level was at altissimo, pitching and keening. His pitched with it. An echo. Her shadow. The dark to her light. North to her south.

He moved in closer.

She swallowed, her wine dropping a fraction.

"Nowhere I've lived has ever smelt like this."

"Because I live out of a suitcase, Sadie."

"Or a soft black bag and battered silver telescope case."

He smiled and it felt good. The best he'd felt all day since leaving her bed. "Or that. The truth is I can't stay in one place longer than about a month before it starts to feel too comfortable, my work suffers and I leave. Relationships follow the exact same pattern. I don't like it when my work suffers. When it suffers—"

"You suffer?"

He moved in closer again and she put the wine on the bench.

"The data I am able to collect, collate, decipher and impart is important."

"To whom?"

"To the entire world."

An eyebrow kicked north. "Wow. That's a lot of pressure."

"I like pressure," said Will, moving in close enough that the tips of his leather shoes prodded her socks. "I live for the pressure. Pressure is my bliss."

Sadie crossed her arms but her feet stayed put. "Will, is this some kind of warning?"

"Sadie, since you came into my life I have no bloody idea what I'm doing."

He slid a hand into Sadie's hair, tucking his hand over the back of her neck. He gave himself a moment to soak in those eyes, the freckles, energy enough to keep this place alight for a week.

"Wait," she said on a whisper, "what are we doing?"

"Again, if you need me to tell you that—"

"Will."

It was the perfect moment to explain to her the margins and objectives, and a deadline.

Instead he ran his thumb over her cheek and leaned towards her. Her mouth opened on a sigh just before he put his lips to hers.

A second later her hands crept up his chest, sliding under his collar and pulling his head closer. She opened to him, pressing her body against his. Making sweet little murmuring sounds as she melted into his arms.

He held her tighter still. So tightly she lifted off the ground. Swinging her around, he sat her on the bench.

Her eyes flashed open and her hands flew away as the cool of the concrete seeped into her jeans. And then she smiled against his lips.

This. This was what he'd been thinking about all day. Coming home to this. The intimacy he'd been avoiding his entire adult life. It was terrifying. It was irresistible.

She pulled back just enough to slide his jacket from his shoulders, letting it drop to the floor.

"You're a bad influence," he murmured as he tried to go in for another kiss.

But she pushed him away, moving to undo the buttons of his shirt, one by slow damn one. Once his shirt joined his jacket she ran a hand over his chest, following the line of the now purple and yellow bruise. "Does it hurt?"

"Not right now."

She laughed, the sound sexy as hell.

Then she kissed the bruise, right at the top, and Will sucked in a breath. He held it still as she pulled him into the cradle of her thighs and kissed him. On the jaw, the cheek, the tip of his nose.

Her kisses were so delicate, so exquisite, he felt as if he could barely hold himself together. As if he might crack right down the middle if he breathed too hard.

But then she touched her lips to his, ran her tongue over the seam and tugged his head to hers and he fell apart anyway.

He'd been overachieving by every quantifiable measure of success. But it had been a straight and narrow road. He hadn't been living until that moment.

Pathways opened up inside of him as he ran his hands over Sadie's hair, as he pressed into her warmth and swallowed her gasp in a kiss that changed his world.

He grabbed her by the backside and lifted her off the cold kitchen bench. She wrapped her arms about his neck and didn't break the kiss for even a breath as he carried her upstairs. But still Will held on tight.

She had a habit of running when the going got tough. Making her feel safe enough to stay would take finesse, timing and patience. The hours he'd spent behind the eyepiece of a telescope attempting to focus on precise celestial bodies light years away proved he had the staying power.

At the top of the stairs he turned left, heading into his room this time.

They never did get around to eating that soup.

"Do you have a warmer coat?"

Sadie looked up from her coffee to find Will had come

home early. Then down at the clothes she'd had on the day before. Her underwear was clean, so she figured that was winning. "I do not."

"Wait here."

"Okay."

Will ducked back upstairs, into his bedroom, and came out with a familiar black tracksuit top.

"Hello, old friend!" she said, putting it on under her jumper, letting the hood fall out of the top. "Now what?"

"Now we go out."

"We can't go out."

"Well, we can't stay here. Not for ever."

"If we go out there someone might see you."

"I've been seen before."

"But they'll see *me*, with you."

"Let them."

He gave her a look then, a look she'd never been given in her life before. Yet she understood it all the same. Deep down in the most primal, private, female part of her she knew.

Will Darcy was staking his claim. Not for ever. He didn't believe in for ever. But for now. Which, for him, was still a very big deal.

"Are you sure about this?"

Will took her by the hand and tugged her into his arms. "I called our friend the Prince this morning."

Whoa. "And said what?"

Will rubbed away the frown that popped up above her nose. "I gave him a brief, G-rated, rundown of your stay. He asked how the soup was. I changed the subject."

She coughed out a laugh.

"We had a long talk about many things and found ourselves in absolute agreement."

"You did?"

They had. "The first thing we agreed on was that the

mourning period was over. The photos of us are true and the world has to get over the fact that they are out there. Time to get on with getting on."

"The palace won't like it."

"The palace can bite me."

"Wow, Will Darcy, them's fighting words."

"I was always good in a fight, even as a kid. Scrappy. Not one for following the rules. I've also never been one to skulk in doorways, and I don't plan on making a habit of it now. So what do you say?"

But she couldn't say a single thing. She was too busy trying to find her feet. Not sure whether to laugh or cry or scream, or turn cartwheels. The only thing she didn't have the urge to do was run. She simply placed her hand in the crook of his arm and smiled.

Outside, the day was glorious. Freezing, as if the first tendrils of real winter were coming, but sunny.

Sadie took a great big, bracing breath. "Are we waiting for the car?"

"I thought we'd walk." And off they went.

Once they hit the end of his street, the crowds began to swell. Tourists and locals. Shoppers and workers. A bustling, noisy, energetic mob.

Being around people once more, for the first couple of minutes Sadie panicked any time someone looked their way, but as Will pointed out landmarks—places he drank coffee, a half-court where he played basketball, the Shard—she began to relax. Besides, no one looked at her twice. Not when she had Will at her side. He drew enough gazes, both admiring and envious, for the both of them.

"So, what do you think?" he asked.

Sadie smiled at Will before realising what he was looking at. A good-sized Tudor building—white with brown trim—lay just ahead.

The Globe Theatre—the modern-day "home" of William Shakespeare.

Sadie wasn't sure she could feel any happier than she did in that moment. Until Will pulled two tickets out of his pocket. *"Much Ado About Nothing*—what do you think?"

Speechless, she nodded. And followed as Will led her inside.

And as the play unfolded before her, a simple, brilliant telling of a complex, bittersweet tale, she knew she was done forcing Shakespeare down the throats of high-school kids who weren't even close to being ready to appreciate the language she loved so dearly.

It was a job she had revelled in for its battles and its victories. A job that had fallen her way. A job people expected her to love.

Just as New York had been something everyone had assumed would be a dream come true.

But defying expectations wasn't such a bad thing. And if it meant following her heart, doing what made her happy, and tapping into her bliss, then even if people didn't quite understand the choice, surely that had to be better than the alternative.

She glanced at Will to find him watching her.

And, not caring if anyone was watching, if anyone knew who they were, she gave him a smile that started at the little place marker he'd burned onto her heart. She slipped her hand through his arm, leant her head on his shoulder and let Beatrice and Benedick sweep her off her feet.

Will could not remember the last time he'd taken a morning off work on purpose. But it had been worth it.

He'd followed the play to a point, but had found Sadie far more entertaining: the spark in her eyes, the grin that near split her face in half and the tears when everything came good. She saw the world like someone who was on earth for the very first time.

She was practically skipping as they left the theatre. "That was amazing. Just...wonderful. It's been so long since I've seen a real, live, professional Shakespearean production not put on by sixteen-year-old kids. I feel like I've been banging my head against a wall for years! That, Will Darcy, was an epiphany. I cannot thank you enough." She threw herself at him then, wrapping him in a hug that took him only a second or two to return. "Now I have to check out the gift shop."

While she did so, Will checked his phone. A dozen calls had come in while his phone had been on silent.

Not wasting time to check the messages, he rang Natalie.

"Hello?"

Will checked his watch. Dammit. It was late over there. "Natalie, apologies. I didn't check the time—I'll call back later."

"No, wait! Give me a second to get to my desk." Much shuffling and banging of doors, a squeak of a desk chair and... "Right. So I've been on to his secretary and she seems to think we've lost our chance but—"

"Sorry. Whose secretary?"

"Ah, the prime minister's." A pause, then, "Did you not get my messages?"

"I've yet to listen—"

"Why on earth? You always check your messages. In fact, you're pedantic to the point of anally retentive. My cousin Brianna read somewhere that men with your looks, your brains and your sex appeal—"

"Natalie."

"Yes. Sorry." A breath, then, "He had space for you this afternoon. At two. Then he was flying out of the country for eight days."

Will checked his watch. It was a little after four.

"Send me the number, I'll call—"

"I've already checked. It's too late, Will. He's gone."

Eyelids lowering, Will swore. Swore some more. Then pressed his phone against his forehead.

"Will? Will, are you there?"

"Thanks for trying, Natalie."

"That's okay. I wish I could have done more."

"It's not your fault," he said, right as Sadie came out of the gift shop, her gaze scanning the area before landing on him. "It's mine."

Something was wrong.

After all the excitement of the play, the sweet thrill of freedom and the hot, burning delight of love that was pulsing through her like radio waves, all the extra layers in the world couldn't have saved her from Will's chill.

Once they were back inside the warehouse, thawing out, she got up the guts to ask, "Will, is everything okay?"

"No, actually."

"What happened?"

"It's nothing. A work matter."

As soon as he mentioned work, she felt him pulling away, heading into a bubble inside his head. Her instinct was to let him, but something bigger made her reach out and clamp a hand around his arm.

"Will, tell me. Maybe I can help."

He looked at her then, the creases at the edges of his eyes deeper, but not from smiling. Her heart slowed, her blood turning sluggish, as if preparing itself for a winter freeze.

"I may have mentioned my old professor at some point."

Her memory skipped and raced until it found the moment she was looking for. "The one who encouraged you to wonder."

"He passed away earlier in the year, not long before your wedding invitation arrived, in fact. Which is by the by. Anyway, he had been point-man for a research grant at our old university for decades. On his death it was marked to shut down. It's cumbersome and prohibitively expensive. But it's also imperative to the long-term success of astronomical research in this country."

"What an amazing legacy."

Will's eyes flashed and she thought she had him back, but he ran a hand up the back of his neck, dislodging her hold on his arm at the same time.

"I was guaranteed a chance to meet with the prime minister to urge him to continue the grant and have been waiting for news of the time. It came through this morning while we were walking. The meeting was set for the same time the play began."

Sadie swallowed, the burn of ignominy tingling all over her skin. "Can't you reschedule? Go bang on his door, right now?"

Will looked down at the floor, hands deep in the pockets of his jeans. What had Hugo said? Will wasn't an island unto himself, he was a planet.

"Will—"

"My work, my achievements, my reputation open doors for me where others wouldn't even get a look-in. But this was my chance. My last chance to truly honour a man who made all that possible. I forgot myself and screwed it up."

Sadie's stomach clutched at the disappointment in his voice. Worse than disappointment. Devastation.

Her throat was like a desert as she said, "It's my fault."

He looked at her then, really at her. And she realised in that moment that he held her heart in his hands.

"It's mine. For thinking I could do this."

Sadie didn't ask what "this" was. She didn't have to. She'd been right with him as this thing between them had played out, unravelling, exploding, taking them over. She'd held his hand on the street, she'd felt his eyes on her as they'd watched the play. They'd both been held in thrall of a moment in time where their worlds had aligned and all things had seemed possible.

He was determined to take the blame, but Sadie knew it was all her. This was what she did. She got intoxicated by possibility, by the chance that this time things would be different. She dragged others along for the ride, only to end up bathing them in her chaos.

She wrapped her arms around herself in an attempt to stop the trembles that were taking her over, years of practice helping her summon a smile from nowhere. "Don't be so hard on yourself. You've been amazing. Heroic even. I know how much you've sacrificed in rescuing this damsel in distress. And if there's anything I can do to make it up to you—"

"You are no damsel, Sadie, and right now I've never felt less heroic in my life."

He gave her a long look. Of ruination and despair. But beneath it all hummed that heat. The magnet that kept pulling them back together even when circumstance, fate and history had tried telling them it wasn't to be.

It felt as if the universe was holding its breath.

Then he took a step away. "You're right. I can't take no for an answer. I need to attempt to fix this. Look, do you mind if I...?"

"Go. Go! I can take care of myself."

"Good. Thank you, Sadie." Then he jogged up the stairs towards his office, pulling the door shut behind him.

And Sadie brought a shaking hand to cover her mouth.

She was in love with Will.

She knew it. She'd spent the morning bathed in it like a divine glow. But even that hadn't been enough to stop her from being his downfall.

Sadie couldn't feel her feet as she made her way to her room. And there she slowly, deliberately, packed her things.

She took off Will's jacket, folded it neatly and put it onto the chair in her room. She made the bed, tucking in the corners like an expert. She grabbed some tissue and wiped down every surface she'd touched.

All she'd ever wanted was to feel safe somewhere. Or with someone. Even while her life raged in chaos around her, she'd felt safer the past three days in Will's company than she could remember feeling ever before. His stoic strength, his quiet confidence, were like a balm to her frenetic soul.

Which was a big part of why loving Will, and leaving him, meant now she was scared. Terrified. Shaken from the top of her head to the tips of her toenails.

But she had to do this. For him.

With one last look around the room she made her way to Will's office.

He was on the phone, pacing, papers strewn across the surface of his desk.

He was an important man doing important work. Work that he believed made him the man he was. Sadie would have begged to differ, but she knew he wouldn't hear it right now even if she stripped naked, sat on him and forced him to listen.

He put his hand over the microphone. "Sadie, sorry, you're going to have to give me some time here."

"I'm going one better." She hitched her bag on her shoulder and he stopped pacing.

Grey clouds swarmed over his face. He opened his mouth, no doubt to tell her she was being dramatic, and maybe she was, but she stopped him with the international sign for stop. "I've called a car service. They'll be here in ten."

Running a hand down his face, he hung up the phone and strode around the desk until they were toe to toe. The creases around his eyes were so deep, so concerned. Frustration poured off him in waves. "Do you really have to do this now?"

"I really do. It's past time. And you know it too."

Hands on hips, he looked over her shoulder, into the middle distance, his big brain working overtime. "I'm not a selfless man, Sadie. I'm not going to make a song and dance out of this. I'm not Hugo."

"I'm very glad you're not Hugo." It ached not to tell him why. To tell him that she loved his particular brand of strength. His stoicism. She loved his stubbornness and his lonesomeness.

She loved him.

"You've been incredible, Will. A good friend to Hugo. A good friend to me. You gave me sanctuary when I needed it most. But you've given up enough to help us. Too much. Today proved that."

She tried to put it into words he'd understand. *Nothing lasts for ever.* But the words wouldn't come. It hurt too much.

Instead she leaned in, placed a hand on the bruise over his heart and kissed him on the cheek. Then, because she wasn't perfect, she took him by the chin, fresh stubble scraping the pads of her fingers, and turned his face so she could kiss his beautiful lips.

He resisted, caught in that vortex of disappointment and frustration. But only for a fraction of a second. Then he hauled her against him and kissed her with everything he had.

If it had been any other man kissing her so that her kneecaps melted, she might have put it down to the urge to get his own way. But Will was not a game player. He was a man of integrity and might.

If she was a betting girl she might have thought that kiss was his way of showing her he was beginning to fall for her too.

But all bets were off. It was time for her to go.

She pulled away, pressed herself back, held herself together by the barest thread. "Thanks, Will. For everything."

He said nothing. No goodbyes. No understanding nods.

But neither did he look like a statue. He looked ravaged, like a man braced against a perfect storm.

Holding that image in her heart, she turned and walked away, down the stairs, out the front door and into the car waiting to take her to the airport. Where she'd take her chances with being recognised, holding her head high.

For she was running again, but this time it wasn't out of fear. This time she was running away for love.

As the tears ran down her face she felt as if she'd done the absolute right thing for the first time in her life.

No one would throw her a parade, or pat her on the head and tell her *well done*. She'd make no new fans out of this. But she knew, and that was what mattered.

CHAPTER TEN

SADIE PARKED HER car under a tree, leapt over the ancient, crumbling brick wall edging the field and walked across the same expanse over which she'd fled not that long ago.

The bottoms of her jeans were soon damp, her boots beginning to chill. But she ploughed on until she found herself standing outside the antechamber, staring up at the façade of the palace.

It was strange to think she had grown up here, and now it only looked like a building. A beautiful building, to be sure, glorious and charming and strong. But it was no longer her home.

Not about to head up to the front door and knock, but also not keen on bumping into anyone in the private quarters, she went with a hunch, pushed her way through the garden brambles and tested the window. It opened easy as pie.

It was ironic to find herself climbing in through the very same window out of which she'd climbed just a few days ago. Or maybe it was necessary. A kind of bookend.

The antechamber was much as she'd left it bar the wedding paraphernalia, which was no doubt at the bottom of a rubbish bin somewhere.

She checked through the door to make sure the coast was clear, then headed off, through the palace.

Five minutes and a few close calls later, Sadie sat huddled beneath the fluffy, double-thick blanket she'd nicked from the back of a couch in the library, secure in her favourite spot in the palace. She was atop the turret of the tallest tower, feet dangling over the side, the country she loved at her feet.

Her gaze tripped over snow-capped mountains, verdant green fields dotted with fluffy black and white sheep. Over the lights of a dozen quaint villages tucked into valleys and sprawled over hillsides.

One of them had to be the village of Bellponte in which she and Will had stayed. If she'd seen the palace from La Tulipe, then surely she could see La Tulipe from here. But she'd never had much of a sense of direction, and couldn't be sure.

Shivering, Sadie tucked her feet up beneath her and wrapped the blanket tighter.

She hadn't realised it at the time, but her life had changed in that chintz-filled tower room. She'd grown up, faced her demons, faced herself. And she'd begun to fall in love.

"Hey."

Sadie sniffed, wiped her cheek against her shoulder and spun to find Hugo framed by the heavy brick doorway.

He said, "Only the Keeper of the Flags is meant to have a key to this spot."

Sadie lifted a finger from its warm cocoon to tap the side of her nose. "I have contacts."

Hugo ambled to Sadie's side. He sat, then swore at the freezing cold of the brick beneath his hands.

Sadie offered him some of her blanket. He refused with a manly shake of the head.

Together, in silence, they looked out over Vallemont as they had a zillion times before. He'd first brought her up here when she was six or seven. She'd also found him here a few weeks back, after Prince Reynaldo had made him the offer he couldn't refuse.

Sadie asked, "How did you know I was here?"

"At least half a dozen people told me they'd seen you sneaking through the palace, heading this way."

"Oh. I thought I'd made it without being seen."

"A running theme in your life of late."

Sadie groaned. "Tell me about it. A few hours ago I thought I'd made it all the way through Heathrow unseen before a pair of Americans asked me for a selfie."

Hugo shot her a smile. "And there I was thinking you were still in London. In fact, I had the funny feeling you were going to be there for some time."

"Nah. This is where I belong." Sadie rested her chin against her knees and glanced at her old friend. "If I hadn't run, would you have gone through with it?"

"Of course," said Hugo without missing a beat.

"Even though you don't love me, and never have."

"I do—"

"Hugo, come on. Does your tummy tighten every time you lay eyes on me? Do you come out in goosebumps if I simply brush your arm? Do you ache for me when we're apart?"

Hugo's silence was answer enough.

"Then consider yourself lucky one of us was smart enough to walk away."

Hugo nodded. "Done." And like that they put the Great Hiccup of their lifelong friendship behind them.

Then, with a bump to her shoulder with his, Hugo asked, "When did you develop such specific parameters for what it means to be in love?"

Sadie bit her lip.

"Because I've never heard you talk that way. You're always so blasé about such things. I'm assuming this is a new development. Very recent, in fact. Days old, at the very most."

"Drop it."

"No, I don't think I will. Why aren't you in London, Sadie?"

If she could have pulled the blanket over her head she would have. But that would have been the old Sadie—make a joke of things, do a little tap dance to distract everyone from anything unpleasant.

So why wasn't she in London? As difficult or ugly as they might be, the new Sadie was all about the truths.

The truth was she might not physically be there, but her heart was. And her head. And she wasn't going to sit there and do nothing about that any more.

She pulled herself to standing and threw Hugo the blanket.

"Come on, get up."

"Why?"

"You and I have some work to do."

A week later Will sat staring at his laptop.

Or *through* his laptop would have been a more fitting description, as the words of the position paper he was attempting to outline were swimming before his eyes.

He could be doing this on a plane to Geneva, where he was due to present his famous "Scenes from the Orion Nebula" lecture the next day. He did some of his best work on planes, alone, uninterrupted, the white noise creating a prefect creative cocoon.

Instead here he sat, in a village pub, with no Wi-Fi and limited phone reception, waiting to feel the satisfied glow that came from one of the best weeks of his career.

An offer had come through on the Orion Nebula game, and he'd sold, tripling his investment overnight.

An array of radio telescopes in Chile had picked up

space noise for a few seconds in the direction of Orion's Belt and he'd been there to hear it.

He'd been offered the European Space Agency's top spot on the Future Commission—focusing on how best to channel research and funding for telescopes to be launched into space.

Best of all, an unknown benefactor had gifted five years to the Templeton Grant. Natalie had connected the call from the prime minister, who'd bashfully agreed to join forces now that he didn't have to justify the initial expense, promising to announce it at the World Science Symposium later that year.

But no glow came.

His phone rang. In pure relief, he answered it without looking at the caller details. "Darcy."

"Where are you?"

Hugo. Will sat up so fast he knocked his beer, the froth sloshing over the rim and onto his laptop.

Mopping it up with a napkin, he said, "Is everything all right? Is she okay?"

Hugo laughed. "Sadie's fine. As far as I know."

"What do you mean, as far as you know? Isn't she with you?"

"Of course she's not with me, you damn fool. In fact— No. Yes. I'm going to say it. She should be with you."

Wincing, Will screwed the napkin into a ball. "You don't know what you're talking about."

"I'm a well-educated man. I have seen the world. And I am a prince. Therefore, I am never wrong."

It was so unlike Hugo to pull the prince card, Will actually coughed out a laugh.

"She left of her own free will," said Will.

"Did you ask her to stay?"

"You know as well as I do that there's no telling her anything. I've never met anyone as stubborn." *As quick to laughter, as emotional, bright, indefatigable, raw, sweet, thoughtful, warm.*

"Hmm. I feel as if I have."

Will tossed the damp napkin onto the table.

Hugo went on. "I have never seen you as relaxed as you were when you were with her. She was the best thing that ever happened to you, my friend. How the hell could you have let her go?"

Will knew Hugo was pushing for a reaction. He was good at it.

"Right back at you," Will gritted out, unsurprised when Hugo laughed down the phone.

"So, where are you?"

Will looked up from his laptop at the rustic walls, the craggy-mountain motif carved into the bar, the framed picture of the reigning Prince of Vallemont on the wall, the pink and rose-gold trim on the bar towels. All he said was, "In a pub."

"Alone?"

Alone. Funny how that word had been his touchstone for so many years. A motivator, a goal. He'd held on to the fact that his aloneness gave him an edge, time and motivation to work hard, to better focus, to give himself over to the study of the whys of the universe.

Now the word felt like an open wound.

"Yes, I'm alone. I just felt the need to stretch my legs."

Stretching them all the way to a small pub in Vallemont. With a view over the thatched rooftops of Bellponte to the top corner of a crumbling hotel with a lopsided Tower Room that looked as though it might fall off the side of the building at any moment.

Will asked, "I am an important man with much work to do. Did you call me for a reason?"

"Go online, stream Vallemontian station, Channel Four, at five o'clock our time."

"And why would I want to do that?"

"Because, old friend, for all the stars and moons and planets and galaxies you have unravelled in your search for the meaning of life, I'd bet the palace it won't compare to what Channel Four is about to teach you."

Will drummed his fingers against the table top and looked up at the TV playing silently above the bar. The logo at the bottom of the screen said Channel Four. If that wasn't a sign he had no idea what was. "Fine. I'll track it down."

"My work here is done," said Hugo, and then he was gone.

Will checked his watch. Fifteen minutes until five.

He closed his laptop and worked on his beer. A low hum of pub chatter and occasional laughter punctuated clinking glassware and the ting of the cash register as Will watched the clock tick down.

Just on five a "special presentation" graphic flashed onto the screen.

A young woman's smiling face mouthed words Will couldn't hear. Closed-caption text scrolled across the bottom of the screen, stating the journalist's name, stipulating that she was a former pupil of the Vallemont School of Drama and therefore a one-time student of Mercedes Gray Leonine, and was happy to be able to facilitate the evening's special event.

And then…there she was.

Will felt his stomach drop away at the sight of her. Her mussed red hair was slicked back and pinned off her face with a clip. Long, sparkly earrings swung against her shoulders and a pale floral top clung to her elegant frame.

She looked different—still, somehow, serene. She looked so beautiful it hurt to blink. And even with the sound turned down he could hear her voice. The bravado.

The humour. The strength. The vulnerability. As if she were sitting right beside him.

God, how he wished she were sitting beside him. How he wished he could touch her, hold her, kiss her, hear her voice for real; watch her animated face as she told a story; watch her quiet face as she listened to one of his.

For a man who didn't believe in wishes, they came so thick and fast he couldn't keep up.

The interviewer leaned forward and the camera pulled out to show Sadie sitting on a white couch in a large, old-fashioned-looking room that was no doubt in the palace. And there Hugo sat, right beside her.

Even without sound it was clear how fond they were of one another. Nothing more. No romantic tension. No sideways glances. Just friendship. And honest remorse at the way things had been handled.

"Turn it up!" someone called from across the room. "The TV—turn it up."

The barkeeper did as asked, and Sadie's voice blasted across the pub.

"Our reasons were private, but we hope you believe us when we say they were just and good. We were blinded by a need to do the right thing; we just…didn't think things through to their logical conclusions. And if a man like Prince Alessandro says he'll marry you it's pretty hard to say no. Just look at him!"

The interviewer laughed. Blushed. A woman at a table behind Will said, "Oh, I'm looking."

"If you take anything from this interview, know that your Prince is one of the very best men you could ever hope to meet. Second-best at worst. He's just not the man for me."

And then Sadie looked into the camera. She looked right into Will's eyes. It was a split second, a blink. But he felt that look as if she'd reached out and grabbed him by the heart and squeezed.

"And you, Prince Alessandro—is Mercedes not the woman for you?"

He smiled, and Sadie turned to him, which was when Will saw the clip in her hair. Silver, sparkly, a shooting star.

Will didn't realise he was on his feet until someone behind him politely asked him to sit down.

"Don't answer that," she said. "He'll just say something charming so as not to hurt my feelings. But I'd have driven the Prince crazy. And Vallemont does not need a crazy prince. Look at Prince Reynaldo—such a benevolent leader, so forward-thinking. So generous."

Will noted that Hugo looked down at that point, hiding a wry smile.

"Not only on a personal level—having always been so kind to me, the daughter of a palace maid. Did you know he's recently personally invested in a number of international grants towards the arts and sciences, making Vallemont not only the most beautiful country in the world, but also one of the most progressive?"

The interviewer looked dutifully amazed. "Well, that is news."

The interviewer then turned to Hugo, asking him a spate of questions that Will barely heard. While Sadie leant back in the chair and breathed out long and slow. Only then did Will see how tired she seemed, the slight smudges under her eyes that even television make-up couldn't quite hide.

Sitting through the rest of the interview was the hardest thing Will had ever done in his entire life, but he had to, in case she had any more hidden messages for him. For that was what the interview had been. That was why Hugo had made him watch.

By the end of the interview it was made very clear that this would be the only time they would talk of it; that they believed their explanation and apologies were done. A great big line had been drawn under the day Sadie left Hugo at the altar. This chapter of the country's history was well and truly closed.

Then it was over.

Will's glass sat in a puddle of condensation next to a very large tip as he dashed from the pub.

Outside, he had no idea which way to turn. He grabbed his phone, jabbed in Hugo's number.

Hugo answered on the first ring. "Hey, mate, how's things?"

"Where is she?" Will asked, walking just to feel as though he was going somewhere.

"Now he's in an all fire rush—"

"Hugo."

Hugo chuckled. "She moved out of the palace the day she came back."

"What's her mother's new address?"

"She's not there either. For now she's taken a room in that dilapidated old hovel you holed her up in for those first couple of days."

And suddenly Will was running, scooting around people blocking his way, leaping over a display of boxes holding masses of pink flowers. His shoes slapped against the uneven pavement, his jacket and scarf flying out behind him.

"Probably a good time to tell you I'm heading away for a while."

Will made a left, realised he'd taken a wrong turn. Spinning on his heel, he made a right instead. "Where are you going?"

"Not sure it matters right now. I just wanted you to know so if you don't hear from me you understand why."

Reading between the lines, Will knew: Hugo had taken the olive branch.

Will turned the corner to find himself facing La Tulipe. The window to the Tower Room was open, the gauzy curtain flapping in the wintry breeze.

His lungs burned from the icy air. His neck itched from the heat of the woollen scarf. And as he shook out his cold fingers he realised he'd left his laptop, his notes, his life's work behind in the pub.

The fact that he felt zero compunction to leave this spot to collect his all-important work was final proof of how fundamentally his world view had broadened. Made room for diversion, for insouciance, for the contents of the room above. And it would still be there when he got around to picking it up. This was Vallemont, after all.

Will breathed out fast and hard. The last of his breath leaving on a laugh.

"Everything all right, Darcy?" Hugo asked over the phone.

"It's been a big few days."

"Tell me about it."

"Promise me something. Next time you agree to marry a girl, you actually go through with it."

Hugo laughed. "I don't think that will be a problem I will ever have to face again."

After a loaded beat, Hugo hung up.

Will put the phone in his pocket and stared up at the open window.

She had left. And he had let her go. Because when you lose enough of the people you love, letting people go became a fallback position.

Only here he was. Because he'd been looking at it all wrong.

Gravity wasn't entirely destructive. It helped hold the entire universe together.

Looking around, he picked up a small stone. He threw

it towards the window, hearing it skitter across the balcony floor.

A few seconds later he picked up another and tried again. This time the stone hit the glass door.

His heart was thundering in his chest by that stage, as if it were trying to kick its way through his ribs.

Then the door moved, the curtains sucking inside the room.

And there she was. Beneath a fluffy pink beanie with a pompom on top, her hair bobbed on her shoulders. Her lips were painted a pretty pale pink. A dark floral dress flared at her wrists and landed just above her knees. Brown tights disappeared into knee-high boots.

"Sadie."

"Quite the aim you have."

"Had to do something when we skipped out on school. Skimming stones at a local lake was right up there."

Her hands gripped the railing. "Were you just passing through?"

"I was, in fact, enjoying a quiet beer in a pub down the way when I saw you on the television."

"You did?" She licked her lips. "Was it any good? I couldn't bring myself to watch."

He moved closer to the building, so that he could see her better. "I liked your hair clip."

Her hand moved to her beanie, her cheeks pinking.

"I do have one question for you though."

She leant her arms against the railing. "What's that?"

"It was Reynaldo behind the Templeton Grant. And you were the one behind Reynaldo."

"That's not a question."

"How on earth did you swing it?"

"Prince Reynaldo put the hard word on a friend of mine once. I figured it was time someone did the same back to him."

"What did you give up in return?"

A slow grin spread across her face. "A promise to never again agree to marry anyone in his family. It was a difficult decision but in the end I felt it was the right one for me."

"Not only for you," he said.

She breathed out hard and fast. Her smile was open and warm, and just like that he let it in. He let her in. Let her fill him up. Take him over. And it was as if he'd opened his eyes fully for the first time in his life.

Had the sky been that blue a moment before? The buildings that many shades of yellow? Did winter ever smell this good?

Will could no longer feel his feet. It was as if gravity had simply stopped working. Only one way to be sure— he moved closer to the building and took a better look at the bricks. He grabbed hold of a couple and gave them a wiggle.

"What do you think you're doing?" she called. "Do not climb up that wall!"

A beat, then, "Well, I can't go in the front door. Janine will see me. And then she'll start quoting *Much Ado About Nothing.* Or she'll want to know how I know the Prince, and I'll never get out of there—"

"Sod it," said Sadie, tossing a leg over the edge of the balcony.

What? No. "You have to be kidding."

"I'm no damsel in distress, remember."

Right. It didn't stop him from standing beneath her with his arms outstretched, ready to catch.

A few of the bricks had seen better days, sending sprays of crumbing shale to hit the ground and turn to dust. But she made it down, feet first, pulling bougainvillaea flowers from the front of her dress.

"You quite done?" he asked, his voice rough.

She looked at him then, her eyes full, her whole body

quaking with the kind of energy that could no doubt be seen from outer space.

Then she was in his arms before he even knew they were moving. The scent of honeysuckle filled his senses, and the grey blah that had held him in its grip the past few days melted away.

And then he took her face in his hands, her sweet, lovely face, and he kissed her. And kissed her. And kissed her. "I should never have let you go. No. Let me start again."

"I thought you started pretty well," she said, her voice a husky croak.

"I was right to let you go. For you can go wherever the hell you want, whenever the hell you want. What I mean is, I should never have let you go without telling you what you have come to mean to me."

"Okay."

"I'm used to being alone."

"Big shock."

He should have known she wouldn't make this easy. But that was what he loved about her.

What he *loved* about her. *He loved her.* Where first there was something that took up no space at all, suddenly he was inundated. Because he, a man who believed in things he could see, measure and explain, was in love.

"What I am trying to say, if you'll shut up and let me, is that I'm used to being alone, the way you are used to being surrounded. Your life is here. Mine is everywhere else. You are an untidy grub—"

"While you are so fastidious I don't know how you manage to leave the house in the morning." Sadie blinked up at him, all sleepy-eyed, as her fingers curled into his hair, tugging at the ends every few seconds, sending shards of electricity right through him.

Screw it.

"I love you, Sadie."

The twirling stopped.

"I am in love with you. I have all the evidence to back it up too. Physical, intellectual, anecdotal. But I don't care. The only important thing is that I feel it, right here."

He slapped a hand over his heart and wished with every ounce of his being that she might believe him. Then, with a rush of inspiration that could only have come from somewhere beyond the realm of his understanding, he brought out the big guns. *"Doubt thou the stars are fire; Doubt that the sun doth move; Doubt truth to be a liar; But never doubt I love."*

A little *Hamlet* right when it counted. She grinned and laughed, tears now streaming down her face. "I don't doubt. I believe it," she said. "I believe you."

To think this alternative reality had been out there in the universe all this time and he'd closed himself off to it. He chided himself as a man of science and vowed to explore every angle of this new discovery.

Starting with Sadie's mouth. Her soft, pink, delicious mouth. The sweetest taste there was.

After an age, she pulled away, straining for breath as she rested her head against his chest. "I love you too, you know."

Will tipped her chin so he could look into her eyes. "I didn't actually. But that is good to know."

She grinned, the grin turning into laughter. Then she let him go, flinging her arms out sideways, tipping her head to the sun. "I'm totally, madly in love with you. Which is crazy, right? That this happened. Imagine if Hugo and I had never come up with our fool plan. Imagine if we'd come to our senses earlier. Imagine if I'd never run. The chances were high that we'd have never met. There's only one possible explanation for it. This was always in the stars."

"Sadie."

"Yes, Will," she said on a sigh as she brought her hands to his shoulders.

"As a man of science, I'm going to pretend I didn't hear a word you said past 'madly in love'. Okay?"

"You do what you need to do. Just know that I do love you. Physically." She lifted onto her toes to place a kiss at the corner of his mouth. "Intellectually." She dragged a kiss over the edge of his jaw. "Anecdotally." With that she bit down on his earlobe.

"Good afternoon."

Sadie slowly edged her teeth away from Will's ear before as one they turned to look over Sadie's shoulder.

A local baker was riding by on his bicycle, a bag of baguettes poking out of the basket at the back. He gave them a jaunty wave.

"Good afternoon," they said as one.

"Just saw your interview on the TV," said the baker, letting his foot drift to the pavement as he pulled to a stop. "Very nicely handled. If the rest of your generation is as savvy as our Prince, then our country is in for a grand future. Now you can hopefully get on with your lives."

Will's hand drifted to Sadie's lower back right as her hand curled around the back of his neck. She said, "Sounds like a plan to me."

With that the baker sat back onto his bike and rolled down the hill, whistling as he went.

Will pressed his lips against Sadie's ear. "Shall we? Get on with our lives?"

She plucked a purple flower from his shoulder, then smiled into his eyes. "Let's."

EPILOGUE

SADIE WOKE UP. Sensing it was still the middle of the night, she thought about rolling over and going back to sleep but instead she stretched, hands and feet reaching for the four corners of her glorious, big new bed.

It took up the entire platform in her bedroom in the Tower Room at La Tulipe. No canopy, no fake ivy, no net curtains. Nothing princessy about it at all.

She'd bought the bed for Will as a gift when they'd moved in. He'd bought her the building to put it in, so fair was fair.

She let her hands and feet relax, her breaths slowing, a smile spreading over her face as she thought about her plans for the coming day.

There was a meeting with the architect and project manager first thing, as refurbishment was beginning in the old foyer next week—the administration offices of the brand-new Vallemont Royal Youth Theatre Company.

As patron, Hugo had requested something dry, esoteric, modern for their first play. As chief financial officer, Natalie had told Hugo to keep his intellectual nose out of things he didn't understand. As front office manager, Janine hadn't stopped smiling long enough to have a decided opinion. As director, Sadie had smiled and nodded and told everyone she'd certainly take his thoughts into consideration.

Rehearsals for *Romeo and Juliet* began that afternoon.

As for the rest of La Tulipe—it would eventually become home. So far, they were living out of the Tower Room and would do for some time. The place was crumbling, with so many add-ons and temporary walls built over the years it would be like a puzzle to undo it all and bring it back to its former glory. But they had time. Years. Their whole lives.

She breathed in deeply and rolled over, ready for sleep to come again.

But something stopped her.

Her eyes sprang open. She sat bolt upright. Weak moonlight poured into the room and she struggled to make out shapes in the semi-darkness. There! By the couch. The overnight bag on the floor.

Will was home.

Sadie leapt out of bed and wrapped a robe around herself—black, soft, Will's—then padded out to the balcony. The night was crystal-clear. The moon a sliver in the sky.

She climbed the new stepladder that had been bolted to the side of the tower, used the turrets to haul herself over the top and landed with her usual lack of finesse.

And there he sat, rubbing a hand over his beard as he finessed the mighty new telescope that took up half the roof. Maia had been retired to their London pad and lived in her own custom-built glassed-in, rooftop conservatory, for ever pointing at the sky.

Will looked up at the reverberation of her landing. He pressed back into the seat and rubbed the eye that had been pressed against the lens. His voice was a familiar deep, wonderful rumble as he said, "Hey."

She couldn't hold back. She ran. And she leapt. He caught her, strong enough not to topple as she launched herself at him.

"When did you get back?" she asked, her voice muffled by the fact she was nestled into his neck.

"An hour ago."

"Why didn't you wake me?"

"You know how you are."

"Like a Labrador puppy, all energy then…deep, deep sleep; yeah, I know. How was the trip?"

Will had spent three days lecturing on his beloved Orion Nebula at Boston University, had hosted an international day of moon-viewing from the northern tip of Alaska, then had headed to London to record a voice-over for a BBC documentary. And it sat so well on him, he looked as if he'd just woken from eight perfect hours of sleep.

The man was a natural phenomenon. No wonder the whole world wanted a piece of him. Thankfully Sadie had grown up with a best friend who was a wanted man. She'd learned to be a good sharer.

"Good," he said. "Great. Some brilliant young minds out there giving me a run for my money. I might even have found the first recipient of the new and improved Templeton Grant."

"Oh, Will, that's so cool."

"Isn't it just?" Will lifted a hand to push Sadie's hair from her face.

Her heart skittered in her chest at his touch. She wondered if it always would. She figured there was a pretty good chance.

She settled on his lap, wrapped her arms about his neck and kissed him. Or he kissed her. They probably met somewhere in the middle, which seemed to be their way, and that was her last thought as sensation took over. Her body was all melting warmth, the chill of the night air a distant memory as they too made up for lost time.

Light years later they pulled apart, Sadie sighing. "Now get back to work. All that data won't record itself. I'll just sit here quietly and do my best not to disturb you." With that she sank her head against his chest.

"I'm not sure my calculations will be entirely reliable."

"No? How about if I do this?" She wriggled a little more until she was sure she was getting the reaction she was after.

Will picked her up as he stood. She laughed, and clung to his neck, as he stepped out of the chair, her voice carrying off into the night, over the top of the village that was now her home—their home—dissipating long before it reached the mountains beyond.

And out there, dark beneath the bright white caps of snow above, the palace slept.

Its story no longer her own.

"Oh?" she said, feigning surprise. "You done for the night?"

"Not even close," Will rumbled as he dropped her feet to the cold stone floor.

He chased her down the ladder and took her to bed, where he made her see stars.

* * * * *

MADDIE FORTUNE'S
PERFECT MAN

NANCY ROBARDS THOMPSON

This book is dedicated to my beloved Samantha,
faithful friend, smiling muse and ambassador
of all dogs. You stole the heart of this cat lady.
Rest in peace, my sweet corgi girl.
I'll miss you every day.

Chapter One

Kenneth Fortunado tapped his champagne flute with a table knife. The *ping, ping, ping* of metal on crystal silenced the small gathering of family and friends, whom he'd summoned to the impromptu afternoon barbecue.

Maddie Fortunado shivered as a frisson of anticipation spiraled through her.

A champagne toast at a barbecue. It can only mean one thing.

Finally.

She'd been dreaming of this day.

"Does everyone have a glass of bubbly?" Kenneth asked. "I have a special announcement."

Maddie plucked a flute off the tray of a passing server and turned expectantly toward her father. Catching his eye, she checked her posture and held her glass high. He flashed her a knowing smile and lifted his flute to her in a private *cheers*, before surveying the small crowd he'd gathered on the back terrace of the Fortunado estate.

"Barbara?" he called. "Barbara, where are you? Where is my lovely wife?"

Her mother did indeed look lovely in her powder-blue sweater set, which she'd paired with ivory silk trousers and her signature double strand of pearls. Barbara waved from the back of the terrace where she appeared to be giving the caterer last-minute instructions.

"Barbara, dear," Kenneth said. "Please join me."

Demonstrating that a Southern woman neither rushed nor allowed herself to be rushed, Barbara held up a ladylike index finger, signaling to Kenneth that she'd be there in a moment, and continued her business with the chef.

Maddie allowed her gaze to meander over to her coworker Zach McCarter, who was talking to her sisters, Schuyler and Valene, and Schuyler's fiancé as everyone waited for Kenneth and Barbara to share their big news. Her toes curled in her navy Jack Rogers sandals. Somehow, Zach managed to look masculine—and sexy as hell—holding the delicate crystal champagne glass by the stem, totally oblivious to the fact that she was watching him.

Her uncle Bill, her mom's brother, whom she hadn't seen in months, had come back to Houston for the announcement at their parents' behest, and was engrossed in conversation with Zach and the group. Obviously, her family didn't think there was anything out of the ordinary that Zach had been included in this day of special news.

Zach, who had until a few weeks ago been the broker in charge of Fortunado Real Estate's San Antonio office, had arrived at the house before Maddie, and her mother—as intuitive as ever—had been in the kitchen and had warned her he was here.

"Oh!" Barbara's hand had flown to her mouth, as if she hadn't meant for the exclamation to escape.

"By the way," she'd said, "before you go out there, I thought you should know your father invited Zach McCarter to be here today."

Maddie's stomach had flip-flopped, then plunged. "Here? For the barbecue?"

Barbara grimaced. "Yes. He's out on the porch. Your father insisted on inviting him, even though I said I thought it wasn't a good idea." Barbara shot Maddie a knowing look. "I hope you don't mind."

"Why would I mind?" Maddie kept her voice level and her poker face firmly fixed.

"Why would you mind?" Barbara had shrugged. "Well, I thought this announcement that your father and I are about to make would've been best kept to just family first. But you know how he is. Once he gets something in his head, there's no talking him out of it. It's best just to go with it."

Happy to have the forewarning, she'd seen Zach before she'd opened the French doors that led out to the terrace. In the split instant when her eyes had picked him out of the group that had grown to include more friends than family, her heart had performed a two-step that had caused her to put her hand to her chest.

She looked at Zach standing there, so comfortable in his own skin, laughing with her sisters. The sheer beauty of him—of them all—made the scene look like it could have been an ad for Ralph Lauren or some other all-American line that featured buff, gorgeous people.

Perfection seemed to come so effortlessly to Zach.

This stolen opportunity to drink in his masculine beauty was a smidgen of unadulterated heaven. From the top of his curly blond head—with hair that was on the longish side, but still looked professional—to the bottom of his six-foot-four-inch frame, he was sheer perfection.

His light blue eyes were slightly downturned and adorably crinkled at the edges when he smiled. Maddie took a moment to pay homage to that strong, structured jawline, to those wide shoulders and his impressive height. He was tall, but so was she and next to him, she felt feminine. His nose was just a little crooked and that scar on his chin that she couldn't see but could visualize were just enough to lend a masculine edge to his classic features. Good thing, too, because with his sun-kissed honey-blond hair, perfected by his convertible BMW, he could easily have been too pretty. But he wasn't. He was perfect.

She watched Schuyler reach up and ruffle Zach's hair. She'd wager that she was telling him that people paid big bucks for highlights like that. Schuyler was always bemoaning the high price of beauty when she migrated back to Houston from Austin every six weeks for hair appointments. That was precisely why Maddie preferred to keep her blond hair natural. She didn't have time to get roped into regular salon appointments for upkeep. The mere thought of the obligation gave her hives.

On a better note, she wished she could freeze this stolen moment and savor it over and over. Because Zach looked particularly gorgeous on this fine Sunday afternoon. There was something especially enticing about the way his light blue eyes crinkled as he laughed at something Schuyler was saying. He was probably humoring her as she went on and on about his highlights. He looked so comfortable in his own sexy skin. He was mesmerizing, and the sight of him sent a quiver down to the pit of her stomach. Maddie fisted her free hand, the one that wasn't holding her champagne, so tightly her nails dug into her palms.

Oh, Zach, you sexy thing.

A wisp of wistful regret skittered through Maddie as she realized he would never be anything more to her than a fantasy. He couldn't even be her secret crush anymore, which had been so easy when he was at the San Antonio office. She'd had a chance to get to know him better since he'd transferred to Houston. But she needed to rein it in if she was going to be his boss, which was about to happen once her father made the big announcement.

Any second now.

But until then, she was free to indulge one last tiny little daydream—

Uh-oh—

She froze as Zach's gaze locked with hers. It happened so fast and the jolt was so gripping, she couldn't look away. It was just as well. In her peripheral vision, she could see that Val was talking to Uncle Bill and Schuyler was talking to her fiancé, Carlo Mendoza, leaving poor Zach unentertained. If she looked away too fast, he might think she hadn't wanted him to catch her watching him. Even though she *hadn't* intended for him to catch her looking. It was best to hold up her end of the subtly flirtatious stare-down, which she did— brilliantly, if she did say so herself—dropping her gaze to her champagne flute for a single beat and then snaring his gaze again.

It was a silent dare to see who would look away first.

She sighed inwardly.

It's been fun, Zach, but now it's time for me to move on.

That's what she was telegraphing to him. He didn't seem to be receiving the message, because if he had, surely, he would've had the good grace to look away.

Instead, he raised his hand to her. She made the same motion in return.

In the end, neither of them lost the challenge because her father called it a draw when he started talking and broke the spell. They both gave him their attention. Her mother was now standing at Kenneth's side and he handed her a glass of champagne.

"My family—" Kenneth gestured toward Maddie and then toward her sisters. "Madeleine, Valene, Schuyler and Carlo. And Zach. Zach, I include you because you are like a son to Barbara and me—like family to all of us."

Family? Maddie blanched. *No. That would make him my brother.*

Of course, Zach had been over to the Fortunado homestead. Since he didn't have family in town, they'd invited him last Thanksgiving.

She'd never think of Zach as a brother. Not with the fantasies she had of him.

Those fantasies were anything but sisterly...

"Speaking of sons," Kenneth continued. "I wish Everett, Connor and Gavin could be here today." Kenneth's gaze scanned the group of well-wishers. "Everett and Lila are away on their honeymoon. Those crazy kids eloped after they saw everything that's involved in putting together a wedding. It's not too late to follow suit, Carlo." Everyone laughed. Schuyler held on tight to Carlo and shook her head as Kenneth continued. "Connor and Gavin couldn't get away since they're coming for Schuyler and Carlo's wedding at the end of the month. But—"

Kenneth stopped and shook his head. A slow smile tipped up the corners of his mouth. "I am a lucky man to be surrounded by so much love." He lifted his glass to Schuyler and Carlo. "To my lovely daughter and her husband-to-be and to all of you. Thank you so much for being here this afternoon. It was a last-minute invitation, but as I told you, it's important to Barbara and me to share our news with you first. You are important to us and we wanted you to hear it first."

Kenneth's smile faded.

"When my mother passed away, it was a wake-up call. Those of you who knew Starlight know she was larger than life. She lived every day to the fullest. Her passing not only gave me pause, it made me stop and take inventory of my life. That inventory revealed that I have a lot of lost time to make up for." He put his arm around Barbara. "Not only that, but our children are all grown. They're getting married and leaving the nest. It's made Barb and me realize we have a lot of living to do. It's time for *us*. However, it's difficult to make time for us when I'm working eighty-hour weeks." He paused and smiled down at Barbara. "Thank you for being patient with me, love."

Barbara kissed his cheek.

"With that in mind," Kenneth said, "I am so pleased to announce that right after Schuyler and Carlo's wedding, I will retire from Fortunado Real Estate."

Even though they were exactly the words Maddie had been expecting, a gasp escaped her throat as she led the gathering in a round of applause, sloshing a little champagne as she clapped.

Barbara held up her hand to silence them. "And I am pleased to announce that right after the big wedding, Kenneth and I will take a second honeymoon. We will be leaving on a four-month cruise around the world. Forty-nine ports of call—thirty-two countries on six continents."

More applause.

Maddie's chest hurt and she realized she'd been holding her breath. She was thrilled for her parents, but she was waiting for the *next part*. The part of the announcement where her father said that he was promoting her, that she would be stepping up as his successor to lead Fortunado Real Estate into the next chapter.

"I booked the cruise and told him the ship would sail on June fourth—with or without him," Barbara said. "I told him I'd be on that boat and I hoped he would be there, too. Because even with all this life inventory, we all know that's the only way I'd ever get him to finally make the leap into retirement."

Maddie inhaled sharply to quell her impatience.

"Now, now, my love," Kenneth said.

Maddie blew out all the air from her lungs. Her heart thudded. She could hear her blood rushing in her ears. Her father put his arm around her mother and lovingly massaged her neck, which made Barbara squirm and swat him away. She'd never been one for public displays of affection.

"Kenneth, not in front of the kids," Barbara said.

Yes, not in front of the kids, Dad. Yuck. Save it for the cruise and get to the rest of the announcement.

Kenneth and Barbara raised their glasses to the small crowd.

"Thank you for helping us celebrate our big decision."

Everyone raised their glasses in return and offered cheers and good words like *congratulations, hear! hear!, to your health and happiness* and *bon voyage.*

But wait… What about the rest… What about the announcement of your successor?

Maddie battled the demons of disappointment as she watched her sisters rush to congratulate their parents with hugs and squeals. She blinked once, twice. Took one more slow, deep breath, doing her best to slay the monster inside.

Okay. So, he wasn't going to announce her promotion now.

It was okay. Really, it was.

She blinked again and reframed. It wasn't that big of a deal that her father hadn't yet announced that she would be his successor.

Maddie let the words ruminate in her brain for a moment.

This afternoon was for her parents. It was a big, big deal for them. It was a huge step for them. Today was about them.

Not her.

Them.

Her cheeks burned as she knocked back the rest of her champagne, draining the half-full glass. She could let them have their day. She *should* let them have their day. Her dad probably wanted to talk to her privately before he made the announcement.

Of course. He wouldn't just announce her promotion without preparing her first.

Today was a day to celebrate Kenneth and Barbara. In fact, she was proud of her dad for not making today all about business. It took a lot of restraint on his part, since he was always all business, all the time. Plus, something so important as her stepping into her father's shoes needed to be discussed. Even though they had already discussed it—in broad terms. But now that his retirement had a fixed date, they would need to discuss her salary. They needed to talk about his expectations. She needed to make sure he understood she wanted complete control. His role would be as support system to her.

Or better yet, he'd stay out of Fortunado Real Estate altogether and enjoy his retirement as she implemented her vision for the company.

Her gaze found Zach again. Like her, he stood just outside of the knot of people clustered around her parents, wishing them well.

Once she took over, she would offer Zach a lovely promotion. It was the least she could do if she couldn't offer him her body— *Stop that.* To date, she'd never offered him her body and now she never would. And that was not the way a boss should think about an employee. Even if said employee was drop-dead gorgeous and flirted outrageously with her. He flirted outrageously with all women. He had a different girl with him every time she saw him. And that's why she needed to focus on what would come next: her promotion. It was a chance to give her all to something bigger than herself—something that would never let her down. That was the way to go.

She would always love Zach, but he would never know it.

That was the price she would pay to secure her future. A future so close she could taste it.

Zach McCarter was honored to be invited to hear his boss's big announcement. From the first minute Zach had joined the Fortunado Real Estate team five years ago, Kenneth Fortunado had made him feel like part of the family. Even so, he felt a little out of place here today. Like a fish out of water among Kenneth's adult children and close friends. However, when his boss welcomed him as part of the family, it would be rude—hell, it would be downright ungrateful—to second-guess the invitation.

His gaze landed on Maddie Fortunado, who was standing apart from her sisters and the others who were clustered around their parents. Only he and Maddie, with her long blond hair and perfect skin, hung back.

She stood with her arms folded, wearing a *Mona Lisa* smile that didn't quite reach her blue eyes. Zach knew she would wait until the scrum had dissipated before going in. He knew this because it's what he'd do. He and Maddie were a lot alike when it came to things like this—and in their approach to business. But their backgrounds were polar opposite.

With her Ivy League education and continental upbringing, Maddie Fortunado was not your standard Texas debutante. She was smart—too smart to concern herself with inconsequential things that didn't matter. She put her Harvard Business School education to good use at Fortunado Real Estate and seemed to live, eat, breathe and sleep her career.

While he and Maddie were philosophically alike, Zach hadn't been born into money. He wasn't implying that Maddie didn't work hard. In fact, he had to hand it to her, she never coasted on the privilege of being the boss's daughter. She was good at her job as vice president of sales. She was always in the office. Every time he was there, so was she. No one could accuse her of not pulling her weight. But at the end of the day, she was the boss's daughter. That's why he had to check any feelings that might have remotely resembled attraction.

And there had been a few.

Zach had worked double time just to get to the starting gate of his career, so that a man like Kenneth Fortunado not only knew his name, but respected him enough to invite him into his home and include him in an occasion like this.

Maddie glanced his way again and he made a face at her. She smiled—as he knew she would. She shook her head and rolled her eyes good-naturedly.

Zach closed the distance between them, walking across the marble back porch, past the koi pond to stand next to her.

"Hey," he said.

"Hey, yourself." She cocked a brow. "I guess they let anyone in here these days."

"Surprised by the announcement?" he asked.

She shrugged. "In some ways, yes, but it's been a long time coming. So, in that regard, no."

"What happens next?" he asked.

"What do you mean?" She raised her chin a fraction of an inch, a tell that she knew something she wasn't sharing.

"If anyone knows what's going to happen with the business after your father retires, it would be you."

She opened her blue eyes wide, obviously feigning cluelessness, but she wasn't very good at it.

"I don't know, Zach. I guess you'll just have to wait for another Fortunado family announcement."

She fisted her hands on her hips and the movement showed off her sleek tanned arms beneath her crisp white sleeveless blouse. She had great arms that were toned and feminine. And long, long legs that could drive a man to distraction if he allowed it. Zach wouldn't allow it. He couldn't allow it, he thought, forbidding himself to glance down.

It was likely that Maddie would be named her father's successor. That meant she would go from being the boss's daughter to being the boss. No matter how alluring he found those long legs, they weren't worth compromising his job. He'd worked too hard to get to where he was today to risk losing it all.

"Everyone, lunch is ready," said Barbara. The crowd around her and Kenneth thinned. "Please help yourselves. We have pulled pork, barbecued brisket, and chicken. I hope you brought your appetites. Because there's plenty of food and I don't want any leftovers."

Schuyler and Carlo were the first ones to approach the buffet. Zach and Maddie continued to hang back and let the other guests and Fortunado siblings go first. No matter how many family functions or Sunday lunches like this one that he'd attended, he always tried to err on the side of politeness. He was thirty-two years old and had been in the business since he was eighteen, but at times like this, he still felt out of place. If he thought about it too hard, the fifteen-year-old boy who was on the outside looking in beckoned him farther back into the periphery, where he would feel more comfortable watching than diving into the middle of everything. He'd outgrown his insecurities, of course. He'd like to think he'd gotten as strong as he was to spite them. Because confidence had been a must to succeed in the real estate business. In fact, in this industry, confidence was everything. But being in the Fortunado home like this, he preferred to stand back and watch the family dynamics. Watch and learn. The natural family rhythm fascinated him. Especially families like this that were so different from what he was used to.

"The food doesn't get any warmer," said Maddie. "You better get it while it's hot. Or at least before my cousin Dale goes through the line."

Maddie nodded toward a tall skinny guy who was still talking to Kenneth.

"He didn't earn the name *the closer* because he's good at sales," Maddie said. "He eats a lot."

"The closer, huh?" Zach said. "That sounds formidable."

"Don't say I didn't warn you."

Maddie motioned for him to join her as she approached the buffet line. He followed. She picked up two plates and offered him one. Her hand brushed his as he accepted it.

"Are you happy at Fortunado, Zach?" she asked.

The non sequitur made him do a mental double take. "Happy?" he repeated. "Of course I'm happy."

"Good to know." Her gaze searched his eyes. There was something in them he didn't understand. Especially when they dipped to his lips for the briefest of seconds.

She bit her bottom lip, a hint of color blossoming in her cheeks, before lifting her eyes to hold his gaze again.

There was something understatedly sexy about her and the realization caught him off guard. He could test these mixed signals she was sending—these cracks in her buttoned-up, businesslike armor that kept him guessing, making him wonder if he was reading her right. And he was usually very good at reading people. He prided himself on it.

But these flirty looks of Maddie's sometimes morphed into stare-downs that became games of chicken to see who would look away first. The accidental brush of hands, and now asking him if he was happy at Fortunado? What was that all about?

"Why?" he asked. "If I was, say, restless, would you be willing to make it worth my while to stay?"

"And how would you propose I make it worth your while?"

She watched him, waiting for his answer as she held out the white china plate for the server to dish up a piece of chicken and a portion of brisket.

He arched a brow, and his gut clenched at the thoughts swirling around his head. He felt as if he were contemplating taking something that didn't belong to him. Like finding a twenty-dollar bill on the sidewalk—you could stuff it in your pocket and walk away...or you could do the right thing and try to find the owner.

She must've read it in his expression.

"You're full of yourself, McCarter." He watched her walk to an empty table off to the side, rather than joining her sisters and Carlo at the one in the middle of the patio.

Zach took his plate of barbecue and followed her, claiming the seat next to her. "Full of myself? That wasn't a very nice thing to say."

Her eyes widened. "You're so sensitive."

"That's me. I'm just a sensitive kind of guy. Isn't that what the ladies want? A sensitive guy?"

She cut a piece of chicken off the bone. Raising the fork to her lips, she stopped short of putting the bite into her mouth, a mischievous smile tipping up the corners of her lips.

"Is that what you tell all the ladies?" Maddie asked. "That you're a sensitive kind of guy?"

Zach flashed his best smile. "Whatever works."

"Whatever works," she repeated. "Is that your philosophy?"

"Nope. Sensitivity is my philosophy. How could you forget?" He made a stabbing gesture in the center of his chest. "I thought we'd finally found something in common. You know, you liking sensitive men and me being sensitive."

She laughed and her cheeks colored. He liked the thought of rattling calm, cool, collected, perfect Madeleine Fortunado. He wanted to get under her skin. Because it was the closest he'd come to ever getting under anything of hers.

Maddie took a sip of her margarita, willing herself to calm down. She was grateful when Schuyler and Carlo moved from their original spot and joined them.

"What's wrong?" Schuyler asked Maddie when they sat down. "What did I miss?"

Zach snared Maddie's gaze and he raised his eyebrow, issuing a challenge for her to explain the conversation.

"Zach will explain." She turned to him and smiled.

"Whatever works." He winked at her and her cheeks colored again.

He cleared his throat. "I was just asking Maddie what she did for fun. You know, I'm starting to get the feeling that all she does is work. She doesn't always work, does she?"

"Pretty much," Schuyler said.

"There has to be something else," he said. "I'm curious about what she likes to do for fun."

Schuyler looked as if she wasn't buying it. "Oh, really? I know my sister works a lot, but you two get together every Friday night at the Thirsty Ox, don't you?"

"Of course we do," Maddie said.

"But that's still work-related," Zach qualified.

"And Zach usually brings a date," Maddie added. "Or he stops by and rushes out to meet a date."

"I didn't realize you noticed," Zach said.

Carlo and Schuyler watched them banter back and forth as if they were the lunchtime entertainment, and Maddie wanted to bolt.

"Even so," he said. "How is it that I don't know much about you? What are your interests outside of the office? When you're not thinking about real estate, what do you think about?"

Maddie felt herself blanch. "That's a little personal, don't you think?"

"No, it's not," Zach said. "Is it? I don't mean to make you uncomfortable. I just want to know you better. I was hoping you would tell me one thing I didn't know." He held up his hands. "But if you'd rather not, it's okay."

Before Maddie could reply, he turned his attention to Carlo and Schuyler.

"Where will you live after you're married?" he asked.

"I'm helping them find a house in Austin," Maddie cut in before her sister could answer. "And I have a dog."

"What?" Zach looked puzzled.

"You asked me to tell you one thing about myself that you didn't know. I have a dog. So, there you go. That's one thing."

Zach nodded. "I didn't know that. Thank you for sharing it with me. What kind of dog?"

Maddie shook her head. "Nope. You said one thing. Now it's your turn. One thing. Start talking, McCarter."

He blinked. "Fair enough. I lived in San Antonio for five years and before that I traveled around a lot."

"I know that about you," Maddie said. "Tell me something I don't know."

"Really?" He wrinkled his brow. "How do you know that?"

Maddie bit the insides of her cheeks. She had to be careful not to tip her hand. A lot of her Zach information had come from perusing his social media accounts, which were usually pretty generic and real estate–oriented, but occasionally a friend of his would post a personal morsel and Maddie would gobble it up like cake. Of course, she'd be mortified if he ever found out that she stalked him on Facebook and Instagram. But, hey, it was a free country, and his social media pages were open to the public. It wasn't as if she'd hacked in or was doing anything devious. It was all completely aboveboard.

Sort of.

Social media was a secret crush resource. It was fair game.

Even so, she would be mortified if he found out.

"I'm sure you mentioned it before," she said nonchalantly. "How else would I know?"

"Is that a tactic to get me to divulge two things about myself to your one?" He looked smug, as if he'd uncovered her diabolical plan.

"Okay. Whatever." Maddie shrugged him off, wanting to quit while she was ahead. "It's not that important."

She immediately regretted how cold her words sounded. If she was good at flirting, she could've gotten some mileage out of their banter. But the truth was, flirting sort of freaked her out. She could do it up to a point, but when he got too close, she choked. When she choked, her defense mechanisms kicked in and she came across as prickly. Because it was so much easier to pretend like she didn't care. It was just as well, she supposed. Because she *shouldn't* care.

But then Zach was sitting there pretending to look wounded and her stomach flipped.

"Ouch!" he said. "I have been put in my place."

No! That's not what I meant. I didn't know what else to say.

Then he smiled and those dimples winked at her. If

her mind had been spinning before, she was at a total loss for words now.

She was glad when his phone rang.

He took it out of his pocket and glanced at the screen. "Sorry, I need to take this call. Excuse me, please?"

She watched him unfold his long body from his place at the table. He answered the call while he was still close enough for Maddie to hear him say, "Hey, how are you?" His voice sounded low and sexy, qualities that suggested he wasn't talking to a client. Her heart fluttered and then sank. She'd heard him on the phone with clients before. This was definitely a girlfriend. Zach had a lot of girlfriends because he was a flirt. He had an easy appeal, especially with women. He flirted with any woman who would flirt back... Not so unlike the way he was flirting with her.

You're not special. He flirts with everyone.

That thought was like a cold glass of water, a reality check to remind herself that she really should stop this nonsense before she embarrassed herself. She was already way out of her element carrying on like she had been.

He was good at what he did. And because he was good at what he did, Maddie needed him on her team at Fortunado Real Estate when she took over for her father.

Priorities. Do not muddy the waters. Remember what's important.

"Speaking of house hunting," Maddie said, looking at her sister.

Schuyler looked puzzled. "We weren't."

"I mentioned it a few minutes ago," Maddie said.

"I have a house to show you. It's not even on the market yet. One of my clients gave me the heads-up. It's a dream house so it'll go fast. When can we go look?"

Schuyler clapped her hands. "Let's go this week. As soon as you can come to Austin." She turned and looked at her husband-to-be. "Carlo, can you take some time off next week?"

"Anything for you, my love." Carlo leaned in and planted a kiss on Schuyler's cheek.

"Okay, then," Maddie said. "I'll call my client and check her availability."

She started to excuse herself from the table, but Zach was already making his way back.

On second thought, maybe the call to the client could wait until after lunch.

Zach caught her eye as he walked back to the table. His long stride was loose and comfortable. Her mind raced, searching for something witty to say after he sat down. She thought about quipping about the call being personal, maybe teasing him about showing his sensitive side. But they'd worn out that joke. Instead, she resorted to the traditional and polite.

"Is everything okay?"

"Sure," he said. "But I do need to go."

Maddie's heart sank.

"But before I go, I want to thank your parents and congratulate them on your father's big decision. But first, Ping-Pong."

Maddie was sure she'd heard him wrong. "Did you say Ping-Pong?"

He flashed that grin and those dimples made Maddie's toes curl in her sandals.

"It was my favorite pastime when I was nine," he said. "I'm sure you didn't know that."

She laughed. *Ping-Pong.*

"No, I didn't know that."

"Do you play?"

"As a matter of fact, I was pretty darn good at it, back in the day."

"We should play sometime," he said.

Maddie drew in a sharp breath and nearly choked. She didn't understand her reaction. He wasn't asking her on a date.

"You two should *totally* play," Schuyler urged. "In fact, I think we still have a Ping-Pong table somewhere around here. Mom never gets rid of anything. She just learns new techniques to masterfully store everything. But I digress. We should have a Ping-Pong date night. It would be so much fun. Totally retro. My money would be on Mads, though. She was pretty good at it. Or at least she was the most competitive out of all of us. She's always hated to lose. She still does."

Maddie impaled her sister with a look, to which Schuyler seemed oblivious.

Not true! Okay, maybe it's a little true.

Even so, she wished Schuyler hadn't said it.

"It's a date, then," Zach said. "The loser will buy the winner's beer one Friday at the Thirsty Ox." He turned and started walking away, but stopped and turned back. "And the loser has to tell the other winner five personal things."

Chapter Two

The next morning, Maddie glanced up from her computer and saw her sister Valene standing in the doorway of her office.

"Do you have a moment?" Val asked. "I have some questions about the McKinney listing on West Pine."

Maddie's eyes flitted to the time at the bottom of her computer screen. When she'd gotten to her desk at 7:30 this morning, her father's executive assistant, Rae Rowley, had phoned and asked her to clear her schedule at 11:00. Maddie had been a jumble of nerves for more than three hours this morning, doing everything she could to distract herself. Why hadn't Val come to her sooner?

The 11:00 meeting was *the meeting*. The one she'd

been waiting for since she'd joined the firm. Probably longer than that—since she was born.

She'd been reading an email about a career day event sponsored by the local school system. She'd volunteered to share everything she knew and loved about the real estate business with elementary schoolkids, but today she was reading the material to distract herself more so than to prepare for the annual event, which was next month.

The diversion had worked because now it was 10:55.

"I'm supposed to meet with Dad in five minutes." She smiled a knowing smile and her younger sister's mouth fell open as realization dawned in her eyes.

"Is this about…?" Val made circles with her hands, as if she were indicating something that was too big to put into words.

"I think so," Maddie said. "I hope so. I guess I'll find out in about—" She glanced at the time again. "Four minutes."

Maddie stood and gathered her leather folio and her lucky Montblanc fountain pen. It had been a gift from her father when he'd promoted her to vice president.

"I'm sorry I can't talk right now. Unless it's super quick and you want to walk and talk. Or we could meet later?"

"Oh, my gosh, don't you worry one bit." Val reached out and gave Maddie's arm a little squeeze. "My questions can wait. This is much more important. This…" She made the all-encompassing hand circles again. "This is our future. Fortunado Real Estate's future.

And I am thrilled that I know about your promotion before anyone else."

Maddie shrugged. "It isn't official just yet."

"We all know it's coming." Valene pulled Maddie into a hug. "Okay, chief. Go in there and show him who's boss."

Val let go and grimaced, shaking her head as if trying to erase the words. "Well, you probably don't need to show Dad you're the boss. He already knows. Oh, you know what I mean."

Sweet Val. She was young and a little naive, but her heart was in the right place and she had such good instincts. It would be a great morale booster for her if Maddie could find some way to reward her—maybe a token promotion—after things settled down. Maddie filed that thought away to revisit soon. Right now, she had a meeting to attend.

She and Val chatted as they walked down the office's main hall toward the formidable double doors at the end of the passageway.

"The long and short of it is the McKinneys and I are wrangling on the listing price for their house," Val said. "They think we should ask $200,000 more than what I'm recommending for the property."

"Did you base the price on comps in the area?" Maddie asked.

Valene shrugged. "Really, there's nothing quite like it in the neighborhood. That's why I need your advice. They say their home is special—"

"Everyone thinks their home is special," Maddie said. "And I'm sure it is, to them. But at that price, we're edging close to $185 per square foot. It would be a record for that neighborhood."

By that time, they'd reached their dad's office and his assistant spoke before Val could. "Your father is expecting you, Ms. Fortunado. Please go in when you're ready."

"Thank you, Rae," Maddie said and turned her attention back to Val. "I'm sure they don't want to price themselves out of the market. I'll stop by your desk after I'm finished and we can figure it out. But I need to go. I don't want to be late."

She hated to leave Valene hanging, but of all people, Val knew it wasn't a good idea to keep their father waiting. Especially not today. Besides, this was a good exercise for Val. If she was going to succeed, and Maddie had all the confidence in the world that she would, her sister needed to learn how to steer the client toward a reasonable listing price. It took practice, but she'd get the hang of it.

"No, you certainly don't want to keep him waiting." Val said the words with a lilting songlike quality. "Not today. Not for this meeting. Good luck."

Maddie breathed through a hitch of anticipation that had become almost Pavlovian since her father had allowed himself to introduce the *R* word into his vocabulary.

Retirement.

He'd committed to it yesterday when he'd made the big announcement. Now he was about to seal the deal by putting the rest of the plan in place.

Lately, her parents had been talking about spending

more time together. They wanted to travel; her father had been promising he would cut his hours. But even after the barbecue, when he hadn't named Maddie as his successor, she wondered if he'd really go through with it. Something felt a little off. One step at a time, she'd reminded herself last night as she'd tossed and turned while reliving the announcement.

She'd never seen her mother as serious as she'd been when she'd said the cruise around the world would sail with or without him. Barbara didn't draw lines in the sand very often, but when she did, she didn't play. That boat was leaving on June 4, and she would be on it with or without him.

Barbara Fortunado was possibly the only thing Kenneth loved more than Fortunado Real Estate. Sure, he loved his kids, but he'd go insane if his wife was away for four months. Still, he was an all-or-nothing man. There would be no semiretirement for him. There was no way he could stay away from the office that long without making a clean break.

Even if he had sealed the deal on his retirement yesterday, this meeting made the slim chance that he might change his mind seem less likely.

"Are you free for lunch?" Val asked. "We could talk about it then."

Maddie glanced at her watch. It was edging on 11:00. Even if Rae hadn't specifically mentioned lunch when she'd called about the meeting, she'd said *clear your schedule*.

"I'm not sure, Val. You know how Dad is. He may

just want to meet, but he may want to go to lunch afterward."

To celebrate.

Her stomach did a triple gainer at the thought.

Finally.

She would insist they get a bottle of champagne. The very best vintage in the cellar. And when he reminded her it was the middle of the day, that they had work to do, she would put her hand on his arm and tell him that he had earned this champagne. It was as much to celebrate his life-changing decision as to celebrate her promotion.

She'd pick up the tab. It would be symbolic of his passing the mantle.

"I don't have anything scheduled this afternoon," Val said. "Let me know when you're free. I'd really like to get back to the McKinneys before the end of the day."

"Of course. Of course." Maddie smiled her most benevolent smile. "I'll see you as soon as I'm free."

After all, Val was Maddie's protégé. Just as their father had trained her, it was up to her to pay it forward and teach Valene everything she knew about the Houston real estate market. Since they were so close in age, it was unlikely that Val would ever head up Fortunado. After all, the company only had room for one president. But Maddie would make sure that Val's hard work was rewarded.

Once Val got more experience, maybe Maddie could make her a vice president? Or CFO?

Val nodded. "Sounds good. Thanks, Maddie. Good luck." She mouthed the words *and congratulations.*

As Maddie turned, she smiled at Rae and walked toward her father's office. All the hard work she'd poured into her job was about to pay off. All the long days and weekends dedicated to business rather than dating and having fun. No, scratch that. Work was fun. It was a sure thing, a solid investment. The harder she worked, the more she proved herself.

She didn't mind chasing after a business deal. In fact, she was in her glory when she was hunting down a deal. She'd latch onto it and stay the fight until she won. But she never chased men. Men were untrustworthy. They were too unpredictable. Giving her all to business was the closest thing to a sure thing she'd ever find.

Work was a solid investment of her time. Unlike the uncertainty of the dating world. Would she like to get married and have a family? Sure. Someday. But right now, Fortunado Real Estate claimed her full attention. The more she proved herself, the more comfortable her father seemed to be about retiring and turning Fortunado Real Estate over to her.

The sound of male voices coming from her father's office snapped her out of her reverie before she gave a staccato rap on his office door.

"Enter," Kenneth said.

When she opened the door, she smiled askance when she saw Zach McCarter sitting in one of the two cordovan leather club chairs across from her father's mahogany desk.

Her father and Zach stood up when they saw her.

"I'm sorry." Maddie glanced at her watch to make sure she had the time right. It was 11:01. "I didn't mean to interrupt. Rae said you were ready to meet with me. I can wait outside while you two finish up."

"No," her father said. "Come in. Come in. Zach is part of this meeting, too. Now that we're all here we can begin."

Maddie's stomach dropped as the men lowered themselves into their seats. Why was Zach part of this meeting? This meeting had nothing to do with Zach.

"Sit down, Maddie." Kenneth Fortunado gestured to the matching leather chair next to Zach.

Her mind raced as she smoothed her black pencil skirt before sitting down.

Maybe today isn't the day. And that's okay. It's fine.

Actually, it wasn't okay, but what other option did she have?

She'd talk to her dad after the meeting and assure him she knew it was hard to relinquish control. After all, if anyone knew that, she did. She'd inherited the tendency to micromanage from the man himself. He probably just needed a little reassurance that Fortunado Real Estate would be fine in her hands. It would be more than fine. It would thrive.

He just needed to bite the bullet and make the decision already.

She tamped down her disappointment by letting her gaze do a quick sweep of Zach in his dress khakis and white button-down, which was open at the collar. As always, he looked effortlessly professional. And gorgeous. Neither too casual nor overly preened. Leave it to him and his broad shoulders and perfect butt to make simple white and beige look like a work of art.

Yes, she'd noticed.

She studied the angle of his cheekbones, the slant of his aquiline nose, the waves of his blond hair and the gleam of his blue, blue bedroom eyes. It was hard not to notice Zach McCarter and all his masculine perfection.

In fact, just last night she'd indulged in a late-night fantasy about Zach's *masculine perfection*—those perfect shoulders and butt. And those dimples. Oh, those dimples.

He was gorgeous. And she was human. And he was totally and completely off-limits, which made him the perfect secret crush. And, well, a guy like Zach never looked at a woman like Maddie, which was fine with her. In fact, it was just the way she liked it. If she was going to be his boss, he could never know about the thoughts that ran through her head.

It wasn't as if he was a mind reader. So, she had nothing to worry about.

Except she was worrying about his presence at this meeting. What was he doing here?

Maddie thought her father would've talked to her separately.

A sinking feeling lodged itself in the pit of her stomach.

Last year, Zach had barely edged out Maddie as Fortunado's top sales producer. This year they were running neck and neck. But it was only May and she fully intended to reclaim the throne. That victory would be the final jewel in the crown after she took over for her father. Of course, she'd been focusing on administrative tasks other than sales—mentoring Valene, learning the advertising and promo end of the business, researching client-building methods, and such. There were only so many hours in the day. She was doing all the extras and almost matching Zach as the top sales producer. It went without saying that if all she did was focus on sales, like Zach did, she'd be running circles around McCarter.

"Thank you for making time to meet with me this morning," her father said, as if either of them would've opted out. "I've been eyeing retirement for a while now. It's taken me a long time to wrap my head around the concept, but with a little help from Barbara, I've finally decided to take the plunge."

He paused for what seemed an eternity and Maddie held perfectly still, resisting the urge to shift in her seat, redistributing her impatience.

Now that sinking feeling was gripping her stomach and attempting to turn it inside out.

"Congratulations, Kenneth," Zach said. "I know it wasn't an easy decision."

"Thank you, Zach. It's been one of the most difficult decisions of my life. This business represents the sum of my life's work. I've invested a lot of sweat equity in this place, building it from the ground up. So, you can imagine that I want to leave the business in the best hands once I step back."

Maddie sensed what was about to happen before her father spelled it out. She wanted to say something, but she didn't want Zach McCarter to glimpse any weakness or uncertainty in her. This was *her* future. *Her* legacy. This wasn't happening—

"I consider the two of you my right-hand people,"

Kenneth continued as Maddie's peripheral vision was overtaken by a white-tinged fog.

You can only have one right hand, Dad. Who is it? Him or me? It's me, dammit. It's me. Why are you doing this?

Her gaze could've singed a hole into her father as she tried in vain to telegraph her feelings to him. But he seemed clueless.

"That's why I've narrowed the candidates for my replacement down to the two of you."

He glanced first at Zach and then at Maddie.

"Maddie?" Kenneth's smile fell. "Are you okay?"

Feeling two sets of eyes on her, Maddie forced her mouth into a smile. "I'm just surprised, Dad. This was the last thing I expected when you asked me to meet with you this morning."

Her father gazed at her a few beats too long and she was sure he sensed her confusion. He was an intuitive man. He had to know that this was not just a surprise, but a personal affront, an insult.

"I thought you would've had some kind of idea," her father said, "since we've discussed the possibility of you running Fortunado in the future."

The possibility.

He'd led her to believe that it was more than just a *possibility*. No, he'd led her to believe that she would step into the position of president of Fortunado Real Estate upon his retirement. Now he couldn't walk it back fast enough.

"I guess I thought you were offering more than a *possibility*," she said.

She had dedicated every bit of her postgraduate self to Fortunado Real Estate. She'd sacrificed her personal life, her dating life, working eighteen-hour days and weekends, making herself available to clients twenty-four hours a day, seven days a week. While her father may not have out-and-out promised her she would be his successor, he had implied it. Besides, Kenneth Fortunado was all about family. Why in the world would he consider turning over the family business to an outsider?

Her father either chose to ignore her remark or pretend as if he hadn't heard it, because he was already moving on. It was a good thing he hadn't pressed her because she wasn't about to say anything more in front of Zach.

Her father leaned forward, his hands folded on his desk. "Barbara and I leave on our cruise on June 4. That means right after the wedding—in approximately two weeks—I will name my successor. If the two of you choose to accept the challenge, one of you will take my place as president of Fortunado Real Estate."

Maddie glanced at Zach, fully expecting him to do the right thing and bow out. She wanted him to hold up his hands and say that it wasn't appropriate, that it wasn't his place to challenge Maddie for what was rightfully hers. Instead, he flashed that perfect smile with those dimples that opened doors and broke hearts. He looked Maddie square in the eyes and said, "I'm in."

His smile was reminiscent of the one he'd given her last night when he'd challenged her to a friendly game of

Ping-Pong. But this was a competition to determine her future—to decide who got control over her birthright.

But damned if her own traitorous heart didn't twist at the sheer rakish beauty of him. That hurt almost as much as the thought of her uncertain future.

"Bring it on," she said, instantly wishing she would've said something a little classier. But he didn't seem to mind. His eyes glinted as if sparked by the competition. She forced her gaze away from the seductive pull of his.

Once upon a time Zach McCarter might have been her secret crush, but now *he* was the competition. As far as she was concerned, he was the enemy.

"Good," said Kenneth, turning his gaze on Maddie. "Maddie, I'm proud of you for rising to the occasion. I must admit that I was worried about how you'd take it. But I have to hand it to you for wanting what's best for the business."

Maddie dug her nails into her palms as she kept the smile fixed on her face. So, he'd worried about how she'd take it, but he hadn't given her the courtesy of a heads-up before this meeting? Oh, yeah, they'd talk about what was best for the *family business* later.

"The real estate business is brutal," said Kenneth. "Whoever takes over Fortunado will likely face much tougher challenges in the years ahead. I want to make sure whoever I choose is up for the long haul."

Ostensibly, he was speaking to both of them, but he was looking at Maddie.

And she'd believed it couldn't possibly get worse.

Were they really going to do this now?

"I'm up for the challenge, Dad." Her voice was clear and her words were crisp. "I didn't realize our family business was up for grabs. You know, open to an outsider."

She was well aware that her words had surpassed crisp and veered into clipped. Her father winced, but she didn't know how Zach reacted because she didn't look at him. But she'd guess that he'd managed to keep a pleasantly stoic poker face. And if she knew what was good for her, she'd compose herself, too.

Her father cleared his throat. "The business is not up for grabs, as you put it. You might be the one I choose if you prove yourself the worthiest."

Prove myself the worthiest? What the hell do you think I've been trying to do my entire adult life?

Her father's words shook her to her very core. After all the hours she'd put in, all the sacrifices she'd made for the good of the company, he still wasn't satisfied that she'd proven herself worthy?

If she didn't know better, she might think that this had more to do with turning over the reins to one of his daughters. His sons weren't interested. So, what did he do? He *adopted* one.

At least she had the good sense to not talk about this now. But they would talk. He had better believe they would talk.

Even in her fury, she had the presence of mind to know that her father wasn't a chauvinist. He'd trained her himself and he'd led her to believe—

She shook away the thought. And she tried to ignore

the little voice that taunted her, reminding her that Zach had outsold her last year.

Not by much, but he'd won.

He'd won and she'd lost.

Kenneth looked from Maddie to Zach and back to Maddie. "Your future is in your own hands," Kenneth said. "You can win the position, but you have to earn it. I'm speaking to both of you."

A sound like white noise buzzed in Maddie's ears.

"I'm a self-made man," Kenneth continued. "I never had anything handed to me. I built this business from the ground up and I want to make sure my successor not only fosters it, but takes it to places I never dreamed possible."

He punctuated the statement with a shrug.

Self-made man? Never had anything handed to him?
Was he kidding?

It took every ounce of Maddie's self-control to keep from reminding him that the Texas Lottery money he'd won hadn't exactly come from hard work and determination. He'd beaten the odds and was lucky enough to choose the right numbers. But she also knew what his retort would be. That he'd invested that money. He hadn't squandered it on all the trappings that a man who'd been raised by a single mother who could barely make ends meet might've been tempted to buy: the fancy house, the expensive cars. She'd heard him tell the story a million times. At face value, a cool million seemed like a lot of money, but it wasn't. In fact, it was just enough to provide a false sense of wealth. After a person lived like a rich man for a few years, all he'd have

left to show for it would be an empty bank account—
and very often he'd be in worse financial shape than
when he'd started.

It was a point of pride for Kenneth that he had been
smart and invested his money. He'd worked hard to
build Fortunado Real Estate into what it was today.

*Yeah, Dad, what about how hard I've worked for
you? What about how much of myself I've invested in
you and Fortunado?*

He glanced at his watch. "I need to leave in a few
moments. I have a lunch appointment and I don't want
to be late. But do you have any questions I can answer
before we adjourn?"

Yeah, Dad, I do. What the hell?

"What are you looking for?" Zach asked. "What's
the criteria?"

Maddie turned and looked at Zach for the first time
since her dad had made the announcement.

Ah! Amateur question, McCarter.

She knew instantly what her father would say before he said it.

Kenneth shrugged. "Show me what you've got.
That's all I'm going to say. Well, that and may the best
man—or woman—win."

Her father held up a finger, his eyes flashing. "Wait.
There is something. You know the Paisley? That new
high-rise Dave Madison is building downtown? I want
Fortunado to be the exclusive agents for that property. I
want you two to work together to land that listing. The
whole building. You need to work together to come up

with a plan to seal the deal. That's an important part of the challenge."

"We're on it." Zach got to his feet, making all the right noises of agreement and understanding. As he shook Kenneth's hand, Maddie stayed in her seat. Zach lingered on the threshold of her father's office, obviously watching to see what she was going to say or do.

Maddie got a little bit of satisfaction from the look on his face when she said, "I need to talk to my father for a moment, Zach. Please excuse us."

"No problem." Zach gave a quick wave of his hand and closed Kenneth's office door behind him.

"How could you do this to me?" She turned to her dad the second they were alone. "I'm your daughter."

She couldn't remember playing this card before. It had been a point of pride to never take advantage of the fact that she was the boss's daughter. She knew she enjoyed a certain level of job security that those without the benefit of Fortunado blood didn't have. But she'd never needed it. She'd worked damn hard to earn the presidency that her father had so unceremoniously announced was up for grabs.

If that's the way he was going to be, then for a few moments she was going to play the family card. She was going to be the boss's daughter because he owed her an explanation—if for nothing else, as to why he'd blindsided her.

She could tell by the look on his face that he could see the depth of her anger.

"I'm sorry, Maddie," he said. "I can understand that this comes as a surprise, but I think you'll appreciate the challenge and rise to the occasion once you have some time to think it through."

She let his words reverberate in the air and took some satisfaction that at least he understood that she was upset.

"I love you," he continued. "I love all my children, but I also don't intend to let you or your siblings get complacent—especially when it comes to the business I've spent my life building. All promotions at Fortunado Real Estate must be earned. I have complete faith that you'll earn yours."

People might have argued that Zach McCarter was a lot of things. One thing they couldn't call him was a quitter. Overly sentimental probably wouldn't be on the list either.

So, why was it, he wondered, as he waited for Maddie at the Blue Moon Cafe, that he couldn't stop thinking about the look on her face when Kenneth had presented the challenge?

This should've been a day to celebrate his shot at the opportunity of a lifetime. This was the payoff for his hard work. Instead, he felt vaguely unsettled thinking about that injured-doe look in Maddie's blue eyes.

She'd probably kick him if she knew he was comparing her to an injured animal. She'd probably buck right up in his face.

But that's what he'd seen and he couldn't get her face out of his head.

This was business. Any other time—any other

person—and Zach wouldn't have given it a second thought. But he had a soft spot for Maddie.

Zach was probably more surprised than Maddie when Kenneth asked them to compete for the position. After all, everyone who worked for Fortunado Real Estate knew that Maddie coveted her father's job. She was the heir apparent, and everyone thought it was a given that she would take over for Kenneth when he retired.

When Kenneth asked him to transfer from San Antonio to the Houston office, Zach knew change was in the air. At first, he thought it was a token gesture to pacify Zach's restlessness. Kenneth seemed good at reading people. Even though Zach hadn't said it, Kenneth had to know that after five years as a broker with Fortunado, it was time for a change, time to open his own real estate office. After all, he was making Fortunado a hell of a lot of money.

Zach had no ties to San Antonio, no family to consider, no reason to not pack up and move to Houston. The move was an opportunity to learn the Houston market, which would be a useful tool once he did strike out on his own. When Kenneth had asked him to come to Houston, he'd said he wanted his senior associates to focus on teamwork, that there was some new construction in the Houston area and he wanted to put together an "A-Team"—Kenneth's words. He hadn't said who else was on his A-Team, but he'd specifically spelled out that he wanted Zach's help assuring that Fortunado would get exclusive listing contracts. Of course, Zach had been up for the challenge, but that teamwork bit threw him. Generally, he worked alone. He rarely partnered with other agents on listings. It wasn't his MO. Of course, it would take teamwork to run a business like Fortunado.

But this—this chance to head Fortunado—it was an unexpected challenge and he liked it. It would take teamwork and maybe this was a good chance for him to prove to himself that he wanted to manage a team rather than flying solo.

It all made sense—the transfer, the invitation to the barbecue where Kenneth announced his intent to retire, and today's meeting where he'd tapped the two of them as front-runners for his position.

The only thing getting in the way of intense satisfaction and immediate strategizing on how to annihilate the competition was that look on Maddie's face.

That's why he'd wanted the two of them to have lunch and sort this out. Kenneth had been smart when he'd tacked on the Paisley addendum. The last thing he needed was for his two top associates to be at war. Not only did they need to sit down and strategize about the Paisley, but they needed to make sure everything was good between them.

Easy for him to say since he was the interloper.

When Maddie walked into the restaurant, their gazes snared. She didn't smile. Her face looked neutral. Again, she seemed to be daring him to look away first—to walk away from the opportunity first.

He stood and watched her walk toward him.

He had two choices: he could bow out or he could go for it. If he chose to go for it, there would be no option but to pull out all the stops, to step up his game. If he stepped up his game, he would win. He always won. It was a point of pride.

Even if this opportunity didn't feel 100 percent right and it felt as if he was preparing to take something that didn't belong to him, Zach McCarter had never been a quitter.

He needed to put his game face on now. That face didn't have to be mean or savage. The mark of a good manager was to deal with conflict and produce as many win-wins as possible—especially in situations like this where there could only be one winner.

Him.

He would need Maddie on his team when that happened.

"Zach," she said, as she reached the table.

"Maddie, thanks for agreeing to meet on such short notice."

He reached for her chair, but she pulled it out herself. "Of course," she said. "There's a lot at stake here."

He nodded.

"That's why it's even more important that we work together," she said.

He wasn't sure what he'd expected, but based on the way she'd received the news not even two hours earlier, her eagerness to work together came as a shock. The woman was full of surprises.

"I'm glad you feel that way," he said. "We're going to make a great team."

Chapter Three

"Ping-Pong is not a date," Maddie said to Schuyler as she drove her sister and Carlo to see a house in the Austin neighborhood of Westlake. She'd driven up to Austin to show them houses and commercial property for a nightclub Carlo wanted to open. Carlo had been looking for months and holding out for exactly the right spot to open his new business. He'd come close a couple of times with property Maddie had shown him. Now that he was getting married, Maddie had a feeling he'd settle down and make a decision on the commercial site.

This trip was a welcome opportunity to get away from the office—to put some space between Zach and herself. If only Schuyler would stop making Zach tag along in spirit. "Or at least it's not the kind of first date I'm interested in."

Liar. If circumstances were different, you'd be happy to pick up trash with Zach McCarter and call it a fun first date.

But the situation was what it was. And it wasn't fun.

"Besides," Maddie added, "I cannot believe you'd even mention Zach McCarter in that context now that Dad has pitted us against each other."

After the disastrous meeting with her father and subsequent tension-charged lunch with Zach, she'd driven home, thrown the basics into an overnight tote and driven the two and a half hours to Austin. Presumably, it was to show Schuyler and Carlo property. But, if she was perfectly honest with herself, it had been for self-preservation.

She'd never been so happy to get out of the office—to get out of town. Because suddenly the entire city of Houston seemed too small to accommodate the dreams and ambitions of both Zach and her.

It was clear one of them had to go.

And it wouldn't be her.

Just because she was working out of town, it didn't mean she would be the one to bow out. They had their marching orders. They would work together to secure the Paisley deal and sell out the luxury high-rise. In fact, she'd taken the initiative to call Dave Madison's assistant and set up a meeting. He was out of town and Monday was his first available. In the meantime, she would help her sister and future brother-in-law. Working outside of the office would give her time to clear her head. It would only make her stronger.

"It's totally a date," her sister said. "He is so gorgeous, Mads. Maybe Dad has a method to his madness. Maybe he's doing this to throw you and Zach together? Remember how at the barbecue he said he thought of him as a son? Maybe he meant son-in-law."

Maddie shook her head. "I don't think so. And Sky, I really don't want to talk about him. Okay?"

Now she was sorry she'd told Schuyler about her father's plan. Even so, Schuyler was still going on about Ping-Pong as a first date.

Maddie white-knuckled the steering wheel. Even her siblings supported Maddie as their father's heir apparent. Her three brothers had chosen careers outside of the real estate industry. Valene was just starting out at Fortunado Real Estate. Schuyler had never shown an interest in the family business. Even though she could've had a role at Fortunado, she'd chosen to follow her own path. She'd confessed that there was a time when she'd felt like the odd sibling out—since both of her sisters had been bitten by the real estate bug—but following her own path had brought Schuyler to the Mendoza Winery, and that's where she'd met her husband-to-be. Now, Schuyler seemed to have made peace with her path in life.

And Maddie's once sure life was upside down.

Beside her, Schuyler sighed. "But you guys would look so cute together."

"We would not look cute together." Maddie's voice was monotone.

We would look gorgeous together.

Mortified that Schuyler was going on and on about this in front of Carlo, Maddie glanced in the rearview mirror. She was relieved to see that he'd put his ear-buds in and was gazing out the passenger window. He seemed to be nodding his head along to the music and not paying one bit of attention to their conversation.

Thank goodness.

This was sister-talk that they should be discussing in private.

"And just to clarify," Schuyler said, "Ping-Pong would be a sweet first date. You need to lighten up, missy."

Schuyler's personality was like a Chinese finger trap. Once she latched onto something, she grabbed even tighter if the other person tried to pull away. The trick was to relax, to lean into it.

Or make her think she'd hurt your feelings.

"Zach didn't mean anything by it. He's probably forgotten all about it, anyway. So, just drop it, okay? Besides, how could I ever date a guy who was after my job? Please don't make me feel any worse than I already do."

Schuyler's face softened. Then she muttered something under her breath that sounded frighteningly like, *There's no wonder Dad passed you over for the promotion.*

"What did you just say?" Maddie demanded. "That was really mean."

Schuyler flinched. "I said, there's no way Zach would pass on that after we caused such a commotion. What was mean about that?"

Maddie stole a look at her sister. Schuyler looked thoroughly stricken.

"I'm sorry," Maddie conceded. "I must've misunderstood."

They rode in silence for a few moments, until Schuyler bounced back.

"We really did cause a commotion over you two matching up at the Ping-Pong table." Schuyler shifted in her seat so that she was facing Maddie, and continued as if she hadn't heard a word Maddie had said. "Mads, you two would be so perfect. If you start dating now, you can bring him to the wedding. You'll look so good in pictures. Like Barbie and Ken."

Maddie rolled her eyes. "I'm about as far from Barbie as a Tonka truck."

"Stop being so hard on yourself," Schuyler said. "He's totally into you. I can feel it. And with a little…" Schuyler reached out and gently toyed with a lock of Maddie's long blond hair. "With just a little spiffing up, you could totally put Barbie to shame. Barbie ain't got nothin' on you, sister."

Maddie made the mistake of glancing at Schuyler and saw her make a gesture that was a combination of double finger guns, a shrug and pursed lips.

"What?" Schuyler laughed. "Don't look at me that way. It's true. But don't be insulted. That wasn't a dig at your looks. You're gorgeous, Mads. But you could be like Hollywood-level *gorge* if you just made a few changes."

Okay. Here we go.

Maddie felt her walls going up. Schuyler was the pretty sister. Maddie had always been the smart sister. Not the smartest *sibling*—her brothers had that sewed up. Valene was the baby, so, somehow, she escaped being compared to any of them.

Lucky Val.

Too bad society often valued looks over substance. Not that Sky lacked substance. She just… Well, sometimes Schuyler got away with things because she was pretty. She smiled and batted her big blue eyes and men turned to putty in her hands.

Sky wasn't manipulative. Not exactly. She didn't have a mean bone in her body. What she did have was this almost childlike, free-spirited quality and a general lack of self-consciousness that allowed her to get away with things that Maddie would never even dream of trying.

Maddie didn't have time to worry about the latest fashions and lipsticks. Classic wardrobe pieces and a no-nonsense grooming routine had always served her well. She wore her long, thick blond hair one length so she could let it dry naturally and pull it back from her face, which was always makeup-free, except for a swipe of clear lip gloss on special occasions. She had been blessed with good skin. So, why take a chance of clogging her pores with makeup she didn't have time to mess with anyway?

"Comparing a woman to Barbie isn't exactly a compliment, Sky. And last I heard, Ken wasn't interested in Barbie. I don't think she's his type, if you know what I mean. Not that there's anything wrong with Ken's preference. You know, love is love is love. I believe in live and let love, whatever floats his boat. Right now, my preference is to focus on work."

Yeah, and look where that had gotten her. A first-class ticket to nowhere. For a split second her life flashed before her eyes and she didn't like what she saw: still single; the spinster sister. Her nieces and nephews would call her Crazy Old Aunt Maddie. Only, instead of cats, she'd have a whole herd of corgis.

When she glanced at Schuyler, her sister was frowning.

"If you ask me," Schuyler said, "I think you're protesting too much, sister dear."

Maddie felt heat bloom at her chest and begin to work its way up.

Maybe, she *was* protesting too much. She was giving herself away. So, she seized the opportunity to grab the layup her sister had presented like a gift.

"I don't remember asking you, Sky. In fact, I have no idea what you're talking about. What am I overprotesting?"

"All I'm saying is you'd have to be dead not to notice how drop-dead gorgeous Zach McCarter is. Or oblivious. Maybe my sister is oblivious." Schuyler directed the comment to Carlo in the back seat, as if Maddie wasn't even there. "A hot guy is interested in her and she's oblivious."

Carlo didn't answer.

Maddie stole another glance in the rearview mirror and was relieved to see that Carlo's earbuds were still in place. He was the one who seemed to be oblivious. Thank God.

"Don't talk about me like I'm not here," Maddie protested. "And don't pull Carlo into this. FYI, when I'm in the office, I focus on my job, I don't ogle my co-workers."

"Are you really so focused on your work that you can't see what's right in front of you?"

Even though Maddie's eyes were glued to the road, she felt her sister's gaze boring into her as the heat that had been confined to her chest crept up her neck until it burned her cheeks.

Schuyler clapped her hands. "Oh, my God. You *do* see him. You like him, don't you?"

For a fraction of a second Maddie felt all her defenses give way and every schoolgirl emotion wash over her face. And even though Schuyler could only see her in profile she obviously saw it, too.

"You are totally into him!" she said. "Carlo, she likes him."

All Maddie could do was shake her head like an idiot.

"Mads, it's okay. There's nothing wrong with having a crush on a guy. I mean, especially at your age."

Maddie slanted a look of death at her sister.

"Thanks for that, Sky. You always know how to make me feel good."

"I didn't mean to upset you," Schuyler said. "You know what I mean."

Yes, she did. And her sister was right. She was twenty-nine years old and single with no romantic prospects. It shouldn't matter. It didn't matter because she was married to her job. Yet, she couldn't even admit that she had a crush on Zach McCarter. And why not? Carlo wasn't listening and Schuyler was a safe confidant. For all her free-spirited ways, she'd also proven herself to be trustworthy—a virtual vault...after she wore you down and made you confess.

For a moment, Maddie let herself wonder if the co-worker excuse was simply another part of her defense mechanism.

It was. She had enough self-awareness to admit that. But it was also true that if she admitted her attraction to Zach and things got weird, she might lose one of the firm's best brokers.

There she was overthinking it again—

But that's why she was good at her job. She thought things through. Where Schuyler would leap and hope the net appeared, Maddie looked at pros and cons from every angle before taking one step.

The overriding fact was, she and Zach had worked together for five years. Albeit, they'd been in different offices. They'd had five years to flirt. They'd had five years to act on any possible feelings or chemistry or electricity—whatever you wanted to label it. If he'd been interested, if he'd had any feelings for her, he would've acted on them by now. He hadn't. Clearly, he wasn't interested.

Even though she'd crushed on him from afar, that ship had sailed. Her father had pitted them against each other and she was going to win the promotion. So, it would be an exercise in frustration to try and start up something now. Even if it wouldn't be wildly inappropriate for the brand-new president to date one of her employees, she wouldn't have any time for a new relationship—or even a date. She would have her hands full with work.

Maddie knew the only way to get Schuyler off her back was to give a little, but lay down the law.

"Of course Zach is gorgeous. Everybody knows Zach is gorgeous. Zach knows Zach is gorgeous. He's simply not my type."

"I don't know, Mads," Schuyler said. "I felt some serious chemistry zinging back and forth between the two of you."

Enough!

For a moment, Maddie was tempted to lash out, to tell her sister that she had much more important things to worry about than handsome faces and zinging chemistry. But she caught herself before she did. She bit her lip a little too hard to make her unkind words dissipate. And good thing. It was her fatal flaw—when she got defensive, when she felt like she'd been backed into a corner, she tended to come out swinging. Being mean to Schuyler would be like kicking a puppy, which she would never do. Her sister didn't have a mean bone in her entire body. If Maddie knew what was good for her she would try to be a little more like her impractical, impetuous little sister.

Really, she knew it was futile to wish she could be more like Schuyler, who lived for the moment and put her heart's desire above all that was practical—hence, her determination to go against their father's wishes and follow a lead she believed would prove that their family, with its Fortunado last name, was related to the infamous Fortune family.

Maddie steered the car off the high road and onto the street of the Westlake neighborhood home she was sure was perfect for Schuyler and Carlo. And not a moment too soon.

"We're here," Maddie announced as she flicked on her right signal and turned onto the brick driveway of a house that looked like a smaller reproduction of a Spanish castle.

She knew her sister well enough to know she was easily distracted by shiny objects. Right on cue, Schuyler's eyes widened and her jaw dropped. "This is it? Oh, Maddie, it's beautiful. It's just perfect. Carlo, look!"

Carlo had pulled out the earbuds and was echoing his fiancée's awe.

There was nothing like a piece of gorgeous real estate to reframe a conversation. Perched high atop a hill, overlooking Lake Austin, this house was a particularly stunning show-stealer. Carlo and his cousins had recently opened Mendoza Winery in the Hill Country and business was booming. Though this estate was at the upper end of the couple's price range, the bank had prequalified them for it.

"This is it," Maddie said, as she took off her seat belt. "First and foremost, the backyard is fenced in for the dogs." Schuyler had recently rescued two little dogs named Stuff and Fluff. "It features four bedrooms, three baths, a gourmet kitchen, with a keeping room, a media center, exercise and sauna, wine cellar and tasting room, pool and spa, a guest apartment, and a three-car garage. Would you like to see inside?"

"What's a keeping room?" Carlo asked.

"It's an open-plan room that flows right off the kitchen," Maddie said.

She let herself out of the car and joined her sister and Carlo, who were staring up at the house like they'd found the Holy Grail.

"Could you see yourselves here?" Maddie asked.

Schuyler nodded. "This is our house, Carlo."

Carlo laughed. "It's impressive, but we haven't even seen the inside yet."

"I know," Schuyler said. "But I just know this is our house."

"Well, come on in and have a look around." Maddie took the lead and started toward the oversize dark wooden double doors.

This was why she loved her job. She was good at it. Matching couples and families with their dream homes was like a sixth sense for her. When she was doing that, and getting a reaction like she'd gotten from Schuyler and Carlo, she was in her glory. Setting up people with houses was so much more comfortable than allowing herself to be matched for a relationship—or pitted against the only man she could've seen herself getting involved with.

It was all for the best. She hadn't always made the best decisions where men were concerned. A lot of time had passed since her last mistake. Nonetheless, it was a lesson learned. That's why even if the electricity between Zach and her burned bright the way Schuyler claimed it did, Maddie had to pull the plug.

* * *

The GPS indicated that Zach's destination was approaching on the left. He turned down the Tim McGraw song that was playing on the radio, flicked on his signal and slowed down before he steered the behemoth of a pickup truck he'd rented for the occasion onto the apron of the driveway, stopping in front of an impressive black iron gate. He pushed the button on the call box. After Zach identified himself, the person connected to the voice on the other end buzzed him in.

As he followed the long, winding gravel road past stands of pine trees and fenced-in pastureland, he took the opportunity to survey what he could see of the property—and it was vast.

With more than three thousand acres of unspoiled Hill Country farmland, the Pomodoro Ranch in Sisterdale was a gem. He already sensed it had been worth the nearly four-hour drive from Houston. Or at least it would be once he secured the listing. He silently vowed that he was not leaving here until he had a signed agreement.

That's why he'd pulled out all the stops and had changed into boots, jeans and a chambray work shirt, which he'd washed three times to take away the just-purchased look of it. The ensemble was far from his usual style, but he figured Jim and Mary Ann Winters, owners of the Pomodoro, would be more comfortable with someone dressed in Texas casual than a guy who arrived in a convertible BMW and looked like he was ready to grab a nine iron and hit the golf course.

He'd also made sure his ride was as much of an accessory as the Stetson sitting on the seat next to him. The Ford F-150 wasn't his Beemer by any stretch of the imagination, but it had proven to be a surprisingly comfortable ride.

The gravel road delivered him in front of a rambling wooden and brick colonial ranch-style house with an awe-inducing six-car garage and double beveled-glass front doors. Zach parked in the generous area in front of the house that was finished in pavers.

Before he'd closed the door to the truck's cab, a man in a cowboy hat, faded, work-worn jeans and a plaid shirt, who looked to be upwards of seventy, had stepped outside and was offering his hand.

"You Zach McCarter?" he drawled.

"Yes, sir. That would be me." He met the man's hand with a firm shake. "Mr. Winters, nice to meet you."

"Thanks for making the drive all the way out here, son," Jim Winters said. "The location scares off some people from the city. I guess you could say that's the first test I've been putting Realtors through since I started interviewing brokers. But I heard you were the very best. Is that the truth?"

"I'll do everything in my power to make sure you're not disappointed."

He wished he could say he was the best, but a certain competitive blue-eyed blonde had been giving him a run for that honor. Lately, the visceral reaction he felt when he thought of her made him realize that if circumstances were different—if he didn't work for her father, if they weren't competing for the same job that would make one of them the boss and leave the other gravely

disappointed—he might want to see what else the two
of them could excel at together. And it wouldn't be anything that could happen at the office.

But he couldn't think about Maddie right now. For
the last few days, since their meeting with Kenneth,
Zach had been telling himself to keep his mind in the
game and his efforts focused on proving that he was
the man for the job. And that started with landing this
listing.

"You up for walking the land?" Jim Winters asked.

"I can't think of anything I'd rather do right now."

The older man nodded. "This ranch has been in my
family for three generations. But my boys moved out
years ago, and they have their own families and lives.
Seems like no one is interested in ranching these days.
That's why Mary Ann and I decided the best thing we
could do is sell the place. Do you think you can find
me a buyer, son?"

Several hours later, Zach parked in an open space
near the front doors of the high-rise building that housed
the Fortunado office. He'd just gotten back to town
after the listing appointment in Sisterdale. It was after
business hours—if the real estate industry had *business hours*. All the top producers worked way beyond
the usual Monday-through-Friday, nine-to-five gig. It
was Friday night and he had about an hour's work left
before he could call it a day. It didn't feel like a sacrifice to Zach. In fact, he felt more at home at the office
than he did at his condo.

First, he wanted to change out of the Wranglers and

chambray work shirt he'd worn to the appointment with
Jim and Mary Ann Winters. His regular outfit of khakis and a button-down was neatly hanging on hangers
on a hook behind his office door. The way he looked at
it, he wasn't being disingenuous by wearing the Wranglers and Stetson, as much as he was giving the clients
what they wanted. And it had worked. He'd landed the
listing. His tenth listing this week.

As he unlocked the front door and secured it behind
him, he noticed a light was on in the office across the
hall from his. Maddie's office.

It shouldn't be a surprise. The only other person who
rivaled him for hours worked was Maddie. He hadn't
seen her car in the parking lot, and thought she might
have called it an early day.

Obviously, he'd miscalculated.

She was fierce, competitive and hungry—eager to
take down her competition and slow to back down.
Those were the perks that came from growing up
wealthy and entitled. She possessed a confidence he'd
never been afforded growing up in the foster care system. His father had worked himself to death—literally—
leaving his mother to raise Zach and his brother on her
own. She died two years later, when Zach was fifteen
and his brother Rich was twenty-one. Technically, Rich
had been old enough to be Zach's guardian, but he said
he wasn't up for the responsibility. For lack of knowing
better and trusting that her oldest son would do right by
his younger brother, their mother had named Rich the
beneficiary of the life insurance policy she'd had through
her job. It had gone a long way toward putting Rich

through law school. The deal was supposed to be once Rich graduated and got established, he would put Zach through college. But in order to get through law school, he'd said he needed to be free to pull all-nighters at the library without the responsibility of a moody, grieving teenage brother who skipped school and got into trouble.

His grandparents were dead and his one aunt and uncle had been estranged from his mother, so Zach had nowhere to go. Whether it was at the behest of the authorities or because Rich didn't know how—or want—to fight for him, Zach ended up in foster care. He bounced around the system. He'd hidden how scared and abandoned he'd felt behind a facade of independence and toughness. The big takeaway from that three-year period of his life was that it was best not to depend on anyone.

But in the end, Zach liked to believe the experience hadn't made him bitter. In fact, he liked to think it had turned him into the man he'd become. He'd learned to not get too close to anyone and only rely on himself. That way, he knew he'd never be let down. Self-reliance had been the only sure thing in his life.

Once that had become ingrained, he'd learned that a smile and a lighthearted demeanor could open doors and give him access to people who could help him pad his bank account. Case in point: who would've ever thought that Kenneth Fortunado would open the door to his empire to somebody who didn't share his blood?

Zach had earned his way to this offer. He hadn't strong-armed or swindled or misled Fortunado into making this offer. He'd simply shown him that he was the best person for the job.

That's why it was even more important to not let the stricken expression on Maddie's face distract him from his goal. Kenneth had said, *May the best man— or woman—win.* Zach refused to feel guilty for trying.

He made his way down the dimly lit hall and paused in the threshold of her office door.

"Did someone forget to tell you you could go home?" he joked.

"What are you talking about?" Maddie said, without missing a beat. "This is home. I thought you'd cut out early—what the hell are you wearing?"

She scrunched up her nose and gave him a once-over from head to toe, then added, "What costume party are you attending?"

"I had an appointment," Zach said.

"Where? Billy Bob's Rodeo Clown School? This is a new look for you. And maybe not quite your style."

He smirked. At least she was still acting like herself. He shouldn't be surprised, he told himself. She was a professional. The Madeleine Fortunado he knew would never let anyone catch her brooding in the office.

"That's one of the reasons I came back to the office," he told her. "To change clothes."

Maddie grimaced. "You really went to your appointment dressed like that?"

"Sure. I bought the hat especially for the occasion." He tipped it onto his head. "Too bad you didn't get to see the truck. It pulled everything together."

She'd been in Austin on business for a few days and

he'd been out of the office closing some deals. They hadn't seen each other since their lunch on Monday.

He was glad to see her acting like herself.

"The truck?" she asked. "What are you talking about?"

She rolled her chair back from her desk and crossed one shapely, tanned leg over the other. The move inched her gray skirt up her leg a bit. Zach dared himself not to let his gaze fall.

"The ranch is over in Sisterdale. I rented a Ford F-150 to complete the ensemble." He gestured to his too-blue Wranglers. "I figured I might as well look the part when I met the client."

Maddie smirked as she smoothed her skirt down. "You know, ranchers can usually smell an imposter a mile away."

He cocked a brow. "Are you suggesting I'm not genuine?"

Maddie gave his ensemble a very slow, obvious head-to-toe perusal. He didn't mind her eyes on him one bit.

With the sleeves pushed up on his forearms, he looked unnervingly natural in that blue work shirt that emphasized his broad shoulders and trim waist where it was tucked into jeans. Damn if those Wranglers didn't fit him like he'd been wearing them for years. He'd finished the ensemble with cowboy boots that somehow were just scuffed enough to look authentic.

This was proof that the guy could wear anything and look hot.

"Given the fact that you drive a sports car and probably spend more money on a single suit than I spend on clothes for the entire year, yes, I'd say this is not a *genuine* look for you."

But damn, you look good—

Maddie bit back the words before they could escape and made a noise that was somewhere between a cough and clearing her throat as she made sure she swallowed them.

"Are you okay?" Zach asked.

Maddie waved him off. "Of course. I just have a tickle in my throat. Please tell me you didn't actually wear the cowboy hat."

"I did wear the cowboy hat. Why? Do you think I shouldn't have?"

That delicious mouth of his had turned up at the corners and Maddie knew he was trying to yank her chain. She was determined to play along, just as she was determined to prove to him that she wasn't the least bit affected by her father's bombshell, that she was secure in the challenge and would succeed easily in claiming what was rightfully hers.

But why Zach? Why did her dad have to challenge her with Zach? If he wanted to prove a point, he could've brought in someone from the outside. He could've poached a competitor or recruited some hotshot who raked in millions of dollars in sales.

No, he'd chosen Zach. Her crush. He didn't know that, of course.

"Maddie?" Zach said. "The hat? Shouldn't I have worn the hat?"

"Only if you wanted to look like an even bigger fool."

He winced. "Next time I'll know better."

"I suppose you bought the belt buckle, too?" Her gaze dropped to the oversize, square silver belt buckle that featured a gold-toned steer head right in the center.

"Yeah." His gaze dropped, too. She knew that he knew that her gaze had fallen due south. She crossed her arms to keep him from seeing the shudder of longing that rippled through her.

"It's a beauty, isn't it?"

Maddie swallowed hard and forced her eyes up.

"So, when are they going to make their decision?" she asked.

He smiled at her and she could've sworn he seemed happy that she'd been looking at him. God, she loved the way his blue eyes crinkled at the corners when he smiled. Eyes like that could sink ships and break hearts.

Right this moment was proof positive of that.

She needed to be careful. He was the enemy. The one person standing between her and everything she'd been working for. Yet, she couldn't resist flirting with him. Hell, forget the flirting. She wanted to walk right up to him and unbutton that blue shirt and see if his abs were as washboard flat as they looked. She wanted to relieve him of that belt with the ridiculous buckle and slip her hands beneath the waistband of those Wranglers and see if his hidden assets looked as promising as advertised.

"What do you mean?" he said.

She bit her bottom lip. "I mean are they talking to other brokers? When are they going to let you know?"

"Of course, they're not talking to other brokers. Do

you think I went to all this trouble and drove all the way out to Sisterdale to walk away without the listing?"

"You got the listing? Dressed like that?"

"Of course I did."

Maddie felt her cheeks flame as a little voice inside her said, *This is why your father is giving him a shot.* The logical part of her knew this was true, even though the emotional part of her swelled up and eclipsed the voice of reason.

She wasn't about to let him know it bothered her.

"Good for you," she said. "I guess it was worth dressing like a greenhorn."

He could have made a comment about going the extra mile and how it might do her some good to get out of her comfort zone and think outside the box like he did.

But he didn't.

All he said was, "Looks that way. Listen, I need to go finish up the paperwork."

"Right," Maddie said. "Are you going to the Thirsty Ox for happy hour?"

On Friday nights, a handful of Houston-area real estate professionals had a standing date to meet for drinks and compare notes. They were supposed to share tips and tricks, but mostly, it was a report card for the week, a show-and-tell as to who'd sold what and had secured the most listings. It was a license to brag and posture, masquerading as cooperative business. He hadn't been part of anything like that in San Antonio.

"That's right." Zach glanced at his watch. "That is tonight. I have to finish my paperwork, and I have a thing later tonight, but I think I can stop by for a few minutes."

It wasn't that he disliked sharing; he just wasn't used to operating that way. This was business. He didn't see how it helped to brag about your clients and closings. But to each his own. In the name of self-correction, he knew being more community-minded could only help him in his effort to win the Fortunado promotion. Kenneth was a social guy. In most regards, it was the only area in which he and Fortunado differed. Zach had always held his business ventures close to the chest, Kenneth's philosophy was that glad-handing only bolstered his business.

Maddie cocked a brow at him. "You have a *thing*? Is that a technical term or a formal occasion?"

He laughed. "Neither. It's just a *thing*. Don't you ever have *things*?"

"Can't say I do," she said. "I'm usually too busy working for that kind of nonsense."

"You need to get out more, Madeleine," he said.

Maddie was pretty in a natural way that some men might overlook, though her natural beauty wasn't lost on him. She had smooth skin, which she didn't hide with makeup. Her clothing usually leaned toward the expensively understated. While her clothes were never flashy or, God forbid, sexy, Zach recognized the good quality of the classics she chose. She usually wore her long blond hair pulled back off her face with a headband or ponytail. Tonight, she'd twisted it on top of her head and secured it with a yellow pencil. He considered ribbing her about her improvised hairstyle in the same fashion in which she'd kidded him about his faux cow-boy ensemble, but he thought better of it. Not tonight. Not when he still had work to do and then he had to go out to real estate show-and-tell.

As he stood there, he realized he wasn't sure how much they should tell the happy hour gang about the way Kenneth was auditioning his replacement.

Maddie was a strong woman. In fact, some consid-ered her downright prickly, which probably added to her untouchable quality. It was something that transcended the unspoken off-limits mandate of her being the boss's daughter. With her Ivy League education and her shel-tered upbringing, a woman like Maddie was way out of his league. Besides, in the little bit of time he had for pleasure, he wasn't looking for anything too serious or heavy. There would be plenty of time for that, after he'd secured his future. For now, he needed to keep his eye on the prize.

"We need to talk about your father's announcement and how we want to handle it if it comes up tonight," he said. "It has the potential to make things uncomfort-able between us, but I want you to know that it doesn't have to be."

"Okay." Her answer was remarkably level and de-void of emotion. He'd hoped that if she had a problem with it or harbored any resentment or lingering animos-ity toward him—Monday at their lunch it was apparent that she wasn't happy with the arrangement—he hoped they could talk it out.

"If you need to say anything to me, now is the time

to say it," he said. "Go ahead. Don't hold back. I can take it."

She looked at him as if he'd sprouted two heads.

"Such as you won't be offended if I tell you how much you're annoying me right now by talking to me instead of letting me get my work done? Is that what you mean?"

Her blue eyes flashed a mischievous glint as she smiled at him. There wasn't a trace of the hurt and animosity he'd sensed days ago. In fact, he half expected her to good-naturedly accuse him of trying to undermine her, but she didn't. So, he took it as his cue to exit.

He smiled back and held up his hands. "Sorry. I'll leave you to your work."

As he started toward his office, she said, "Zach?"

He turned back to her. "Yes?"

"You know I intend to win. What are you going to do when I do? I mean… Will you stay?"

They both needed to get to work. He wasn't going to stand here and go back and forth about who was going to win. They both wanted it.

"Honestly? I don't see how I could stay if I don't get the promotion. So, that means we're both in it to win it."

"I guess we are," she said. "Bring it on."

Chapter Four

Bring it on?

Maddie cringed inwardly as she replayed the conversation she'd had with Zach an hour ago in the office. She shouldn't have said it—again. It made her sound bitter and spiteful...and uncool. Not that she'd ever been cool a single day in her life.

She should've just kept playing it cool. But once again, she'd tacked on those final three words: *Bring it on.*

If Zach was going to leave Fortunado if—when— she won the promotion, then she might as well kiss him and get it out of her system.

She inhaled sharply at the rogue thought. She blinked and took a gulp of beer, glancing around the Thirsty Ox looking for colleagues, as if they might be able to read her mind if they were close by. The thought was ridiculous. Both thoughts were ridiculous: mind-reading colleagues and kissing Zach to get him out of her system.

But was it such a bad idea?

She was going to win. He was going to leave—and who could blame him? If Zach bested her for the promotion, would she really want to stay around? It wasn't that either of them were sore losers. It was a matter of principle, of self-preservation.

If he was going to leave anyway, why not just kiss him now and get it out of her system? Then she would be able to clear her mind—cleanse it of all lustful Zach McCarter thoughts—and better focus on the colossal task ahead of her. Because once she kissed Zach, it would be like popping a balloon. The illusion would be debunked. The great and powerful Oz would be exposed to be a mere mortal.

If that were true, then why were her lips tingling at the thought of tasting his, and her girl parts bucking for more than a kiss?

Oh, hell.

She crossed her legs, trying to stanch the need. Even though she thought she might want more, she told herself one taste would be enough to send her feelings for him into a downward spiral. That's how it had always worked in the past. A big buildup, only for the fireworks to fizzle out with a pitiful whimper.

Kissing Zach would be no exception.

Where is everyone?

Now, more than ever, she needed the distraction of colleagues talking shop. She'd arrived at the Thirsty

Ox a little later than usual since she'd been late getting out of the office. Usually, she was the first one here on Friday nights, single-handedly holding down the fort until the rest of their group arrived. But as she was wrapping up her day at the office, she'd figured some-one else could man up and hold the tables—usually the three six-toppers in the center of the pub. But when she'd walked in, she was surprised to discover she was, as always, the first to arrive.

The Thirsty Ox was their place of choice. There was an English pub in the front, where people could meet and order drinks and pub fare. In the back was a full-service restaurant. The casual atmosphere and de-licious food made it a popular place, and it was busy every day of the week, but at Friday happy hour, it was a madhouse.

By this time, they were all usually on their second or third beers, the ones who'd decided to stay later were considering adjourning to the restaurant in the back where they could enjoy offerings such as fish and chips and shepherd's pie. The ones who were just doing a drive-by were contemplating their departure.

Where was everyone?

She glanced around the place, its Tudor décor em-bellished with neon beer signs and perennial Christmas tree lights. The pub buzzed with groups playing darts and shooting pool amid the noisy music. But Maddie recognized no one—or had somehow missed them. It was a casual arrangement. No one RSVP'd, and not ev-eryone could make it every week, but there had never been an instance in the five or so years that they'd been meeting that everyone had been absent on the same night.

Everyone except for her. Because this was her big night out every week.

A little voice deep inside hollered up from the darkness, *You're twenty-nine years old. What if you've put all your eggs in one basket for nothing? If Zach wins, what will you do?*

Zach wasn't going to win. Kissing him would be her lucky charm, the motivator that would drive her over the finish line.

But what was she going to do? Walk up and plant a big smacker on him?

That's romantic.

There's nothing romantic about this.

Her lady parts begged to differ. *There could be.*

She got up from the bar and glanced in the back to see if her colleagues had skipped happy hour and headed straight to dinner. When she didn't see anyone, she grabbed a table for four that was newly open. Maybe others were late, or maybe they had other plans. Her sister Val had a date tonight. Maybe everyone had dates tonight. Zach had mentioned that he had plans. Maybe after the unceremonious brush-off she'd given him, he'd decided to skip happy hour and go straight to his thing that he had this evening.

Maybe she was the only one who didn't have a personal life outside of the office.

Maddie took another pull from the long-neck beer bottle, which she'd purchased just as happy hour was winding down. If no one showed by the time she finished her drink, she'd call it a night.

Why was she taking this so personally? The Friday night meet-up wasn't mandatory. It wasn't as if the lot of them had blown off her personal party. But she always looked forward to these get-togethers. It was the one time during the week that she let down her hair and blew off steam.

She really did need to get a life, didn't she?

Work had been her life. It was her boyfriend, her lover. She'd been so focused on climbing the corporate ladder, she hadn't had time to meet men and date. What a fool she'd been.

Her mind kept replaying her father telling her that there was no guarantee, that just because she was his daughter, he wasn't going to hand her the job.

All promotions must be earned.

When had she given him the impression that she was just sitting there waiting for him to hand it to her? That was the humiliating and maddening part. Maddie thought she was showing him her best by putting in eighteen-hour days, working weekends and forgoing vacations and dating. Obviously, her best wasn't good enough.

It'd been good enough to earn her the title of vice president of sales. Zach hadn't earned that title. He was just an associate broker who had a higher level of certification and experience than a basic real estate agent. Granted, he worked hard, but she was *family*. Even if her father thought they both had worked hard and saw the need for a tiebreaker, wouldn't blood win out in the end? How could he potentially pass her over for an outsider?

"Excuse me," said a guy who was part of a large rowdy group a few tables over. "Mind if I take a couple of these chairs?"

"I do mind," Maddie snapped, but tacked on a smile to ease the bluntness of her words. "I'm expecting friends."

Did he really think she came here by herself on a Friday night to have a beer alone at a table for four in the middle of a busy pub? Obviously so.

"Sorry," he murmured. As he turned to walk away, she called him back.

"On second thought," she said. "You can have them. I don't think I'm going to stay much longer."

"What about your friends?" he asked.

Apparently, they're not coming. They'd either been in and out of the place before she'd arrived or she was the only agent with free time on her hands on a Friday night. She could do the solo-girl bit at home, where she was more comfortable and looked less lonely.

"I guess they'll just have to fend for themselves."

The guy's concern lasted about as long as it took his biceps to bulge as he lifted two of the three chairs like he was curling dumbbells. "Cool."

As he walked away with the chairs, someone else came up behind Maddie and put a hand on one of the chairs. Without looking up, she said, "Sorry, someone else is using that chair."

"Who?" asked a familiar voice. "Did you bring a date?"

Her gaze snapped up as Zach sat down in the chair before the guy could return to claim it.

"No, I didn't bring a date," Maddie said. "I gave away the chairs since no one showed up tonight. He's coming back for that one, too."

"He can't have it. I'm using it," he said. "Where is everyone else?"

"Since I'm not the one in charge of this week's RSVPs, your guess is as good as mine."

Zach flinched and she realized she sounded snarky. She didn't mean to. He didn't deserve it.

"Do you want to talk?" he said.

"Talk about what?"

He arched a brow at her in a knowing look and she got the feeling that his patience wasn't infinite. That was fine. She didn't need the charity of his good nature. They were, after all, competitors.

She'd told Zach to *bring it on.*

Ugh.

One of them would win and the other would lose. It was that simple. Anything she divulged—including how unfair, how sexist, how messed up this whole situation felt—would just be tipping her hand. She would be confessing her own self-doubt and that would give him a big advantage.

She wouldn't say anything, but that didn't stop her from feeling every bit of outrage and disappointment. Nor did it stop the endless loop of inner monologue that played in her head.

On top of that, she was mad at herself for letting Zach get under her skin.

Winning should've been enough of an incentive to stay focused, to not let him get to her. But here he was with his sexy eyes and those adorable dimples and he was just making things worse. She should do something to take back her power—something that would give her no choice but to channel all her angry, petulant energy away from those lips and into winning.

"Are you sure there isn't something you want to talk about?" he asked.

As if he didn't know.

"What's there to talk about?"

He laughed. "Okay. I get it. You don't want to talk about it. But just an hour ago in the office, you seemed fine. Now you seem angry."

"I'm not angry. Why would I be angry?" she answered as a server came to take his drink order. The petite twentysomething blonde took on a dreamy quality when Zach smiled at her. Maddie couldn't blame her. Zach had that effect on most women under the age of ninety-five.

"I'll get this round," he said. "What are you drinking?"

"Don't you have a date tonight?" Maddie reminded him.

"A date?" he said as if he didn't understand. "I have plans later, but I don't know if I'd call it a date. What do you want to drink?"

She asked for another beer and Zach ordered the same along with a basket of the restaurant's homemade sweet potato chips.

A Mumford & Sons–type band took the stage and

started playing a loud folksy British-sounding tune. A group of four women stood up and began singing along and clapping with their arms over their heads. Someone in the room let out a long, loud whistle.

Maddie was looking around the room, everywhere but at him.

When the server left, she asked, "Are you meeting a woman?"

"Does it matter?"

"Well, I know I wouldn't appreciate it if a guy showed up for a date with beer breath."

"Good to know. I'll use some mouthwash."

"So, it is a date, then," she said, as if she'd tricked him into the confession.

"So, it does matter to you, then," he answered, a wide grin overtaking his handsome face.

The words were on the tip of her tongue. She tried to bite them back, but she was too late.

"And what if it does?"

In a split second, everything happened in slow motion. Zach's jaw dropped... and she leaned in and kissed him.

It was a whisper of a kiss, so unexpected—even to herself—that she felt his surprise as she braced her hands against his chest. But then, like sweet milk chocolate melting in the heat of the sun, his hard mouth softened and he kissed her back. He took control of the kiss, slowly at first, with lips and hints of tongue, his arms on her back.

His mouth tasted of mint and it fused with the hoppy flavor of the beer she'd been drinking. There was something else, an indefinable flavor that was uniquely him—something which she suddenly realized she'd been craving her entire life. She leaned in closer, not wanting the kiss to end. As if reading her mind, he slid his arms up to her neck, and opened his mouth, deepening the kiss, pulling her closer and sliding his hands into her hair.

The kiss faded into a gradual—almost reluctant— parting of lips, a tentative reclaiming of personal space, a cautious *oh,* Scheisse, *what do we do now?*

In the seconds that followed, she realized that the one kiss that she thought would cure her wasn't working that way at all.

She pressed her fingers to her lips.

As it turned out, kissing Zach to get him out of her system might not have been the cure-all she thought it would be. In fact, it might have opened Pandora's box.

Clearly, she hadn't thought this through as carefully as she'd thought she had; she'd simply reacted, followed her instincts, allowed the pin that held her heart together to be drawn to the steel magnet that was him. If she'd thought it through, common sense would've stopped her from doing something so imprudent. Something so deliciously, divinely, toe-curlingly stupid.

She took a deep breath and reminded herself that now the die was cast. With one kiss, she'd sealed their fate: she had to win and he had to go.

Maddie stood up. "I have to go."

No, he has to go. I have to leave.

"No, you don't," he said. "Because we have some

things we need to talk about. You can't just kiss me
and run away."

She grabbed her purse and fled the bar like Cinder-
ella running against midnight.

"Maddie," Zach said. "Don't leave."

But the noisy pub swallowed up his words before
they could reach her. Not that it would've done any
good if she'd heard him.

With her kiss fresh on his lips, he had to go after
her. He stood and pulled a twenty out of his wallet and
handed it to the bemused waitress who'd come with
their drinks. "Keep the change."

He took a few steps away from the table and scanned
the area between him and the door. The place wasn't
that big, but he didn't see her.

Madeleine Fortunado was a complicated woman.
She was well-bred, but she had a fiery temper. She was
fluent in three languages, but she drank American beer
from a bottle—in an English pub. She wore very little makeup but she dressed in expensive classics. She
had all the quiet tells of a woman who had been raised
with every advantage, but she rarely called attention
to herself.

Except when she was spontaneously kissing him.

Sure, she was fun to flirt with and, on a very super-
ficial level, he'd thought about dating her, but he'd ruled
it out just as fast because she was the boss's daughter.
But damn…he'd never wanted her in a physical way.
Until now.

Until she'd leaned in and kissed him and thrown his

equilibrium and everything he thought he knew about her out the window.

She wasn't at the bar. It was a safe bet that she'd already made it out the door.

He made it outside just as she reached her car.

"Maddie, wait." He sprinted toward her.

He was always in charge of himself. Usually, he had the upper hand with women. The bottom line was he had to so that he didn't give the women he saw the wrong idea. He had no room in his life for a relationship right now. Maybe someday, but not right now. That's why he never let it get that far. That's why he never got emotionally involved. He walked away before anything could take root. Maybe it was a chicken and egg thing. Maybe he could walk away because nothing had taken root. Not in a very long time. But that was another lifetime ago, before he was who he was now. That relationship had only reinforced the importance of not letting himself get too deeply involved. He'd learned that with his family when his folks died. His family had never been there for him.

He reached her just as she fished her keys out of her purse.

"Hey, what are you doing?"

She looked at him like he was crazy.

He should've let her go.

He should've just let her get in her car and drive away.

"I'm leaving?" she said like he was a dolt. And he was, for trying to make her stay.

He needed time to think, needed to put together the

right words. But standing there with the taste of her on his lips, he couldn't think. All he could do was feel and that was a dangerous thing.

"Don't go," he said over the merriment of a group of people who looked like they were ready to party as they made their way toward the building. She shot him a questioning look that was half surprise and half question. *What do you want from me?* She hitched her purse up onto her shoulder.

"Let's take a walk," he said. "Let's get out of here."

Night had already fallen on downtown Houston and the air had turned chilly. Maddie crossed her arms in front of her and was rubbing them.

"Are you cold?" he asked. "I wish I had a jacket to offer you. If you're uncomfortable, we don't have to walk."

She arched a brow. He read her expression to mean that the kiss had made this an uncomfortable situation. Yet here they were, neither of them acting very anxious to make an exit.

"What do you want, Zach?"

"I want to talk about what just happened in there."

She opened her mouth as if to say something, but stopped and shook her head.

"I'm sorry about that. I shouldn't have kissed you."

Now he was the one who was at a loss for words, when he should've said, *Yeah, and I shouldn't have kissed you back.*

Maddie took a step forward. "I suppose walking might help warm me up," she said over her shoulder at him.

Zach could think of several other ways that he could help her warm up, but none of them involved activities the two of them could do in public. God, that kiss really had done something to him. But it was just a kiss, he told himself.

That was the thing, though. It hadn't felt like *just a kiss*.

"Where do you want to go?" she asked when he stepped up beside her.

"Let's walk to the Paisley."

Her eyes widened for a moment, but then she visibly relaxed. "That's a great idea. It's just down the way."

"I know." He smiled at her. "It seems like neutral ground."

She nodded and locked her car with her key fob.

They were different in so many ways—she was all about family and connections, while he was a loner by nature—but they connected via business. And kissing, it seemed.

They started walking down Main Street, keeping silent and maintaining a safe distance between them until they reached the construction site.

Maddie was the one who broke the silence. "I kissed you because you said you weren't staying."

"I'm staying if I win the promotion," he said. "In all fairness, I should tell you I don't intend to lose."

"If you win, I'm not staying," she said. "So, either way, it was a goodbye kiss."

They sat down on the concrete steps leading up to the high-rise's front doors. The building looked finished on the outside, but the builder was still in the process of finishing the inside. The building was located in a popular area with lots of downtown nightlife, so a steady stream of people filed by on their way to the various clubs and restaurants.

"You'd really leave your family's business?" he asked her.

She slanted him a look. "Of course. How could I stay if my own father passes me over for a promotion? Never mind. You wouldn't understand."

She waved him away and crossed her arms.

"What makes you think that I wouldn't understand?" he challenged.

She laughed. It wasn't a condescending sound, more of a note of exasperation.

"Of course you couldn't understand. I do appreciate your attempt at empathy, but you have no idea what it's like when your father doesn't take you seriously."

She paused, but he sensed she wasn't finished. So, he let her continue.

"Everyone takes Zach McCarter seriously. All you have to do is smile and people—yes, both men and women—are putty in your hands and you can mold them and form them as you see fit. My father included. Somehow you've managed to wrap him around your little finger."

She blinked at him as if her words had surprised even herself.

"Are you finished?" he asked.

She shrugged.

"You have a point," he said. "I don't know what it's like for my father not to take me seriously. My father died when I was thirteen years old. My mother died two years later. My brother was too angry at the world or too self-absorbed to want the responsibility of raising me. So, he gave me away and let me cool my heels for the next three years in the foster care system."

Maddie's face had gone ashen. "Zach, I'm sorry. I didn't know."

"Of course you didn't know. Not many people do. It's not something I advertise, but I'm not ashamed of it either. That experience made me into the man I am today."

Maddie looked down, and for a moment the two of them sat in silence on the steps of the Paisley. The sound of people on the sidewalk in front of them, the building that would determine their future to their backs.

Why had he just told her that? He'd never shared that piece of himself with any other business associate. In fact, the only person he could remember opening up to was Sharla Grasse, the only woman who'd broken his heart. All those years ago.

"You shouldn't be ashamed of who you are," Maddie said. "You can't help it."

They were quiet again.

"So, that's another thing I didn't know about you," she said.

He nodded. "That means you're up one. You owe me one."

"Okay..." she said, drawing out the word as if she was thinking. "Something you don't know about me is I'm ashamed of myself for carrying on about my father. I must sound like an entitled brat to you."

He turned to her and shook his head. "You're human.

I can imagine how it would be to be in your shoes. It would suck. You were expecting one outcome and you were disappointed by the way your father handled it. Something I do know about you is you're a hard worker. You would be very deserving of this promotion. If—" He stopped and held up a finger as if to make a point. "Let me emphasize the word *if*—because I'm not giving up and I'm not letting up. If you get it, it will be because you earned it and not because your father handed it to you."

She started to say something, but Zach opened his fingers and held up his palm to stop her. "Something else you don't know about me is I think you have the advantage in this little contest we're in. I don't know that your father even knows it, but it's true."

She looked troubled.

"That's not true," she said.

"Maybe it's not, but I think it is. Now I'm one up on you. It's your turn to tell me something I don't know about you."

She laughed. "Well, whatever the case. Technically, that last one didn't count as a something I don't know about you. It was something you're thinking, but not something truly about you. So, I'll see you that one and raise you one. I think you're an incredibly kind, caring person. I think you have an incredible outlook and love of life despite what you've been through."

She had a small mole just below her right eye. How had he never noticed it before? It made her even more beautiful. Tonight, he'd noticed a lot of things about her he'd never taken the time to slow down and see. Those lips…those eyes…the fact that her teeth were perfect, but her nose was just slightly less than so. He drank her in greedily, wanting to commit to memory every single detail of how she looked at this very moment in the dusky May twilight, with her guard down. He wanted to lean in and kiss her—take one more taste, see if he remembered right and this time memorize how she tasted, how perfectly their mouths fit together, how the chemistry that had always buzzed between them turned into white-hot electricity when they kissed.

"Are you and your brother close now?" she asked.

The bluntness of her question pulled him off the ledge, kept him from leaning in and kissing her again. Had she sensed that was what he was about to do and searched for a question to kill the mood? If so, she'd chosen the perfect one. It was the verbal equivalent of a bucket of cold water.

"If that's too nosy, you don't have to answer," she said.

"I don't mind. No, we're not close. My brother and I haven't spoken in more than a decade."

Her brow knit into a look of concern. He could see the wheels turning.

"You're probably wondering why, if he's my only family, we're not close."

She nodded. "Yes, that's exactly what I was thinking. I mean, I come from this big, crazy, sometimes downright obnoxious family and I can't think of a single thing anyone could do that would make us estranged. If any of us had a problem that big, the other ones would lock us in a room until we'd worked it out. That is if we didn't insist on working it out ourselves."

"It's not that dramatic," Zach said. "In fact, it's actually rather anticlimactic. He never had time for me when I needed him. Once I got out and started making my way in the world we were both too busy to bother."

She squinted at him and gave her head a quick shake.

"I don't understand. Does he live in California or someplace far away?"

Zach chuckled. "Actually, he lives in Austin."

"What?" Maddie said. "You two were living in the same state and you didn't bother to get together? What are you not telling me? There has to be more to this that you're not saying."

There was, and for a solid minute he looked at her, remembering Sharla and how she'd left him after he'd unloaded his past on her. In one regard, Maddie was right. Zach knew he had a way with people. As long as he smiled and brought the sunshine, they were pretty much putty in his hands, as Maddie had said. But the minute things got too heavy, people left. People didn't like to be burdened.

"Zach, tell me. I mean, you've already told me this much. You might as well tell me the rest."

"Okay, tell me if you'd lock yourself in a room to work this one out. Before our mom died, she made my brother the beneficiary of a life insurance policy. It wasn't a lot of money, but it was enough. Enough for him to raise me. She made him promise to take care of me. Granted, he was barely of age. He didn't know anything about raising a punk teenage kid who was skipping school and getting into trouble. When things got too heavy for him to handle, and child services started poking around, telling him he could be held legally responsible for my truancy, he let them take me and put me in foster care."

Zach shook his head bitterly. "He said it was for the best. He was trying to put himself through college. When I asked about the money, he said after he got through law school, he'd put me through college if I kept my nose clean. There was always an *if*…and there was always a reason why it was never a good time to make good on his promise. He had too many bills, he was getting married, his kids needed braces. But the truth was he had his career and his family and his boat and fancy car. His lifestyle had probably expanded to the outer limits of his income, but he never made good on that promise. He took the money our mother left us and ran."

Maddie was looking at him as if he'd confessed his brother was an extraterrestrial. "How could he do that?"

"It sounds really sordid, doesn't it?" He hated her look of pity. "I don't know why I unloaded all that on you."

"Zach, you needed to tell someone. I'm sorry that happened to you."

He waved her off. "You don't need to be sorry. I've obviously done all right for myself. I asked him for help. He wasn't in the position to do it. It was fine. Like I said, fending for myself made me the person I am today. So, it's all good. No need to worry about me."

Except that he wanted to pull her into his arms and taste her lips again. She should worry about that.

Her kiss had unleashed a need in him that was proving difficult to ignore. He wanted to lean in and kiss her again. Hell, that wasn't all he wanted to do.

If Maddie knew what was good for her, she'd stay far away from him.

They'd had a moment. That was all.

They'd kissed and it couldn't be undone.

After she and Zach had parted ways the night before, Maddie had made a pit stop at the Kroger where she'd purchased a package of Oreo cookies and a pint of Ben & Jerry's Cherry Garcia, which she'd opted for over her usual go-to flavor, Half Baked, because it seemed to mock the very problem that had driven her to the junk food in the first place.

What kind of a half-baked notion had made her think it was a good idea to kiss Zach McCarter?

He'd been so nice to her afterward, too. Her heart thudded hard against her breastbone as she remembered the tenderness in his gaze. At one point, she'd wondered if he might kiss her again. Against all that was sane and good, she'd wanted him to. But he didn't.

Which was both the best and worst thing that could have happened.

Why did he have to be so nice? Especially after he'd suffered his own hardships? Why couldn't he have acted like a jackass and tried to move in for more? She would've put a stop to it in a big hurry. Or why couldn't he at least have let her walk away so she could've gone home and eaten her feelings in that emergency first aid of ice cream and cookies? If he would've let her walk away, she would've driven away feeling self-righteously superior that her suspicions about him had been confirmed: he was a player and a scoundrel, a wheeler-dealer who wasn't interested in her and only interested in winning.

Instead, he'd been concerned about her. He'd confessed her father's arrangement had surprised him as much as it had surprised her. For a few moments after they'd parted, she'd wondered if his confession had been a ploy, a means to play her by making her feel sorry for him. The rich girl would still have opportunities if she didn't get the promotion, but the poor man—though, now he wasn't a poor man by any means—was simply reaping the rewards of a life of hard work.

If he was trying to play her, he was being subtle. If he was being sincere, it was so sad to think that he had a brother to whom he hadn't spoken in over a decade. Sometimes men could be so stubborn. Surely, Zach wouldn't have made up a story about what drove him and his brother apart. But if they were each other's only family, and both of them were doing well, couldn't they sit down and talk things out? Sure, it was easy for her to play armchair referee. She'd been raised with every advantage, but even if the worst happened and her father hired Zach over her, even if she left Fortunado to start up her own venture, which she most certainly would do if it came to that, she would not allow it to drive a wedge between her and her dad. Nothing was worth more than family.

She couldn't stop thinking about what Zach had said about his brother.

His name was Rich and he was an attorney in Austin. She turned on the desktop computer in her home office. When it was fully booted, she searched for Richard McCarter, attorney.

The first item the search engine offered was the law offices of McCarter and Black.

Bingo.

Rich was easy to pick out of a photo of the firm's partners. He was a slightly older, less handsome version of Zach. Zach had obviously been the brother who had been blessed with the lion's share of the handsome genes. Not that Rich wasn't handsome.

There was another photo—a family photo used for an ad for Richard McCarter's run for city council—a failed bid, a bit more research showed. Even so, it showed him smiling up from a blue picnic blanket that was spread out beneath an ancient oak tree. A pretty brunette and three kids who looked to be in elementary and middle school surrounded him. For all intents and purposes, he looked like the quintessential family man. Of course, anyone could portray themselves however they wanted in a staged photo, but at face value, the guy looked like his family was important to him.

If so, how could he shut out his brother?

A plan was forming in the outer reaches of her mind. Lately, she'd been coming up with a lot of half-baked ideas—believing her father would promote her without making her jump through hoops, kissing Zach... Oh, yes, she seemed to be full of foolish ideas lately. What was one more, especially if she could help reunite a family? Yes, a definite plan was starting to take shape. Maybe she could play mediator to get Zach and his brother talking again.

A lot could change in a decade.

As she prepared to go over to her parents' house to meet her sisters—Carlo was out of town this weekend and Schuyler was driving in to spend a couple of days with family—she started scheming. She needed to go back to Austin for the closing of Carlo and Schuyler's house. They'd put in an offer on the mini Spanish castle overlooking Lake Austin and the seller had accepted it. Since it was a cash sale, they were due to close next week, right before the wedding. And she needed to show them more commercial properties to consider for the nightclub. While she was there, she might just have to pay Rich McCarter a visit and assess the damage.

More immediately, she needed to prepare herself to see her father. She needed to have a new mind-set. Today, she would put aside her wounded pride and re-double her determination to win the promotion. Sitting around feeling sorry for herself wasn't going to do her any good.

For that matter, neither was boycotting her favorite Ben & Jerry's ice cream flavor. The Cherry Garcia was delicious, of course, but not nearly as satisfying as Half Baked. This morning, as she tossed the empty ice-cream pint into the trash and sequestered the remaining Oreos in a zippered plastic bag, she was feeling bloated and unsatisfied, with a craving for cookie dough and brownie bites—and another taste of Zach.

She set the bag of cookies next to her purse so she wouldn't forget to take them to her parents' house, where she, Val and Schuyler were converging for a sisters' weekend. She seriously considered another Kroger stop before meeting them. They deserved ice cream— even though Schuyler had been last-minute wedding dieting.

Maddie put her hand on her stomach. To nip that temptation in the bud, she plucked the pint out of the trash and surveyed the nutritional panel.

After adding up the caloric count, she dropped the container like it was burning her fingers. Nearly five hundred calories and an entire day's worth of fat grams in one pitiful pity-party-for-one. And that didn't include the Oreos.

Zach's kiss had been much sweeter.

She blinked away the thought and reminded herself that she'd have to work out extra hard on Monday since she wouldn't have time to hit the gym this weekend. It would be good to have an outlet for her pent-up emotions.

Zach McCarter didn't stand a chance.

"Bring it on," she murmured to Ramona, her two-year-old corgi, who had padded into the kitchen and was leaning against Maddie's leg as if showing her solidarity. Maddie leaned down and scratched the little dog behind her ear. The animal stared up at her with soulful eyes as if trying to understand what she was saying.

"I know," Maddie said. "The whole thing doesn't make any sense to me either. What can I do other than give it my best shot?"

The dog plopped down on top of Maddie's foot. "At least I know you're on my side, Ramona. But we must go now. You're coming with me to Grandma's house. We're going to spend some time with Aunt Schuyler and Aunt Val. Doesn't that sound like fun?"

Maddie gently extricated her foot and bent down to give the little dog one more scratch, relishing the silky softness of her velvety sienna ear before attaching the leash. Ramona gazed up at her lovingly. Maddie grabbed her purse and the bag of Oreos and headed out the door.

Chapter Five

Forty-five minutes later, Maddie got out of her white Volvo, smoothed her yellow sundress and walked around to the passenger side to free Ramona from her doggie seat belt, and fetch her parcels. A small bag contained her dog's food, dishes, treats and toys, and another larger shopping bag contained the bag of Oreos and a dozen assorted cupcakes from Moonbeam Bakery, the home of Houston's most delicious baked goods. She'd resisted a Ben & Jerry's run, but this occasion called for cupcakes.

Val's car wasn't in the driveway yet, but Schuyler's sleek red BMW was parked front and center and Maddie smiled at the thought of having some sister time. Since Schuyler had moved to Austin and she and Val worked so darn much, times like this were fewer and farther between.

Seriously, when was the last time she'd taken an entire Saturday off? Even though she intended to win the promotion, the pragmatic side of her wondered if maybe this episode with Zach and the promotion was the universe's way to teach her about balance. Really, she couldn't go on the way she'd been going. It made her realize that if all the material things were stripped away, what would she have? She'd have her family, of course, but her parents were prepping for the second chapter of their lives and her little sister was getting married.

Forty years down the road did she want to be Crazy Old Aunt Maddie? Did she want her siblings and future nieces and nephews whispering about her behind her back, calling her the spinster sister?

No.

In that spirit, today would be about fun. As she closed the distance between the driveway and the grand front porch, her phone pinged, alerting her that a new message had come in. Reflexively, she glanced at it as she walked toward the huge wooden double doors of her parents' home, but resisted checking it. She had her hands full with precious cargo. She certainly didn't want to upset the cupcakes before her sisters had a chance to ooh and aah over the little works of art, and gripe and curse her for bringing them because they were trying to diet.

But in the end, they'd eat them—between the four of them—Schuyler, Val, their mother and herself, they'd probably polish them off.

She might even offer one to her dad to prove she harbored no ill feelings over the Zach situation.

Liar.

She braced herself for the likelihood that before the weekend was through, she and her sisters would probably ponder how their father could, in his right mind, consider turning the family business over to Zach. It would feel good to have them rally around her.

But she wouldn't tell them she'd kissed Zach. Because she probably wouldn't be able to fashion a poker face that didn't betray how much she'd loved that kiss.

If the girls started dissing Zach and their dad too much, she would remind them that this was in her power. She had this. She wouldn't allow their dad to turn the company over to Zach or anyone else who wasn't part of the family. It suddenly dawned on her that maybe this whole competition was nothing but a charade. Her father's way of posing one last challenge.

She breathed in the sweet smell of a sunny spring day and redoubled her determination to accept this situation for what it was: one last hoop for her to jump through, manufactured by Kenneth Fortunado before he turned loose his life's work for a life of leisure.

She couldn't stop thinking of how Zach and his brother had let money come between them. Even if her own pride was hurt by the way her father had handled things, Maddie put herself in his shoes. She knew turning over the company had to be hard for her dad. A wave of sympathy tenderized the anger she'd been chewing on all week. Letting go of his empire wasn't easy. She couldn't—or at least she shouldn't—blame him for flexing his power muscles one more time. In the effort of being a good daughter, she would not only give him this, she would prove to him that he had nothing to worry about.

Maddie let herself and Ramona in the front door and followed the sound of voices and puppy barks.

"Fluff and Stuff are here!" Maddie told her dog. "Are you excited to play with your cousins?" Ramona answered with an excited bark and quickened her pace, her nails clicking on the hardwood floors as she trotted toward the kitchen. That's where she found her mother and Schuyler seated at the marble island with a bunch of brochures spread out in front of them. Schuyler's puppies played rough-and-tumble on the expansive kitchen floor.

The little dogs stopped their acrobatics as they sensed Ramona enter the room. Soon the three dogs were happily chasing each other around like long-lost friends.

Unfortunately, the same air of goodwill wasn't flowing between Schuyler and Barbara. In fact, the tension was nearly palpable and Maddie quickly realized they were engaged in a lively debate about wedding flowers.

"I really think we should scrap the orchids and opt for extra peonies," their mother said. "Peonies will hold up much better than orchids. They're so fragile. You don't want your flowers to be drooping before you walk down the aisle."

"But I like the clean, simple look of orchids. It completely changes my vision if we don't have orchids. Peonies are so froufrou."

"Hi," Maddie said. Both women turned toward her.

"Hi, honey," Barbara said. "I'm glad you're here. And where is my little granddog Ramona?"

Ramona yipped and broke away from the pack only long enough to put her front paws on Barbara's leg. Barbara reached down and gave her a loving scratch behind the ears.

Ramona seemed like a welcome distraction, even if it was just momentary. "Schuyler and I were just putting the finishing touches on the flowers for the wedding," Barbara said. "Come in and tell us your thoughts."

The wedding was right around the corner. Schuyler and their mother were past the point of fun and ready for the big day to get here. Reading between the lines, Maddie knew what her mother really meant was, *Come in and be the tiebreaker.*

Where was Val when she needed her?

"My knowledge of flowers is basically roses are red, violets are blue," Maddie said. "Although, I always thought violets were purple. But maybe that proves that I'm a disaster when it comes to color or at the very least I'm color-blind."

"You are not a disaster when it comes to color," her mother said. "As a matter of fact, you're very good at it. Look at all those homes you've staged and sold. If that's not proof, then I don't know what is. I've been telling your father that." Barbara arched her brows. Her expression made it clear that she did not approve of the way her husband had handled things. Of course, Barbara Fortunado was a mama bear personified. She couldn't stand to see her babies hurt, and it gave Maddie a great deal of satisfaction to know that her mother was on her side.

Her mother never shied away from voicing her opinion—
like with Schuyler's wedding flowers—but when it came
to things that involved her kids, she was also their best
advocate. Fiercely loyal, she would go to the mat for her
babies. If Maddie knew her mother as well as she believed she did, Barbara probably hadn't minced words
when she'd voiced her disapproval to her husband. However, Barbara was also a Southern lady. Southern ladies
did not talk ill of their husbands to anyone—especially
not to their daughters.

"Come in." Barbara's stool scraped the hardwood
kitchen floor as she pushed it away and stood. She took
the cupcakes and Oreos out of Maddie's hands, un-
bagged them, and placed them on the island.

The zippered bag of cookies seemed to scream that
Maddie had recently binged. For a second she contemplated pretending like she'd brought them as a garnish
and sticking one in each of the cupcakes' fluffy icing.
But she wasn't sure Oreo would go with the various fla-
vors. No, she was better off leaving well enough alone.

She was a connoisseur, not Martha Stewart. She
knew her strengths and her limits, and that was a
strength she was proud of.

"Sit down," her mother told her. "Try some of these
stuffed mushrooms and brisket-wrapped asparagus that
the caterer sent all the way from Austin with Schuyler
for us to try."

Schuyler and Carlo were getting married in the
sculpture garden at the Mendoza Winery in Austin,
which Carlo and his cousins had purchased last year.
The reception would be catered by La Viña, the win-

ery's restaurant that overlooked the vineyard. It would be a stunning evening.

Maddie's heart twisted. She was so happy for her sister and she didn't begrudge her one single second of the happiness she'd found with Carlo and the thrill of feeling like a princess as she planned this once-in-a-lifetime event. But since her father had dropped the bomb, Maddie had to admit, beneath the anger, she'd discovered a gaping hole. Something was missing from her life and when she saw how happy and complete Schuyler looked after meeting the love of her life, Maddie wanted the same for herself.

Or at least she did in theory. In reality, allowing herself to lose control and fall in love was a scary prospect.

"All the way from Austin, huh?" Maddie asked.

Schuyler nodded. "They sent them in one of those insulated bags so they'd stay warm. I think they're delicious. What does my maid of honor think?"

"They look fabulous," Maddie said and helped herself to a mushroom.

"Let me fix you a glass of iced tea." Barbara was fussing over her just a little too much. It made Maddie wonder if her mom was overcompensating for her dad's promotion challenge. Kenneth Fortunado might be the head of his real estate empire, but there was no mistake that Barbara ruled the roost at home. Maddie wished she could've been a fly on the wall when her mother had first heard the news. Although Barbara was never one to interfere in her husband's business matters, she held an MBA and was an astute businesswoman in her own right. She ran the Fortunado Foundation, working with the financial gurus who oversaw the nonprofit's vast portfolio and beneficiaries, which mostly consisted of women and children.

"How are you, honey?" Concern was etched on Barbara's face as she slid a large glass of tea, complete with lemon round and mint sprig, in front of Maddie, who was still standing. "Are you doing okay?"

"I'm fine, Mom." Maddie squared her shoulders and smiled as if she hadn't noticed her mother's pained look. "How are you?"

She bit into a spear of asparagus.

"Just fine, sweetheart. I'm so happy to have all my girls here today. Or at least we will be once Val arrives."

Maddie nodded. "These are great, Sky. I vote yes on both."

Barbara was peering at her with a look that registered somewhere between motherly concern and tiptoeing on eggshells. It was as if she might be able to spot the crack in Maddie's facade if she looked closely enough. But all cracks and bruises had been carefully patched and concealed. Her mother would be hard-pressed to detect even a hint of damage.

Schuyler seemed oblivious to her mother's delicate questioning.

"Whatcha got there, Mads?" she asked, eyeing the items their mom had placed on the granite island.

"Cookies and Moonbeam Bakery cupcakes." Maddie reached for the box and slid it down to her sister.

Schuyler held up her fingers in the sign of the cross. "You she-devil! Keep those cupcakes away from me.

You know I'm trying to diet so I can fit into my wedding gown. How could you?"

"If you lose any more weight, your wedding gown is going to fall off," Maddie said. "Come on, Sky, it's a girls' weekend. We deserve a treat."

"Yes, we do," Barbara said, as she untied the light blue ribbon with the trademark white stars. Their mother lifted the lid and inhaled deeply. "My, oh, my, they smell good. I call dibs on the sweet tea cake with lemon icing."

Schuyler scrunched up her nose. "And you brought us a half-eaten package of cookies? Are the Moonbeam cupcakes just a Trojan horse to hide the fact that you're trying to unload all your leftover sweets on us?"

"No, Schuyler." Maddie flashed a mischievous smile at her sister. "You don't have to eat them. There will be more for us, right, Mom?"

Except, that was exactly why she'd brought the cookies to her parents' house, to get them out of her own house.

Schuyler reached over and helped herself to a cookie. She separated it, exposing the creamy center, which she scraped with her teeth.

"Save some for the rest of us," Maddie chided, snatching one for herself.

"Girls," their mom reprimanded.

Even though this was the way Maddie and her sister had always communicated—they gently sparred—they didn't mean anything bad by it. They certainly didn't wish each other any harm. They were simply as different as the tortoise and the hare—in every regard—and this was one of the ways they celebrated their differences.

"Maddie, why don't you put the cookies and cupcakes on a plate?" Barbara reached into the cabinet and pulled out a colorful ceramic platter she'd purchased in Italy on one of the rare vacations she'd managed to coerce her husband into taking. She handed it to her daughter, who prepared to do as her mother suggested.

"Where's Carlo this weekend?" Maddie asked, happy to change the subject.

"He's in Napa this weekend, taking care of some vineyard business before the wedding."

A quip about when Dad was going to meet with Carlo to arrange the final payoff for his agreeing to marry Schuyler played through Maddie's head. Even though it was meant as good-natured teasing, she stopped short of saying it because it might sound mean. As much as she and her sister loved to banter, Maddie feared that would cross the line. At worst, it might hurt Schuyler's feelings; at best it might make Maddie look jealous. And she was. Sort of. Well, not the begrudging type of jealous, simply the type that wished she had someone who loved her as much as Carlo loved Schuyler.

"Napa?" Maddie echoed. "I'm surprised that you didn't go with him. Napa is gorgeous this time of year."

"It's always gorgeous," Schuyler said, "and there will be plenty of opportunities for us to visit in the future, but this might be my last chance for a sisters' weekend while I'm still single."

Schuyler had made it clear that instead of a party-hard bachelorette party, she wanted a nice, quiet pampering weekend with her sisters.

It suddenly dawned on Maddie that *this* was that weekend.

Had she been so self-absorbed that she'd nearly forgotten her sister's bachelorette party? God love Schuyler for being willing to meet her halfway—and with such a good nature, too. Her sister had taken it upon herself to show up. The least she could do was provide the bachelorette weekend of her sister's dreams.

At that moment, they heard Val sing, "Hello!" from the hallway. Like magic, she appeared with a bouquet of pink and gold balloons and a shopping bag from the liquor store.

"Where's my favorite bride-to-be?" she said. "Are you ready for a sisters' weekend of a lifetime?"

Val set down the bag and fished out a beauty pageant–type sash that aptly said *Bride-To-Be* in gold glitter, along with a plastic tiara with rhinestones and a strip of baby pink marabou at the base. Schuyler squealed.

"Let's get this party started," Val said. "I brought the champagne. And I got us fancy glasses."

Val set out four bottles of Veuve Clicquot rosé and four painted wine goblets, that were customized to each of the women present.

Schuyler's, of course, said *Bride-To-Be*. Their mother's glass said *MOB Boss*—MOB meaning mother of the bride. Maddie's was Maid of Honor, but should've said *Self-absorbed Slacker*; and Val's said *Favorite Sister*.

Not only did Val deserve that title, but Maddie wanted to add *Goddess* and *Lifesaver*. Her little sister had saved the day and she was making it appear that she and Maddie had planned everything this way.

She was humbled. Even though she hadn't forgotten Schuyler's visit, she had been so caught up in her own issues that she'd been failing on her maid of honor duties. But Val—fabulous, wonderful Val—had quietly picked up the slack.

Maybe she didn't have it as together as she thought. Maybe she still needed to grow a little bit—rather than being fully formed and perfectly ready to step into the Fortunado president's role. If she could forget her sister's bachelorette party, she needed to take a step back and see what else she was missing. But not now. She'd already spent too much time focused inward. She wasn't going to do that this weekend. But she did file away an urgent mandate to do some serious inventory at the beginning of the week.

Schuyler opened the first bottle of sparkling rosé with a loud *pop* of the cork. It caused the champagne to foam up out of the bottle and spill down over the neck.

"Oh, Schuyler," Barbara good-naturedly reprimanded. "Let me get a dishcloth to clean up that mess."

"No, Mom," Maddie said. "You relax. I'll get it."

Barbara put a hand on her oldest daughter's shoulder. "Oh, honey. Let me do it. You've been working so hard with all that your father has put on you this week."

Maddie silenced her mother with a nearly imperceptible shake of her head. Thank goodness, the astute woman caught on. The last thing they needed right now was for the attention to be diverted from Schuyler to the race for the Fortunado presidency. The last thing

Maddie wanted to deal with right now was Schuyler peppering her with questions about Zach.

Too late.

"Speaking of working hard," Schuyler said. "How's everything with Zach? Have you two had that Ping-Pong date yet?"

"No, we haven't." Maddie kept her voice light. "Is there anything special you want to do this weekend, Sky?"

"I swung by the Thirsty Ox last night," Val said as she gave her sister a knowing look. "I saw that you and Zach were the only ones from our usual group. So, I didn't stay. The two of you looked pretty intense."

Val arched a brow before she picked up the bottle and started serving the champagne.

Val had seen them? *Oh, crap. What else did she see?*

And why was she bringing it up? She was in dire danger of losing her "favorite sister" status if she wasn't careful.

"So, you and Zach were getting intense at the Thirsty Ox last night?" Schuyler's mouth fell open and her eyes were huge and greedy.

"Yes, a bunch of us always go there for happy hour on Friday nights." Maddie shrugged it off like it was no big deal and let her gaze fall to her mother who was mopping up the spilled pink champagne and watching the scene unfold like she had a ringside seat at the roller derby.

"But it was just you and Zach. And Val says you were getting intense." Schuyler raised an eyebrow. "What exactly does that mean, Mads? And more important, is there something brewing that we should know about? Come on, Maddie. Spill it. I'm the bride-to-be. This is my party. I demand to know."

Oh, there was something brewing, all right. Only, not in the way her sister was insinuating.

An emotional storm was brewing. A storm of gargantuan proportions. If Val saw her kissing Zach—and judging by how coy she was acting, Maddie had a sinking feeling she had seen them—Maddie predicted there might be some squalls this weekend.

"Calm down, Bridezilla." Maddie rolled her eyes at her sister. "I've already told you he's not my type."

Schuyler scrunched up her pretty face. "Well, okay. Since you brought it up, what *is* your type, Mads?"

"My type doesn't really matter because I haven't even had time to think about what my type would be." *Liar. It's Zach.* "Even if I knew, I'm too busy working to date."

"I don't buy that." Schuyler squinted at Maddie.

Maddie shrugged. "Sorry to disappoint you, but that's my life right now. I'm happy for you and Carlo. You found each other. You're going to marry the love of your life and that's great. But you know what, Sky? I'm perfectly happy with my life the way it is."

Double liar. Maddie purposely avoided eye contact with her mother since the woman sometimes possessed the uncanny ability to read her mind.

"But you're bringing a date to the wedding, right?" Schuyler was undeterred.

"Probably not." She took a bite of her cookie.

"Why not?"

"Did you not hear what I just said? I'm not bringing just anyone to a family wedding and I certainly don't have time to go out and meet someone now."

"You should ask Zach," Schuyler said.

The way Maddie's breath hitched at the suggestion made her swallow wrong and choke on her cookie.

Barbara clapped Maddie on the back.

"Mom, I'm fine. I just—" Another round of coughing preempted Maddie's words.

"Here." Barbara thrust her glass of sparkling rosé at Maddie. "Drink this."

Grateful for the diversion, Maddie took the champagne and took a long swallow. The bubbles tickled her nose and burned the back of her throat, making her eyes water.

"Gosh, I didn't mean to get you all choked up," Schuyler said. "Who knew that the mere mention of Zach McCarter would do that."

As Maddie blinked away the moisture that had gathered in her eyes during her coughing fit, a stifling heat settled around her. It had her pulling at her dress and trying to ignore the way the searing heat burned her cheeks.

"Even more reason that you should bring him as your date to the wedding," Schuyler said.

"And on that note," Maddie said, "I think we need to have a toast."

Barbara jumped up. "And after that I'll just go put these extra bottles in the spare refrigerator. I wouldn't want them to get warm."

The Fortunado women held up their glasses. "To a

fun weekend together," Maddie said, trying to infuse enough happiness into her voice that it would sway them to change the subject. "And to family, the most important thing in the world."

After they clinked glasses, Barbara snagged an Oreo off the plate and popped it into her mouth. Before she grabbed the unopened three bottles and walked out of the kitchen, she turned to her daughters. "You girls behave yourself. And, Schuyler, eat a cupcake and don't bully your sister about bringing a date. This may be your weekend, but it doesn't give you a license to abandon your manners."

Maddie could have kissed her mom. She loved her sister, but sometimes Schuyler had a one-track mind. Like a bulldog with a bone, she could latch onto things and not give up. Case in point: Schuyler was happily engaged to Carlo Mendoza and therefore thought everyone should be as happily in love as she and Carlo.

Nice idea in theory, but not exactly practical for the rest of the nonromantics of the world. But you might as well speak Latin to Schuyler instead of trying to explain this concept. She couldn't seem to comprehend that not everyone was destined to meet their soul mate.

If only.

Barbara had no more than cleared the kitchen when Schuyler set down her glass and turned to Maddie.

"I know you've been super busy with work. But you're free this weekend." Schuyler's eyes had a certain glint that scared Maddie.

"No, I'm not free. It's your bachelorette party. It's

our sisters' weekend. I'm very busy—we are going to be busy—and I wouldn't have it any other way."

She would be crazy busy next week working a whole lot more since it was the final week to put the finishing touch on the Paisley proposal and reel in the deal so she could secure her future.

"I know that," Schuyler said. "And I appreciate that you're devoting a whole weekend to me when you have so much on your plate. So, I'm going to make it extra simple for you. You know what I want to do tonight?"

"I'm afraid to ask, but I have a feeling you're about to tell us."

"You're darn right I am." Schuyler knocked back the champagne that was in her glass and held it out for Val to pour some more. "I want to play Ping-Pong tonight."

Oh, no, she wasn't—

"And I want one gorgeous guy to come over and play with us."

Schuyler bit her bottom lip and looked as if she might explode with delight as she milked the situation for all it was worth.

"Val, would you be a sweetheart and call Zach Mc-Carter and ask him to join us tonight?"

"Maddie brought cupcakes." Schuyler thrust the open box at Zach, and Maddie wanted to hide under the Ping-Pong table. "Try one."

"I'd love to sample your sweets," he said, his eyes locking with Maddie's, and damned if she didn't feel the heat flood her cheeks again.

It was a game to him.

Well, two could play that game.

"Right here? In my parents' house? Aren't you brave."

She held his gaze and watched him mentally back-pedal.

Sort of.

"I never have been able to resist a good cupcake. How did you know they were my favorite?"

She couldn't take her eyes off his as he bit into it. She hated herself for melting just a little on the inside. And, wow, nice of her sisters to be so facilitating. Calling him up and somehow persuading him to drop everything to come over for cupcakes and Ping-Pong. Were they in middle school?

Maddie glanced at them, but they were pretending to be engrossed in a conversation of their own.

After what transpired last night, this was possibly the most awkward situation she'd been in in a long time. She didn't know whether to curse her sisters for making it happen or pledge her undying gratitude.

This was either the beginning of something disastrous...or something very, very good.

Chapter Six

"Ready to get down to business?" Zach asked after he'd finished his cupcake—dark chocolate with mocha icing. "Best three of five? Winner of each round is the person who reaches ten first."

Standing in the Fortunado recreation room, staring across the long green tennis table at Maddie, Zach couldn't imagine any place else he'd rather be right now. Even with Schuyler and Val sitting on the sidelines, lost in conversation about who knew what, not really paying attention.

"Sure." Maddie grimaced at Schuyler. "The winner can play the guest of honor."

Schuyler pointedly stared at Val, acting completely engrossed in their conversation.

When Val had called him and extended the invitation to come over—to play Ping-Pong, of all things—he wondered if this was a setup orchestrated by the sisters on behalf of Maddie. What had she told them? He'd had other plans, but he had immediately rescheduled them.

Why not? He hadn't engaged in a good round of table tennis in years. It seemed like a good way to break the ice after the events of the previous night. Even if Maddie's sisters had in mind a personal outcome for Maddie and him, he would steer this get-together another way. It would be a fun, nonthreatening way to get him and Maddie back on the business track. They were meeting with Dave Madison, the developer of the Paisley, first thing Monday morning. It would be a good opportunity to go over their strategy so that their Monday meeting with Madison would be seamless and, most important, successful. They had one week before the wedding, one week before Kenneth would make his decision.

"You serve first." Zach tossed the ball across the table to Maddie. She caught it with a deft swipe of her left hand and proceeded to bounce the ball on the table with the paddle, showing off her skills.

Maddie was quieter than usual. Almost to the point of seeming that she didn't want him there. Zach was feeling a little subdued himself. That was even more reason that they needed to get over the quicksand of awkwardness and back on stable ground. He was happy to be the one to lead the way.

"Now you're just showing off." Zach picked up the beer Schuyler had offered him when he'd arrived. "Where are your parents?"

"They're out tonight." She rolled her eyes. "Disappointed that you won't get to try to score some personal points with Daddy?"

"No, just having flashbacks to high school," he said. "Playing Ping-Pong and drinking beer while the parents are out."

"Is that how you spent your Saturday nights?" Maddie asked.

"Embarrassingly, yes. Quite a few."

They laughed.

"So, you were a nerd, Zach?" she said.

"Be careful how you toss around that word," he said. "I seem to remember someone saying your past is steeped in the game, too."

"I love nerd couples," Schuyler said from the sidelines.

Both Zach's and Maddie's heads swiveled to look at her.

"Schuyler." Maddie glared at her sister. "Can you not?"

Ah, so there was an ulterior motive.

Zach didn't hate the idea.

He hadn't been completely immune to that kiss. If he was honest, it had taken everything in his power to stop himself from leaning in and kissing her again.

He'd woken up this morning thinking about that kiss and—

"Prepare to be annihilated, McCarter."

A second after the warning, Maddie served, sending the ball over the net with lightning-quick precision. He barely had time to raise his paddle before it bounced off the edge of the table.

"One, zip," Maddie said.

"Hey, I thought we were both supposed to be ready before we started," Zach protested as he put down his beer, retrieved the ball and rolled it across the table to her.

"McCarter, I'm always ready. I thought you were, too. Obviously, I was mistaken."

"You're always ready," Zach repeated. "That's one of the things I like about you."

"Let's get this over with," she said, making the ball dance with several whacks of the paddle.

"Do you have somewhere you need to be?" he asked, noting the edge in her voice.

"Tonight is my sister's bachelorette party. The last thing I planned on doing was playing a match of Ping-Pong with you."

She really didn't want to be here. She didn't want him there either. "The last thing, huh? Well, at least I was on your list, even if I was the last thing."

She shot him a perplexed look. "I have no idea what you're talking about. I planned a party. You weren't invited."

She leaned forward to launch her second serve and a hint of cleavage peeked out of her top. Zach tore his eyes away.

"Ouch," he said, returning the ball like he meant business. "That's mean. Do you want me to leave?" They volleyed several rounds. "When Val invited me over, I didn't realize you had other plans. I'll go."

Maddie looked up and the ball she'd returned hit the net.

"I always finish what I start," she said.

"Do you?" He gave her a knowing look and her cheeks flushed a pretty shade of pink.

She lifted her chin a notch. "Always. Your serve."

The raw look in her eyes coupled with the memory of her kiss made him imagine exactly how they might finish that kiss. If they were going to finish what they'd started, it would have to go a lot further than a kiss.

He answered by slamming the ball across the table. She returned it with equal force.

Innuendo was not the way to get them back on steady business ground. He tried a more direct approach.

"I had lunch with Dave Madison today."

Maddie missed the ball, but rather than going after it, she set down her paddle on the table. "He's out of town. How could you have had lunch with him?"

"He got back last night. Dave and I go way back."

She put her hands on her hips. Zach noticed that somewhere along the way, Val and Schuyler had left the room. "You didn't tell me you're BFFs with Dave Madison."

"I don't know if I'd go so far as to call him my BFF."

"Quit being flippant."

"I'd say calling Dave my BFF has quite a bit of *flip* to it."

"Why didn't you tell me, Zach? Why were you keeping that little tidbit to yourself?"

"I just told you."

"Did you know this last night?"

"I did."

"You kissed me and you didn't bother to inform me

you were meeting with Dave or, even better, invite me to join you?"

"If I recall, you were the one who initiated the kiss."

Her cheeks flushed again, but this time her eyes flashed. "Don't change the subject. Zach, we promised that we were going to work together on this project. Withholding information like that is not working together. I think you should go."

"I think we need to sit down and talk about this before we meet on Monday. If not, we're not going to bring our A game."

"I wanted to trust you, but I guess you're no better than anyone else who is out for himself. So much for working together."

Reading between the lines, he could take her *no better than anyone else* comment as she was comparing him to his brother, Rich. She didn't say it, but the suggestion was there. Or maybe that was still a tender spot with him. Either way—whether she was stealthily punching below the belt or he was drawing his own conclusion—it stung. He should've never confided in her—or anyone—but mostly her. Because for some reason, Maddie Fortunado made him feel emotionally vulnerable in a way he hadn't felt in years.

Why else would he have come over here so eagerly, rearranging his Saturday evening plans so he could see her under the guise of an asinine game like Ping-Pong?

"It's two-one," Zach said. "If you quit now, I win. You'll owe me five *one things*."

"Because this is all just a game to you, isn't it?" She

looked him up and down and he'd never felt so naked and exposed. Was that how she saw him?

"Fine, Zach. You win. That's all you wanted. It seems to be the only thing that's important to you."

It's not the only *thing.*

She started to walk out of the room.

"Maddie, stop. Come back, please. I didn't tell you because I knew you would want to come."

She whirled around. The intensity of her glare nearly leveled him.

"Wow. Thanks for that, Zach." Her voice dripped with sarcasm. "I feel so much better now that I know your true intentions."

"That's out of context. Let me finish."

He looked up at the ceiling, trying to gather his thoughts. Never had a woman had the ability to rattle him like she did. He prided himself on being unshakable. How the hell did she do that?

Why the hell are you letting her do it?

"Dave and I go way back. I knew him from Dallas when I was there. Long before I started working for Fortunado. I wanted to use this lunch to ease into the subject of us taking over as the exclusive listing agents for the Paisley. If you would've come, it would've obviously been a business lunch. You and I are work associates. What was I supposed to say? 'This is Maddie Fortunado. She and I want your business?' It wasn't that kind of lunch. I couldn't bring you. It's not like you're my girlfriend."

The nanosecond the words left his mouth, he knew he'd put his foot in it deep.

Jackass.

"No, I'm not your girlfriend," Maddie said. "Let's just get that straight right now. I'm sure I have absolutely nothing in common with the women you date. Therefore, you and I have nothing in common beyond work. You bring your A game on Monday and I'll bring mine. We should be perfectly fine. Goodbye, Zach."

She wasn't his girlfriend. If it hadn't been clear before, it was perfectly clear now. And so was the fact that she had embarrassed herself by kissing him.

Every time she thought she had the upper hand, Zach surprised her and came out of nowhere with a better, stronger plan.

Case in point: his clandestine lunchtime meeting with Dave Madison.

"I still can't believe you made him leave," Schuyler said as they sat in the living room after Zach's departure. "Val and I left you two alone so you could get cozy, not so you could pick a fight and kick him out."

"I had a good reason for kicking him out," Maddie said, rubbing a rough spot on one of her fingernails.

Schuyler swatted her hand. "Stop picking at your nails. Forget that I'm the bride-to-be, we are taking *you* to get a manicure tomorrow."

Maddie crossed her arms, tucking her offending fingers under her arms. Her hands could use some attention. Her entire life could use a makeover right about now.

She explained what had happened—how she and Zach had had a deal that they would work together.

Yet, he had not only cut her out, he'd completely kept her in the dark.

"So, let me get this straight," Val said. "He went behind your back and met with Madison? Without you?"

Maddie nodded. At least someone understood why she was so upset.

"Did he have a good reason?"

"He said it was a *personal* lunch," Maddie said. "He was meeting a *friend*."

Zach McCarter was great at playing the *friend* card.

"He said he wanted to ease into talking about the deal. But we all know that if Dave Madison has a meeting with Zach and me on the books for Monday he's going to ask him what it's about. I know they discussed business. Now I can't trust him to have told me everything. Maybe he's keeping an ace up his sleeve for Dad."

Val squinted at her as if she wasn't completely siding with Maddie.

"What?" Maddie said as Schuyler sat down beside her with a nail file and a small bottle. She extracted Maddie's left hand and began rubbing oil on her cuticles.

"I know you might not like this," Val said tentatively. "But would you have been comfortable attending that lunch?"

Yes, because if Zach had invited me, it might have meant that he wanted me to be part of his life outside of the office. First, the kiss, next, lunch with his friend... who also happened to hold the key to a promotion for one of us.

Maddie shrugged. "I don't know what I think anymore. All I know is I've always believed that nice guys finish last and somewhere along the way, I've gotten soft. But no more."

"Maybe you just need to view this as an opportunity that will set you one step closer to clinching the deal," Val said.

"I mean, the guy does have a personal life outside the office, right?" Schuyler said.

There was a certain look in Val's eyes and while Schuyler was engrossed with salvaging Maddie's nails, Maddie did her best to silently telegraph a message to Val: *Do not, under any circumstances, reveal what you saw last night at the Thirsty Ox.*

"Zach was so sneaky about it," Maddie said. "Now I don't know if I can trust him to be fair about everything."

"Business is never fair, Mads," Val said. "You taught me that. Now, love is a different story. You have to trust the man you love one-hundred percent."

Schuyler's head popped up. She had a gleam in her eyes. "And are we talking business or love here? That makes all the difference in the world."

"We are talking business," Maddie said. "One hundred percent business and only business."

Val eyed her skeptically.

"That's the unsettling part," Maddie said before Val could out her. "My life is one hundred percent business. And then Dad yanked the rug out from under me…"

Maddie's eyes began to well up with tears. Geez, what was wrong with her? When had she gone so soft?

All it took was one "Oh, honey" and a hug from

Schuyler before the full-blown waterworks started flowing.

"I have sacrificed everything for Fortunado Real Estate," Maddie said, as she let the tears roll down her cheeks. "I haven't dated. I haven't had fun outside of Friday happy hour at the Thirsty Ox. I've put my life on hold and now I'm twenty-nine years old and what do I have? What if all that sacrifice has been for nothing? What if I never have what you have with Carlo, Sky?"

The emptiness inside her felt cavernous. She was tempted to fill it with the rest of the cookies and cupcakes, which her sisters had moved to the living room coffee table after Zach had gone. She glanced at the plate and contemplated doing a face-plant in the cupcakes and drowning her sorrows. But then she'd just hate herself for losing what little control she had left.

She swiped at a tear and sucked in a deep breath.

She couldn't tell if her sisters' silence made it better or worse. At least they were giving her time to get a grip on herself.

She so needed to get over Zach McCarter. Any lingering feelings should have died the minute her father had announced his plans. Despite tonight's throwback feel, she wasn't in high school. She was a grown woman who needed to remember that the object of her desire— the *former* object of her desire—was now the person who stood between her and her life's plan.

As Schuyler resumed conditioning Maddie's cuticles, Val started the movie *13 Going on 30*. As her sisters lost themselves in the movie, Maddie allowed herself to remember her kiss with Zach one last time.

What a dreadfully bad idea that had been.

She wasn't anything like the women he dated. The women she'd seen Zach with were pretty—stunning, even. Trophy wife material.

Ugh. How boring an existence would that be?

Your one job was to look gorgeous and never, ever grow old. Or fat. That meant hours spent in hair salons. And forsaking Moonbeam Bakery cupcakes.

That would never happen.

Even if she had to be a little curvier than what might be considered socially acceptable. She wasn't fat, but she loved her sweets.

She and Moonbeam had a pledge: 'til death do we part.

Schuyler's Barbie and Ken comment sprang to mind.

With her free hand, Maddie reached up and rubbed the ends of her hair between her thumb and index finger.

If she'd been Zach's girlfriend or even girlfriend material, he would've brought her to that lunch with Dave Madison. But she wasn't his girlfriend.

Was Dave Madison cut from the same cloth? If Maddie somehow transformed into a stunner, would she be able to regain the lead that she felt had slipped away in one afternoon?

She was starting to realize that even if she had been working hard all these years, maybe she needed to do more. Obviously, she needed to do more.

Her appearance, for example. What would happen if she made just a little more effort in that area? Not the amount of time a professional trophy wife spent, of course. Who had time for that? But what if she did

more? Got those highlights Schuyler had been talking about? They were coming into summer. She could
ask the hairdresser to make it subtle. Subtle and professional. As much as she loved being outside, they'd
probably fade naturally.

Her sisters laughed at a part in the movie as Maddie
scrolled through her phone checking her email.

An e-newsletter from Robinson Computers caught
her eye.

She opened it.

Carlo's cousin Alejandro Mendoza was married to
Olivia Fortune Robinson, one of the heiresses of Robinson Computers. Carlo had introduced Maddie to the
couple and she had sold them a house.

Based on something their grandmother had said to
Schuyler before she passed away, Schuyler had a theory that their dad, Kenneth, and Olivia's father, Gerald Robinson aka Jerome Fortune, were half brothers,
which would make Olivia their half cousin. Kenneth
hadn't been very keen on Schuyler pursuing her hunch.
Plus, at the time, Maddie had been more concerned
with matching Olivia and Alejandro with their perfect
house and making a sale. At best, it would've been un-
professional to ask a client if their grandfather had had
an affair with her grandmother, making them related.
So, Maddie hadn't even been tempted to go down that
path. Regardless of the intrigue, Maddie found Olivia,
who was just as business savvy as she was beautiful,
to be a fascinating woman.

She'd read business and lifestyle profiles on her. If
Maddie hadn't had such a blinding case of tunnel vi-

sion, she might have noticed then that Olivia was a woman who had it all.

She was the perfect combination of trophy wife beautiful (though she was by no means a helpless damsel) and whip smart. She was beautiful but men still took her seriously.

Suddenly, realization dawned and opened her eyes to a whole world of possibility.

Maddie sat up straight. Why hadn't she thought of this before?

"Hey, guys," Maddie said. "Can I ask you a question?"

"Sure," Schuyler said without taking her eyes off the screen.

Val paused the movie and Schuyler blinked as if coming out of a trance.

"I need you to be completely honest with me."

They nodded and Maddie braced herself for brutal honesty. "Do you think the way I look is keeping me from succeeding in business? I mean, do I need a makeover?"

Maddie could hear virtual crickets during the silence as her sisters looked at each other, no doubt daring each other to speak first.

"Well, I guess your silence speaks volumes," Maddie said. "I asked you to be honest. You're not going to hurt my feelings if you say I do. Because here's what I'm thinking. Zach already has Dave Madison on his side. I need to pull out all the stops if I'm going to win the promotion. That includes making myself the very best I can be—in all areas.

"I've always put so much energy into my work performance, believing that hard work was all that matters. But look at me. I've never put much effort into my appearance. Sure, I dress for business—smart, tailored separates that allow me to present a pulled-together, no-nonsense image. But I've never bothered with makeup. Actually, I've never had the patience to learn how to use it, and I guess I never wanted to attract the type of men who valued a woman for her looks. And more important, men don't have to change their appearance to be taken seriously in business." Before she went on a tangent about gender inequality, she brought herself back to the topic.

"Look at me. I'm boring. I'm like a blank canvas that no one notices. But Zach… Last evening he came into the office all decked out in a rancher getup."

"What?" Schuyler asked. "What do you mean?"

Val shook her head, looking disappointed. "How did I miss that?"

"He had a lead that a rancher down in Sisterdale was looking to list his property. Not only did he buy Wranglers and cowboy boots, he rented a Ford F-150."

"Wranglers?" Schuyler mused. "God, I'll bet he looked hot."

He did.

"You see?" Maddie said. "He changed his appearance and you start objectifying him."

Schuyler and Val squinted at her, looking like they weren't quite buying what she was trying to sell.

"Okay, maybe that's not quite the same thing, but—"

"Did he get the listing?" Val asked.

Maddie grumbled under her breath. "Yes, but that's beside the point."

"No, it's not," said Val. "Not at all. Think about it. He wanted the listing. He did what he needed to do to get it—"

"And now he can worry about being objectified all the way to the bank," Schuyler added, looking pleased with herself.

Val laughed. "Well, something like that. What I'm trying to say is just because you put on a little lipstick, it doesn't mean you lose your integrity. You can change the words to the Eleanor Roosevelt quote to say, *the only person who can make you feel objectified is you.*"

Obviously, Val wasn't just the baby of the family. Right now, she seemed like the wisest of all her siblings. Her little sister was right.

Maddie had never been insecure. In fact, before her father's big shake-up that had her doubting everything, she would've considered herself the most confident of the siblings—or at least the most confident of her sisters. How was it that she was a mess contemplating mascara and blush?

"So, I think I need a makeover," she finally said.

Schuyler nearly fell over herself getting off the couch. "I'm going to get my makeup bag. Don't move."

"Sky, no," Maddie protested. "Come back and watch the rest of the movie."

"No, how many times have we seen that movie?" she said. "And I'm sure we'll end up watching it dozens of times in the future. But catching my big sister in the mood to let me put makeup on her face may be a once-in-a-lifetime opportunity. I need to strike while the iron is hot."

"We can do it tomorrow," Maddie said. "I'm really not in the mood to do it tonight. Besides, this weekend is supposed to be about you. And it feels like all the attention has been focused on me. I'm really sorry about that."

"Nonsense," said Sky. "This weekend is already turning into exactly the kind of weekend I wanted—time with my sisters. Now, it's my party and I say we're going to give you a makeover. So, sit tight. I'll be right back."

Since Maddie needed to stop by the office the next morning, she opted to go home for the night. She and her sisters were going to brunch Sunday morning, but Maddie decided it would be a good idea to sleep at her own house so that she could shower, change clothes and get an early start. Truth be told, she could probably shower, dress and get in and out of the office before her sisters were even ready to go.

On her way home that night, wearing the makeover that Schuyler had given her, she wondered if she should stop by the twenty-four-hour drugstore and pick up the things that her sister had used on her.

Maddie had to admit the makeup felt surprisingly good on her face and looked more natural than she'd thought possible. She'd envisioned makeup to feel heavy and irritating, like a mask or an unnatural coating of wax that would smudge and drip as she got hot and irritable under its weight.

Not so.

Maddie couldn't even feel it.

She looked like herself. Only better. More polished and pulled together than she'd ever looked in her entire life.

Who knew?

When Maddie had expressed her surprise and joy, her sisters had carefully made all the right noises, telling her she was beautiful just the way she was—only with a little help she was knockdown, drop-dead gorgeous.

"Do you know who you look like?" Schuyler had asked. "Val, who does she look like? You must see it. OMG, tell me you see it. She looks like Blake Lively. Do you know how long I've wanted to put just a little bit of makeup on your face? Not that you're not perfectly fine without it. But who wants to be perfectly fine when you can be gorgeous? Isn't she gorgeous, Val?"

In her exuberance, Schuyler hadn't even given Val a chance to get a word in.

"She looks just like Blake Lively. Wow! I can't believe I never noticed your potential."

Maddie chuckled at the memory as she drove home. At a stoplight, she adjusted the rearview mirror so she could glance at herself. It wasn't out of vanity as much as it was disbelief and...happiness.

What would Zach do if he could see me now? Would he be eager to take me to lunch with a guy like Dave Madison?

The neon sign of a twenty-four-hour drugstore caught Maddie's eye. She glanced at the clock on her dashboard. It was after midnight, but impulse had her flipping on her turn signal and steering her car into the parking lot.

Schuyler had insisted that after brunch they were going to go shopping for cosmetics for Maddie. She was going to get a professional beauty advisor at one of the high-end department stores to recreate the look for her and teach her about good skin care.

"You'll need to remove your makeup every night and start with a nice fresh, moisturized face every morning," Schuyler had said. "You need a lot of product. Oh, you are going to make some lucky beauty advisor very happy tomorrow. It's going to be a great sale, because you need everything."

No. Not everything. Baby steps, Sky. Baby steps.

She would remove her makeup every night because she didn't want to ruin her skin, but she'd keep the mild cleansing bar her dermatologist had recommended. She didn't have time for a complicated beauty regime that called for dozens of little jars, tubes and bottles and made her bathroom counter look like her own personal cosmetics department.

Plus, with the way Schuyler was talking, it sounded like it would take hours to get everything redone. Tomorrow would be about Schuyler. Not about Maddie.

As she entered the drugstore, she picked up a shopping basket to hold her treasures. On her way to the cosmetics aisle, she recalled the steps that Schuyler had painstakingly explained.

Pheew, she thought as she surveyed the options that took up the entire length of mirrored wall and the shelves behind her. She believed in choice, but this was overwhelming.

What was the brand that Schuyler had used?

She looked around to see if she could spot a store clerk to help her, but remembered it was midnight. She was lucky the place was open. A couple of rows behind her a gaggle of girls who looked barely old enough to be out this late, much less old enough to buy wine, were giggling over the labels.

Nope. If she was going to do this, she was in this alone.

Come on. It can't be that hard. You can do this. Just pick out some things and go home.

She picked up a bottle of foundation that claimed it created a dewy glow.

She matched a bottle to her inner arm. It was the lightest shade. That reinforced that she really needed to get out of the office and get some color. But this would have to do for now because she didn't want an orangey ridge at the base of her jawline. She wanted to look natural.

Like herself, only better.

In addition to foundation, she chose a plum-brown eye shadow—because Schuyler said a slightly purplish brown would bring out the blue of her eyes. She put a black eyeliner pencil in her basket, along with black mascara—very simple.

See, this wasn't so hard.

She decided that she wouldn't mind a bolder color lipstick. She perused the different shades—every color under the rainbow. Literally.

Who wore blue lipstick?

She recalled the girl who worked the counter at the dry cleaner where Maddie took her clothes. Her lipstick had been an iridescent navy. In a strange, individualistic way, the girl wore it well. Obviously, that's what makeup was about—discovering your comfort level and wearing the product with confidence.

She needed a lipstick that conveyed she was a strong, powerful businesswoman.

Red.

Red was a power color.

They didn't have testers. She had to trust the color swatches on the end of the tubes. She chose one called Million Dollar Red.

Blush. She chose a package of powder blusher she thought was the right shade.

Schuyler had started to teach her how to use dark and shimmery light powders to contour her face—to give the illusion of sharper cheekbones and a smaller nose—but Maddie had called it quits.

"Let me learn the basic techniques before you try to turn me into a master sculptor," she had insisted.

Remarkably, Schuyler had agreed.

By the time she brought home her treasures, Maddie was too keyed up to sleep. She took one last lingering look at the way Schuyler had done her makeup. She even snapped a couple of selfies with her smartphone and then she washed her face.

She had to get up early to get in and out of the office in time to meet Val and Schuyler for brunch. So, she put on her pajamas and went to bed even though she wasn't the least bit tired.

She did her breathing exercises, inhaling for four counts, holding the breath for seven counts, and exhaling for eight counts. Even after ten rounds, she couldn't quiet her noisy mind.

Thoughts kept jumping from kissing Zach, to arguing with Zach, to whether she would run into Zach at the office so they could smooth things out before their meeting on Monday morning. If Dave Madison sensed that there was tension in the air, it might compromise the deal. Dave would need to be sure that Zach and Maddie could work together, and while Maddie still didn't appreciate Zach not being completely up front with her, she needed to get past it. She needed to turn it around to her advantage.

She sat up in bed and turned on the lamp on the bedside table. Looking slightly annoyed, Ramona opened one sleepy eye but didn't move from her pillow bed on the floor next to Maddie's bed. There was no sense lying there stewing over it.

"Sorry, girl. Go back to sleep. At least someone is getting some rest tonight."

Maddie swung her legs over the side of the bed and padded over to the en suite bath. Her cosmetics were lying on the built-in vanity counter still in the bag. She sat down at the vanity, opened the packages and lined them up till they looked like soldiers at the ready. Soldiers that would help her win this battle.

She opened the bottle of foundation and poured a dab

out onto the back of her hand, as she'd seen Schuyler do, and began applying the opaque liquid to her face.

She'd purposely opted to go a little lighter to look more natural—but had she gone too light?

It didn't look like what Sky had put on her.

It was late, but Maddie was wide-awake and eager to try on the rest so that she'd know what she was facing in the morning before she went into the office. Because, of course, if Zach was in the office, she'd want him to see the new her while she pretended that she was still the old her.

She picked up the brown eye shadow next. In contrast to the base makeup, it looked much darker than it had appeared in the packaging.

After poking herself in the eye with the mascara wand, which made her eyes water—and water—and water—and getting overzealous with the red lipstick, she couldn't decide if she looked more like a scary clown or Heath Ledger's Joker.

Oh, this was bad.

Obviously, it was *that* hard to make makeup look effortless and natural.

As she scrubbed her face clean, she decided that maybe she needed more practice before she debuted her new look.

She towel dried her face then rubbed her index finger over her red-tinged lips. The lipstick had feathered beyond the boundaries, forming a ring around her mouth that looked as if she'd been eating a cherry snow cone. She hoped she hadn't permanently stained them. It was almost 2:00 a.m. At this rate, she'd do well to get five hours' sleep if she got up in time to make it to the office and back to meet her sisters.

She climbed back into bed and drifted asleep dreaming up a plan that would allow her to make things right with Zach and win the promotion.

Chapter Seven

Zach had a potential buyer for the Winters ranch in Sisterdale. He'd let Jim and Mary Ann know that he was bringing Joanna and Gary Everly by around eleven thirty. He'd rented the truck again. It comfortably seated six, so the three of them would have plenty of room for the long trip.

The Everlys were meeting him at the office at seven thirty Sunday morning. He'd stopped by the bakery and picked up a dozen donuts and three cups of coffee for the trip. He was fifteen minutes early, which gave him just enough time to go inside and grab the spec sheet for the property. When he pulled into the parking lot and saw Maddie's white Volvo, his stomach tightened—and not in an altogether bad way.

She'd been right last night—or at least partially

right—when she'd said he hadn't been up front with her about meeting Dave Madison for lunch. He should've told her before he went. He was glad to have this opportunity to clear the air before seeing her tomorrow.

He let himself in the office and announced himself so as not to scare her, since she probably wasn't expecting anyone this early in the morning.

"Maddie?" he called from the hallway. He could hear the clicking sound of someone working on a computer keyboard. The *click-click-clickity-click* stopped the moment he'd spoken, but she didn't say anything.

"Hey," he said when he appeared in her office doorway. "I just wanted to let you know I was here. I'm meeting some clients. So, I'll be leaving in a few minutes."

"Are you showing the property down in Sisterdale?" she asked, eyeing him up and down.

"How did you know?" he asked.

"The cowboy costume."

"Yeah. My Sisterdale uniform. I'm driving some potential buyers out there today."

Maddie's gaze made a slow perusal of his body starting from his head, working its way down to his boots and back up again. When their gazes finally met, there was a hungry look in her eyes.

"Well, now that you've undressed me with your eyes…" he said.

"Zach," she said. "Don't."

"Don't do what, Maddie?"

The pink of her cheeks deepened. Her lips looked particularly alluring this morning. He wondered how he'd never noticed before, never *seen* her before. But now he couldn't unsee her and he didn't want to.

That kiss had awakened something in him—an undeniable attraction, a dormant hunger. And he was dying for another taste. He was dying for her. He wanted to pull her close and strip away every barrier between them.

"I should have told you about my meeting with Dave Madison before I went. I don't know why I didn't, other than I'm not used to considering others when I work. I've always flown solo—in work and in my personal life. Which brings me to the real point. I don't think my lunch with Dave Madison is the problem here."

"Of course it is," she snapped a little too fast. "I mean, but not anymore. I appreciate you seeing my point of view. So, we're good."

She waved him away and turned her body squarely toward her computer and started typing. She was focusing a little too hard on the screen. She seemed to be taking great pains not to look at him.

"Are we okay, Maddie?"

"Sure. Your client will probably be here any minute now, and I have to get my work done. I'm meeting Schuyler and Val for brunch. We need to salvage what's left of her bachelorette weekend."

He leaned his hip on her desk, intending to show her he wasn't in a hurry to leave her. "You do realize Val called me and invited me over last night, right? I didn't just show up."

She frowned at him. "Of course."

"Then, if my lunch with Dave Madison and my

crashing your party last night aren't the problems, I can think of only one other thing that could be bothering you."

She pushed her chair away from her desk with a swift shove and leaned toward him. "Why would you think something is bothering me, Zach?"

"First of all, your tone."

She crossed her arms. "Sorry. My mom used to say, 'You don't hear you the way others hear you.'" Something in her demeanor softened. "I don't mean to sound bitchy. I'm really not a bitch, Zach."

"I know you're not."

She gave a one-shoulder shrug. "Wouldn't qualities that come across as bitchy be applauded if I were a man? Or maybe not applauded. They wouldn't even be noticed."

Their gazes fused for a combustible instant.

He noticed her. He wanted to tell her he noticed her, that he couldn't take his eyes off her, but the faint sound of someone knocking on the front door broke the spell and pulled him back into the here and now.

"That's my clients," he said. "They're early."

"You better not keep them waiting, then."

Maddie scooted her chair back to her desk and glanced at her computer monitor again, the color still high on her pretty cheeks.

What almost happened there? If Joanna and Gary Everly hadn't arrived early he would've leaned in and kissed her. He'd wanted to kiss her. But he hadn't been as fearless as she'd been that night at the Thirsty Ox. Now they were out of time.

"For the record, I don't think you're bitchy," he said. "I think you're passionate. Don't ever apologize for, or feel bad about, being passionate."

He thought she was passionate.

Passionate.

It might've been the nicest compliment anyone had ever paid her.

"Earth to Maddie?" Schuyler said. "Armand wants to know if you'd like another bloody Mary?"

Maddie realized her sisters and the very handsome waiter, who had been flirting with them since the moment he'd introduced himself, were staring at her.

Maddie glanced down, unsure whether her glass was full or empty or somewhere in between, saw that there was only a splash at the bottom.

"Yes, please. That would be lovely."

"You're in a good mood today," Val said. "A little dreamy, but I don't know when I've seen you so relaxed."

Maddie smiled and shrugged. "Really? Why wouldn't I be happy when I get the chance to hang out with my sisters?"

Schuyler and Val exchanged dubious looks.

"Since you went home last night," Schuyler said, "I was afraid you were mad at me for asking Zach to come over last night."

Maddie feigned confusion. "Why would I be mad?" She hadn't been happy about it. But if her sisters hadn't meddled and she and Zach hadn't argued, they wouldn't have made up this morning. If not for them, she might never have known that he thought she was *passionate*.

"Even if I was upset—which I'm not, I promise— I wouldn't spoil the last day of our girls' weekend by pouting. And speaking of, after we try on our brides-maid dresses, what would you like to do this after-noon, Sky? We could go wander around the Japanese Gardens, or I hear that they just opened a brand-new exhibit of the French Impressionist painters at the Mu-seum of Fine Arts. Or there's that new movie with Zoe Kazan that looks great."

"All of those options sound great." Schuyler sipped the fresh bloody Mary the waiter had stealthily set in front of her. "I think we'd just better stick with shop-ping today. I wish we had more time, but I still have some things to pull together for the wedding. Can you believe Carlo and I will be married in less than a week?" Schuyler wrung her hands.

"Are you nervous?" Val asked.

A wistful smile overtook Schuyler's face. "Not re-ally nervous as much as I'm excited. I just want every-thing to be perfect. I keep thinking of little things I've forgotten."

"You know nothing is perfect," said Maddie. "But the imperfections will give you fabulous stories to tell later. You've hired the best wedding planner in Texas. She'll handle those little things and she'll have your back. So, you should use this last week of singlehood to relax."

"She's not going to make sure I have the perfect thing to wear on my wedding night," Schuyler said. "I need to find something. I can't believe I almost forgot."

"But what about all the gorgeous things you got at your lingerie shower?" Val asked.

"I know," Schuyler said. "Every single thing was gorgeous, but I have something specific in mind. Do you all mind if we go to the Galleria after the dress fittings so I can look?"

"The bride's wish is our command," said Maddie.

"You are sneaky." Maddie slanted a glance at Schuyler, who smiled a victorious smile.

Schuyler hadn't wanted to come to the Galleria to find a perfect piece of lingerie to wear on her wedding night. It had been an ambush to get Maddie into the cosmetics department and into the chair she now sat in for a professional makeover.

If she'd poked herself in the eye three times last night applying a simple coat of mascara, how on earth was she going to replicate the fine line that Cheryl, the makeup artist, had just drawn on her right eyelid? And Maddie had to attempt it with one eye closed? It made her hands shake contemplating the idea. If she created a distraction, could she make a getaway?

"Here," Cheryl said, handing Maddie the slim brush. "You do the other eye. You'll see how easily it glides on."

Maddie waved her off. "You've done such a nice job with my makeup, I don't want to ruin it."

"But you see, that's just it," Cheryl said. "Try it, you'll see that it's virtually foolproof."

Foolproof? Hahaha!

Maddie was tempted to counter with her scary clown

tale from the night before, but suddenly, arguing her point felt more exhausting than just trying. She accepted the brush, leaned in to the mirror and followed Cheryl's instructions.

To Maddie's amazement and utter delight, the liner went on as magically as Cheryl had promised. And then, so did the mascara and lipstick.

As Cheryl stepped back and surveyed the results, Schuyler and Val voiced their approval.

The woman handed Maddie a hand mirror. "Simple, fresh and natural. Best of all, this look is fast and easy to do."

If Schuyler's impromptu makeover had been good, this one was nothing short of astounding.

"She'll take everything," Schuyler said with a sweep of her hand as if reading her mind.

Cheryl smiled at Maddie. "I promise this look will take you less than seven minutes in the morning. Just think, a whole new gorgeous you in less time than it takes to brew a cup of coffee."

A whole new me. That's something.

What was important was how much Schuyler seemed to be reveling in the idea that Maddie was amenable to not only wearing makeup at her wedding, but learning how to make it a part of her daily routine. She got the distinct feeling that even though her sister was too kind to come right out and say it, Maddie's professional makeover may have been one of the missing parts that Schuyler had been fretting over during brunch.

Maddie felt a little selfish pretending she was doing this all for Schuyler. Sure, she was a big part of the reason, but an anxious giddiness was forming in the pit of her stomach as she contemplated seeing Zach tomorrow morning.

What would Zach think of a more polished, passionate Maddie?

"While we're at it," Schuyler said when Cheryl went to package her purchases, "let's talk about your wardrobe."

"My wardrobe is just fine," Maddie said. "It's all from Brooks Brothers. I love that brand. It's one-stop shopping. Quick and efficient. Angie has been my specialist since I got back to Houston after college. She calls me once a year and reminds me it's time to come in. She lays out an assortment of classic pieces I can mix and match and has them ready for me to try on. She shows me how I can get two weeks' worth of outfits out of five or so pieces."

Schuyler and Val looked amused, but not at all impressed.

"Yes, we're familiar with your style, Mads," said Val.

Her sisters exchanged a look.

"Boring," Schuyler sang under her breath.

"You really should think about working some color and pattern into your neutrals," Val said.

"Or scrapping the neutrals altogether and getting a new wardrobe with some pizzazz," Schuyler said.

Uh-oh. Had she created a monster by letting Schuyler herd her into the makeover chair?

"Hey, my neutrals are fine," Maddie said. "And I do pair them with colorful blouses every once in a while. And what about my teal dress? That's colorful. My wardrobe is easy. One less thing to worry about in the morning, especially now that I'll have to dedicate time to makeup."

"Seven minutes, Mads," Schuyler said. "Seven minutes will hardly derail your schedule." She waved her hand, as if shooing away Maddie's argument. "I know of a shop that helps disadvantaged women get back into the workplace that would love to have your neutrals. You'll be getting new clothes to go with your new look. Believe me, after I get through with you, you're going to thank me when you see yourself. But first, after we finish here, we're going to get your hair cut—"

"No!" Maddie insisted, as she paid for her cosmetics. "That's where I draw the line. You are not touching my hair."

It turned out that Schuyler didn't lay a hand on Maddie's hair, but Jade, the stylist Sky still traveled from Austin to Houston to see every six weeks, ended up having her way with Maddie's locks.

It was a mystery how Jade managed to be available at the exact moment that the Fortunado sisters arrived, since Sky often bemoaned how she had to book her appointments months out.

Maddie was beginning to sense a conspiracy, but she had to admit it was fun seeing herself transform right before her own eyes. It was a learning experience and a reminder that sometimes the old way of doing things needed a little sprucing up.

Jade listened to Maddie's concern for needing low-maintenance hair.

"I don't play well with round brushes and blow-dryers," Maddie told her. "If I tried to use one of those brushes, I'd probably get it stuck in my hair and have to cut it out. I don't have the time or the inclination to learn. So, let's not do anything that requires styling."

Jade assured her she would give her a style even better and more low maintenance than her current do.

First, she gave Maddie some strategically placed highlights to frame her face and give her hair some dimension. After Jade washed out the bleach, she trimmed off about three inches and cut in long layers, which Jade promised would give Maddie's thick hair more bounce. And, yes, she would still be able to pull it back into her signature ponytail.

"Just look at you," Jade exclaimed, after all was said and done. "You're stunning. I mean, you are knock-down, drop-dead gorgeous, girl. Why on earth would you want to hide these tresses in a pony? That's a sin."

For the first time ever, Maddie wondered the same thing. Her hair felt lighter and bouncier. When she ran her fingers through it, it was silky to the touch and fell neatly back into place. Suddenly, it seemed a heck of a lot more professional than a ponytail.

Val stayed behind to have Jade work her magic on her hair, while Schuyler dragged Maddie to Hattie's Boutique for a look at her spring collection.

Even though Schuyler had been living in Austin for the past several months, she still knew all the best places to shop in Houston. Schuyler seemed to be having so much fun with their shopping adventure that Maddie embraced the possibility that they would be visiting each and every one of her sister's favorite shops. For the first time in her life, she was enjoying shopping.

The funky, fashion-forward boutiques were a far cry from Brooks Brothers' professional offerings.

It was like taking a trip to a foreign country. It wasn't necessarily her lifestyle, but she could embrace it for an afternoon. When in Rome…or when in boho boutiques… do as your sisters do. She'd never minded investing in classic pieces that would outlast trends and time, but some of the trendiest pieces Schuyler and the shopgirls picked out for her cost three times her normal purchases.

These clothes were expensive and attention-grabbing.

Unlike her glamorous, sassy sister, who had been more like their late grandmother—whom they'd all called Glammy after a childhood speech impediment caused Schuyler to mispronounce *Grammy*—Maddie wanted to wear the clothes. She didn't want loud colors and screaming patterns to wear her.

Such as the red, orange and yellow Emilio Pucci shift dress Schuyler was handing Maddie over the louvered dressing room door.

"Oh, no," Maddie said. "Not this one." She opened the door a crack and peeked out. Schuyler was wearing a black-and-florescent-pink maxi dress that played tricks on Maddie's vision. The dress suited her sister. But this Pucci number… "It's too bright. If I wore this, someone would mistake me for a stolen Picasso painting."

"That's right," Schuyler said. "With your body and legs, you'll look definitely like a work of art in this dress. Put it on and come out so I can see you in it."

Schuyler let go of the clothes hanger. Rather than

letting the crazy dress fall to the floor, Maddie caught it and closed the fitting room door. She eyed the getup. It wasn't her at all. She held the dress up to her body and looked in the mirror to prove that point—that it was exactly the opposite of everything she stood for. It was loud and obnoxiously bright. It was attention-seeking and...*fun*.

With her new makeup and freer, lighter, looser hair, it looked fun.

She couldn't help but try to imagine Zach's face if she showed up to their meeting tomorrow morning wearing a dress like this.

No. I couldn't. I'd feel too conspicuous. It's so not me.

That's when a little voice in her head said, *If you keep doing what you're doing, you'll keep getting what you're getting.* Like not having her body of work be good enough to win a promotion on its own. Or like having to kiss a guy first and have him seem like he was interested, but hang back enough to make her wonder if he was interested or if it was just flirty business as usual.

Or even worse, if he'd upped the flirting ante simply to throw her off her game.

But he'd called her *passionate*. She was passionate about her job. About Zach. He'd recognized the fire in her, even when she hadn't seen it herself—or at least known what to call it.

She'd called it bitchy. He'd called it passionate.

A passionate woman shouldn't be afraid to take a risk. At least not with something as low-risk as clothes.

She slipped the dress over her head, loving the expensive feel of the silky fabric as it glided down her body. She fluffed her hair, which fell back into place perfectly, and adjusted the dress so that it sat right on her.

Oh, no.

It was too short and so bright it bordered on vulgar. Sort of. It did call attention to itself. To her.

"Do you have it on?" Schuyler called.

But it also skimmed her curves as if Pucci had made it just for her. It hit her about three inches above the knees, which automatically made it inappropriate for the office, but… If she looked at it through another lens, a different lens, it was a playful romp of a dress that might be fun to wear after hours.

As if she ever went out. Other than Fridays at the Thirsty Ox, her after hours were spent at home with Ramona. Her little dog loved her just the way she was. In fact, the garish pattern might scare her.

And that was one of the dumbest lies she'd ever told herself.

A knock sounded on the dressing room door. "Open up, Mads. I want to see the dress on you."

Feeling overwhelmingly shy and completely out of her element, Maddie opened the dressing room door a crack. Schuyler took it from there and yanked it the rest of the way open.

"Oh, my gosh, look at you!" Schuyler *squeed*. Maddie had heard the word *squee* used before—usually in a text from one of her sisters, but until that moment, she'd never actually heard the sound. The noise Schuyler was making was most definitely a *squee*.

"You look absolutely gorge." Schuyler clapped her hands and bounced a little in her enthusiasm. "Turn around."

Schuyler made a circular motion with her index finger and Maddie complied, feeling strangely giddy at her sister's reaction.

"You have to get this dress, Mads. We are not leaving here without it."

"I don't know, Sky."

Schuyler grabbed Maddie's hand and pulled her over to a set of three-way mirrors at the end of the rectangular dressing room.

"Look at you. Just look at you."

Schuyler clasped her hands together and held them under her chin in a way that reminded Maddie so much of Glammy it almost took her breath away. Glammy, who'd been their father's mother, hadn't even been gone a year, but of all the siblings, Schuyler had inherited her tendency toward the overly dramatic, just like Glammy.

Before their grandmother died, she had set Schuyler on a mission to prove that the Fortunado crew was related to the infamous Fortunes, a vast, wealthy family who, due to Jerome Fortune's affairs, had ever-expanding branches in the southeast and England. But their father had put a hard stop to Schuyler's digging, saying he was proud of his background and who he'd become without any help from the Fortunes. He was a self-made man who had parlayed a lottery win into a real estate empire. Glammy, whose name had been Mary before she'd changed it to Starlight, had single-handedly raised him without help from her only son's father. Anytime anyone questioned Kenneth Fortunado about his father, he claimed he didn't know who his dad was and didn't care. Since Glammy's passing, speculation was that Julius Fortune, Jerome's father, was his biological father, but Kenneth maintained he didn't care if that was the truth. He had his six kids and his wife—and he certainly had enough money that he didn't need any Fortune money. He had instructed everyone to leave well enough alone.

"Maddie?" Schuyler said. "Are you okay?"

Maddie shook her head. "Yeah, sure. For a moment there you reminded me so much of Glammy it knocked the breath out of me."

"Oh." Schuyler drew in an audible breath that hitched and her eyes welled. Maddie was afraid that her sister might start crying. All of her siblings had loved Glammy, but Schuyler was the closest to her. Like two peas in a pod. Schuyler had said the only reason her wedding wouldn't be perfect was because Glammy wouldn't be here to see it.

To help her sister regain her composure, Maddie said, "Would this dress be appropriate for work?"

She knew it wasn't, but the bulldog had dropped her bone and Maddie was delivering it to her so she could get a better grip.

Schuyler drew in another shaky breath, but this time she focused her gaze on the dress.

"No, not for work. But it would be perfect for the rehearsal dinner. Come with me. There's an adorable hot pink Kate Spade fit and flare out here I want you to see.

It has a jewel neckline and it's sleeveless so it will be perfect for this summer when the weather turns warm."

Schuyler found her sister's size and sent her toward the fitting room. The pink dress was cute—for Schuyler. But it was such a departure from what Maddie was used to. Even so, she tried it on.

With the help of the sales associate, Schuyler pulled several more dresses that she deemed fun, fashionable and work-appropriate for Maddie. She also pulled a pair of strappy gold sandals. Her sister might have been wasting her calling working as special events coordinator for the Mendoza Winery. With her affinity and flare for fashion, she should have her own boutique.

The Kate Spade fit like a dream and Maddie had to admit that the vibrant shades and geometric patterns of the other selections were pretty. Actually, they were downright exquisite, but she didn't feel 100 percent natural when she tried them on. But the pink dress felt as if it were made for her.

"You look great," Schuyler insisted. "Do you think I would steer you wrong?"

"Not on purpose."

"Oh, please." Her sister rolled her eyes. "Get the yellow-and-orange Pucci for the rehearsal dinner and, for now, just get one new dress for work. I vote for the Kate Spade. You're going to feel so drab when you try to go back to your old boring neutrals that you'll be back to buy a whole new wardrobe. How much do you want to bet?"

Maddie frowned at herself in the three-way mirror.

"I just don't know, Sky. It's a lot of change all at once. I don't even look like myself anymore."

"You look like you, only better. It really isn't that drastic because you've always been beautiful. But just more like a blank canvas waiting for someone to come in and paint you at your very best."

They locked eyes in the mirror.

"You don't believe me?" Schuyler asked. "Go put that pink Kate Spade back on. I'll be right back. Come out into the store when you're dressed."

Maddie squinted at Schuyler. "What are you up to?"

"Just shoo." Schuyler made a sweeping gesture with her hand. "Go change and meet me by the sales desk."

By the time Maddie emerged dressed in the pink number, Schuyler had assembled a panel of six guys.

"Guys, meet my sister Maddie. Isn't she hot?"

What the hell?

As the guys murmured their agreement, Maddie shot daggers at Schuyler with her eyes. What were they supposed to say being put on the spot like that?

This was one of the most awkward moments of her life. Almost as awkward as the aftermath of kissing Zach. She wanted to duck behind the sales desk or run out the front door. She would've if she hadn't been wearing the unpaid-for dress. Instead, she turned to go change.

"Where do you think you're going?" Schuyler asked.

"Away from here."

"That's just rude," Schuyler said. "These guys want to meet you. Don't you, guys?"

Again, they murmured their agreement.

"Maddie is single, but works too much. So, she doesn't get out a lot. I want a show of hands. If you saw my sister out somewhere wearing this dress, would you ask her out? Raise your hand if you would."

To Maddie's flummoxed surprise, all six hands went up.

She felt her face flame. Judging by the intensity, it was probably the same color as her dress. If not brighter.

Bride-to-be or not, she was going to kill her sister.

"This has been very awkward," Maddie said to the guys. "Thank you for being so nice. I apologize on behalf of my sister. You all have been great sports, but you're free to go now."

One guy left, but the other five stayed. The tallest one with dark hair said, "Can I get your number?"

My number?

For the first time, Maddie allowed herself to really look at the guy. He was cute, but he looked a little young.

"What's your name?" Maddie asked.

"Drew," the guy answered.

Maddie smiled at him. "Drew, you're a sweetheart. Do you mind if I ask how old you are?"

He chuckled. "Nineteen."

"Ah, nineteen." Maddie mustered her best smile as she turned to her sister. "Drew is nineteen, Schuyler."

"So, what," Schuyler countered. "He has good taste."

"Drew, if I were five years younger I'd go out with you in a heartbeat." Okay, maybe seven years younger. But she didn't need to tell Drew that. She didn't want to hurt his feelings after he'd put himself on the line like that. "But I'm too old for you. You need someone a little more age appropriate."

"It's okay. I dig older chicks. What are you, like thirty-four?"

I'm twenty-nine and you're a child. Go back to the playground.

"Thirty-four, huh?" She shot Schuyler another scalding look. "Something like that. It was nice to meet you. It was nice to meet all of you."

She turned around and felt like she was doing the walk of shame to the dressing room, where she locked herself in and contemplated not coming out. She had a protein bar in her purse and a half-full bottle of water that Jade had given her at the salon. She could live quite comfortably in here.

She took her time changing and hanging up the dozen dresses she'd tried on. The entire time she gave herself a pep talk. Schuyler was only trying to help. She really did mean well. And the guys had been nice. They'd all raised their hands when polled about whether they'd date her. Why did this feel so humiliating? It should bolster her self-esteem.

She lowered herself onto the fabric-covered bench and sat with the feeling for a moment. Really, *humiliating* wasn't the right word. Sure, she'd been jolted out of her comfort zone. But that wasn't necessarily a bad thing. In fact, she thought as she looked at herself in the mirror, a lot of good had come from today.

Even if Drew, the one who dug older chicks, had aged her by five years, she should be flattered by his clumsy compliment. In fact, all the guys had been flattering.

So, what was wrong here?

Why was this not settling very well with her?

Because they're not Zach.

The realization made her breath hitch and the pit of her stomach tingle in a way that only happened when she thought of Zach.

"Chin up, buttercup." Schuyler's voice carried through the louvered door. "Six out of six dudes surveyed say Madeleine Fortunado is a hot tamale. But she needs to work on her game. For the record, they didn't say that. I added that part, and you know it's true. I can help you with that, too. But one step at a time."

They're not Zach.

What was she going to do?

She touched the hem of the pink Kate Spade dress and rubbed the fabric between her fingers before looking at the price tag.

Yikes. It cost more than the price of two of her usual pieces and she really couldn't mix and match it with anything. If she tried to pair it with one of her blazers, she'd look like she'd borrowed one of Zach's sports coats.

Zach.

Did he think she dressed manly? Not really manly as much as conservatively. Neutral. What was it Schuyler called it? Boring.

Maddie liked things straightforward, in fashion and in life. She liked things to match. When things didn't match up or varied from her well-ordered plans, it threw her off-kilter.

Maybe the reason Zach threw off her equilibrium—

and threw her off-kilter—the way he did was because he messed with her well-ordered system. He made her think and feel things that didn't have a place in her world.

Maybe she should buy the dresses—the pink Kate Spade and the yellow-and-orange Pucci. She'd wear the Pucci to the rehearsal dinner to make Sky happy. She'd get the gold sandals, too. And maybe she'd get the pink dress and wear that little number into the office tomorrow.

She knew she was good at what she did. No amount of makeup or pretty dresses could disprove that truth. But now she had to admit there was room for improvement. For a different approach.

Another knock sounded on the door. "Mads, are you okay in there? Don't be mad at me."

Maddie opened the door. "I'm not mad at you, Sky, but thanks for the most mortifying afternoon of my life." She turned and gave her sister a hug. "And the best afternoon of my life, too."

Schuyler hugged her back and then pulled away holding Maddie at arm's length. "Look at you. You're like a beautiful butterfly who has burst from her cocoon."

"It's a chrysalis."

"What did you say?" Schuyler asked.

"A butterfly emerges from a chrysalis, not a cocoon."

Schuyler waved her off. "Okay, whatever. You're like the duckling who has finally blossomed into the swan."

She started to explain that ducks and swans were two different birds, but she stopped herself.

"All right, Miss Simile, let's not get carried away."

Schuyler laughed. "We just have one last thing to do before my work here is done. We're going to get manis and pedis. Then you will be the complete package."

As they walked into the nail salon, Schuyler said, "Three of those dudes gave me their phone numbers and want you to call them."

"Three including Drew?"

"No, three other than Drew. He wanted to ask you out. So, technically, all six thought you were hot, and four of the six were willing to put their money where their mouth was. Are you going to call them?"

Maddie had to admit it was flattering, but... "No, I'm old-fashioned when it comes to calling guys."

But not making the first move to kiss a guy. Well, not just any guy. Zach.

"What do you mean?" Schuyler asked.

"I don't call guys. They call me."

Schuyler frowned at her. "I should have given those guys your number. Or... I could call them for you. That's what a great, loving sister I am."

"No, of course, I didn't want you to give them my number. And don't you dare call any of them. In fact, give me their numbers right now."

Maddie held out her hand but Schuyler clutched the paper tightly and held it out of Maddie's reach. "Only if you promise you'll call one of them and ask them to be your plus-one to the wedding."

Maddie's jaw fell open. "Are you crazy? I don't know those guys. Why would I invite them to an important family event? And a wedding that's out of town, for that matter."

Schuyler shrugged. "Fair enough, but who are you going to bring? I have you down as bringing a plus-one."

"There's a simple fix for that," Maddie said, as she climbed into the pedicure chair. "Take my plus-one off the list."

"Too late. I've already made the seating chart. All the names are written in gold script on a big piece of framed Plexiglas. It says Maddie Fortunado's plus-one. It can't be changed without scrapping the entire board and having it redone."

"What if someone cancels?" Maddie said over the sound of running water. The nail technicians were filling the footbaths and it was a little hard to talk over the sound.

"They'd better not cancel," Schuyler shot back. "Carlo and I kept the guest list small because we want our wedding to be intimate and elegant. Every single person who attends is someone special to us."

"Such as the six guys you dragged in off the street?" Maddie snarked. "Which one is the most special? I'd love for you to rank them in order."

Schuyler rolled her eyes, but Maddie sensed that she might have gone too far. "I gave you a plus-one because I wanted you to have a good time. Mads, I worry about you. Now that our brothers and I have moved away, and Mom and Dad are going to be traveling more, it's just you and Val."

Maddie braced herself for Schuyler to mention the fact that she had put all her eggs in one Fortunado Real

Estate basket and now that basket was proving to have some holes in it. She decided to cut her off at the pass.

"If I don't win this promotion, I'm going to leave Fortunado."

Schuyler didn't look surprised. "I can't say I blame you. Will you stay in town?"

Maddie shrugged. "I don't know. Maybe not. I haven't thought that far ahead. Dad hasn't announced his decision yet and I'm trying to stay positive."

"You're selling a lot of property in Austin lately. Why don't you move there— Oh, I almost forgot! Act surprised when he calls you, but Carlo is super interested in that last location you showed us. The one near the university. He thinks it'd make a great spot for the nightclub. He wants to make an offer before we leave for our honeymoon. But you didn't hear it from me."

"That's good news. Now I'll completely forget you said anything about it."

"So, if you win," Schuyler said, "what's Zach going to do? Because I can't imagine that Dad would really turn over the business to someone who isn't family."

"He says he's leaving if he doesn't get the promotion."

Schuyler's eyes got wide. "Like leave-leave? Leave town? Or just leave the company?"

Maddie shrugged. "He hasn't said one way or the other. But either way it would be bad. If he stays, he'd be smart to open his own office. But he'd be Fortunado's direct competition. And if he left, well…"

Maddie drew in a deep breath and closed her eyes for a moment. She hadn't wanted to think about that either.

She could see so many ways that Zach was the better man for the job. He was so connected—even only being in Houston for a few months. He just seemed to have a way of making things work. Either way, it was a lose-lose proposition. Either way she was going to lose the only man she'd been interested in in a very long time. If she hadn't loved and respected her father as much as she did, she'd be cursing him for messing up everything. For messing up her life.

Schuyler shook her head. "Well, that's no good. How are you two nincompoops ever going to get together if you're not even in the same town?" She let out a sigh. "I still say you two are perfect for each other."

Maddie slanted a glance at Schuyler, who had full-on relaxed into her pedi. She had cranked up the massage function on the chair, which was nearly in full recline.

She looked so happy. Maddie was thrilled for her. But it wasn't the first time that she wished she could be a little more like her free-spirited little sister. Schuyler always had faith that things would work out—and they usually did. Maddie simply couldn't act without over-thinking all the ramifications.

By the time she thought everything through, she was nearly paralyzed with indecision. So, to appear decisive and in control, she usually defaulted to what was comfortable.

If you keep doing what you're doing, you'll keep getting what you're getting.

"Sky, may I confide in you?" Maddie asked.

"You'd better." Schuyler returned her chair to the up-right position so that she was sitting as straight as the big leatherette chairs would allow. Maddie was sorry she'd disturbed her.

"Relax," Maddie said. "Put your chair back the way it was. What I have to say is really not a big deal."

Liar. It's a huge deal, if you'd only open up.

Just leap. Stop overthinking.

"This is about Zach, isn't it?"

Maddie froze, if only to keep herself from shaking her head and changing the subject.

"Don't be shy about it, about him, Maddie."

Maddie tried to say something, but she couldn't force out the words that were lodged in the back of her throat.

Schuyler cocked a brow. A cheeky expression claimed her face. "It's a good thing I love Carlo so much, because if I didn't I'd set my cap for Zach McCarter."

That was all it took to dislodge the lump in Maddie's throat. She laughed so hard her eyes started to well. "Set your cap? Who are you? Jane Austen?"

Schuyler beamed at the appreciation for her joke. "I made you laugh."

"Yes, you did," Maddie said.

"That's just it," Schuyler said. "You should be laughing more, smiling more. Lately, the only time I see you laugh and smile is when you're around Zach. Otherwise you're wound tighter than Zach's ass."

"Schuyler." Maddie glanced at the nail techs who were deep in quiet conversation with each other and seemed to not be listening to them. Thank God.

"You have to admit he does have a great ass," Schuyler said. "I've noticed. No disrespect to Carlo, who has a nice ass, too. I want you to have a nice ass of your own, Mads. I mean, a guy of your own with a nice ass."

Maddie pressed her hand to her mouth to stifle her laughter. She didn't want to draw any more attention to them. "Okay. Okay. Okay. I'd love that."

"So, you're saying you've noticed Zach's great butt?"

Maddie glanced around the nail salon. It was so late in the day that there was only one other pair of women in the place and they were seated at the other end of the row of pedicure chairs not paying the least bit of attention to the sisters' conversation.

"You have, haven't you?" Schuyler wiggled her brows.

"Okay, yes. I've noticed. Who wouldn't notice?"

"Right? A person would have to be dead not to," Schuyler said. "A few minutes ago, you said you were going to confide in me about something. Dish."

Of course, Schuyler wouldn't forget a juicy offer like that. But the most important thing was that despite her sister's free-spirited ways and her tendency to make jokes about trivial matters—or to use humor to draw Maddie out of her shell—Schuyler was a great confidant. If Maddie asked her not to repeat something, Schuyler was more solid than Fort Knox.

Maddie had learned the hard way that if she didn't issue a caveat and specifically ask her not to say anything about something, all bets were off. In fact, bets would favor Schuyler repeating exactly what she'd heard—at the most inopportune time.

"So, this is just between us, okay?" Maddie said.

Schuyler leaned in and drew her thumb and forefinger over her lips, indicating that her lips were zipped.

Maddie recounted the events of Friday night at the Thirsty Ox and how she'd kissed Zach.

Actually, it felt good to throw caution to the wind and giggle about her crush with her sister. Schuyler's eyes were huge and her mouth formed a perfect O. Maddie wasn't surprised that her admission had rendered her sister momentarily speechless.

Momentarily.

"You kissed Zach?"

Maddie nodded and heat washed over her cheeks.

"And he came over Saturday night," Schuyler said.

Maddie nodded again.

"He really seemed like he was into you."

"I don't know about that."

"Well, I do. You have to ask him to the wedding, Mads."

Maddie shook her head. "No, I can't. It's not a good idea. The whole point behind the kiss was to get him out of my system."

Schuyler winced and shot Maddie an incredulous look.

"Don't judge me," Maddie said. "When you look at the facts, it only makes sense. One of us will win this promotion. The other one is leaving. Getting involved wouldn't work. That's assuming he's even interested in getting involved. Zach is a first-class flirt, Sky. So, I'm more inclined to believe that the kiss didn't mean anything to him. I kissed him because I've always had a thing for him and this way, no matter what happens, now I won't wonder what it would've been like. I guess you could say it was my consolation prize."

"No!" Schuyler shouted. Their techs looked up and the women at the other end of the row darted alarmed glances down their way.

"Sorry," Schuyler said. "Just trying to talk some sense into my sister. As you were."

The women gazed at them warily, as if they were looking at a couple of unpredictable animals.

"Schuyler, *shhhh*," Maddie admonished.

"There will be no consolation prizes here. You will not just settle for a stolen kiss. You will win the whole thing. You deserve to have everything you want."

Maddie envied her sister's Pollyanna spirit, but Maddie knew Sky was the dreamer and she was the realist.

"It is what it is," Maddie said.

"No, it is what you make it. Why is it so difficult for you to admit that there could be something between the two of you if you'd just open your heart and try? Why don't you try to figure out a way to win the promotion *and* Zach?"

Maddie's heart kicked against her rib cage.

Thump-thump, thump-thump, thump-thump.

"Why? Because I hate losing," Maddie said. "And taking a chance on Zach and missing the mark would hurt too much."

Chapter Eight

Monday morning was off to a bad start. Dave Madison had called while Zach was in the shower and left a message canceling their meeting that morning. Dave said that yesterday he'd been called away on business in Dallas and he wasn't able to make it back.

Zach wondered if the important piece of business that had detained him was blond or brunette.

Now he was left to do the dirty work: telling Maddie that Dave had canceled. Hearing the news this close to Kenneth's deadline and the fact that he'd called Zach, not Maddie, was not going to go over well. Especially since Maddie already believed Zach was trying to ingratiate himself to her detriment.

To help smooth things over, he'd stopped on his way in and picked up a couple of bagels and two café mochas. His plan was for the two of them to spend the morning strategizing. Under the guise of wanting to compare schedules with Maddie, he'd waited to call Dave back to reschedule. Maybe that would appease her.

Why was he taking such pains to be nice? It was his instinct to call Dave right back, verbally rough him up for canceling at the last minute and then make him feel as if he owed him. That's how business was done.

He went straight to Maddie's office without even stopping by his own. He knew she was there because her white Volvo was parked in its usual spot. Funny how the sight of her car now sparked an instant reaction in him when he saw it.

When he got to her office, her head was bowed as she read something on her desk. It dawned on him that her hair, which she normally wore in a ponytail, was down and covered her profile. Her hair looked shiny and a little bit shorter and fuller. His mouth went dry at the vision of her in bed with him—naked and on top—leaning toward him as he ran his hands through those wild, silky locks, pulling her closer as they rode the wave together—

He cleared his throat and knocked on the door frame with the hand that held the small bag of bagels.

She looked up and smiled at him.

Damn.

She looked…different. Somehow.

The woman who sat in her chair was gorgeous. What was different about her? Her hair, for one. But could a haircut really change a person that much? She looked different to the point that he almost couldn't believe she was the same woman.

"Good morning." He managed to spit the words out. "You changed your hair."

She leaned her face on her chin and flirted with her eyes. "You noticed."

"Yeah. Looks great."

She was in such a good mood, he hated to spoil it with the news that Madison had begged off on their meeting.

"Whatcha got there?" she asked, gesturing to the bag and tray of cups he was carrying.

"Breakfast. Are you hungry?"

"You know me, I can always eat."

She was definitely the same Maddie. But he'd never seen her like this. How had he never noticed how gorgeous she was? It wasn't just the hair.

Or was it?

"You should wear your hair down more often. It looks great."

"Thanks." She reached up and toyed with a piece of her hair.

He'd read in one of the body language books he studied that when a woman played with her hair, it was a tell suggesting she was attracted to the person she was talking to.

The feeling's mutual.

Was it a workplace taboo to comment so much on her appearance? He couldn't help it, and she didn't seem to be taking offense. She'd kissed him...

"I hope you like mochas," he said, as he handed her one of the cups.

"What's not to love. Thanks, but don't you think we'd better take this on the road with us so we're not late for the meeting?"

He slid into the chair across from her desk as she wheeled her chair back and stood up. He noticed the dress she was wearing—the very hot, very pink dress—yes, very hot. It had a flirty little skirt that hit well above her knee and moved when she did. The top of her dress fit her like a glove and even though the neckline wasn't plunging or revealing, it showcased her breasts in a way that had him shifting in his seat.

He took a sip of scalding coffee, burning his mouth and bringing his mind back to the task at hand. There had always been something about her. Something beautifully untouchable that made her feel out of his league and caused him to hang back rather than swoop in as he did with the other women he dated. He'd be smart to stick to business.

"Bad news," he said. "Dave Madison canceled the meeting this morning."

"Very funny." She hitched her handbag up on her arm.

"I'm serious."

The smile that initially suggested she would play along with his prank fell. "You're not kidding?"

Zach shook his head.

Maddie dropped her purse and sank into her office chair. "Why? And when did you find out?"

"This morning," Zach said. "Madison left a message."

She pulled her phone out of her purse and looked at it, then skimmed it onto her desk. "He didn't leave me a message."

"He probably figured I'd let you know."

Maddie *harrumphed*. "Because the two of you are such good buddies. It would've been nice if he could've given me the courtesy of a phone call. Does he want to reschedule?"

"He didn't say." Zach had predicted Maddie wouldn't receive the news well. "All he said was he was called out of town yesterday and wouldn't make it back by our meeting. Why don't you call him and reschedule for us? If you want to. I'm not asking you to schedule my appointments."

"I get it." Her face softened. "And I appreciate it. I've been calling him, but I haven't made contact with him. He seems more comfortable communicating through you. I was looking forward to this face-to-face so I could meet him and we could establish a business relationship. He's a hard guy to pin down."

Zach nodded. "That's how he operates. He's good at what he does, builds a solid product, but he marches to his own tune. Be prepared for that."

Maddie picked up her coffee and sipped it. He could see the wheels turning in her head.

"What does your week look like?" she asked.

"Just schedule the meeting as soon as you can and I'll make it work."

"Thanks, Zach. It's a tight week for me because

Schuyler's wedding is on Saturday. I'd planned on going to Austin on Wednesday. I hope he'll be back tomorrow."

Since Schuyler didn't work for Fortunado Real Estate, she'd only invited the people she knew well. At the barbecue where her father had made his big announcement, she'd apologized to Zach for not inviting him and explained that she and Carlo were trying to keep the wedding intimate with just their family and closest friends.

He understood.

Maddie looked down and toyed with the top of her coffee cup. "I owe you an apology," she said. "Since we're coming down to the wire before Kenneth makes his decision on who he's promoting, for a moment, I was thinking ugly thoughts of you. I wondered if the meeting being canceled was some kind of a dirty deal or a double cross to put yourself in better position for the promotion."

She looked up. "Now I know I was wrong. I think I've been wrong about you all along."

He smiled. "I don't operate like that, Maddie. I know this challenge your father has issued has put us in an uncomfortable position, but I don't believe in stepping on people to better myself. Or bettering myself to the detriment of other people."

"I believe you. You operate that way because of what your brother did to you, right?"

Zach shrugged. He didn't like to talk about his past, but for some strange reason, he wasn't annoyed by Maddie bringing it up. It meant she understood him.

"Probably. But it's in the past."

"Have you ever thought of sitting down and talking to him? How long has it been now?"

Zach shrugged again.

"That would be…" His words trailed off. He couldn't recall off the top of his head, because he'd put Rich out of his mind. "I wouldn't know what to say to him. I don't even know how he would receive me if I looked him up."

Despite all his success, all the money he'd earned and saved and invested, family was the one thing money couldn't buy. It was a rare and precious commodity. He was moved by Maddie's commitment to family. She could've easily let this challenge come between her father and her. It could've caused a big rift right before Schuyler's wedding. But Maddie had her head on straight enough to keep that from happening.

Needing to change the subject, he shot her his most mischievous smile. "What other misconceptions have you had about me?"

She returned an equally suggestive—almost naughty—smile. It pierced him in the most delicious way.

"That doesn't matter now," she said. "But I think I still owe you a few *one things*."

"As a matter of fact, you do."

"Even though I really shouldn't have to pay up from the Ping-Pong match because we never finished. But I do have one thing for you now."

He smiled. He could've resorted to the safety of their usual banter, insisting that she'd forfeited the game so

he had won fair and square. But who won and who forfeited wasn't important right now. "Do tell."

"One thing you don't know about me is..." Her voice
sounded shaky, and she looked uncertain, like she might
back out of telling him what she'd planned on saying.
But then she took a deep breath. "What you don't know
is, I'd love for you to be my plus-one to Schuyler and
Carlo's wedding. Will you go with me?"

After Maddie realized she wanted Zach to be her
date to the wedding, she'd promptly overthought it and
prepared herself for the possibility that he might not
want to go.

If that was the case, she'd been prepared to tell him
that it was important to Schuyler for her to bring a date,
but bringing someone she didn't know well, someone
who didn't know her family, might make a statement
she didn't want to make. At the very worst it might take
some of the attention off Schuyler because her nosy
family would be so curious about who she'd brought.
Was it a serious relationship? Was Maddie the next
bride-to-be? What a headache. So, she'd decided Zach
would be the best bet. Plus, she strategized, after working on this project together, if they went to the wedding
together they would present a united front to Kenneth,
proving that no matter who won the promotion, they
could work together for the sake of Fortunado Real Estate. Never mind how they'd both declared they would
leave Fortunado if they didn't get the job.

As it turned out, she hadn't needed all the reasons

and strategies she'd prepared. Zach had answered her with a simple, "Thanks. I'd love to be your date."

Date.

He'd actually said he would be her *date*.

Maddie had been so breathless and giddy, it had been almost impossible to contain it. So, she'd shooed him from the office saying she had work to do. At the top of her list? The call to Dave Madison.

Her giddiness had been brought back down to earth with a resounding thud when she'd gotten his voice mail. She'd left a message imploring him to meet them the following day—Tuesday. She disconnected with the sinking feeling that her message had just disappeared into the big, black hole that seemed to have swallowed any interest Madison had in partnering with Fortunado.

The next call she'd placed had been to Richard Mc-Carter, Zach's brother. Since Zach was going to be in Austin for the wedding and Rich lived in Austin, Maddie decided it couldn't hurt to let Rich know that Zach would be in the area over the weekend.

Maddie had gotten through to Rich on the first call. She was certain it had been a good sign.

"Hello, Rich, my name is Madeleine Fortunado. Your brother, Zach, is a good friend of mine and I was hoping you had a moment to talk."

She'd been heartened when he'd sounded eager to hear about his brother. Without sharing any details, Maddie had simply relayed that Zach didn't know she was calling, but she was certain he would be willing to talk to him. She gave him Zach's cell number and hung up hoping for the best.

However, when Tuesday had passed and Friday arrived without a call from Dave Madison, Maddie was afraid that Fortunado's opportunity might be slipping through her fingertips.

"Have you heard from Dave Madison?" she asked Zach on Friday morning when he arrived in Austin for the wedding. Maddie had been there since Wednesday playing handmaiden to Schuyler.

"I haven't heard a word from him. I was hoping you had. The guy can be such a flake sometimes. He's creative and busy and he has the attention span of a gnat. I told you he operates on his own schedule. I'm sure he'll get back to us when he's ready."

"I know, but time is ticking," Maddie said. "Do you think he's jacking us around? Maybe he's contracted with someone else? I wish I knew one way or the other so that we can make a plan B for my father. I've been in touch with Blue Circle Portfolio. They're the ones looking at developing that land in the theater district and if we can nail that down, maybe my dad will forgive us for not landing the Paisley."

"Yeah, that's great," Zach said, as he stared at his cell phone.

"Well, it wouldn't really be great," Maddie said. "But at least we won't go to my dad empty handed. Maybe he will give us more time to woo Dave. What are you looking at? I get the feeling that you're not all here this morning."

Zach laughed and scrubbed his face with his palms. "Sorry. I'm not really all here. The strangest thing happened." He laughed again. This time Maddie detected an air of disbelief in the sound.

"What is it?" Maddie said. "Everything okay?"

"Uh, yeah. Maybe. I don't really know. My brother called me last night. I haven't heard from the guy in more than a decade and he called me out of the blue the night before I'm supposed to be in Austin. You wouldn't know anything about that, would you?"

Maddie turned her attention to her cup of coffee. *"Maay-be."* She winced as she looked up and flashed an apologetic smile at him. "Please don't be mad at me, Zach. I'm only trying to help. I just thought since you were going to be here and he lives here and—"

"It's okay," Zach said. "He sounded...good on the phone. He's eager to talk. We're meeting for lunch today at 12:30. I'll let you know how it goes tonight at the rehearsal dinner."

As Zach steered his BMW into the parking lot of the restaurant where he was meeting his brother, he realized he was nervous.

This didn't have to mean anything. But it could mean everything.

He'd spent his entire adult life pursuing money, romancing his bank account. He'd scored his financial goals. On this side of the conquest, the most important thing he'd learned was all the money in the world couldn't fill the emptiness inside him. Spending time with the Fortunado family, watching their dynamics, seeing how they navigated the sometimes-stormy waters of family relations, made him want the one thing that money couldn't buy.

Granted, he could get married someday and have a family of his own. Lately, when his mind went there, when he started thinking of ditching the lone wolf gig and opening his heart to someone, Maddie was the one his heart kept coming back to. She was fiery and passionate and she had a heart of gold.

If not for her, he wouldn't be sitting here psyching himself up to see his brother—a family member he thought was lost forever.

Zach recognized Rich the moment he walked into the restaurant. His brother had taken a table in the crowded bar area. Zach figured that Rich had chosen that table to cut down on the awkwardness of this first meeting. It was better than being stuck in a corner at a quiet table for two possibly with nothing to say to each other.

When Zach reached the table, Rich shook his hand. "Good to see you, Zach. You're looking well."

Zach returned the pleasantries and they made small talk about the real estate industry and Rich's law practice and his wife and kids until the servers cleared away their lunch plates.

Zach had prepared himself for the lunch to wrap up without a conversation of any emotional depth. Hell, he had gone into this without any expectations. It was the only way to keep from getting hurt. But Rich surprised him when he said, "I don't know when I've ever been as happy to talk to someone as I was when you took my call."

He added, "I'd love to meet your girlfriend, Maddie, someday. She seems pretty remarkable."

Zach didn't correct Rich's use of the word *girlfriend*. And, of course, Maddie was remarkable. She had changed his life in the few weeks that he'd allowed her in. He would be damn lucky to have the privilege to call her his girlfriend.

"I've often thought if I could have one do-over in life, I would go back to when Mom died and I'd do everything completely different. I should have fought for you, Zach."

And just like that, all the walls fell.

"I know I wasn't the easiest kid to deal with," Zach told him. "In fact, I was a pain in the ass. Looking back, I guess I can't blame you for trying to get me into the hands of someone who could rein me in. Since you were my guardian, the police were threatening to put you in jail if I didn't go to school. I was so mad at the world for the lousy hand we'd been dealt, I didn't care about anyone or anything."

"And I don't blame you for hating me even more after you went into foster care."

Zach took a long swallow of his sweet tea, buying time to weigh his words. But he kept coming back to honesty. He and Rich seemed like they were on a good path, but one lunch wasn't going to heal more than fifteen years of estrangement. Unless he said what he needed to say, this reconciliation wouldn't heal them. It would scab over with the truth of his feelings festering inside.

"I'm not going to lie," Zach said. "I hated you for it.

I guess I hated you right up until I realized that your sending me away may have been the formative experience I needed. It's made me who I am today."

It had also made him untrusting and guarded and hesitant to get too close to people because in his experience, he'd found out the only person he could rely on in life was himself. But he was learning to trust. His heart was thawing. Thanks in large part to Maddie and the Fortunado family.

The face-to-face meeting with Rich was a huge step toward embracing the family he wanted. Maybe. Or maybe he shouldn't invest too much of himself too fast until he could see where this was going. They were both older now, both set in their ways and in their routines. Rich had a family—he'd shown Zach pictures, but he hadn't mentioned anything about introductions. He had no idea if he'd even told his wife they were meeting today. But Zach knew he was getting way ahead of himself. He would be content to take today for what it was.

Rich nodded his understanding. "I feel like I owe you something to make up for the tuition I didn't come through with when you needed it."

Zach froze.

Money. It always came back to money. Money ruined everything.

The last time Zach had seen Rich he'd swallowed his pride and asked his brother for help. He'd needed money for college and since Rich was already through law school and building his practice, Zach had reminded him of their mother's wishes for the insurance money. She'd only left the policy in Rich's name because he was the adult at the time. Their mom had thought she was making it easier on her boys that way, that she was keeping their inheritance—as humble as it was—from getting tied up in court where they'd spend more on attorney's fees than the policy was worth. Little did she know she was setting up her sons for estrangement.

Rich hung his head. "When you came around I was going through tough times. I know that isn't an excuse, but it's what was happening."

Rich reached into his shirt pocket and pulled out a fat envelope. "This may be too little too late, because it sounds like you're doing more than all right for yourself, but this is the amount of money that was owed to you. It's cash. So, don't be flashing it around."

Rich laid the envelope on the table. Zach kept his hands folded, afraid that if he touched the money he might turn to stone. He didn't want money. He didn't need it now. It wasn't why he came here.

"And I want to give you something else," his brother added, "to make up for the lost interest. It's something you deserve much more than I do." He pulled out a small black box and pushed it across the table toward Zach.

"What's this?"

"It's Mom's engagement ring. I figure if you ever get around to asking that Maddie to marry you, this might come in handy."

"I told him I didn't want the money," Zach told Maddie in the hotel bar after the rehearsal dinner was over. The story was too involved to get into during dinner. Plus, they'd been seated at long tables and everyone was talking and toasting the bride and groom. It wouldn't have been appropriate to bring up something so personal during the festivities. "But Rich wouldn't take no for an answer. He wouldn't take it back. It's not a lot, but it was cash and he told me to invest it and use it for my kids' college someday when I have kids."

He didn't tell Maddie about Rich giving him their mother's engagement ring, which he'd accepted with no compunction. It was a piece of his mother. All these years he'd never had anything that belonged to her. Even if the ring stayed in a safe-deposit box, at least he would have one thing that had been hers.

"How did you leave things?" Maddie asked.

"We're going to see each other in a couple of months. I may come and play golf. He says he gets to Houston every so often on business. We just left it open. No pressure, but with the feeling that we're going to try. That we both want to try."

"That's great," Maddie said as she sipped her brandy.

"When I first found out you'd called him, I should be honest, I wasn't very happy. But now I can't thank you enough. You gave me back my family."

"I just made the call," she said. "You did the rest. I'm just glad you didn't think I was being too pushy and butting in where I shouldn't."

"Are you kidding?"

Their gazes caught and something sensual and electric passed between them. They were sitting next to each other on a small settee that forced them to sit close enough that he could smell her delicate perfume. She was wearing a wild orange-and-yellow patterned mini-dress that was different from anything he'd ever seen her wear. Come to think of it, other than that tight, hot-pink dress, he couldn't remember the clothes she'd worn in the past. They faded into the background when he envisioned her in his mind's eye. All he saw was her beautiful face and her hair.

She was wearing it down tonight. He ached to reach out and touch it, to run his hands through it and pull her close.

She'd been different since that day she'd asked him to be her plus-one. Or maybe he was seeing her differently. The only thing he knew for sure was that he wanted her.

"I've been thinking about what you said last Sunday when we were in the office."

Maddie squinted at him, racking her brain, as if she was trying to remember what she'd said to him.

"What did I say? I hope I was nice."

He smiled and shrugged, remembering the banter that had led to the crux of what he wanted to say to her tonight.

"You said you didn't mean to be bitchy. And I said I'd never thought of you like that. You're passionate and fiery. That's what I've always noticed about you, Maddie."

He couldn't help himself. He reached out and stroked his thumb over her cheekbone. "I can't help but notice you. You're smart and beautiful. And I think I'm falling for you."

He allowed himself to thread his fingers through her hair. It was as soft and silky as he'd thought it would be. He slid his hand to the nape of her neck and gently urged her into his arms and lowered his mouth to hers. He drank in the sweet taste of her. She tasted like the apples from the Calvados she'd been sipping. The fruit mingled with the taste of the deep, rich coffee that they'd enjoyed after dinner, and there was a hint of cinnamon and spice. He deepened the kiss, needing as little space between them as possible. The feel of her curves pressed against him made him want things he hadn't allowed himself to even think about in a very long time. Not just sex. Not just the physical release that so often came out of the unspoken agreement that long before morning the spell would be broken. Never at his place because he wanted control over the situation. He'd never wanted to open his world to anyone else because it came with too much risk. He'd never wanted to until now. He wanted to take her up to his room and help her out of that sexy little dress and show her exactly how much he wanted her.

Maddie had opened a need in him that was so great it was nearly all-consuming.

"Come with me," she whispered. "I want to show you something."

Of course he followed. He would've followed her anywhere.

She led him to the end of one of the old hotel's hallways. She pressed her fingers to her lips. "Shh."

She looked down the hallway before opening a door—an old closet of some sort that was empty and big enough for just the two of them—that he hadn't noticed because the door was covered in the same old-fashioned wallpaper that was on the walls. She tugged him inside and shut the door.

"How did you know about this place?" he asked.

She answered him with a kiss so passionate that it ignited such a strong need in him that it almost overpowered him.

He wasn't sure how long they made out in the closet because he lost all track of time. It could have been hours or moments, but soon it was apparent that all they were going to do was kiss if they stayed there. The space was cozy and not conducive to lifting her up and... Besides, the door didn't lock, and despite how much he wanted her, he didn't want their first time to be like this. He wanted to savor her. He wanted to unwrap her slowly and treat her like the rare and valuable gift she was.

"Let's take this upstairs," he said in her ear. "I want you to stay with me tonight, Maddie."

Zach's hands cupped her bottom and he pulled her in close so that their bodies were flush, curve melting into muscle, muscle supporting curve. It was hard to tell where his body ended and hers began.

He liked it that way and he wanted to explore every inch of her.

Maddie let her head fall back, which pressed her even closer into his erection. He kissed the soft expanse of her neck and was tempted to slip his hands under that short little dress so that he could explore her breasts— Hell, he wanted to get rid of that dress and all the other barriers between them and bury himself in her until she cried out. But that was the need she brought out in him.

Slow down.

"Come up to my room." He kissed her again, hoping she wouldn't refuse. His hands found their way to the hem of her dress and began making a slow migration up the bare skin of her hip, past the thin strap of her thong, to her waist. He pulled back just enough so that his hand could find the underside of her breast.

Breathless, she broke the kiss, but kept her mouth a whisper away from his. "We need to stop."

Stop?

"God, Maddie, you're driving me crazy. I want you. I want you upstairs and in my bed."

"I want you, too. You have no idea how much. But I can't tonight. I promise we will finish what we've started here. But I promised Schuyler I'd stay with her tonight to keep her from sneaking out and seeing Carlo and being relegated to a life of bad luck."

"Bad luck? What are you talking about?" Regretfully, Zach tugged her dress back into place and put his hand on her back, trying to give them some time to cool down before they exited their hideout.

"It's bad luck for the bride and groom to see each other before the ceremony on their wedding day. It's part of my job as maid of honor to ensure my sister's happiness."

He cupped her face with his hands. "So, maid of honor duty calls?" he said between tiny kisses on her lips, her temple, her eyes—purposely avoiding her neck because if he revisited that sensitive area at the base of her ear, it might be the undoing of both of them.

After he delivered her to the hotel's bridal suite, they made out in the hallway.

"We could stay right here," he whispered in her ear. "I could help you stand guard."

Maddie opened her mouth wider and deepened the kiss. Teasing her, he pulled back, giving himself just enough room to say, "If we're out here, Schuyler won't be able to go anywhere."

Maddie laughed, low and sexy, against his mouth. The sound vibrated inside him and stoked the fire even hotter.

Then Schuyler opened the door. "Maddie, is that you? Oh!"

She slammed the door as fast as she'd opened it, calling, "Get a room, you two. But do it tomorrow night, after I'm married, because seeing you two makes me want to go see Carlo."

"I have to go," Maddie told him.

"I wish you didn't."

"Me, too, but we'll have tomorrow. And all day long, we'll know what's going to happen at the end of the night."

She kissed him again.

"If you keep this up, I'm not going to leave."

He took her hands in his and kissed her fingers one by one. "I'd better go. We don't want to have the fate of your sister's marriage on our heads. Sounds like it could cause a whole lot of bad karma."

Maddie laughed. "She would personally deliver that lot of bad karma to us. I guarantee it."

Still holding her hands, Zach took a step back. "Good

night." The words *I love you* were on the tip of his tongue, but he bit them back because they surprised him. Jolted him. But then Maddie smiled her naughty smile and it turned him inside out.

"I probably won't be able to see you until the reception because tomorrow I'll be my sister's keeper. But I'll leave you with this thought. Every time you see me tomorrow, every time you think of me, remember what's going to happen tomorrow night."

She kissed him one more time and turned to let herself inside the suite.

"We may not make it through the reception," he said.

"I hope not." She closed the door, leaving him hot and bothered and counting the hours.

Five minutes later, Zach was unlocking his own hotel room door three floors below the bridal suite when his phone rang. He thought it would be Maddie and pondered the possibility of phone sex as a consolation for having to go their separate ways tonight.

He closed the door and was preparing to ask her what color that thong was that he'd met in the closet tonight. He'd keep it lighthearted and playful. That way it would either get things started or they could laugh about it before they said good-night. But then he saw Dave Madison's name lit up on the LED screen.

Zach muttered an expletive under his breath. Why the hell was Dave Madison calling at this hour?

Zach answered the call. "Madison, it's 1:00 a.m. You'd better have a damn good reason for calling at this hour."

"Dude! I'm in Australia. I'm all messed up on time. I thought it would be late morning there."

"It's not."

"Yeah, I have no idea what the time difference is. I hope I'm not interrupting anything important."

"If something important was happening, you wouldn't be talking to me right now."

"Sorry to hear that. You losing your mojo?"

Tomorrow.

He heard Maddie's voice in his head, remembered the look in her eyes as she blew that final kiss good-night.

"Why are you calling, Madison? What do you want?"

"Lighten up, dude. I'm calling with good news. I know you're under a deadline. I wanted to let you know I'm making you the exclusive listing agent for the Paisley."

Madison rattled off some terms he required for the deal. Zach countered on some of the more unreasonable ones. Madison easily acquiesced because he knew they were unreasonable but always tried to push the envelope. The guy was always trying to spin a deal in his favor, but he also knew that Zach wouldn't put up with his crap. He also knew that Zach was the best in the business and could sell out the building faster than anyone in Houston.

"I'll run this past my listing partner, Maddie Fortunado, and I'll get back with you first thing tomorrow. Good?"

"Uh, no. I don't know who this Fortunado chick is,

but I'm offering *you* this deal. Not her. You. Exclusively."

"First, she's not a chick. She's a damn good businesswoman. She's part of the Fortunado Real Estate family. That's the brokerage I work for."

He started to say she'd be running the place very soon, but stopped short. The thought surprised even him.

"Yeah, well, she's been annoying the crap out of me with all her phone calls. So—"

Zach uttered another expletive. "If you'd call her back she wouldn't have to keep calling you."

Dave Madison was starting to annoy the crap out of him. Nobody put Maddie down like that and got away with it.

"All right, whatever. My offer stands firm. I'm happy to bring you on board. The chick can bring in buyers, but she's not part of the deal."

By 5:00 p.m., Maddie was wearing the cardinal-red gown Schuyler had chosen for her. The color matched the rest of the bridesmaids, but since she was the maid of honor, the style was different.

Maddie loved her dress. Adored it. The cut flattered her in all the right places. The silky red fabric caressed her skin and made her feel beautiful and sexy. Most of all, she couldn't wait for Zach to take it off her tonight, when they were both finally rewarded for their patience.

She was falling for him. No, past tense. She had fallen for him, and hard.

Maddie was in love with Zach.

She'd talk to her father and make him work out something so that they both could stay. They both brought different strengths to the table. Fortunado needed them both.

In the meantime, she wasn't going to coast on her love for Zach. She was going to keep calling Dave Madison until he finally took her call. Zach clearly had the advantage since he knew Dave, but he'd stepped back on this, giving her a chance to bring something to the table. Zach had hooked Dave; now she was going to do her part and reel in the Paisley.

Schuyler was in the shower preparing to get ready for the eight o'clock ceremony. That meant Maddie had about fifteen minutes to herself. She fished her phone out of her evening bag and dialed Dave.

To Maddie's utter surprise, just when she thought the call was about to go to voice mail, he picked up on the fourth ring.

"Yeah?" He sounded groggy, as if she'd awakened him from a sound sleep.

"Mr. Madison? Dave? This is Maddie Fortunado—"

The grogginess gave way to a string of expletives that had Maddie holding the phone away from her ear. "I'm in Sydney. You woke me up. What the hell do you want from me?"

Her first inclination was to apologize and tell him she'd call back later. But how in the world was she supposed to know where he was when he couldn't even show her the courtesy of returning her calls—even if it was to tell her he wasn't interested?

"I'm calling about Fortunado Real Estate selling the units in the Paisley. I've left you a number of—"

"I know you have and I haven't called you back for a reason. I've given that contract to Zach McCarter. I'm good here, okay. Stop calling me."

Maddie dropped the phone before she could hang up. It slid under the bed.

As she bent down to fish it out with shaking hands, the full magnitude of Dave's words hit. He'd given the listing to Zach? She'd fallen hook, line and sinker for McCarter's game.

Chapter Nine

Schuyler was a beautiful bride in her mermaid-style gown that hugged her curves, showing them off to their best and flaring out at the knees for a dramatic effect. It was quintessentially Schuyler: sexy and dramatic.

The outdoor wedding had been ethereally romantic in the Mendoza Winery's sculpture garden with its rosebushes and views. The manicured lawn seemed to stretch on for miles, but the area where the ceremony took place, in front of the Spanish-tiled fountain, was adorned with orchids provided by the florist, which enhanced the rose garden that was in full bloom. The flowers, which were lit to perfection, seemed to be at their splendoring best when the couple exchanged their vows under an inky, starry sky.

It was everything Maddie could've wished for her

sister: perfect weather, supportive guests and a loving soul mate in handsome Carlo Mendoza.

It almost made a girl believe in love again.

Well, except for the love part.

Schuyler had found her perfect man, but once again, for Maddie, love had delivered a sharp, poisonous sting.

The mere thought of having to face Zach broke her heart all over again every time she thought about it. That meant the best thing she could do was steer clear of him for as long as possible. All she needed to do was stick it out until the end of the reception and she could drive back to Houston tonight.

Since she was part of the wedding party, it had been easy for her to avoid Zach until the reception. Now that the ceremony was over, the photos were shot and the bridal party and newlyweds had been introduced, it would take some skillful maneuvering to circumvent him without creating a scene.

She wouldn't cause a scene.

He was the last person on earth she wanted to see right now, but she wouldn't ruin her sister's otherwise perfect night.

As the caterers buzzed around with the passed hors d'oeuvres, Maddie saw her father, but, to her relief, there was no sign of Zach.

"Hi, Dad," she said as enthusiastically as she could muster.

"Madeleine, light of my life and apple of my eye. You look beautiful. How are you, honey?"

It wasn't the same cautious, tentative *how are you* subtext: how is the business arrangement going? It was a genuine greeting from a man who was genuinely happy to be celebrating his daughter's wedding day.

"Couldn't be better," she said.

Liar.

"I'm glad to hear that," he said. "Me, too. Lovely wedding, isn't it? You girls did a great job putting this little shindig together."

She knew he was in a good mood because he didn't even joke about how much the *little shindig* was setting him back. She half expected him to make a crack about having to call off retirement to pay the wedding bills, but he didn't.

Instead, when a waiter came by with a tray of champagne, Kenneth snagged two flutes off the tray and handed one to Maddie.

"Thank you, Dad."

"I take it that you and Zach are getting along well," he said. "Isn't he your date? Where is he?"

Maddie groaned inwardly.

Here we go.

No. We're not going to talk about this right now.

"I don't know where he is."

I don't care. As long as you're here and he doesn't appear to be in this ballroom, I don't care where he is or what he's doing.

"I was pleased when Schuyler mentioned that you two might be getting close."

Maddie choked on her drink. "She said what?"

"She mentioned that romance might be in the air. I must say, I approve. Zach McCarter is son-in-law material."

Oh, no, he is not. He is a backstabbing, double-crossing turd.

Never in her entire life had she ever talked about romance with her father. And she didn't plan to start now. He was so very off base about this one. She hated to pull out the big guns, but she needed to put a hard stop to this conversation.

"Speaking of sons-in-law, now that Schuyler is married to Carlo, I guess it will be more difficult to keep our possible connection to the Fortunes quiet for much longer since the Fortunes and Mendozas seem to be inextricably intertwined."

Her father frowned, all traces of the earlier good humor vanishing from his face.

Welcome to my world, Dad.

"My feelings about the Fortunes remain the same. I am still not interested in fostering a relationship with them and I am not encouraging our family to reach out to them. Maddie, you know I've never been fully convinced of the connection. Your grandmother changed our last name when I was a young child. Her name was Mary Johnson. She changed our last name to Fortunado because it was a form of the name she believed we deserved but couldn't claim. That's how we ended up with the Fortunado moniker. Even so, we're Johnsons, not Fortunes. But let's just suppose by some crackpot shot we were related—that Schuyler's right when she suggests that Gerald Robinson and I share the same father, Julius Fortune. The dad, Julius, has been dead a long time.

"Even if it was true, I don't see any benefit in pursuing the connection. From all accounts, I've heard Gerald Robinson—or Jerome Fortune, or whatever his name is—is a cold, hard, cheating SOB. I don't even want to meet him. Why in the world would I claim him as family? Let's leave well enough alone."

"I think that's a great idea, Dad." Maddie gestured to Barbara, who was walking their way. "I think Mom's looking for you."

Kenneth brightened. "Oh, yes, of course. You have a lovely night, Madeleine. Don't worry. Your day to be a bride will come. Hopefully, very soon?"

Maddie kept her expression neutral. It had been a harsh means of stopping the Zach talk, but it had done the trick. Because of that, she was going to let his last comment roll right off her back. She walked over to her three brothers and Lila Clark Fortunado, who were sitting together at a table.

"Hey, guys," Maddie said, pulling out one of the empty chairs.

"Hey, sis." Connor Fortunado stood and hugged Maddie. Since Carlo had so many brothers and cousins, there hadn't been room in the bridal party for her brothers, but, Maddie figured, the upside to that was it gave them more time to talk.

"You're looking good, Mads," said Gavin. "You clean up nicely."

"When did y'all get in?" she asked, aware that Zach had just entered La Viña, the restaurant connected to the Mendoza Winery that was catering the reception.

Gavin had gotten in last night. Having recently returned from their honeymoon, Everett and his new bride, Lila, had flown in this morning.

Against her better judgment, she let her eyes scan the room. She wondered where Zach was. She'd lost sight of him while she was talking to her brothers. Zach was probably spinning another business deal that was bound to make her look bad. It certainly seemed as if he had no interest in anything but business. And that was fine. She wasn't doing business this weekend. She was taking time off to live life, celebrating her sister's marriage.

She laughed at a story Everett and Lila told about their time in Las Vegas, where they'd eloped. As thrilled as she was for her brother, she couldn't stop searching for Zach. She couldn't help but be on her guard. Odd that she hadn't seen him at the reception so far. He seemed to be gone.

So was their father.

"Where's Dad?" she asked.

"He's with Carlo." Everett gestured toward the large window that reached from the hardwood floor to the arched oak-paneled ceiling, offering a breathtaking view of the sculpture gardens. She spotted Carlo and her dad on the winery's lower terrace, enjoying brandy, cigars and deep conversation. The sculpture garden's soft lighting gently illuminated them.

"That looks like a serious talk," Maddie said to Everett. Even though Carlo had taken the old-fashioned approach and asked their father for Schuyler's hand before he proposed, Maddie was certain their father was taking this opportunity to lay down the law, giving Carlo the "you hurt my daughter, I hurt you" talk. She chuckled to herself. If she'd learned nothing more from her parents, it was the importance of family. You might fuss and squabble, but family had your back. Family never double-crossed you. At least not the members of the Fortunado family.

She glanced around for Schuyler, wanting to joke that their father was telling Carlo that now that he'd married Sky, all sales were final. No refunds. No exchanges.

The Fortunado family, she laughed to herself. It was sort of like the mafia without the crime. Now that Carlo had married into the family, there was no getting out. He was one of them for life.

But Carlo was clearly in love with Schuyler. If her dad was having the *scary* talk with him, good-natured Carlo was smiling and nodding and appeared to be humoring Kenneth like a good son-in-law. Carlo had never wanted anything from her father—except his blessing to marry Schuyler. He wasn't interested in the real estate business, as he and his cousins owned the winery and the restaurant where they were right now.

Maybe her dad was right. Maybe the Fortunados had everything they needed in each other. Maybe it wasn't worth the risk to try and merge their family with the enormous Fortune family—or anyone else. When Glammy had been alive, Kenneth used to joke that with the nine of them they had enough to form a baseball team. "Who needs more?" he used to say. But since Glammy was gone and Schuyler had been hot on the scent of proving that Julius Fortune was their grandfather, which would make them related to the Fortunes, their father had been more adamant than ever about closing ranks.

With Carlo as part of the family, they were back up to nine. Actually, since Everett had married Lila, they had their team and a spare. Maybe it was best to leave well enough alone, because when you trusted too easily, sometimes—oftentimes—you got burned.

Maddie felt a pang of envy for Schuyler and Carlo's and Everett and Lila's good fortunes at having found their soul mates.

She hated herself because her gaze unwittingly searched again for Zach. Not in the longing way she had in the past. This time it was out of self-preservation. It was out of keeping your friends close, and keeping your enemies in sight always.

Last night, after that kiss, she'd let herself believe that Zach was her Carlo. She could imagine him asking her father for her hand, promising that he would love and cherish her for the rest of his days…planning a future with her, instead of stealing her future from her.

She watched her father and Carlo shake hands. The satisfied look on her new brother-in-law's face hinted that the talk went well. Her father wasn't hard to get along with. He was a straight shooter who played by the rules and demanded the same from everyone else.

Kenneth had no more than made it inside La Viña when Zach appeared. As if from out of nowhere, he was right there, shaking her father's hand. Kenneth was slapping him on the back in a way that made the anger that had been simmering in the pit of her stomach boil. There was no denying that Zach looked handsome in his tux. The mere sight of him made her melt a little inside in a way that had nothing to do with how mad she was. And that made her furious with herself.

Fantasies were for people who chose to sit on the sidelines and dream. Delusions were for people who allowed themselves to be taken advantage of.

That wasn't going to happen to her again.

Enough with the self-pity. She needed to be proactive and figure out what she was going to do next. She was a strong woman. Strong women didn't play the victim. Strong women didn't make excuses or point fingers. Zach had won. Even if it wasn't fair and square, he'd won, and the sooner she wrapped her mind around it and decided her next move, the better off she'd be.

In the meantime, she wasn't going to sit there and watch Zach McCarter glad-hand her father.

Instead, she grabbed her brother Gavin's hand. "Dance with me."

The band was playing a catchy eighties song and Gavin obliged without hesitation and followed her to the dance floor.

The music was too loud to carry on a conversation while dancing, which made it perfect, because Maddie didn't want to talk. She needed to burn off some of her rage before she did something stupid.

The problem was her father wouldn't see anything wrong with Zach's tactics to secure the Paisley deal. Maddie knew Zach hadn't gone about it honorably or honestly, but he'd sealed the deal when she couldn't even get Dave Madison to return her call. The only way

Dave Madison would go with Fortunado as the exclusive brokerage was if Zach was in charge. That was the bottom line. It was all that mattered.

It was a slap in the face, but the deal was done.

Zach had won.

Plain and simple. She didn't like it. She didn't like the way he did business or the way he'd manipulated her to get what he wanted. Scratch that. She hated herself for allowing him to manipulate her. She'd let her heart get in the way. She'd trusted him when she never should've let him get that close.

"Mind if I cut in?"

Zach was standing on the dance floor tapping Gavin on the shoulder.

"That's okay," she said. "I'm tired and I want to get something to drink."

She walked away and for lack of anywhere else to go, she went to the ladies' room. She couldn't cut out early and go back to the hotel because she was her sister's maid of honor; she still had to make a toast. She needed to be there for her sister until Schuyler and Carlo drove off into the night. That meant she couldn't hang out in the bathroom for the rest of the night either.

She checked her reflection in the mirror, adjusting the neckline of the red gown Schuyler had chosen for her to wear tonight. It was a pretty dress, even if it was bright. The red lipstick she'd purchased that night at the drugstore matched perfectly. Schuyler had informed her that red lipstick was the hardest color to apply because of the hyperpigmentation. It wasn't as noticeable when a lighter color went on crooked or bled outside of the lip line, but red was nearly impossible to mask…without a lip liner and a little bit of practice.

Armed with the proper tools, Maddie had mastered red and looked darn good, if she did say so herself.

And she intended to keep giving herself these pep talks until she felt like herself again.

She was the only one in the ladies' room. So, she looked at herself in the mirror and said, "You can do this. You will get through this. Right now, do it for Schuyler. And soon you will be fine."

She checked her posture and as she pulled open the door, she nearly ran into her friend Billie Pemberton, a real estate agent and family friend who lived in Austin.

"Maddie, hi!" Billie said, as she gave her a quick embrace. "You look gorgeous and the wedding was just beautiful. Schuyler and Carlo seem so happy. They almost make you believe in love, don't they?"

Maddie forced herself to laugh. "I don't know if I'd go that far, but I'm so happy for my sister and Carlo."

"I hear that you and Zach McCarter are an item."

Maddie racked her brain trying to figure out how Billie would know Zach, but everyone in Texas seemed to know Zach. It was a small world and seemed to be getting smaller and smaller as the years flew by.

"We're just friends. This weekend is strictly work-related."

"That's good," Billie said. "He's a good-looking guy, but it would be awkward if you crossed that line—if you know what I mean—and things didn't work out. You know something always happens. Love is so overrated, even the guys who seem perfect wind up disappointing in the end."

"That's the truth," Maddie said. "It was great running into you, Billie. I'm sure I'll see you again before the night is over."

When Maddie stepped out of the ladies' room, the music was loud and thumping. She caught a glimpse of her sister out on the dance floor with Carlo. They looked like they were having the time of their lives and didn't look like they needed Maddie for anything.

She needed some fresh air and decided it was a good time to step outside. She exited the side door and walked down to the sculpture garden where Carlo and Schuyler had been married a few hours earlier.

The event coordinators had removed the Chiavari chairs and the sculpture gardens had been returned to their original splendor. The lush roses perfumed the air and the babbling fountain provided a soundtrack for her senses that eased a bit of the angst she'd been suffering.

And to think, if she hadn't promised Schuyler she'd stay with her last night, she might have taken Zach back to her room.

If she was feeling this bad after just a kiss...

No, she wasn't going to go there.

She walked over to the edge of the gardens, to the place where area gave way to the sweep of green grass that led to the vineyards, and stood there until she began to feel a chill from the cool night air. She crossed her arms and rubbed them, trying to warm up.

"Are you cold?" asked a too-familiar deep voice that

made Maddie's stomach lurch and fall. "Take my jacket. It's chilly out here."

"No thank you," she told Zach. "I was just going inside." Maddie turned to walk away.

"Are you avoiding me tonight?"

"I don't really want to talk to you right now, Zach."

"Maddie, what's the matter? Are you mad at me?"

She stopped and whirled around. "You're really going to stand there and pretend like nothing is wrong?"

Zach stared back at her. "What are you talking about?"

Maddie looked around, making sure they were alone before she quietly lit into him.

"I finally got ahold of Dave Madison. It helps if you catch him when he's sleeping. Either that or he picked up because he thought someone else was calling. Probably that, because he wasn't very thrilled to hear from me. He said he'd already talked to you and the two of you had worked out the details about the Paisley. He informed me that you're going to be handling the listings. Exclusively. Congratulations, Zach. That's quite a coup. What's next? A hostile takeover? Oh, wait, you won't have to because now my father is going to make you the president of Fortunado Real Estate."

She gave him a round of applause.

"It's not as bad as it seems, Maddie. I promise."

"Frankly, Zach, from my vantage point, it couldn't look much worse. When were you planning on telling me? Or were you staging your big reveal to be in front of my father? Oh, wait, that's probably what you were talking to him about earlier."

"Maddie, listen to me—"

"No, Zach, you listen to me. I can't believe you would stoop so low. No, you know what I can't believe? I can't believe that I would fall for somebody who would stoop so low."

She turned around and walked away from him as fast as her stiletto heels would carry her.

"When I was talking to your father earlier, I told him I was withdrawing myself from consideration for the promotion. The job belongs to you, Maddie."

She stopped abruptly, and turned around. "Wait, what? You're withdrawing? What do you plan to do with the Paisley listing? You know you have a noncompete clause. You can't just *take* everything."

"I'm going to stay as long as it takes to sell out the Paisley and then I'm going to marry you, if you'll have me."

She was so angry that her ears were ringing from the blood that had been rushing and the sound of her heartbeat echoing. She thought he'd just said he wanted to marry her. Surely, she was mistaken.

"What did you just say?"

By this time, he'd closed the gap between them and there was no mistaking when he pulled out a small black box from his coat pocket and held it out like an offering.

"I said, I want to marry you if you'll have me. Because I love you."

He opened the box and showed her the small sapphire surrounded by diamonds. "I know it's not big or showy, but it belonged to my mother. When Rich and

I met yesterday, I told him about you and he could tell from looking at me that I was in love with you."

The world was whirling around Maddie, but Zach, standing there holding out that beautiful ring, was clearly, sharply in focus.

"Are you going to say something?" he asked.

Every fiber of her entire being was begging her to say *yes*, to throw her arms around him and kiss him so hard and so long that they would be each other's only source of air. But the practical Maddie, the one who was still feeling compromised, spoke instead.

"But, Zach, what happened with Dave Madison? He made it sound like he didn't want Fortunado, like he only wanted you."

"I handled Dave. I told him without Fortunado, there is no me. But I also realized without you Fortunado wouldn't be the same. At least not for me. I still believe your dad would've given you the promotion in the end, but—"

Maddie smiled. "So, you're withdrawing because you're afraid of losing?"

He smiled back. "You bet I am. I'm afraid of losing you. So, what do you say?" He got down on one knee. "Madeleine Fortunado, will you make me the happiest man in the world and marry me?"

"Yes!" She threw her arms around him and kissed him so hard the rest of the world disappeared.

An hour later, Maddie joined all the other single ladies and lined up inside La Viña for Schuyler's bouquet toss. Even though Maddie was newly engaged, she didn't want to steal Schuyler's thunder by breaking the news at the wedding. She and Zach would wait until Schuyler and Carlo returned from their honeymoon and they'd call the family together and make a big announcement of their own. They'd have to Face-Time her parents since they'd be out to sea on their big cruise. But they already knew. Zach had pulled Kenneth aside and asked his permission to marry his daughter. Then he'd found Barbara and both of her parents had given their resounding blessing.

So, she stood waiting happily for the toss. Before Schuyler threw her flowers, she turned around and looked Maddie in the eyes and mouthed the words, *These are for you*. But when she tossed the bouquet, it split in two.

Maddie caught half and the other part landed right in Billie Pemberton's hands.

"Oh, for God's sake," Billie muttered under her breath, but loud enough for Maddie to hear.

"It's a sign, Billie," Maddie said. "We're next."

"I don't think so," Billie grumbled.

Zach appeared and swept Maddie into his arms. "It's most definitely a sign. Just wait."

Epilogue

The next morning, as Maddie awoke, she kept her eyes closed.

She'd had the best dreams, the sexiest dreams, in which she and Zach had stayed up until the sunrise making love. They couldn't get enough of each other.

A strong arm pulled her in close to his rock-solid, naked body, confirming that what had happened after the wedding was prime-time real life. Her eyes fluttered open and she saw the gorgeous sapphire and diamond ring on her finger.

"For a few seconds, I worried that I'd dreamed everything," she said. "But here you are."

"Here we are," he said. "Let me show you just how real everything was last night."

He entered her gently and they spent the rest of the morning making slow, tender love.

Afterward, as they lay together, tangled and spent, Maddie said, "I want to tell you one thing you don't know about me."

He propped up on his elbow and trailed his thumb over her cheekbone and across her kiss-swollen lower lip. "Tell me something I don't know."

"I love you, Zach McCarter. I've been in love with you from the first moment I saw you. And I don't know if I adequately expressed it but, last night, you made me the happiest woman in the world when you asked me to be your wife. Now I have a surprise for you."

"My love, you are full of surprises."

"While you were catching the garter, I was talking to my father. I suggested that he let both of us run Fortunado Real Estate."

Zach raised his brows.

"Think about it," Maddie said. "You and I bring different strengths to the table. What would be better than us joining forces at work and at home?"

He pulled her tighter into his arms. "It's true, we do complete each other. But we can talk about business later. Right now, I have one thing I want to tell you that you might not know."

"Oh, yeah? What is it?"

"I love you even more right now than I did when you said you'd be my wife."

* * * * *

MILLS & BOON

Coming next month

MISS WHITE AND THE SEVENTH HEIR
Jennifer Faye

Of all the bedrooms, why did she have to pick that one?

Trey frowned as he struggled to get all five suitcases up the stairs. The woman really needed to learn how to pack lighter.

At the top of the steps, he paused. It was a good thing he exercised daily. He rolled the cases back down the hallway to the very familiar bedroom. The door was still ajar.

"Sage, it's just me." He would have knocked but his hands were full trying to keep a hold on all of the luggage.

There was no response. Maybe she'd decided to explore the rest of the house. Or perhaps she was standing out on the balcony. It was one of his favorite spots to clear his head.

But two steps into the room, he stopped.

There was Sage stretched across his bed. Her long dark hair was splayed across the comforter. He knew he shouldn't stare, but he couldn't help himself. She was so beautiful. And the look on her face as she was sleeping was one of utter peace. It was a look he'd never noticed during her wakeful hours. If you knew her, you could see something was always weighing on her mind. And he'd hazard a guess that it went much deeper than the trouble with the magazine.

Though he hated to admit it, he was impressed with the new format that she'd rolled out for the magazine. But he wasn't ready to back down on his campaign to close the magazine's doors. None of it changed the fact that to hurt his father in the same manner that he'd hurt him, the magazine had to go. It had been his objective for so many years. He never thought he'd be in a position to make it happen—but now as the new CEO of QTR International, he was in the perfect position to make his father understand in some small way the pain his absence had inflicted on him.

Trey's thoughts returned to the gorgeous woman lying on his bed sound asleep. She was the innocent party— the bystander that would get hurt—and he had no idea how to protect her. The only thing he did know was that the longer he kept up this pretense of being her assistant instead of the heir to the QTR empire—the worse it was going to be when the truth finally won out—and it would. The truth always came to light—sometimes at the most inopportune times.

Continue reading
MISS WHITE AND THE SEVENTH HEIR
Jennifer Faye

Available next month
www.millsandboon.co.uk

LET'S TALK
Romance

For exclusive extracts, competitions
and special offers, find us online:

f facebook.com/millsandboon

◎ @millsandboonuk

y @millsandboon

Or get in touch on 0844 844 1351*

For all the latest titles coming soon, visit
millsandboon.co.uk/nextmonth